INTERDICTED SPACE

by

GILLIAN ANDREWS

Interstellar Enforcement Agency

(Book Two)

ISBN: 978-84-09-17130-9

DEPÓSITO LEGAL: DL PM 1577-2019

COPYRIGHT AUTOR Y EDITOR @ GILLIAN ANDREWS 2019

PRIMERA IMPRESION 2019

1.0

Illustration @Tom Edwards

TomEdwardsDesign.com

1

I almost jumped out of my skin as the ansible implant I now carried in my brain flared into life. It must have been about three times too loud. I flailed at my head in a stupidly futile attempt to turn it down. It may have made me look pretty stupid, because our resident apprentice Chyzar fell about laughing.

I finally remembered that I had been told to graduate it by pressing on the bone directly behind my left ear. The noise abated to something faintly bearable.

I treated Zenzara to what I felt was a disapproving and dignified stare. It had zero effect.

"Mallivan here," I said hesitantly, hoping I had got the knack of speaking silently within my head.

The screeching inside my grey cells abated slightly. A rather cross-sounding voice replied. *"Haven't you heard anything I've said?"*

"Sorry, Supreme. Teething troubles with the ansible."

"Get them sorted, then. We don't have time for that sort of thing."

"Is there a problem?"

"You are needed out East, as soon as you can get there."

"Understood. What is the problem?"

"What is your current position?"

"We are five days south of Talscharin, in the Landau Rift."

"Good. Get yourselves to Peliss first. You will stop there to pick up three passengers. They will be carrying further orders for you."

I hesitated. "Could we make that Waypoint Station, Supreme? I have some ... err ... parts waiting for us at Waypoint. If we are to undertake a long journey I would like to have those ... parts on board."

There was a pause. "I don't see why not. It will make little difference to the transit ship. The time to rendezvous would be the same."

"Very well, Supreme. I'm assuming this operation has been approved by the Macer Legacy?"

"It has. The Legacy has still not been supplied with ansible connectivity. The Macers have requested external feeds only. They do not wish to embed implants in their bodies. We have shipped an industrial unit to Ulon Prime and it should be installed within the week. In the meantime, you will be receiving their orders via the Supreme Council on Tyzar, as now."

"Understood, Supreme. We will get underway immediately."

"Do so. This is a matter of some urgency."

I mentally switched off, looking around at the others. "Well, that was interesting."

"I told you to test your ansible connection, Ryler Mallivan Bell," Zenzie said. "You always put things off."

"That's simply not true!" I felt indignant. "I forgot."

She made a noise that sounded like a shuttle in reverse.

I decided my best plan would be to ignore her. She was, after all, only eight. Unfortunately she was also the only representative in the Major Shells of the trans-stellar race known as the Chakrans. And she knew it.

The last straw was that she was bound to me by the Savior Protocols. I had unwisely saved her life some months earlier, something I might have thought twice about had I known I would be stuck with her for the rest of my days.

The Tyzarans have a protocol that they must dedicate their lives to anyone who saves theirs. And when I say dedicate, I mean dedicate. Zenzara sticks to me closer than my own shadow. It can get very annoying. I repeat; she is only eight. Eight-year-olds are not always as logical as you would like them to be.

On the other hand, she is very quick with a thoria and her nivala and has already saved my life more than once.

Now she sobered up. Her crest was almost vertical – a sure sign that we were going into danger. Tyzarans have a sixth sense about this.

"Who are we picking up?" she asked in a suspicious tone.

"How should I know? Supreme Oznard didn't tell me." I pressed my hand to the comlink. "Continue course to Waypoint. Time of journey estimated at ...?" I looked over at Neema, currently at the pilot's station.

"...Two days ten hours," she told me promptly.

Zenzie was still not prepared to let it go. "Where are we going after Waypoint?" she asked.

"East."

"Vaer Nova?"

"I don't know."

There was a long silence. Sammy and Mel exchanged glances. Our last encounters with the Vaers from Vaer Nova had not gone well. Not gone well at all. I had lost my family's ship and the two Enif members of our crew had been leveraged out of their life's work. They had lost the entire works of Eshaan. Not only that, but what the Vaers stole could never come back to the market, so that work was lost to the Enif culture forever.

I turned to Denaraz, the Tyzaran who had originally been placed on board *Nivala* to protect Zenzara, but who had gradually become a valued member of the crew. "Are you getting the same vibe?"

He didn't have to answer. He was. His two crests were vertical.

There are three civilizations that could be classified as 'East'. Macers and Vaers, both from the Great Shell; and Nepheals in the Atlas Shell. It wouldn't be the Macers on Ulon Prime because the Supreme Council had spoken about them. So. Either the Vaers or the Nepheals. I knew which one I would prefer.

It was only a few hours later that I was recalled to the bridge from the pool, where I was attempting to break my record over sixty laps. I know that it sounds as if *Nivala* is a luxury ship, but that is only to people who know nothing about space travel. The one thing you need to have plenty of on a spaceship is water. It is used for fuel and we need it to drink. So it has to be stored somewhere. The other thing desperately needed in space is a way to keep your astronauts fit. Water tank ... need for fitness. It hadn't taken a lightbulb moment to fit the two together. Most spaceships nowadays had what was charitably referred to as a swimming pool. Though the fact was more prosaic ... a large metal storage tank with a retractable cover.

I was still rubbing at my hair with a towel when I got to the bridge. Mel stood up to give me the captain's seat. I waved her back. I wasn't planning on staying long enough to keep it warm for her. "What's up?"

She pointed to the screen. "Two freighters, one Vaer and one Spacelander. Both are over the emissions level."

We could only stop one, but it was a no-brainer. The Vaers had not signed the Ulon Accords and were not part of the Interstellar Alliance that we represented. Although we were now the official Interstellar Enforcement Agency, they would ignore us and possibly even fire on us. I picked the Spacelander freighter. The Vaers slowly edged out of our range and then accelerated away.

"Bunch of pirates!" said Sammy.

He was not wrong. Any Vaer ship this far away from the Great Shell was probably a privateer. Vaers are extremely bellicose, and the very worst of them were banished many centuries ago from the original homeworld, Vaer Prime, and sent to Vaer Nova. Once there, the worst of *those* were banished again to the Southern Continent, where they formed the Sellica faction. Those who stayed in the Northern Continent became the Propter faction. Vaer Nova has little to no agriculture or mineral deposits, so they were all forced to take to the skies. The

Original Vaers from Vaer prime had effectively shot themselves in the foot, because what they had really done was encourage outright piracy. However, since all ships registered on Vaer Nova are required to pay a tax to their so-called government, the term considered more accurate is privateer.

Vaer privateers are hostile and resentful of the other species in the Major Shells. They have developed technologically advanced weapons, which they stockpile unashamedly. They are also not above trading some of the worst of these to anyone with funds.

If you wanted to find the dregs of the Major Shells, you would take a visit to Vaer Nova. Though you would be sure to arm yourself beforehand. On Nova, life costs exactly the price the market puts on it. It is just one more commodity.

As to the original planet of Vaer Prime, it has isolated itself completely. No aliens are allowed to set foot on it, and its inhabitants are thought to still live in a restrictive, semi-feudal system where the state reigns supreme. There is great mistrust between the two planets, now bitter enemies. Nova Vaers frequently attack Vaer Prime shipping and its citizens. Because of this, the only interstellar trading with any of the Vaers is through the black market.

The Vaers are descended from a long line of predatory birds. They look like it too. They have sharp eyes and sharper beaks. They are large … about the size of three humans. They have an imposing look about them.

They also believe they are superior to the other species in the Major Shells, especially those that descend from prey animals. They scorn the Nepheals, who are terrified of them. For the Vaers, the Nepheals are simply meat on the hoof.

Vaers are intensely proud and haughty. Their own language is impossible to speak for the other species, except the Avaraks, who can manage most of the glottal sounds.

"I wish we had jurisdiction over them," I murmured.

"That day will come." Neema sounded sure of herself, but I wondered.

I had heard that the privateers from Vaer Nova had been expanding their horizons. Their ships had been seen out as far as the Far Dust. I hoped it wasn't true, though we would probably never know. They kept themselves very much to themselves.

I shook my head as we dropped out of ZEPH drive in front of the other ship, which was trundling along at EM speed. "Open a channel to the Spacelander vessel, please."

Neema's fingers flashed over the console in front of her. Then she nodded.

I cleared my throat. "Spacelander vessel, this is the Interstellar Enforcement Agency. You are contravening seven interstellar contamination regulations. Your emissions are registering scale 86 on the toxicity radian level. Kindly pull over and come to a full stop in space."

The ship seemed to be trying to accelerate.

I exchanged a glance with Sammy. He grinned and gave half a shrug. "If that's what they want …" He moved over to the weapons com, which was linked directly to the weapons bridge one deck down. Denaraz was on duty there. "Prepare to fire warning shots."

Denaraz's disembodied voice replied rather economically, "Ready."

"Fire one shot to pass 500 yards across her bows."

Nivala gave the slimmest of shudders as the shot was fired. There was a long pause, then a yelp and a squawk of static from the freighter. "What the krikk do you think you are playing at?"

I re-opened the link on the communications panel. "Unmarked freighter. If you do not comply with our orders, you will be stopped by force. I don't think I have to tell you what that will do to your ship …?"

There was an indignant splutter back, which then resolved when a second voice, calmer than the first, spoke. "Interstellar Enforcement Agency, please withhold fire. We are complying with your orders."

Somebody on the other ship forgot to cut the connexion. We heard quite a few curses and reflections on our collective parentage. But they were slowing down.

I pressed my finger on the transmit button. "Understood, unmarked freighter. We will wait."

We stuck to them like Geigas on a phyonwe tree as they slowly decelerated until their ship came to a standstill. I aimed the bows of *Nivala* at their midships. I realized at that point that I was still dripping wet. "Sammy, can you take a team over there? Since these new regulations have only just come into force, just inspect the ship and give them a warning. We don't want to be heavy-handed. Meeting us can be a bit traumatic."

Sammy rolled his eyes. "Speak for yourself." He began to giggle at his own joke, a habit of his I have been trying to cure him of. At Interstellar Enforcement, we need to keep our dignity. It is an uphill struggle. None of us had much to start with.

I waved him away. He nodded to Anzany and Neema. They stood up with him.

My resident conscience naturally felt she had to speak. "Do you think we have time for this, Mallivan Bell?"

I gave a sigh. I was pretty sure most captains didn't have eight-year-olds questioning every decision. Perhaps that is how they manage to end up with that gravitas I seem to lack. Though all this was still new to me.

She went on, "Didn't the Supreme say with all speed?"

"She did. However, our main function from now on is going to be to ensure emissions are kept to a minimum. I don't think half an hour now is going to make much difference."

I hoped that was true. I am forever putting my foot straight into my mouth.

Zenzie gave me an 'are-you-sure-you-know-what-you-are-talking-about' look. I ignored it. I get a lot of those, too.

Mel frowned. "Funny thing. I still can't see a name anywhere on that freighter. And there seems to be no identifying registration."

"Yes, that is odd. I have never heard of a Spacelander vessel not being registered."

"Surely the Space Trust insists on it?"

I nodded. "It does. Any vessel not showing the correct identifying marks is considered pirate." I suddenly began to have doubts. Maybe I should have gone myself. I hoped I hadn't sent Sammy and the girls into any trouble.

It was too late to change anything. *Nivala* is a small ship and they were already flying the smaller shuttle out of the bow doors of our cargo bay.

At least I had sent them by shuttle. We could have docked onto the freighter, but I am a little loath to do that, especially with vessels unknown to any of us.

I got Sammy on the vid link. "Watch yourselves. There are no markings whatsoever on that ship."

"Sure, boss." Sammy wasn't going to worry about a little thing like that. "We'll be back in a jiffy."

Zenzara's heavy wrinkles deepened. "Jiffy?" she asked.

"Soon."

"Then why not say 'soon'?" she demanded.

I rolled my eyes. I don't know if all children go through a 'why' phase, but hers was driving me crazy. She was always wanting to know how everything worked, why things were the way they were, how much I knew about the inner workings of the most mundane things.

Inevitably, I never knew enough. I think I had plummeted in her regard when I failed to explain to her satisfaction how an efficient onboard sewage evacuation system worked.

Holding it to such an intense spotlight made my knowledge superficial. She did it without even realizing it, with a child's innocent interest in her surroundings, but it made it hard to be complacent about anything. I found it disheartening. Tyzarans are about twice as intelligent as Spacelanders, so they can make us look pretty dumb in comparison.

There was a crackle and the vid-screen in front of us flashed. Sammy's face came up. He looked even glummer than he usually did.

"Err ... Rye ... err ... Mallivan ... you aren't going to like this much."

My stomach sank. "Go ahead, Agazed." Time to be more formal, clearly.

"This ship is the replacement vessel for *Faraday*, and is captained by one Gunnar Mallivan Bell. It is in transit for Mallivan, for new registry, which is why it has no markings currently. Captain Gunnar Mallivan assures me that a full overhaul will be undertaken when he reaches *Bellaris* Shipstation."

Of all the ships in all of space! My uncle! *Faraday* is the ship I lost to the Vaers. My family hasn't forgiven me. Yet. They may not ever forgive me. This was not good. Not good at all.

Sammy wasn't finished. "The ... err ... captain would like a word with you."

I bet he would. My uncle Gunnar wasn't one to mince his words. I cringed a little. But there was no delaying it. No sugar coating of pills. "Put him on."

"I might have known it would be you. Wasn't it enough to give away the family ship? Now you think you can swan over here and fine us?" The gruff accusatory voice brought up childhood memories.

I rubbed a hand across my chin. "Uncle Gunnar, a pleasure to see you, as always."

"Wish I could say the same. You needn't think you can come back to the Landau Rift and throw your weight about, because you can't. We don't even want to see you. Have you any idea what you have put your mother through? Do you even care?"

"Of course I care. The loss of the *Faraday* was not something I planned. Uncle, I—"

"—Do you know that she has been ill? I haven't seen you calling to see how she is."

That was a low blow. He knew perfectly well that my mother had been refusing all my calls. I frowned. Surely my sister Sibby would have been in contact with me if my mother had been unwell?

"What is the matter with her?"

He huffed. "As if you care! Your actions nearly killed her!"

That is my mother's side of the family. They may have a slight affinity for drama. I sighed again. "I had no choice, Uncle Gunnar."

"There is always a choice. Your choices led you to that situation."

No, actually they didn't, Uncle, but I wasn't going to say so. Truth be told, once the Terrans decided to fire on *Commorancy* and destroy her, my life took a direction I had no input in. I became space flotsam. Stuff happens.

But my family would never see it like that, and who am I to blame them? I allowed our most valuable ship to be commandeered by the Vaers. I nearly bankrupted the family. I could see their point of view. In fact, I felt lucky that my sister Sibby was still speaking to me.

This conversation was pointless. I was aware of the rest of *Nivala's* bridge crew waiting for me to explain. I wasn't going to. Anything I could say was only going to make things worse.

"Nice to see you, Uncle. Please do make sure that those emissions are brought down to Interstellar spaceworthy standards before she sets out again. Give my regards to the rest of the family. Mallivan out." I stabbed at the button to cut the connexion.

Zenzie was staring at me, her crest drooping. "That wasn't fair of him."

"Maybe not." I didn't feel like talking. "I am going to finish the time trial I was in the middle of. Get the shuttle back on board and resume course for Waypoint."

I took my anger to the pool and unleashed it on the water. Lap after lap helped the frustration to dissipate, but didn't lighten my savage mood. Fighting the water as if it were an adversary instead of a friend didn't help my time trial, either.

2

We reached Waypoint a couple of days later, and docked relatively quickly in the huge space station's outer facility.

Before we could even organize crew downtime on the station, we had visitors at our airlock. They strode through our corridors with an entitlement that automatically put my back up. I don't like people so convinced of their own worth, so sure of their own opinions. In my experience, it goes with the strange preconception that their skin is worth more than yours. Take Captain Tevis. Great example. You just knew that, whatever happened, he would have withdrawn to somewhere safe and sound, close to those who were making it happen, but not close enough to be in danger.

My face must have shown my thoughts, because the tall Tyzaran woman in front of me stopped and her crest twitched. I pasted on a welcoming smile.

"Supreme Oznard. I wasn't expecting to see you here. A pleasure to see you again." Not.

She inclined her head graciously. "Captain Mallivan. I hope you and your crew are well."

She meant she hoped Zenzara was well. The rest of us were negligible to her.

"Mallivan, please. We don't go in for titles on this ship. Chy Zylarian is well, thank you." I wasn't going to play her game.

She raised one elegant eyebrow. "That is good news. I hope to speak to her shortly."

"Of cour—" I turned to motion Zenzie forwards only to find that she had disappeared. Sammy, who was standing immediately behind me, gave me a grin and a shrug. Great. *Now* she vanishes! "—se, Supreme. I will ask the Chyzar to attend you after our business is concluded."

"Thank you, Captain." She straightened up into crisp business mode and naturally ignored my wishes not to be addressed as captain. "Is the ship in optimal condition for a trip to Nephealis?"

I could feel my shoulders relax. Nephealis! Not Vaer Nova. That, at least, was very good news. "I believe so, Supreme. With a little provisioning."

"Excellent. Now, I would like you to meet the two consultants who will be travelling with you to Nephealis. They are accompanied by Spokesdesignate ..."

"Xynia. I remember. How ... err ... nice to meet you again."

Xynia stared down at me in a challenging sort of way. "I am sure that my time on board will be of use to you and also to our new Chyzar. I shall be able to instruct her in some detail of the protocols that must now accompany her new status."

My grin wasn't faked. This was going to be interesting. "I am sure she will appreciate your help, Spokesdesignate. I know just how much she must have missed such instruction."

A chortle from behind my back was turned into a cough. Xynia squinted past me, as if to single out the culprit and reprimand him or her.

"Are these ... visitors ... to remain on Nephealis?" I asked.

"No. They are to conclude their lecture there and then will require that you drop them off on Ulon Prime. They will stay briefly with the Macers until a ship can be sent to pick them up."

"Yes, Spokesdesignate Xynia. I ... I was unaware that the Macers had facilities for off-world visitors."

"They have now constructed one or two simple modules that can accommodate alien visitors for short periods. The main problem is the lack of options for food."

True. If you didn't eat kelp, Ulon Prime would be a bit of a challenge. There was, literally, nothing else available on the whole water planet. Rather them than me.

"Understood, Spokesdesignate." I looked beyond her as the other two visitors appeared through the airlock.

"Welcome to —" The words stuck in my throat. I think I may have made a sort of groaning noise. I stood, staring, momentarily struck dumb.

"Hello, Rye!" He looked exactly as I remembered him. Insouciant and full of bravado. He swaggered through the airlock as if he owned the world. Bull Cunningham.

He extended his hand.

I regarded it as I might a snake. "Cunningham."

He was grinning past me, showing a lot of teeth. "Mel, my love. Long time no see. And is that Sammy? How's the leg, Sambo? Nice to see you are all well. I wasn't sure you would make it off that asteroid."

Of course he wasn't. He is the one who had made sure we were left stranded on it in the first place.

Sammy made a sound like a drain. He hated being called Sambo. "Hello, Bully-boy," he snapped. "Might have known you would turn up like a bad penny."

"Now, now. No need to be snarky." He spread his arms wide. "I thought you would all be glad to see me." He put on a sad face. "I am disappointed."

Sammy pressed his lips together.

I held my hand out to the other man who had entered. "Mallivan Bell. Nice to meet you."

He returned my grasp firmly. "Ramesh Chandrayanan."

There was a shocked silence. We all knew who this was. The Terran scientist who had invented the RAMP missiles that very nearly destroyed the universe.

He immediately picked up on our doubt and gave a laugh. "Don't worry. I am not here to invent more doomsday weapons. When I came up with the RAMPs I was unaware of the danger they would pose.

"I have been on Tyzar for the last couple of months, where they have been tutoring me on their latest quantum breakthroughs. Now I am being sent to Nephealis, where I am to give a lecture ... I think they call it a *Dialectis* ... on the subject."

"I see." I didn't. I had heard the one about 'keep your friends close but your enemies closer', but I wasn't at all sure I subscribed to it. I was surprised that the Tyzarans hadn't chucked this guy into a dungeon somewhere and thrown away the key. I wasn't sure how I felt about Xynia turning up again either. She was the Tyzaran we had suspected of treason, of selling the new Tyzaran ZEPH drive to the Omnistate.

So Chandrayanan was now on our side. That, at least, was good news. If it was true. For some reason my subconscious was telling me to be wary. Of all the new visitors.

"Welcome aboard. I ... I am surprised at the company you keep."

His thick eyebrows twitched. "Bull Cunningham? My companion? Oh, he wanted to come. He was given Omnial status. I am lucky to have such an illustrious Terran at my side. They don't give away Omnial status to just anyone, you know."

No, they didn't. They gave it away to traitors who lied and cheated their way into people's ships in order to steal technology and pass it on to their governments. Personally, I thought having Bull Cunningham by your side to protect you was a highly risky thing to do. Too much like getting into a cage with a crocodile. Was he here to protect Chandrayanan or to eliminate him if he got overfriendly with the Tyzarans or the Nepheals? I certainly wouldn't put it past him.

I turned to escort our visitors to their quarters. *Nivala* has two guest cabins, one on the starboard side of the pool on the middle deck, one on the port side. The two men would have to share. I couldn't see Xynia bunking up with either of them.

I may have brushed Bull's shoulder as I passed. I wished it had been his head. My adrenaline had spiked.

I showed Xynia to her cabin first. She thanked me and then asked me when we could get underway.

"I had hoped to give the crew some free time on station," I told her. "In any case, we need to take on supplies. The journey from here to Nephealis will take us over five weeks. With a trip of that length and three extra mouths to feed, we cannot leave before restocking."

The corners of her mouth turned down. "Very well, but please keep it to as little time as possible. We do not have time to waste."

"Shall we say two days? That is the minimum I will need to make sure we can cross both ways safely. I know we can resupply some of the requirements at the Nepheal Gyre, but I don't want to depend on that. Information about the type of supplies they can give us is very sketchy."

"You have never been to Nephealis yourself?"

I shook my head. "Nobody I know has. As Spacelanders we tend to stay in the Landau rift. Of course, work sometimes takes us into the Bifold shell and the local Shell, but the Atlas Shell is uncharted territory for almost all of us."

Xynia pursed her lips. "It is new for me, too. Only about ten of my fellow Tyzarans have ever had the honor of visiting Nephealis."

I inclined my head. "We should be able to leave two days from now. Shall we say at midday?"

"That will be adequate. Thank you."

"Do you have any further instructions for us? This whole operation seems rather ... unusual, to say the least."

"I have no further instructions."

"Then, if you will excuse me, I have to contact the chandler's depot on Waypoint."

Zenzie collared me as soon as I set foot on the upper deck. "What is she doing here?" she hissed. "She was the traitor!"

"We think. We can't be sure. If the members of the Supreme Council have sent her here, I guess we must have been wrong."

"Can't you get rid of her?"

"No."

The Tyzaran girl treated me to a disgusted look. "I have a good mind to sneak out onto Waypoint and stay here."

"You are welcome to do just that," I said in a placid tone.

She glared at me and her fingers splayed. "You know I can't!"

"No? That Savior Protocol is very inconvenient, isn't it?"

This time she really did hiss. "You are enjoying this, Mallivan Bell, are you not?"

I took a quick step back. "She says she will teach you how to behave as the new Chyzar."

"I know how to behave as the new Chyzar!" Her voice came out as a wail.

"The voyage will only be five or six weeks."

"Five or six WEEKS?" Her crest was completely vertical.

"Thereabouts."

She blew out more air than I would have thought her slim little body could hold. "You did this on purpose!"

I held up both hands. "Now, be reasonable. How could I have known she was coming on board? None of this has anything to do with me. And if it did, I certainly wouldn't have let Bull Cunningham take one step on board *Nivala*, now would I?"

She stood silently for a moment. Then she dropped her head. "No."

I was beginning to feel sorry for her. "Look, Xynia can't expect to see you whenever she likes. Why don't we schedule two hours a day? We can say you have other lessons and duties that take up the rest of your time. We will get Denaraz to confirm that for you. He can up the number of defense lessons and I will give you a shift with the pilots."

She didn't like it, but I could see that she was coming around. "I suppose. All the same, I don't like sharing a ship with Xynia, and I certainly don't like sharing a ship with Bull Cunningham. I don't like or trust her, and bad things tend to happen when he is around."

"Tell me about it."

She frowned. "I was doing."

"Yes, I know. I mean ... oh, never mind. I am going ashore. Do you want to come?"

She gave me a pitying look. "As if I would let you go without me. Who knows what could happen out there?"

I was beginning to think it might be safer on Waypoint Station than it was on the *Nivala*. I really didn't like where this was going.

Sammy, Mel, Denaraz and I took the first shore leave, with Zenzara accompanying us, of course. She bounded along in front of us happily, pleased to be off the ship and keen to experiment new places.

"Where are we going, Mallivan?" she asked in an excited voice.

"The Station Lounge."

"Why?"

"I am hoping to meet up with someone."

"Someone I will like?"

"Maybe."

I had already ordered all of the parts and provisions we would need from the various wholesalers that operated out of Waypoint Station. But there was still one vital part I was missing. I hoped it was still here. This was the second time I had tried to pick it up.

We walked into the enormous lounge and looked around. There must have been some hundred tables dotted around the space, and the multitude of plants hid many of the occupants. It was almost like a setting from Old Earth.

Then I heard it. Or rather, it heard me and reacted.

Zenzie covered her ears and then looked around. "What is that noise?"

An unmistakable high-pitched whine dominated all the noise of the chatter of many voices.

Sammy and Mel both grinned. They knew what it was.

"Scout?" asked Sammy. "Did you get Sibeal to bring him?"

I nodded. "We need him. He is an integral part of my crew."

Sibby must have spotted us, because at that moment a large animal barreled up to us, the high pitched whining noise still coming out of his mouth. He was the size of a large Earth dog and covered with long bristles, currently lying back against the bare skin. His head finished in two concentric sets of teeth. One was small and internal, the other consisted of large curved teeth that almost resembled tusks.

He threw himself at my legs and began to twist in and out, rubbing his snout against me.

I dropped to my knees. "Scout! How are you boy? Great to see you!" I tugged at his large ears – something he loves.

Zenzie was entranced. "Is that a Geiga? A real one?"

I nodded. She sat with a thump on the floor and threw her arms around his neck. He snuffled at her face and wagged his short stumpy tail like crazy.

"He likes you! That is good, because I was planning on putting you on Geiga-walking duty once we get on board *Nivala*."

"He's yours? He's going to stay?" Her eyes lit up. "Fantastic! Of course I will walk him."

"You can teach him to swim."

"Really? Yes. Yes!"

A cool voice broke in on us. "Going to say hello to your sister, too, Mall, or is it all about the Geiga?"

Only one person has ever called me Mall. "Sibby!" I stood up hastily and gave my sister a tight hug. "Thanks for bringing him. I'm sorry I left you hanging last time. Things just didn't work out."

She laughed and hugged me back. "That's OK, Mall. I did some shopping, had a bit of a break. Frankly, it was good to get away from all of the bemoaning."

"Bad, was it?"

"Worse than bad. They seem to think you did it on purpose."

"I know. We just had a run-in with Uncle Gunnar. He said our mother was ill?"

"Pfft! She says she is, but she's well enough to stride up and down cursing you. Well enough to organize the purchase of a vessel that was being auctioned off for debt repayment."

I rolled my eyes. "And looked it. That thing was hobbling along in space. They are going to have to invest a small fortune in time and money to get it up to family standards."

"They know. Uncle Gunnar is taking over as captain."

That stung. I knew somebody would have to, of course, but hearing that I had been so easily replaced was a bit of a blow to my pride. I shook my head. There could be no pretending it was not all my fault in the first place. I had to let go.

Sibby squeezed my arm. Her sympathy actually brought tears to my eyes. I gave a ferocious frown. "Why didn't they ask you?"

"You know why."

"It's crazy. You would think that we could have evolved more in space. Instead of which, we are going backwards." I had an idea. "Sibby, why don't you join us on *Nivala*? You would be great here. We could use your skills, too." Sibeal was a highly rated nanotech engineer. "And we don't have those silly prejudices about sticking rigidly to tradition."

In the Landau Rift, the eldest female Spacelander child is brought up to be one thing and one thing only: the Prime. In our culture, each family resides on a large, almost sedentary, spaceship known as a shipstation. My family's is called *Bellaris*.

These shipstations are inevitably run by one woman, the matriarch of the family. She is known as the Prime, and is the one responsible for the upbringing of the new generations, investment and all matters relating to finance.

In my family, Sibby is the matriarch in waiting. She is the heir. She will take over when my mother dies or cannot continue. She will be *Bellaris* Prime. Her path was decided by custom when she was only two. I have always felt sorry for her, because she really loves to travel.

She can't take over the new ship, because it is considered too much of a risk for the future matriarch of the Mallivan family. She is supposed to wait on *Bellaris*, learning more and more about all aspects of the family business.

Sibby gave Mel a sad smile. "I wish I could."

Mel walked over to her and put one arm around her. They had been friends all their lives. "I wish you could too, Sibby."

"I know." She patted Mel's hand. "Tell me, how are you doing?"

Mel grinned. "Better. When your dear brother isn't pointing guns at my head, that is."

Mel suffers from Claustronetia, a fear of being encased in steel in spaceships. Mel is not the heir to a matriarch, so she was expected to go to space and become captain of one of the Estamain family ships. Her father had shown his tremendous disappointment in her all her life. She had gradually had her self-confidence battered down until she was only able to board a ship once every few years, for the mandatory ship training courses. That is why she had been on *Commorancy* with us.

She had come a long way. I knew she wasn't comfortable on *Nivala*; that would be too much to ask. But she was now able to be an efficient member of the crew. And I thought she was improving all the time. Of course, being in a relationship with Sammy helped that. Mel was coming into her own.

Sibby slapped at my arm. "You didn't!"

"I don't remember doing any such thing!"

There was a chorus of disbelief.

I knew perfectly well that I had. She froze up when we were facing the Avaraks, and I had to get her to move. You would have done it, too. In any case, it didn't do her any harm, now did it? She is much better shipside than she ever was before. She should thank me.

I vocalized this thought.

Mel's mouth formed a large 'O' of sheer disbelief. "You have got to be kidding me!"

"Well," I pointed out, most reasonably, it seemed to me, "here you are! On a ship, happy as a grig." I looked at my nails and blew on them. "You're welcome."

Mel dove at me so unexpectedly that she nearly knocked me over.

Scout, the Geiga, who doesn't like people attacking me, gave one horribly sharp pinging note of warning before he fell static, facing the threat. It is what Geigas do.

He froze with his snout pointing directly at her. His bristles were all sticking out of his body at right angles. He resembled a pin cushion. His snout and his tail were sticking out to front and back.

Zenzie gave a cry as the burgeoning bristles brushed her backwards. She tumbled over and knocked into a table behind her.

"Mallivan!" she shouted. "What are you doing?"

That seemed most unfair. "You shouldn't clutch animals around their necks. This is what happens."

She was glaring at me as she picked herself up.

Mel reached over to give her a hand. "Sibby," she said, "I don't think you have met our resident Chyzar, also your brother's shadow."

I shrugged at the look my sister gave me. "It's complicated."

Sibby shook Zenzie's hand. "A pleasure to meet you."

Zenzie tipped her head to one side. "You look like Mallivan. But ... softer."

"Thank you. I like to think so."

"I like you. Will you come with us?"

I know my sister well. She was tempted. Very tempted. I held my breath. Please, Sibby. Please, break free of all the expectations.

Then she shook her head. "I can't Zenzie. I'm sorry."

I looked down. Some things never changed. I honestly had no idea how she could face going back to the dormant life on *Bellaris*. I had hated it, and I'm pretty sure she did too.

She caught my gaze and gave a short wave of her hand, as if to push the doubts away. "Where are you off to next?"

Zenzara brightened. "Nephealis."

"Really? That is quite a journey."

Scout bumped at my legs again, now satisfied that the danger was over. I leant down to scratch behind one ear. There was one spot he adored.

He gave a sigh of happiness and collapsed next to the chair I had chosen to sit on. I was very glad to have him back.

Geigas come from the Polar Shell, out beyond Tyzar. Their home star is Geiga, a bright blue-white primary. They live underground and are short-sighted, but have acute echolocation combined with hyper-developed hearing. Their bodies are long and covered in long hard hairs that can protrude all over their bodies for up to a foot. They have a huge set of teeth, and are quite scary.

Geigas, if untrained, can be very aggressive, and some 400 years ago the original Spacelander settlers used them for mole-fighting, a supposed sport that has now been banned for generations.

They also used to be used in uncharted mining to stand as guardians against local predators, as a Geiga can detect danger remotely. When alarmed, a Geiga gives a particular pinging noise that is quite unmistakable and will always turn to face the danger it detects. Some Spacelander families still keep Geigas as pets, however, and providing they are given a suitable habitat and enough exercise, the Animal Institute allows this, but their living conditions are frequently inspected.

I have had Scout since he was a baby. I found him quivering in the back of a filthy cage on Tevan 321, one of the Space Trust's less wholesome planets. He had obviously been smuggled illegally out of Geiga. He was far too small to be on his own, and he was giving off a continual keening noise that was driving the rest of the animals in the shop mad. The shop owner had been standing over the cage with a large knife, about to put an end to the infernal racket the baby Geiga was emitting.

I had pushed the knife out of his hands, and bent down to the Geiga's height. The little animal had shuffled close to the warmth it felt from my hands and had stilled.

The silence had seemed thick in that horrible shop. I had turned to the owner. "How much?"

He had licked his lips. "Five hundred credits." Universal credits are the standard currency in most areas of the Major Shells.

I gave him three hundred. He threw in the cage, delighted to have turned a loss around.

I made sure the Tevan authorities knew about his activities. He had to have connections to the Vaers. Only a Vaer would have ripped a cub away from its mother.

The poor thing had been nearly dead. I stayed up with it for a week, until it finally regained enough weight to be viable.

Since then we had rarely been separated. Scout's hypersensitivity gave me time to react to delicate situations. I kept him warm and contented, gave him the fruit and vegetables that form a Geiga's staple diet, and even tried to obtain phyonwe fruit for him from time to time.

"Scout, we are going to Nephealis. You are going to be in seventh heaven. That is where all the phyonwe fruit comes from."

He gave a pleased grunt and turned over on his back, presenting his large belly to be scratched. He was happy. We were back together again. Scout didn't ask for much. I was glad Sibby had managed to get him off *Faraday* before the ship was removed.

Zenzie was already tugging at Sibby's hand. "Will you come to see *Nivala*? Please?"

Sibby is used to children. She helps take care of our own six. They are a year younger than Zenzie. The good thing about the Spacelander system of artificial reproduction is that all your children are the same age, which gives them a great childhood with plenty of brothers and sisters to play with. Sibby looked down on Zenzie and smiled. "Of course I will. I was hoping you would ask."

We strolled back to the ship, chatting as we went, with Scout checking out the corridor in front of us. His tail was twitching from side to side now, a sure sign of contentment.

Supreme Oznard was waiting for us at the airlock. "I hope that isn't the part you were waiting for," she said sourly.

"Oh! No! Of course not. Err ... This is my sister, Sibeal. She has brought some necessary provisions from the Mallivan system, and I asked her to take advantage of the journey to bring my Geiga." There was no reason to tell the Tyzaran woman that the 'provisions' consisted of most of my clothes, some paper books I had been given as a teenager and a couple of boxes of accumulated junk. Sibby had rescued them from being summarily thrown out of an airlock. I got the feeling that, if my mother had had any say in the matter, I would have followed suit.

"I see." Oznard said. Scout snuffed at her feet and sneezed, causing the member of the Supreme Council to jump back. Zenzie giggled, then looked studiously at the deck plating.

It was enough to draw the Supreme's attention. "Chy Zylarian! I have been hoping to have a discussion with you. Perhaps you would be so kind as to come to my quarters on the spacestation?"

Zenzie looked at me, her face falling. I nodded. "Chy Zylarian will attend you in ... shall we say in a couple of hours? She needs to change for such an important meeting, and Denaraz will wish to accompany her, for her own safety."

"Of course. They will find me in Suite 1001 on the tenth floor."

Zenzie had opened her mouth, but I nudged at her to close it again. "She will be there."

Oznard gave another baffled look at Scout and then withdrew, gingerly giving him a wide berth. Scout lifted his snout and sniffed at the air. He sneezed again. He wasn't impressed with the tall Tyzaran.

"I don't want to go."

"Of course you don't."

"Then why should I?"

"Come on, Zenzara. You know why. You are brighter than that."

She blew out air. "Oh, all right. I suppose I will have to go. But being a Chyzar sucks!" She flashed her claws in and out at me to make sure I had picked up on her bad temper and then stomped off along the passageway towards her quarters.

Scout flattened his ears and watched her go. I picked up the bag containing his brushes and leashes and led him to my own quarters. Sibby brought up the rear carrying his bed. We soon got him settled in with a couple of apples.

I sat on my bed and Sibby splayed over the chair by the small desk. "What's it like at home?" I asked. As soon as the words came out I knew that it was no longer home to me, and probably never would be again. *Nivala* was my home now.

Sibby looked sad. "She's been on a rampage ever since you told her about *Faraday*. The day they came for the ship she tried to keep them off with a pulser."

"She would. I felt terrible to cause the family so much pain and loss."

"Tell me what happened."

It took me an hour to get through the whole sorry story. I hated myself for not somehow managing to stand up to the Vaers, not having turned the tables around sooner than we did.

Sibby reached out to touch my hand. "You couldn't have done anything else, Mall. It wasn't your fault. You did what you had to in order to save the people you were with. It was the right call. Never think it wasn't."

I found I was actually shaking. "Thank you, Sibby."

She smiled again. "And you have a new life now. A good life, from what I have seen?"

"Yes." I was surprised as I realized that it was a better life. I was in a ship I loved, with people I got on well with, doing something really useful. I wouldn't change back, even if I could.

"You see? It all worked out in the end."

"Not for you, Sibby. You are on the receiving end of all her spleen. I am so sorry to have caused so much trouble."

For the first time I saw wrinkles across my sister's forehead. "I know, Rye. But there is nothing you can do about it now. My place is on *Bellaris*. I have to be there. I don't want to leave the children to grow up with such resentment." The corners of her mouth turned down. "I would like to get away more, but until she calms down a little I can't. In another year or so, when all this is in our past, well, then I will come and stay on this pretty little ship. If you will have me?"

"Are you kidding? You will always have a place here. Always."

We hugged each other and then stood up.

Scout barely looked up as we left the cabin. He was well settled in to his new abode.

As soon as we stepped out of the cabin we almost tripped over Zenzara.

The girl had been propped up against a nearby bulkhead. "I was waiting to show you around."

I checked my watch. "Just half an hour, Zenzie. You have an appointment after that, remember?"

Her look was scornful. "I haven't forgotten. Denaraz is picking me up in any case, so I can hardly forget."

I patted her on the head, something she detests, and walked past them to the bridge. I had been neglecting my duties, and there were a million and one things that I needed to do to get the ship ready.

As I left I could just hear Zenzie ushering my sister into the gymnasium. "You will never believe the size of this," she was saying. "And it is famous. We held the peace talks that ended the Terran war here."

"Did you really? And were you present for that ..."

I walked out of hearing. But I was glad they were getting on. Zenzie was going to be alongside me until I died. I hoped Sibby would stay close, too. There had only ever been the two of us. The third *Bellaris* embryo from my mother and father's stock had died in infancy so we never got to meet him. And the three siblings that were sent to my father's family shipstation had been all male. They grew up in Rasseny, half-way across the Landau Rift. I had never met them.

So any day I saw Sibby was a good day.

Today certainly had been.

3

We pulled away from Waypoint two days later, fully provisioned and with as many spares as I could stash into the various store cupboards. Supreme Oznard had departed before us, in transit to Ulon Prime. Zenzie had been reticent about her visit with the Supreme. According to Denaraz, Oznard had spent most of the time lecturing our new Chyzar about her lack of due decorum. I wished I had been there.

With the Supreme gone, Sibby was the only one who had come to see us off. I waved out of the airlock hatch as Mel slid us out of the dock.

My sister grew smaller and smaller as the spacestation vanished into the distance. I felt a heavy sadness in my stomach. I wondered when I would see her again.

Eshaan was standing beside me. It was examining my face. The Enif clicked a little, sounding almost motherly. "You care for your sister?"

"I do. She is family."

"Didjal is my family."

"Yes."

It nodded sagely. "Family makes your footprint stronger."

It was a strange thing to say, but I understood what it meant. It was true. "How is the painting going, Eshaan?"

It seemed to hesitate. "I am painting. Yet perhaps there is still something missing in my work."

"I am sorry to hear that."

"I thought that it would be easy to express all these new things that have happened around us, but it is not. I fear that the fault is in me. I have not yet let go of the resentment I have towards the Vaers. I think that, until I do, my art will not reach what is known on Enifa as the golden standard."

He had a point. It was no good holding on to the past. Had I let go of *Faraday*? Really? Had I accepted that it wasn't my fault?

I knew I hadn't. It was going to take much longer than the few months that had passed. It might take me years. One day I hoped I would forgive myself. With a flash I realized something else; I would have to forgive my mother too. Forgive her for the lack of empathy, for the refusal to listen, for the rigid judgement she had displayed.

"I am going for a swim. Do you want to come?"

Eshaan paled under his usual shiny black. "We Enif do not swim."

"Don't you? Oh, sorry, I probably should have known that. How do you exercise then, when on ship?" Now I thought about it, I had never seen either Didjal or Eshaan training.

"Our muscles do not require training. We have an optimal system at all times."

Some people got all the luck. "You mean you never have to take care of yourselves?"

Eshaan tilted its head. "Run around the decks, as you do? Swim? Go to the gym? No."

This was hard to get my head around. "So, even when you are old, you never become weak?"

"You *do*? How strange."

That made me think. I could feel a headache coming on. "How do your bodies keep at optimal state?"

"Older cells are transformed to young cells. Do you not have this ability?"

"I wish! So you never work out?"

"It has always seemed a repetitively boring pastime to me. I thought you other species found it fun."

I was gaping at the injustice of it all. "You mean you could just lounge around all day on a couch and still win a marathon three weeks later?"

"I am unfamiliar with the terms, but if you are asking if I am stronger and fitter than you currently are, the answer is yes."

"So what do you die of?"

"We die when the ability to transform our cells is lost. This is a catastrophic event in our lives. It leads to immediate death, as I am sure you can imagine it would, if all of the cells in your body were to die concurrently and have no replacements."

"I get why you would call that catastrophic. But I was told that Enif always die in their pairs. I mean, that if you die then Didjal would too."

"Of course. Enif pairs share everything. If I were to lose the ability to rejuvenate at a cellular level, Didjal would share its ability with me, putting both of us in the 'State of Enlightenment'."

Eshaan realized that I was still finding it hard to understand. It gave me an almost exasperated look, before deciding to explain further.

"Enif decline very suddenly. If it weren't for their *faliif*, their partner, they would die within minutes of this happening. However, if their *faliif* connects physically with them, so as to combine cells in one circuit, they can postpone this effect. However, it does mean that both of them will die, at the same time.

"We usually pass from health to death in 24 hours, sometimes much less. This change is heralded by a heightening and intensifying of all our cordotonal organs. We enter into a heightened state of awareness, which we call enlightenment.

"We commune together for those last hours, and only the nearest *Belofiin* may join briefly with the dying pair close to the end to record any lasting insights for posterity." Eshaan gave the Enif equivalent of a smile. "In some cases there can be substantial insight into really important philosophical questions.

"The *Belofiin* will then bless them both, and withdraw to wait solemnly for the joint death. This is a happy event, as it is said that *faliif* truly join in the moment of their death, becoming one soul forever.

"On Enifa, their local group would rejoice and celebrate such a union for two whole days. Of course from the day of their death their names are also joined into one, to celebrate this transition to an eternal union."

"I had no idea."

"I thought you knew. In our case, Didjal and Eshaan will become Dishaan after our death. Any works I finish that are accepted into the golden standard will be attributed to that name."

I was beginning to realize that I may not have taken a sufficient interest in the various races now living on *Nivala*. I stared at the floor, feeling slightly ashamed of myself. "Well, I know not to invite you to go swimming with me!"

Eshaan's carapace thrummed, a sort of Enif equivalent of laughter. At least, I hoped it was. "It is a failing. Enif hate water. We are scared of what you call swimming. I could drown if you threw me in the pool."

The Enif always seemed so strong. Yet they were terrified of water.

"Would you like me to teach you?"

It looked down at me with something like pity. "No, thank you, Captain." Then Eshaan loped away with its usual strange gait.

"Huh!" You learn something every day.

I made a mental note to try to have a conversation like this with all the members of the crew.

I was waiting to take the lift down to the middle deck and the pool when Bull Cunningham sauntered over. I was not particularly anxious to have a conversation with him. I felt I didn't need to know any more about him. What I did know was quite enough, thank you very much.

"Rye. Going swimming?"

"Yes. No."

"Look, you would have done the same thing."

"No I wouldn't."

"Sure you would. If they told you it was for the good of your world. That it was so important your name would go down in history."

"No I wouldn't."

He shook his head sadly. "You are just deluding yourself. In any case, you have this ship now. It all turned out for the best, didn't it?"

A fist came out from nowhere and hit him full in the face.

I'm afraid it was mine.

I launched myself at him and my momentum took him down to the floor.

I probably wouldn't have got close to him if I hadn't taken him completely by surprise, but as it was, he was unable to cover himself quickly enough. By the time he got his large hands to where they could be of use to him, the bone in his nose had taken on a very fetching turn to the right and his face was bleeding profusely.

I felt a savage pride run right through me. It was great.

We both scrambled on the metal decking to get the dominant position. He won, because he weighed quite a lot more than I did.

He had just raised his large hand to rearrange my nose just like I had done his, when a flashing shadow hurtled past my eye and buried itself in his neck.

He gave a sharp cry and fell backwards back onto the decking. "Get her off me!" he cried, as her claws came out and raked down the side closest to her. "Ow! Get this crazy animal away from me!"

I managed to get to my feet. My knuckles were probably going to need time in the Zeroth triage chamber, but I really didn't care. I just wished I had hit him even harder. How dare he suggest that all the deaths in that miserable confrontation were 'all for the best'? What sort of monster could say such a thing?

Denaraz pushed me aside and weighed into the melee in front of me. He put in a long arm to pull out a disheveled Zenzara, who immediately turned on him.

She was spitting with rage and it took her a few moments to react. Eventually her crest dropped. "Why did you stop me? He was going to hurt Mallivan!"

Denaraz indicated Bull's nose. "I think it might have been the other way around," he suggested drily.

He turned to me. "Is it wise to attack your guests, Captain?"

And, just like that, I realized what I had done. My skin flushed red with mortification. What had I done?

"Chy Zylarian. Captain Mallivan."

It would be, naturally. The voice of the one person I would have liked to be a million miles away. Xynia! Tell me she didn't witness what had just happened!

"Will you both come to my cabin, please. I would like to discuss ... recent events."

Shells! She had.

I gave a deep sigh. This might be the end of my journey as head of the Interstellar Enforcement Agency. I followed the spokesdesignate. I felt about half the size I had.

Zenzie's crest drooped as she shuffled along beside me. "You tell me not to attack people!" she hissed. "Then you do the same yourself!"

"I am not proud of it," I murmured. "I should have walked away."

"Why?"

"Because I am old. I am supposed to be able to control impulses like that."

"He said that the lives lost because of him didn't matter."

I ground my back teeth together. "He did."

She got a mulish look on her small face. "Then I am glad you battered his nose. He deserved that, and much more."

"Maybe. But I should have been a better person."

"Bah!" Bettering yourself was not something that had come up on Zenzie's radar.

Denaraz tried to stop the spokesdesignate. "The captain was provoked, Xynia," he stammered, as he hustled to keep up with her.

She stopped dead. We all threw on the brakes to avoid piling into her.

"There is no justification possible for an attack on a guest, Denaraz," she snapped.

"You are wrong. There was no justification for the comment Cunningham made. He is a guest on this ship and he insulted all of its crew with his comment."

Her crest twitched. "You believe the guest was at fault?"

"I do, Spokesdesignate."

She turned a dubious face towards him. He was, after all, now ranked above her. She was obliged to listen to him. He had a direct ansible to the Supreme Council; she did not. At least, we didn't think she had. But then, what did we know?

"Explain please."

"The guest offered an act of deliberate provocation, Xynia. Mallivan was obliged, by the social mores of the Spacelander people, to address such an insult. Because of the savior protocols, Zenzara was forced to enter the fray to protect Mallivan. There is no wrong here."

Her eyes were flashing. "Is there any reason I should not report this to Supreme Oznard herself?"

Denaraz straightened to his full height, and his two crests came fully vertical. "You will, if you must," he said in a stiff voice. "However, I would just point out that, as senior Tyzaran official on this ship, I believe that would be my prerogative."

She was silent for at least thirty seconds. She pursed her lips. Then she stared down at Zenzara's lined little face. She gave a sigh. "Oh, very well. I can't pretend to understand the social niceties of foreign races, after all. If you feel there was no real wrongdoing then I suppose I must concur with your findings."

Izan kept the stiff demeanor. He bowed curtly to her. "I appreciate that, Xynia."

She sniffed, but walked away, leaving the three of us to stare at each other.

"Thanks." I was still red in the face. I had to behave with more dignity in the future, however many buttons Bull managed to press.

"Think nothing of it." Izan grinned. "I would have done the same thing."

"No, you wouldn't. And I shouldn't have either. It won't happen again."

He winked at me. "Perhaps better if it doesn't. Xynia seems to have ingratiated herself with the Supreme Council, after all. We don't know what is going on here. I think it would be sensible to avoid any confrontation if possible."

"Yes. I shan't do it again. I appreciate it, Denaraz."

Zenzie was tapping her foot on the floor. "Well, I don't see that you did anything wrong," she told me. "He is a cold-blooded murderer."

Denaraz looked at the ceiling. "Maybe. But you are the sole representative of a race of nonlocal beings, Zenzara. Don't you see it is beneath your dignity to roll around on the floor trying to scratch people?"

"I don't. I am obligated by the Savior protocols to save Mallivan Bell, remember."

He sighed. "How could I forget?"

He was right. I had to think of Zenzara as well. As Chyzar, she was now a really important member of our crew. I had to become a better captain. A better person.

"I'm going swimming," I told them.

"And Zenzara is going to the protocol class with Xynia," said Denaraz.

There was a cry of despair from Zenzie. "Noooo!"

Denaraz plucked her to her feet and patted her down. "'Fraid so," he told her in a sympathetic tone. "And I am coming too, just to make sure you behave."

She huffed, muttering something about being the Chyzar and above such things. Her words were ignored as Denaraz ushered her before him towards the spokesdesignate's cabin. She looked at me for help, but I shook my head. Zenzie really needed some better guidance. I certainly wasn't the right person to teach anybody. I had some lessons to learn myself.

She stuck her tongue out at me. So much for Chyzar dignity. I rolled my eyes and made my way to the pool. Perhaps I should ask Xynia to give me lessons in diplomacy as well.

I kept well clear of Bull Cunningham after that. Although it was a long voyage, this was not particularly difficult. His job was to stay close to Chandrayanan, and Chandrayanan practically lived in his cabin. The man was a bit of a recluse; he avoided any social contact whatsoever.

Strangely, Didjal spent as much time as it could in his company. It told me privately that it had never seen anyone with that level of intelligence. It spent every spare minute it could with the man, until Bull Cunningham put a stop to any visits.

I asked the Enif what it thought about that.

Didjal tapped its carapace. "Cunningham has no understanding of the sort of science Chandrayanan is attempting. It is like watching a fish trying to breathe air. He has attached himself to the scientist because he thinks it will be beneficial to him. Once Chandrayanan told him that I was capable of understanding the physics behind his research, Cunningham took good care to keep me as far away as he could."

"They don't want you to find out what they are doing."

"It would appear that way.

"Is this Chandrayanan doing important work?"

"Important? More than that. He said it could be world-changing."

I tipped my head to one side. "Is that why we are going to Nephealis?"

"Maybe. He told me it was to give a talk, but it is true that the real experts in what he is studying are there. Even the Tyzarans can't hold a candle to the Nepheals in the study of spacetime itself."

"What could be so world-shattering about his research?"

"It has to do with quantum nonlocality and entanglement. Unfortunately, I I couldn't find out any further details. My access was curtailed as soon as Cunningham realized I was able to understand the research."

"Are they working for us?"

The Enif frowned. "Us? You mean the Interstellar Enforcement Agency? I don't think so."

"No, I meant us, the Alliance, as opposed to the Terrans."

Didjal tapped his carapace again, more thoughtfully. "I think they may be working with the Tyzarans. I guess that means that they are helping the Interstellar Agency." It didn't sound very convinced.

Neither was I. Could the Tyzarans be planning to mine his knowledge of this new technology? Did they want it for themselves? Is that why Xynia now appeared to be on excellent terms with the Supreme Council? Instead of being accused of treason, she had certainly been rewarded with a closer link to her government. It was, I thought, even possible that she had been acting on their instructions all along. That would explain why action had never been taken against her. The thought made me catch my breath.

I thought about it for a few minutes, before realizing that the Enif was still staring at me, waiting. "Thank you Didjal. That was a very good point. Can you keep me up to date if you observe anything more? I hate the idea that Bull Cunningham knows more about what is happening on this ship than I do."

"Of course, Captain."

I went to find Denaraz. He was executing a routine on the asymmetric bars in the gymnasium. His hands were covered in white chalk.

I waited until he had finished before asking him about the Terran scientist. He confirmed everything Didjal had told me. "I tried to visit a couple of times, when Didj told me about their research area, but I also was told that it wasn't convenient. Cunningham does not want anybody else to find out what they are planning," he told me.

"It seems to me that Chandrayanan might be in some danger."

"Really? Why?"

"Well, if he is working for the Alliance now, it is not inconceivable that his erstwhile colleagues on Earth may want him back. And then there are the Vaers."

"You think they might make some sort of attempt to snatch him?"

"It had occurred to me, yes. They must have heard about the RAMP missiles, and know that he was the brain behind them. That makes him an asset to anyone who has an interest in the latest armament. We know the Nova Vaers have that." I shifted from one foot to the other, wondering whether to broach my doubts. I had to trust him. He had already saved my life more than once. I told him about my fear that the Tyzarans might be more involved than they were admitting.

His face got longer and longer as he listened.

"So you think my people are betraying the Alliance? You think they will keep all this for themselves?"

"I think it a possibility. Don't you?"

His face struggled with itself. "Yes, damn it, I suppose it is!"

"It would explain why Xynia was never accused of treason."

His expression got even blacker. "If my people betray the statutes of the Alliance I will gouge this ansible implant out of my head with my bare hands!"

"Yes. So will I." In my case it would be a relief. I had had nothing but trouble with the thing since it had been implanted.

He pressed his lips together, steepling his fingers over them. "I see. In that case I think I will make sure I am well armed at all times."

"I think we all should be. I will get some emergency protocols in place. Chandrayanan can go into the crawl tubing under the pool."

He looked suddenly alarmed. "What about Zenzie? She needs to be protected. She would be another asset to any of the dissident races."

"I don't think she would agree to go into the crawl tubing again. She swore not to after she spent three weeks down there with Segaton last time the Vaers attacked. Plus, you have to protect Zenzie; she has to protect me. That effectively bonds us together. Hopefully it would be enough in the event of an attack."

"Cunningham?"

"Cunningham can do whatever he wants. But we need to make sure we don't turn our backs on him. He has a history of betraying people."

"I know what he has done. I will not allow him to gain the upper hand, you can be sure."

"Zenzie and the crew need to know all of our plans."

"Then Xynia will too."

I didn't like that. "Xynia is not part of our crew. We do not know what intentions the Supreme Council has in this matter. She may have orders we know nothing about."

"You may be right. I do not trust her. However, if something happens involving Zenzara, then we may need the spokesdesignate. She is an excellent fighter, and she would give her life for the Chyzar without even thinking about it. Any Tyzaran official would, traitor or not."

I shook my head. The possibility that they might have deliberately sold the ZEPH drive to the Omnistate meant that the Supreme Council could no longer be trusted. I couldn't escape the suspicion that they may have wanted to trade the ZEPH technology for the groundbreaking RAMP missile technology that the Omnistate had developed. It was a sobering thought. If that were true, the members of the Supreme Council were far more self-serving than I had previously thought. It would not have surprised me in the least. In my limited experience, governments could prioritize weaponization over social reforms.

Even though it frustrated me to have to include the spokesdesignate, I knew he was right. Ostensibly she was in charge of the mission. I could not hold back without proof. I gave in. "Very well. I will keep her in the loop. Thanks Izan. You had better get back to your routine."

He nodded, placing both hands into a canvas container of chalk. Then he slapped them together to get rid of the loose powder.

I watched as he lifted himself effortlessly up onto the lower bar of the two. No wonder he was in such good shape; he was very good at it, moving from the lower to the higher bar with such fluidity that at times it was hard to track him. Asymmetric bars are good on a ship. They provide a comprehensive workout in a relatively small space while also allowing the athlete to gain a sensation of spatial freedom that often doesn't exist on long journeys. Most ships have them.

The first sign that we had been right to anticipate danger came out of the blue, two days later. There was a sudden jolt and the whole ship fell out of ZEPH drive.

Nivala shuddered to a forced stop. The bridge and engine crew rushed to identify what had happened. By then we were in full alert. The scientist had been hurriedly pushed into the crawl tubing under the pool. He would be accompanied by Seyal and a large pulser weapon. Naturally, it had proved impossible to keep Cunningham from the scientist, so he was in the junction between crawl spaces too. Chandrayanan's bulky research documents had been hurriedly stuffed into a case and he had taken it down with him, together with both his and Bull's luggage. As far as our attackers were concerned, our only guest was Xynia.

Although the Vaers surrounded us within minutes, they didn't have everything their way. Denaraz and Anzany were on duty at the weapons station, directly below the main bridge. They got several shots off even as we were lurching out of ZEPH drive. I could feel *Nivala's* vibrations as the ABlasers fired.

I passed Seyal as I raced for the main bridge. She had Segaton strapped to her body in a sort of cummerbund that she used as a baby wrap. She was on her way to join the two Terrans.

"Make sure they stay put, will you?" I shouted to her.

She waved her pistol and nodded grimly. She would keep them there by force if necessary. She was useful wherever we put her. Apart from learning at a rate that surprised us all, people consistently underestimated her. That had given us advantages in the past. I was pretty sure it would give us more in the future.

I was pleased to find the bridge crew all on station when I arrived. Sammy and Mel had been on duty, and Neema got there even before me.

There were three ships, and they weren't messing about. They were attempting to position one to port, one to starboard and one directly in front of us.

I punched the communication relay to connect with Denaraz. "Concentrate our fire power on the front one! They are trying to box us in."

A grunt acknowledged my order. Our weapons began to fire.

I next contacted the engine room. "Didj? What's up? Damage report!"

"We were forced out of ZEPH drive, Captain."

"How long to get back on line?"

"At least an hour."

Not good. We certainly didn't have an hour.

Zenzie had run onto the bridge at the same time as I had. She was my shadow; I expected nothing less from her. She was standing beside me, crest rigid as she stared at the vid screen in front of us.

"Do you see that?" she asked, squinting slightly at the image.

"No, what?"

"There!" She pointed. "Where the wings meet the fuselage. See? There, now!"

I tried, but it was hopeless. "I can't see anything. What is it?"

"It looks like a puff of smoke. We hit him! I think there is something on fire there."

"Starboard or port?"

"Port. Yes, I am sure. There is something burning, just where the wing meets the main section."

"Well spotted." I passed the news on to the weapons bridge. Almost immediately, an ABlaser pulse shot out from *Nivala's* main array, targeting the weakened spot.

There was the briefest of all flashes of light, nothing for several long seconds, then a whole sheet of fuselage exploded out into space. Both Sammy and I whooped. That should keep them busy for a time.

"Mel, duck us under that damaged ship and tuck us behind it. We will use it as a shield."

"Sure." She executed the maneuver flawlessly. I couldn't have done better myself. The hesitant girl crippled by fear of space was gone, at least temporarily. I hardly recognized this fiercely competent person that had taken her place.

"Great going, Mel!"

She smiled at me. "That guy won't be firing on us any time soon. He has problems of his own to worry about. Two left."

We were still trying to defend ourselves when the high pitched ping of a Geiga interrupted us. I looked down quickly. Scout was pointing to the rear of the ship, tail stiffly out, snout indicating danger.

We had not seen any shuttles approaching. "They are trying to break in through one of the airlocks!" I grabbed a ZR and raced past the lift.

I skidded onto the cross corridor where most of the cabins were and looked to the left and then to the right. There were airlocks on both sides.

There was nobody outside either of them. I checked Scout. He was indicating downwards. They were on the middle deck.

The only good news was that fully grown Vaers could not fit into the crawl tubes. That meant that they couldn't get to Chandrayanan very easily, assuming that is who they were looking for, and that they would have to use the lifts to move from one deck to another. I lunged for the nearest wall comlink. "Cut off power to the lifts!"

"Done!" It was Neema's voice.

I began to relax. I tore open the nearest hatch and shot down the vertical tube with Zenzara at my heels. They were trapped on that one deck. I could hear shouting between them. It sounded as if three or four Vaers had successfully boarded our ship.

They had figured out that we would be coming at them from the vertical crawl tubing. We began to receive fire from what sounded like a hand-held ultrapulse. I remember feeling confused, because of course the ultrapulse is a Terran weapon. So what were the Vaers doing using it?

I squinted down. I could see a large Vaer arm shoved through one of the tube hatches. He couldn't get any more of his body through the hole. His phalanges held a large weapon and he was firing blindly, indiscriminately upwards at us.

Both Zenzie and I were hit by the shot. We tumbled down the rest of the ladder to land in an ignominious heap at the bottom of the shaft. He swapped arms, reached in and snatched Zenzie from my prone body, pulling her out into the main corridor. One minute I was groaning because of her weight on top of me, the next I was groaning because I couldn't feel her weight on top of me.

The arm reappeared, now reattached to a hand-held ultrapulse once more. The Vaer couldn't even get his head through the hatch, so he was back to waving it about indiscriminately. My ears had not deceived me then. The Vaer had somehow got hold of the most advanced Terran weapons. I contemplated what that meant. Then, belatedly, I realized that I was about to be eliminated, so it didn't really matter what that meant. There just might be a better way to spend my last few seconds in this universe.

I waited for my life to flash by me. It didn't. All I could think of was that they had Zenzie, and that the gun in my face seemed enormous at such close quarters. I felt sick to my soul. I had actually taken Zenzara to them. How stupid was that?

No final prayers had occurred to me either. The only thing that happened is that my heart flooded with useless adrenaline and the reptilian part of my brain screamed at me to escape. Yeah. Thanks. Would if I could. You try diving down a crawl tube immediately after being hit by an ultrapulse. I'd like to see you try it. I managed to shuffle a few inches to the right. It literally took all of the energy I had left, and I collapsed after I had done it.

The gun had prodded around the empty space but now had found my stomach. It prodded again, checking the consistency of the obstruction. I work out quite hard, so I like to think it was a good muscle tone.

Not good enough to fool the Vaer into thinking it was an inanimate object. The gun settled directly at my sternum.

I closed my eyes and waited for the flash. I knew it would be the last thing I ever experienced. Damn! Not the way I had been hoping to go.

The flash, when it did come, seemed dimmer than I had been expecting.

I waited for the pain to flare up, or to cease, or whatever death feels like.

There was a scuffling and the hand holding the weapon began to edge out of the hatch in jerky movement. Back, pause, back, pause. I took a cautious breath. It didn't ooze out of any holes in my lungs, so I took another one. The breathing apparatus still seemed to work.

The arm and the gun finally disappeared out of the hatch. There was a slight pause, and then Seyal's head appeared in the gap. She still had Segaton bound to her chest. "Captain? Are you all right?"

"Now I am," I gasped, trying not to use up the small amount of energy that was slowly seeping back.

"I will get you out in a moment. Please wait where you are."

That was a surplus request, if ever I had heard one. I just gave a weary nod.

She took it as agreement, and her head withdrew from the hole. I thought I heard intense whispering, then the hatch closed behind her and the wheel locking mechanism snapped back into place.

I don't know how long I lay there before I recovered the use of my limbs. It felt like hours, but I guess it must have been around ten minutes. Even then, I wasn't sure that I would be much use in any fight.

Still, I also wasn't going to leave Zenzara and Seyal to wrangle with Vaer intruders on their own. Denaraz and Anzany were on this deck, but I had no idea what had happened to them. I had to make myself move, make myself become useful again.

I managed to pull myself over to the hatch. I found it hard to open the locking mechanism, with no place to use for leverage. At last, I managed to turn the wheel.

I edged the hatch open by degrees, unsure of what I would find on the other side. I lay the ZR on the decking with my right hand, ready to fire if need be, and peeked out.

There was nobody awake in that stretch of the corridor, as far as I could see. The only presence was that of a large Vaer. He was lying quite neatly along the centre of the corridor. He was unconscious, and looked as if he would remain that way for quite some time. Seyal had successfully taken out one of the opposition. Good for her. I wondered if she had taken the time to straighten him up so tidily. Probably. Seyal disliked disorder.

I pulled myself through the hatch and stood up. It took me a few seconds to steady myself, to dispel the vertigo that swept through me.

I heard shots towards the weapons bridge, so I crept forward in that direction. Every step helped to centre me, helped to recover from the ultrapulse that had hit me. I think it must have just skimmed the soles of my feet and then my chest, because I was up and walking. Not too many people can say that after an ultrapulse has been fired at them. I hoped Zenzie was all right as well.

I snuck along the passageway, passing first the kitchen and then the dining room, on the left. To the right I saw the lift, still out of use. Good. The other two decks should be fine. If the Vaers hadn't invaded them as well.

I couldn't know. Not from here. What I needed to do was to solve the current situation on my deck, and then expand out to the rest of the ship.

So I edged towards the airlock separating the weapons bridge from the hallway. It was open. Not a good sign, I thought to myself. If I had been Izan, it was the first thing I would have locked. The fact that he hadn't didn't bode well for him.

I ducked behind the bulkhead and tried to tilt my head around the opening.

I saw a stalemate situation.

Denaraz and Anzany were slumped on the floor, being covered by an angry Vaer. They looked very much the worse for wear, I thought, though most of it looked to be from hand to hand combat. You had to be crazy to go hand to hand against a Vaer. They are three times our size and extremely vicious.

Zenzara was lying on the deck, unconscious or worse. She wasn't moving.

And Seyal was facing up to the remaining Vaer, a loaded ZP in her hand. She was holding it unwaveringly at his head.

"Put the ultrapulse down," she was saying, in her slow, steady tone.

The Vaer was looking amazed. "You are an Avarak female!" he said, a tone of great disdain seeping into his voice. "A female! They are weak!"

"Try me," she said in her usual calm voice. "I have every intention of killing you, I can assure you."

You could see the cogs turning inside the Vaer's head. He did not believe her. I could have told him he should, but he was just too darn set in his ways to think that her soft voice could in any way damage him.

He took a large step towards her. "I am sure you do not want to use that thing," he said, in what her probably perceived as a persuasive voice. "You have a baby."

"You are correct. I do not want to."

His lower beak twisted. "I thought not." He took another step closer. She shot him.

"But I will."

The Vaer gave a squawk of pain, twisting as he fell heavily. The other

Vaer snapped around and loosed off an ultrapulse at Seyal.

She shrieked and ducked, turning rapidly to protect Segaton from the blast. That meant she was unable to avoid it altogether. It winged her in the shoulder. She was spun around by the force of it.

By then I had brought my own gun to bear and had taken out the last Vaer. I managed to get him full in his chest, and though I was unsure of whether a ZR pistol could permanently damage a fully-grown Vaer, this one was definitely out for the count.

I checked Seyal. Despite her injury she was now holding her own pulser to the head of the downed Vaer. He was conscious, but looking pretty pissed with his current situation.

I nodded to her. I needed to get back to the Vaer shuttle that had brought them over. I raised an eyebrow at the bodies and then at Seyal.

She nodded. "I will not let them get up, Mallivan Bell. Go. I will be fine here."

"Thank you Seyal. You did great!"

She looked uncomfortable. "I am a member of the crew. I wish to be a useful member."

"You are! You saved my life. I owe you one."

Her forehead crinkled. "How can you owe a life?" she questioned. "A life cannot be passed on, like a shoe or a coat."

"Not a life. A life-sized favor. That is what I owe you."

"I do not understand. How big is a life-sized favor?"

"Don't worry about it, Seyal. We will know it when we see it."

Another voice broke in on us. "A life-sized favor is the Savior Protocol." Zenzie was beginning to come around.

Seyal's brow cleared. "Then that is good. You mean you will protect me. 'Have my back', as you Spacelanders say?"

"I mean exactly that."

"Does that extend to my son? To Segaton?"

"Of course it does."

"Then I am happy to have saved your life, Mallivan Bell. If anything happens to me I would not want my son to be alone."

"He wouldn't be. He is part of this crew now. It is his home, too. Not that anything is going to happen to you," I finished hastily.

"Thank you. Now, please go and secure the ship."

"What did you do with the visitors?"

She lowered her head. "I'm afraid I wasn't able to reach them, Captain. I trust that they are still in good health." She looked worried.

She had saved my life. "You did great, Seyal. Thank you. Zenzara, are you all right?"

"Yes, Mallivan, I am fine." She carefully took the ultrapulse weapon out of the Vaer's slack hand. She shuffled away from him and pointed it at the other Vaer. "We will make sure they do no more harm."

I slipped back through the hatchway, but I wasn't alone. A very battered Denaraz had staggered to his feet while we were speaking.

"I will come with you," he muttered, blinking deeply in an attempt to clear his vision. I don't think it worked

I looked past him and saw that Anzany was stirring too. That was great news. "Any help welcome," I assured him. "We don't know how many of these Vaers are left in the shuttle."

He gave a curt nod. "What are we waiting for?"

I turned to Seyal. "You might like to drag that Vaer you left in the passageway in here. We don't want him to wake up and go stumbling around on his own."

"Of course. I had forgotten about him."

"Will you be able to manage?"

She lifted her head. "Certainly. Vaers are large, but not more than Avarak males."

That was true. Vaers were shaped differently and were slightly larger than Avarak males, but for sheer bulk, the Avaraks would probably win any day.

Denaraz and I slipped out into the passageway and walked stealthily past the prone Vaer. As we passed, Denaraz raised one eyebrow. "You?"

"Seyal."

He looked at the way the body had been placed. "Of course. You wouldn't have neatened him up like that."

"I wouldn't."

The passageway ended in another corridor, this one at right angles to it. This was the corridor that led to the sick bay to starboard, the spa to port, and a storage bay in between.

We didn't know if the breach had been to port or starboard, so we peered warily around the corner that marked the ending of the central pool area.

All appeared normal to port. We looked along the corridor in the other direction. The airlock by the sickbay had been breached and was still open. There was one burly Vaer standing on guard outside.

We were considering what to do when Zenzara breezed past both of us hopping and skipping.

My jaw dropped. I tried to grab her as she went past. So did Izan, but she twisted very nimbly and managed to evade our hands. We did the only thing we could under the circumstances: duck back around the corner.

Zenzie hopped, skipped and jumped her way along the passageway, crooning a happy little song to herself as she went.

There was a rustle at the end of the corridor as the Vaer must have pointed his ultrapulse directly at her.

The skipping stopped. A little girl voice made its way back to us, its tone full of innocent wonder.

"Hello? Are you a guest too? What's your name?"

The silence indicated the difficulty the Vaer was having processing his next move. I sympathized. I knew from experience that however much you might be tempted to shoot Zenzie, it was not as easy as it seemed.

"Why are you here?"

I could almost see the childlike smile she would be assuming. "I live here." There was the sound of more jumping and skipping. "Do you want to skip with me?"

"Vaers do not skip," he pronounced in a serious voice.

"That's a pity," she replied, butter wouldn't melt in her mouth. "I do."

"Who are you? We came to see a young Tyzaran girl."

"Did you? That must be me. I am the only one on this ship. Did you bring me a present?" More sounds of skipping.

Vaers are very sharp. They make a lot of money because of it. This one must have been the exception. "Yes," he said after some thought. "I have a present for you. On the shuttle."

Talk about led through the nose. I was amazed he couldn't see through her antics.

There was a trill of girly excitement. "A present? Show me! Show me!" The two voices vanished into the shuttle.

Izan and I crept down the passageway and into the Vaer shuttle. It was a moment to close the airlock separating us from *Nivala*.

The Vaer that had taken Zenzie inside had to have heard. Vaer hearing is exceptional. He could hardly have missed the airlock closing.

There was a strangled cry and the sound of a large body hitting the decking. Then Zenzie's voice filtered along the passageway to us.

"Mallivan? Denaraz?"

We hurried along to her position, to find her standing over the Vaer. She must have used her thoria as soon as he turned back towards the airlock. The thong was wrapped around his legs. He was struggling to get up.

Denaraz leaned down and applied a ZR on stun. The Vaer guard glowered up at us for the split second he was still conscious. Then the head dropped to the metal deck and hit, making a surprisingly heavy clanging sound.

I quickly checked the rest of the shuttle. There was nobody else on board. I made my way back to the other two.

"Don't you ever do something like that again," I snapped.

Zenzara opened her eyes wide. "Like what?"

"Don't think you can play your tricks on me, young lady. I thought I told you to stay with Seyal."

She stiffened. "You may be captain of the *Nivala*, but that doesn't mean you can give me orders."

"Yes, actually, it does."

She attempted to brush away the truth, using one hand. "The Savior Protocols trump your being captain."

"No, they don't."

"Anyway, Anzany woke up and so they didn't need me. I thought I would do a better job than you two. You would have got yourselves shot."

Denaraz looked insulted. I must admit, it was irritating that she seemed to look on us as two bumbling fools.

"The same thing could have happened to you."

"No it couldn't. They want me alive. They know I am the Chyzar. I was never in any danger."

The irritating thing about Zenzara Zylarian is that she is invariably right. It makes her insufferable sometimes.

Denaraz had finished immobilizing the Vaer captive by this time. He was now firmly bound to one of the hatches. Even if he regained consciousness, he wouldn't be going anywhere. "Right. What next?"

We looked at each other, then a slow grin spread over all our faces at the same time. We had a Vaer shuttle.

"Now, what to do with it, that is the question," I murmured.

"Indeed." Denaraz stroked his chin. "It does seem a pity not to make good use of it. Especially since the other shuttles could take us out easily if they wanted to."

Zenzie was stepping from foot to foot, looking eager. "Yes! Let's do something really cool!"

Fine to say, but I couldn't see a way forward. We were surrounded by ships bigger than ours, with very effective weapons we couldn't counter.

"I don't suppose your connexion to the Chakrans is live right now?" I asked.

Zenzara shook her head. "They've gone silent. They haven't contacted me since that stuff with Admiral Ellison. Though I can still feel them."

"Pity. It would be useful if you had them on speed dial."

"I think they are trying to build a permanent connexion with me. It just seems to be taking a lot of time."

"Then we will have to get ourselves out of this."

"Yes. I don't think the Chakrans would consider us to be worth their intervention in any case. What is your plan?"

"We need to check the airlocks on all the other decks. The Vaers may have sent more shuttles over."

"Especially if they realized that we could cut the power to the lifts and we don't have flights of stairs to fit them."

"True. We'll check that out first, and then wing it."

Denaraz looked pained. I gave him the 'what's-up-with-you' look.

He sighed, in a resigned sort of way. "I don't know what 'wing it' means, but it seems to me that we don't have a plan."

"O ye of little faith! Of course we have a plan."

"And ...?"

"And what?"

"And what is the plan?"

"Err ... We are going to ... err ..." Luckily, it came to me in a flash. There was no way to win in a straight fight, so we had to do it another way. We could try to mislead them. We could give them what they wanted. Yes. Brilliant. It might not work, but I really couldn't see what else we could do. "... err ... we are going to make them think ... or wonder, at the very least, if the person they came here to get has been killed."

I turned to Zenzie. "You get to Didjal, as fast as you can. Tell it I need this ..." I wrote down something on a piece of paper, "... and this, and this. Then do as it says. Then come back here and tell me what it says."

She was bemused, but obediently got up. "OK Mallivan. I guess it is another one of your crazy ideas."

I smiled. "It is. And it might not work."

"I never think they will." She ran out of the shuttle.

I explained my idea to Izan. He and I spent the waiting time setting the whole thing up. If it was to work it was going to have to look good.

It took around ten minutes before Zenzie was back. She was clutching a large metal box in front of her and a smaller electronic device. "Didjal says this will work. We just have to plug this device in, here. Then we place the box as near as possible to the fuel dump. I have to be at one of the tight-beams on *Nivala*. The device can pilot this thing automatically. That will have to be from *Nivala's* bridge. Didjal has already hacked into the systems."

Good enough. "Right. Denaraz, you go with Zenzie to the vid-screen on the weapons bridge. I will head back to the bridge on *Nivala*."

They nodded. I touched Zenzie on the shoulder. "You know what to do?"

She shrank from my gesture. She must have thought it was patronizing. "Of course. I'm not mentally challenged, you now."

I muttered. She whipped around. "What did you say?" Her crest flew upright in outrage.

"Nothing." I held both hands up. "Just clearing my throat." That wasn't true, but it wasn't the moment to challenge anybody, either.

She didn't believe me, but I had left her nowhere to take it. "Hmm. Just as well," she grumbled, before leading the way out of the shuttle.

I too left the Vaer shuttle, closing the airlock firmly on my way out. I didn't release the captive Vaer, and found myself feeling bad about that as I left. But there simply wasn't time for more. He had chosen his loyalties, and they were going to be the death of him. It didn't make me feel good about myself. I hesitated. And went back. I couldn't deliberately leave him to die, however much I resented and disliked the Vaer race in general. I grimaced and dragged him along the decking towards the airlock. I confess I didn't worry very much whether I was chipping a feather here and there. And his beak might have snagged on the corners once or twice. What do you expect? I try to be a good person, but I'm not *that* good. I was sweating like a pig by the time I tussled him over the airlock to *Nivala*, and was able to turn the closing wheel to its locking position.

I wasn't going to drag him one single inch more than I had to. I let him lie just on the other side of the airlock, and tied him pretty hastily to the inside bulkhead, making sure he couldn't reach anything critical.

Then I slipped inside the crawl tubes and made my way up the crawl ladders to the deck above.

I was still worried that the Vaers might have sent more than one shuttle over, that the upper deck might also have been targeted. I only opened the hatch a chink, in case the bridge area had been taken over again.

Luckily, there were no signs of any such thing. All seemed deceptively quiet. Even so, I was careful as I crept past the saloon towards the bridge.

In the end it was friendly fire that nearly finished me off. I stuck my head around the corner of the bridge and almost got it shot off.

There was a cry of surprise. "Rye! Sorry! Is that you?"

I put one hand to my head and pulled away singed hair. "No, it is the abominable snowman," I snapped. "Why did you shoot at me?"

Mel went pink. "Why didn't you say who you were? I thought you were one of the Vaers."

"Well, I'm not."

"Yes. I can see that *now*. Of course I can. But I didn't know *then*, did I?"

I nodded to Neema, who was at her usual station, before glaring at Mel and then at Sammy. "You two are trigger happy. You need to work on that."

"We will," said Sammy at the same time as Mel denied any wrongdoing. "It was your fault for sneaking around."

I shook my head. "Never mind. I need to get at the pilot's console."

Sammy slid out of his station. "Be my guest."

I settled in front of the console, and pressed one of the comlinks down. "Bridge to the Chyzar!"

"Captain?" It was Zenzie's voice, in an urgent whisper. It seemed to be coming from the Vaer shuttle. Didjal had done a great job.

"Chy Zylarian! Are you safe?"

"Yes." Her voice was hardly more than a murmur. "They have not hurt me. They haven't found my comlink yet. They thought I was unconscious. Please come. I don't want to stay here! I am ... frightened." There was a scraping sound, and her voice came back on the comlink. "They are coming! They know that I am awake! Captain, please—" There was another crackle on the line, the sound of heavy boots and then a loud crack followed by complete silence.

I saw that the shuttle was undocking from *Nivala*.

"Chy Zylarian? Chy Zylarian?"

But there was no further reply. The shuttle had now turned away from *Nivala*. Suddenly, it began to pile on the acceleration, choosing a vector radially outward from the ship.

"We have lost her," I sentenced, using my best voice of doom. I turned to smile at Sammy and Mel who were shocked. Even Neema was staring at me with her jaw slack. I took my hand off the comlink. "That went well." I pressed the communication button to the weapons bridge. "Denaraz. Prepare to fire on that shuttle. Three salvos should do it."

"It had better," came back the gruff reply. "That's all we have, at least for immediate deployment."

"What ... what ...?" Mel's forehead was creased. "You ... you can't ..."

"And there they go!" I grinned and pointed at the screen. The plotter was showing all three Vaer ships turning to cover the fleeing shuttle. Leaving us free, they formed a barrier on the line they thought we would fire through. The two untouched ships were accelerating away from us. "They bought it. Didjal was able to boost the comlink so that they could pick it up."

Sammy grinned. "A put-up job?"

"Well, of course." I rolled my eyes. "You don't think I would really let them take Zenzie away?" Not that I hadn't been tempted to get rid of her myself, of course.

"It sounded like it."

"It was meant to. I knew they would be monitoring our comlink wavelengths."

The Vaer ships were powering up to reduce the distance to their shuttle.

I pressed the button again. "Fire first grouping!"

Four missiles shot off in the direction of the Vaer shuttle. I watched, curious to see what the Vaers would do.

They were very well trained in space maneuvers. The two escorting ships turned as one to protect the shuttle that they thought Zenzie was on. Each ship concentrated its fire power on eliminating one of the torpedoes. Even the damaged vessel managed to get a bearing on one of the two remaining missiles.

Almost immediately three of the four missiles were destroyed. But that left them scrambling for the last one.

"Fire again!" I told Denaraz. "Second grouping!"

Another salvo of four space torpedoes jolted the fuselage as they departed from *Nivala*.

That should give them more of a headache, I hoped.

It did. As the first Vaer ship brought its attention back to the new missiles, the second of them managed to pick off the previous remaining missile shortly before impact.

"Fire again! Third grouping!"

Denaraz obliged. "That's your lot, for now."

I made waving movements with one hand. "Take us out of here, Mel. As fast as you can, and as far as you can."

Mel nodded. I waited to make sure we could reach ZEPH drive, and then turned back to watch whether the last battery of torpedoes would be enough.

The Vaers had successfully picked off the last of the second grouping as well, but they left it so late that the fleeing shuttle was buffeted by the resultant explosion. Now they were really in trouble. The Vaer ship that we had damaged earlier had fallen to one side. It seemed unable to bring guns to bear on any targets whatsoever. The other was having difficulty in retargeting the new volley of threats in time.

I held my breath, hoping that at least one of the last salvo of four would get through. I had a back-up plan in place, but it would be more satisfying if one of the missiles hit the shuttle. Artistically speaking, it would be more convincing.

We were accelerating away fast. Mel was pushing *Nivala* as hard as she could. I hoped that Didjal would be able to keep the engines running. We certainly didn't need a breakdown right now.

I had to crank up the magnification on the vid-screen.

I held my breath. The last operative Vaer ship managed to take out a missile. That left three final missiles still on target. They fired again, but missed. They were getting nervous.

The first ship recovered long enough to take out the second missile, but the remaining two were arrowing in on the shuttle.

I gasped as the second ship succeeded. One of the two remaining missiles disappeared in a haze of white light. Then I smiled. There was no time for them to get the last torpedo.

I pressed another button, to talk to Denaraz. "On three! One ..." I squinted at the screen. I couldn't distinguish any distance between the last missile and the shuttle. "Two ..."

The first ship gave one of the neatest turns I have ever seen in space, and fired off an ultrapulse. The beam intersected with the missile only about fifty feet from the shuttle itself. There was a huge flash.

"Three ..."

And another, even larger flash. The shuttle disintegrated.

I turned away. Now we had to get out of here fast enough to discourage pursuit, although I hoped that the Vaers would have bought the deception.

A rather plaintive voice came across the comlink. It was Seyal. "Err ... You haven't forgotten we have three Vaers down here, have you?"

"No, of course not!" I had. "I'll be right down."

Shells! What to do with three Vaers, especially since the rest of their people now hopefully believed that both Zenzara and possibly our two Flatlander guests had gone to their makers. I rubbed my nose, thinking.

Mel was giving me her smug look. She thought I had screwed up. Well, she should try to think stuff like this out in seconds. It wasn't easy. "You try it!" I told her.

She looked surprised. "I didn't say anything!"

"You didn't have to."

"You can't blame a person for their face," she grumbled.

"You shouldn't wear a face like that, should she, Sammy?"

Mel swiveled around to face her partner, who put on a deer-in-the-headlights look. He raised his hands in surrender. "Hey, I haven't said anything!"

I tutted.

Mel swiveled back.

I shrugged, as if to say, "See, I told you so!"

She opened her mouth, but I rolled my eyes. "Whatever." I got up and tried to give her a stern stare. "Keep this speed up. Change course as soon as we are out of range for those Vaer ships. And when you do that, make the new course close to somewhere we can drop these Vaer captives off at."

I left, smiling as I heard Mel pick on Sammy. "You could have said something, Sammy!"

His voice was bewildered. "What was I supposed to say?"

I lost the rest of Mel's comment, but the gist seemed to be that boyfriends were only put on this world to support their girlfriends.

Now that the lifts were in operation again, I whisked down to the engine room to check on Didjal and Eshaan. They were fine. Didjal was busy coaxing the large engines to keep up the good work, and Eshaan was doing the ostrich walk with baby Segaton. Because of his elongated tarsus, he could bob up and down with each step far more than I would have been able to. Segaton clearly found it soothing; he was fast asleep, one small hand reaching up towards the Enif's glossy shoulder.

I was able to pick up a heavy-duty trolley from the cargo bay. I was done with dragging dead weights around. I just managed to fit it into the lift and take it up to the middle deck.

I untethered the Vaer that was lying by the airlock and manhandled him pretty crudely onto the trolley. He was still out for the count, so I didn't have to worry too much about controlling him.

On the way to the weapons bridge, I stopped off at guest cabin two, briefly parking my loaded trolley outside the door.

Spokesdesignate Xynia should have been sequestered in her quarters for all the recent events. We had decided that she should take no part in any of this.

However, I could find no trace of her in her quarters. I gave a sigh. Of course she hadn't stayed where she was supposed to be. I began to search around the ship for her, finally finding her hiding in the crawl-tubing space under the swimming pool. She had decided to join the two Terrans.

I noticed that she was casually carrying a large ultrapulse pistol. I must have raised an eyebrow, because she followed the direction of my gaze and gave a small laugh.

"I thought I would come down here to protect our visitors," she said. "We wouldn't want them wandering about getting into danger, now would we?"

There was a certain emphasis on her words that surprised me, but I didn't have time to wonder about it at the time. I needed her to stand guard over the Vaers. We were running short on hands.

She agreed to watch over them, though I can't say I saw much enthusiasm.We rearranged her cabin to resemble a transit area. I left my first Vaer with her and then I made my way to the weapons bay, my trolley trundling loudly before me.

Two of the Vaers were awake, being guarded still by Seyal and Anzany. I loaded up the unconscious one and co-opted Anzany to escort the two who were awake to Xynia's quarters.

As we reached Xynia's rooms, the unconscious Vaer began to come to. He hauled himself up off the trolley and was promptly sick all over Xynia's table. *That* made her nose wrinkle up in distaste. I was hard put not to grin.

Finally, we trussed them all up together. I hoped that we could find somewhere suitable to drop them off before long. If not, we would have to feed them. Vaers are big. Supplies are limited. In any case, there would be no relaxing on board *Nivala* until we had got rid of them.

I made my way back to the bridge wondering if I was being too soft.

Should I just have chucked them out of the space hatch? From the fear deep in their eyes, that is what they had been expecting. It is what they had probably done to many of their own captives. The Vaer way, if you like. They had done nothing to make me want to be lenient with them.

Yet I knew that I couldn't act like that. The Interstellar Enforcement Agency had been put into place to represent the law in the Major Shells. It was early days, but it was crystal clear to me that part of our job would be to try to stop the indiscriminate killing that species like the Vaer were wont to carry out. We weren't going to be able to do that by imitating them. I was glad I had saved the fourth Vaer. It might not make a difference to the universe, but it made a difference to me. And to him, presumably. It felt good. The right direction for the Major Shells to take.

Most of us had not come out unscathed from that little skirmish. The Zeroth chambers were needed as we journeyed away from the point of ambush. With Xynia covering the prisoners, we were able to take it in turns. Nobody had life-threatening injuries. We had been lucky to escape. Very lucky. But what worried me most was that I had been wrong. Their target had not been the scientist after all. It had most definitely been Zenzara. That concerned me. Again, I felt there was a bigger picture we were missing pieces of.

Mel's update, when it came, was a big relief. We had left the Vaer ships far behind. They had fallen back to search for survivors in the wreckage of the shuttle. She was certain that we were out of range of their sensor arrays, and was about to change course. She suggested dropping the four captives off at the Pallis Ring. The Pallis Ring is the site of an ancient supernova explosion. It happened so long ago that it is now actually an area of formation of new stars. These haven't really been explored in depth yet, since there are no signs of evolved animal life. The systems are too young for that. However, there are two or three with young planets in orbit.

"They can be dropped on Epsilon CCR1057," Mel told me. "I think there is an automatic relay station somewhere on the planet. They should survive there and will eventually be able to get back to Vaer Nova."

"Set a course, then. Can't *wait* to offload them."

I ignored Mel's pointed suggestion that we might offload other people at the same time. Claustronetics often get a little grumpy, I find.

4

We arrived at the Nephealis Gyre without further incident, apart from the day that Zenzie attempted to glue Xynia's door shut. Luckily, Denaraz was in the hallway at the time and managed to avert an international incident. Zenzara was brought up in front of the captain – me – and was given a good talking to. She was unrepentant and even angry that her plan had been thwarted, huffily insisting that Denaraz had no right to interfere. It took some time and effort to make her see the error of her ways.

Apart from that, the journey was uneventful. Chandrayanan and Cunningham kept themselves very much to themselves and we detected no pursuit by Vaers or any other species. I was glad. I was not the only one to have come out of the last encounter slightly the worse for wear, and it was pleasant to be given recuperation time.

As we approached Nephealis there was almost a festive atmosphere on board *Nivala*. We felt happy to be this close to a place most of us had never even dreamed of visiting. The general feeling on board was that down time on the Gyre would be interesting and well-earned.

The Nephealis Gyre hung in space. It was huge. As the export platform for all their phyonwe fruit production, there were vast areas of freight. Tucked into the other side of the station we could see the fleet of light cruisers that the Nepheals used as their front defense line. They were sleek but tall ships, built to accommodate their owners. The ships resembled their makers – elegant and slim.

Nephealis is a light gravity world, much smaller than most. It is extremely mountainous and rocky, with very abrupt terrain. Very little food can grow on such land. Their main source of food is the fruit of the phyonwe tree. These hardy trees are very tall and grow in rocky areas on the sides of mountain slopes.

Because of these tall trees that are their staple source of food, Nepheals have developed long legs and necks about the length of my arm. They normally walk upright, on their two hind legs, but when endangered will drop to all fours since that enables their slim bodies to reach higher speeds. Their heads are elongated and goat-like, but they have very intelligent eyes. Their feet and hands have large, strong, thin digits to provide good traction across their loose, rocky world.

Nepheals, when attacked, will move startlingly quickly. They can jump across accidents in the terrain, such as quite large rivers. They are prone, however, to break legs, especially in higher gravity environments. They are so large that it is difficult for them to find shelter, which is why speed was important to their survival. The threat of extinction at the beaks of huge rapacious birds has left them with an ingrained fear that survives even after thousands of years. Their almost phobic dislike of the Vaers is well-known. They believe the Vaers to be descendents of the race of predators that decimated the Nepheals.

Their civilization once nearly disappeared during a decade of blight which killed almost all of the phyonwe trees. The Northern Nepheals, desperate to survive, discovered how to fashion tools out of the pliable bark. They managed to save some seeds, and from that point on they began to cultivate the lower, flatter lands. Their species developed in leaps and bounds after that.

Modern day Nepheals are believed to be only two thirds the size of their ancestors, and have shorter necks. They still present a strange sight, however. They are twice as tall as any other species, skeletally thin, and their faces are long and narrow, with a greenish tinge of skin.

Living up to 200 years, they are important members of the Major Shells, fiercely protective of environmental issues, but uninterested in political maneuvering. They dislike the Terrans and the Avaraks for their lack of respect of their environment, and intensely mistrust and dislike the Vaers. One of their greatest insults is "You could have feathers" or "He speaks through a beak."

They are able to understand all sides of an argument, which makes them valuable negotiators and intermediaries. Their civilization is advanced, and they appreciate music and art. They especially value Enif art, having an affinity for the Enif aesthetic.

Their speech is reasoned and sensible and they dislike shows of emotion. Deference and form is important to them and they expect to discourse uninterruptedly. It is considered rude to break into somebody's speech.

Their voices are mellow and almost seductive, and they have all studied logic, ethics, cosmology and metaphysics. They are the most knowledgeable species, in general, in all the Shells.

Nepheals are slow to pronounce, but fair to a fault. They are able to speak, having vocal chords, and in fact are able to pick up languages very quickly. All Nepheals are bilingual in Standard and Nepheale.

We docked at the berth assigned, which was about half way between the freight and the military areas. Then we assembled at the port hatch on the upper level. Zenzara, Denaraz, Seyal and I had agreed to stay on board the ship. The others, after the standard greeting, were to have a full day and night of R & R.

Before that, we were going to have to put up with a formal ceremony of welcome.

Spokesdesignate Xynia stood aloofly off to one side, flanked by Chandrayanan and Cunningham. Cunningham was wearing the dress ribbon of insignia of his Omnial status. He would, of course. The rest of us were standing four paces behind them.

A large creature with kind eyes approached at a stately gait. It was followed by an entourage of about ten other Nepheals, all looking dignified and solemn.

Xynia stepped forward and inclined her head. There was a small pause, then the leading Nepheal dipped its own long head slowly.

"Welcome to the Nephealis Gyre," it said, in a smooth voice.

"Thank you. I have brought the Terran scientist, Ramesh Chandrayanan."

Chandrayanan didn't bother to acknowledge the Nepheals. He moved forward though, and lifted his chin. I guess, being so much cleverer than the rest of us, he thought himself infinitely superior. He probably was, but it wasn't the best way to make friends.

Bull stepped forwards too. He gave a small bow to the Nepheals. "Pleasure to be here."

None of the rest of us said anything. However, a Nepheal to the right of the original speaker, a specimen that was much smaller, walked straight past Xynia's group and up to Zenzara. It lowered its head to sniff delicately at her.

"You are the Chyzar," it said, almost reverently. "I am Danaa. I have been assigned to your company."

Zenzara curtsied to it. "Pleased to meet you, Danaa. Are you a male or a female?"

Danaa gave a thin wheezy sort of sound. It may have been laughter. "I am, like you, young and female. That is why I was chosen. We are honored to welcome a representative of the Chakran people."

Zenzie blushed, much to my surprise. I didn't think she was capable of it. "Well, I'm not sure I could call myself a representative, exactly. I ... I am not able to contact them at will yet."

"We understand that they spoke through you during the war?"

"They did, yes, but they haven't done since then."

Danaa brushed away such objections. "The Chakrans have never interacted with any other species before. Previous Chyzars have only been able to pass on vague impressions. You are the single most important individual in the Major Shells. I am to protect you while you are here, with my life if necessary, and I hope that I shall become your friend."

Chandrayanan and Bull Cunningham were glaring at Zenzara. I don't think they appreciated being upstaged by an eight-year-old.

The original speaker lowered his large head again. "I hope that you will accompany us for a small welcome party we have prepared? May I introduce myself? My name is Caerae. I am a male. I am currently the leader of the Nepheals on the Gyre."

Xynia stepped forwards. "That would be most welcome. Thank you."

Caerae included all of us in his glance. "I hope all members of the crew will attend. There are many delicacies, though of course, most of them have been made of—"

The rest of the sentence got cut off, because an animal shape bulldozed past me and tore down the curved corridor that led away from our docking bay and into the station proper. The Nphealis Gyre is a wheel-shaped station, There are three concentric rings each one smaller than the previous one, connected by 'spokes' leading to a central organizational area, a bit like an ancient wooden ship's wheel.

I gave a cry and lunged after the shape, managing to touch its tail but not grab hold of it. It gave a high-pitched squeak of great excitement and vanished along one of the 'spokes' of the space station.

"Scout! Come back here! Oh, krikk!" I had a sinking feeling in my stomach. This might not be the way to start a new relationship off well.

Caerae's eyes opened wide. "You have a Geiga!" He was quite shocked.

I tried to look conciliatory. "Yes. I'm sorry. He must have smelt phyonwe fruit. He has been cooped up for far too long on the ship. I should have locked him up, I guess, but I forgot about him. Anyway, not to worry. He will just head for the refreshment table."

Caerae was still staring at me as if he couldn't believe my stupidity.

"Honestly, he won't cause any damage. He'll just mosey over to the phyonwe table and snaffle whatever he can." I gave a whistle to show willing, though I was pretty sure Scout would ignore any signals I might make right now. Not with phyonwe fruit in his sights. He can be somewhat determined. Geigas do like their food.

"Why would you bring a Geiga to Nephealis? Surely you know we are the sole producers of phyonwe fruit?"

"Well, of course I do. In fact, I thought it would be a nice treat for him. He likes the stuff so much."

Caerae looked down his long nose at me. His expression told me that I had not come up to expectations. "Do you realize that just one pair of Geigas on the planet could destroy all our crops of phyonwe in ten years? At their optimal rate of reproduction, it could be even sooner."

Xynia shot me a look that promised retribution in the future. I shrugged. How was I supposed to know my Geiga would be *animalis non grata*? They should put a notice up.

"Scout has no female to mate with. And we are not on the planet of Nephealis. We are on a space station. It is impossible for him to procreate here! Look, let me find him and bring him back to my ship. I will make sure he can't get off the ship. I do apologize."

He sighed. "The important thing is to get the Geiga under control," he said, rather accusingly.

There was a mad rush towards the refreshments room. Nepheals and guests jostled each other in their haste to neutralize poor old Scout. We thundered down the passageway and erupted into the area where all the refreshments had been laid out.

Scout was on top of the main table, small tail wagging in frantic pleasure as he snarfed down as many phyonwe fruits as possible. He gave us all a quick upwards look, decided that we did not, after all, present much of a danger, wagged his little tail some more, and lowered his head into the cake he was in the process of destroying, giving every sign of being in seventh heaven.

In the few minutes it had taken us to catch up with him, he had left a wake of destruction over the laden table.

I stopped and began to laugh. It was amazing how much damage one Geiga could do to a refreshments table. It looked like a bomb had hit it.

Xynia glared at me.

I bit my lip and strode up to Scout, seizing him around his fat middle and plucking him firmly away from his banquet. He responded with frantic little squeals of displeasure, squirming to get out of my arms.

He was quite a handful. Geigas are large animals and are pretty strong. I had quite the job holding him. To make things worse, he had realized that he was not going to get any more of the feast, and had upped the sound level. Geigas can screech pretty loudly when they want to. A couple of the hosts had covered their ears. Most of them were staring at me in disbelief. I gave the rest of the company an apologetic look and retreated with my burden to the ship.

That could have gone better.

I guess I could have locked Scout in my cabin.

I did it now, scolding him. Then I made my way back to the bridge. I wasn't eager to face more of Xynia's criticism; I probably wasn't the most popular person on the Nepheal Gyre. It might be more prudent to wait for the others on *Nivala*, I decided.

Zenzie was the first back. She could never leave my side for long. She tumbled onto the bridge giggling and chatting to her new friend, Danaa. The tall Nepheal girl was only just able to fit comfortably without hitting her head on the ceiling. I could see why the Nepheal ships were so large.

Zenzie shook her head at me. "You certainly spoiled their welcome party!"

"That was Scout!" I spread my hands. "It wasn't my fault!"

She gave me a raised eyebrow. Coming from somebody who had recently tried to glue Xynia's door shut, that was a bit rich. I bristled. "They should tell people not to bring their Geigas!"

Danaa was giving that high pitched wheezy thing again. "You are a very interesting Spacelander."

I wasn't sure what she meant, so I ignored the comment. "How is it going? Will we be able to get away soon?"

Danaa now seemed surprised. "Get away?"

"Yes. Our mission was to deliver the scientist and his ... fellow travelers ... safely to you. We did that. As soon as he has delivered his speech, we will be getting back to the Landau Rift."

"You do not wish to stay here? To familiarize yourself with our culture?"

My nose may have wrinkled. I am still learning about being diplomatic. "Oh! Yes! Yes, of course I would love the chance to find out more about the Nepheals. I —"

"—Because my aunt would like to meet the Chyzar."

Zenzara gave a jump of excitement. "On Nephealis itself? Oh, yes please!" She turned to me. "Say we can go, Mallivan! Please? Please?"

Danaa looked happy. "Great! She is in retreat in the mountains, as she has been looking after my new baby cousin. Special dispensation has been given for you and the Chyzar to visit a female retreat." She puffed out with pride. "You will be the only foreigners ever to have done that."

I thought back to what I had read about the race. Nepheal mothers-to-be retire to the wilderness in the mountains, where large retreats have been build in modern times. They voluntarily separate from their community since, in ancestral times, the newly born attracted the interest of the predators and thus brought danger to the community.

The newly born are tended to in relative isolation by their mothers until they can run almost as fast as the pack, which is around one year old.

During this time, both parents individually dedicate their spare time to illumination as a symbol of their mutual love and dedication, each trying to write a thesis that will enhance the knowledge of the species. A meaningful thesis is considered to be a testament to the profundity of their love for their newly-born child, and so are extremely important. Most of the advances in understanding have come through this custom. This is one of the main reasons that the Nepheals have developed so far, so quickly. They are bright and have the best grasp of Quantum Ontology in all the Major Shells.

A great celebration is held when a mother brings her offspring back to the fold. It is known as *Phaala*. *Phaala* is when one of these theses is read to a peer council. This is the day that the young are welcomed into their home lives, when the Nepheal celebrate the successful raising of another member of their race.

At the *Phaala*, the young Nepheal is inscribed in a state register and his or her lineage is traced back to the olden times. This is then immortalized for future generations to study. The two theses by the parents welcoming their offspring to the tribe are also annotated in the inscription.

There could be no doubt that to be allowed to visit a retreat was a signal honor. Not one that could possibly be denied. Not that I would want to. The only thing that concerned me was Scout. I didn't see how I could leave him on his own shut in my cabin.

The Nepheal girl must have read my mind. "You will be allowed to bring the Geiga," she told me. "My aunt was surprised to hear about him. She has never seen one."

"Will Scout be welcome on your planet? I thought Caerae said that Geigas were banned."

"They are. However, we have informed the Board of Elders that he belongs to the Chyzar, and they have given a special exemption. You will, however, be required to keep him under control at all times."

I gave Zenzara a meaning look. She ignored me. Her sense of ownership was fluid, to say the least. She probably did think of Scout as being hers, or at least partially hers. She certainly took him for walks every day, and he was always very happy to see her. In any case, who was I to think something as unique as a Geiga could be owned? They are living organisms, not inanimate objects.

"I see. That sounds amazing, Danaa. When are we to go, and what are the rest of my crew to do while we are down on the planet?"

She frowned. The lighter green spots on her forehead clustered closer together. "They are to stay on the Gyre. But Caerae said that they will be very welcome to enjoy our entertainment hubs."

My crew would certainly not complain about shore leave with entertainment hubs. But I was not so sure about Denaraz. His job was to stay close to the Chyzar at all times.

"There will be three of us."

Danaa looked alarmed. She skittered away on her painfully thin legs. "No! Only the Chyzar and you may go."

I shook my head. "I don't think we can agree to that. The Chyzar has a protector – apart from myself."

Zenzara gave me an incredulous look, which told me what she thought of my abilities to protect her. She glared. "I don't need to be looked after. If you remember, *I* am the one who is supposed to look after *you*."

"I know that, but Denaraz will expect to be allowed to remain close to you. You know that."

She shrugged. "The Supreme can say whatever they want. I do not require their help and I certainly do not require their protection."

Danaa showed her teeth. I hoped it was meant to be a smile. "That's settled then."

The two girls left the bridge so that Zenzie could give Danaa a tour of the ship. That left me to deal with Denaraz, who was the next person back.

His crest stiffened when I told him of the plans. "I can't allow that!" he said flatly. "I must go with you."

"Good luck with that one. Zenzara doesn't want you, and the Nepheals will only allow *me* to go down to the surface of the planet with her. They know *I* have to go – the savior protocols won't allow her to go without me."

Izan blew out air in frustration. "It would help if she listened to the Supreme."

"Yes. But she won't."

He scratched his chin. "No. She won't. Well, I suppose there is nothing I can do about it."

"Actually, I think it may be no bad thing. I don't trust Chandrayanan, and I certainly don't trust Bull. Or Xynia, for that matter. Somebody needs to keep a very close eye on them, and you would be my person of choice."

He regarded me thoughtfully. "Hmm. You might be right." His eyes looked concerned. I think he was beginning to wonder just how far the Supreme Council had participated in recent events.

He wasn't the only one. My own suspicions had been getting stronger and stronger. I decided to mention them again. "Doesn't it strike you as odd that the scientist who invented the RAMP missiles just happens to have ended up in Tyzaran custody? That he is being escorted politely around the Shells giving lectures?"

"The Supreme gave him the option of working for them, under strict supervision, or being interned in a secure facility for the rest of his life."

"So, if he wanted to continue with his studies, he had no choice but to accept?"

"The Supreme consider him to be the single most important scientific mind since Einstein. I was told that they were reluctant to mentally castrate him. They thought his contributions to science could be huge, so they decided to make him work where they could supervise him, but allow him to continue."

"If he shared his work with them?"

Denaraz looked pained. "I hope that wasn't the condition. They told me that his work would benefit the whole Alliance."

I snorted. "You do realize that it is almost certain that your Supreme did a deal with the Terrans?"

He gave a grimace. "The ZEPH drive for the RAMP technology. Yes, I am horribly afraid that they might have done. It would explain why Xynia is still a spokesdesignate and not in jail. She would have been acting under orders from the Supreme Council."

"So what is their motivation now? Now that they have the RAMP technology but it turned out to be useless."

His eyes flickered sideways as he pondered that question. Then I saw him connect the dots. "Chandrayanan has something else of importance. Something else they want!"

"Yes, I think so. I have the feeling your government is very much pursuing its own interests." My shoulders fell. "I just don't know how or why. And I have no proof." I chewed on my lip. "I think you need to stay here. We have no idea if this whole visit is just a front for something else or not, but somebody should be keeping an eye on things up here. I will talk to the rest of the crew as well. We will split them into three groups for leave, so there are always enough people on *Nivala* to be able to move quickly."

He sighed again. "I don't like it, but you may be right. I am, after all, paid by the Interstellar Enforcement Agency now. I no longer report back solely to the Supreme Council." His face was more wrinkled than usual. The split loyalties he was feeling were making him uncomfortable. I couldn't blame him.

"Good. That makes me feel much better about going down there. In any case, we both have the ansible connection, right?"

'*Right.*' I heard his answer in my brain. He was testing the connection. I winced, but pinged him back to show receipt. It was good to know that I wouldn't be completely isolated down on the planet.

5

We landed under a brilliant sun on Nephealis proper. I walked down the ramp of the Nepheal shuttle and shaded my eyes as I looked around.

These were the flatlands. And they were beautiful. The pastures that stretched out before me were covered with olive gray bushes and sparse trees.

Scout, attached to me by a firm chain that only terminated in leather near my hand, where he could not champ through it, lifted his snout and sniffed the air. Then he gave a lunge towards the nearest tree that almost pulled me off my feet.

Zenzie started to laugh, and even Danaa gave one of her wheezes. I scrambled to get my balance back and finally managed to get Scout under control. He gave me a very baleful stare, unable to understand why I would keep him away from a banquet.

There was a rustle of interest from the Nepheals who had gathered around the shuttle ramp. I guess they had never seen a Geiga before. I saw one or two of them pointing and more than one frowning their fear and displeasure. I twisted the leather part of his lead around and around my wrist. He was going nowhere without me, I decided. I didn't think he would be safe here, although I knew that the Nepheals are great ambassadors for the environment and value all life. They abhor violence and would never knowingly kill anything.

A warm breeze came off the surrounding land. I saw that the dirt track was rocky and of a reddish color. Everything was dry and the earth was cracked and parched.

Far in the distance, reaching high into the sky, were the white-tipped mountains. The snow caps were small, showing how difficult Nephealis found it to squeeze moisture out of the cloudless sky. Water was a valuable resource here.

Caerae had exited the shuttle behind us. He now led us towards the waiting group of dignitaries. We were introduced to several members of the Board of Elders. These Nepheals were paler than the rest of the race. Their green skin was tinged with white, especially around their long faces. The spots across their foreheads had grown larger, fusing into lines.

We bowed before them, following Caerae and Danaa's leads.

They chatted to both of us, and several of them even admired Scout, who promptly rolled over onto his back to leave his ample tummy exposed for scratching. His little tail batted at the dirt track as venerable Nepheals bent creakily down to touch the creature most of them had never seen before.

Caerae, who had been cooler toward me since the incident of the welcome party, began to chuckle. I raised one eyebrow in his direction.

"I have never seen an Elder so intrigued," he confided. "These Geigas are our most enthusiastic customers, yet we have never seen one set foot – hoof – on Nephealis before. You are already changing us, Chyzar."

Zenzara nodded graciously, instantly relegating my role to attendant. "For the better, I hope?"

"Oh, certainly. We live in isolation from the rest of the Major Shells, as you know. We are still afraid of our own fragility."

"But you are probably the most intelligent species in the Shells."

"And one of the most vulnerable."

I thought it was time I spoke up. "Now you are members of the Interstellar Alliance. The other races will protect you."

He didn't seem convinced. "Unfortunately, it still takes weeks for the other races to reach us here. Any predators would be long gone by the time the rest of the Alliance was able to reach us."

He was not wrong. Again, I wondered why the Supreme Council had sent the scientist here. It seemed to me to be the height of imprudence. He was to remain onboard *Nivala*, up at the Gyre, until his lecture, but it might still put the Nepheals in danger. I wondered what secrets his mind was hiding.

I found myself looking around for transport, but there was none. I felt my spirits sink. The Nepheals had a long stride. No doubt the miles would vanish under their paces, but Zenzara and I were going to struggle to keep up if we were to depend only on our own relatively short legs.

Danaa herself shifted from one spindly leg to the other. She was eager to leave. "Normally no men are allowed in the retreats," she told us. "They are the exclusive province of the females of our species, and the young under one year old. However, authorization has been granted for Captain Mallivan. Since he is a Spacelander, he is not considered to be a true male."

Well, thanks. That was rude. "Thanks," I said.

She widened her mouth. "You're welcome."

I shot Zenzie a look. She returned it with angelic innocence. Great.

"Are we going or not?" I demanded.

"Of course. We will be accompanied to the foothills by a group of twenty protectors, as the females of our species are. Then we will have to make our own way from there up the mountain to the retreat. You will love it. The views are out of this world."

I tried to smile. "Wonderful."

Zenzie was truly excited. "How long will that part take us? The part where we are alone?"

Danaa pressed her long lips together, highlighting the small whiskers of hair just underneath them. "If I were on my own, about one day. With you? Two or three, I expect."

It kept getting better. Nothing I felt more like than a hike. I wondered what the Supreme Council would make of the whole ship being halted for two weeks while I scuttled up and down mountains. I had already sent them a message about the Vaer attack, but was waiting for a reply. Perhaps I should check back with them and explain the further delay. I frowned as I tried to reach Tyzar through the ansible implant in my skull. I expected the usual interference that set off the violent headaches. I got nothing. No signal seemed to be getting through at all. Perhaps ansibles were blocked on Nephealis.

We set off. We did have to walk on our own two feet, and there were no technological advances to help us along. Still, I quickly came to realize that walking in half gravity was much, much easier. It was actually quite fun. You could push off with one foot and almost sail across the terrain. It took some moments to get used to, but meant that you didn't tire so much as you would have on a full gravity planet. Even so, if Zenzie had been a full-grown Tyzaran she would have outstripped me easily. As it was, we were pretty evenly matched, though Zenzie had far more stamina. She insisted on bouncing up and down as she walked, trying to see how far she could jump. Danaa danced around Zenzie, pointing out interesting landmarks and places as we walked.

I turned to one of the protectors. "Are there no land-based vehicles on Nephealis?"

They stared at me. "Of course there are. We are one of the most advanced species in the Shells!"

"Yes. Yet we are walking towards the mountains ...?"

He was confused for a moment. Then he realized what I was asking. "Ah, you are wondering why there are no vehicles for this excursion. That is because the retreat is a sacred rite of passage. Females of our species have taken this road for thousands of years. As a mark of respect to the past, we always walk ... as they did. It honors our ancestors, brings us closer to our heritage."

"I see." And I did. It made perfect sense. I just wished I didn't have to honor them quite so much. After all, they were not my ancestors. However, it was clear that envoys such as myself would be required to show the utmost respect for Nepheal customs. This was probably going to be my life from now on. I marched on, keeping my head down and trying to make sure I at least kept up with Zenzara.

The landscape was flat for the whole of that first day. All you could see was the wispy grass, the low bushes and the tall phyonwe trees that were scattered all over the place.

Scout trotted along beside me, head down, delighting in the extraordinary smells he was picking up from this strange planet, although he pulled hard every time we passed near one of the trees. He kept up well, too, despite his stumpy legs. I guess having six of them helps. My two were already aching, and I was delighted when we reached a low building built of wood.

"This is where we leave you," said the Nepheal I had spoken to earlier. "We will stay here for the night, then set back to the city at dawn. You will move on." He pointed to the huge mountain that soared up behind the building. "You will continue on to the female camp. It is just beyond the summit of that mountain, which is known as Ayaala. The Ayaala Retreat is one of our most ancient and most prestigious. Some of the best theses in our culture have come out of Ayaala. I wish you a productive and thoughtful journey."

"Thank you for your kindness."

"Will the Geiga be able to climb so far?"

I think he was really asking if I would manage it, but he was too diplomatic to ask me directly.

"I am sure that he will. It will take longer than usual, though."

He huffed in total agreement. "Our females are very fast."

I gave him a sideways look, but he was simply looking proud. This ancient race had deep-seated roots to their origins. I was beginning to identify with their sense of belonging to the earth, to the land around us. For some reason, Nephealis was having an effect on me.

We were assigned bunks in the low building. Mine was in a sort of cubbyhole, and consisted of a hanging hammock. I had seen pictures of them in ancient texts, but never experienced one myself.

I fell out twice before getting the hang of settling oneself in a balanced way. Once in and stable, it was reasonably comfortable. I tested it for a few moments and then went to find the others.

To my amazement, there were no other beds except the hammocks for Zenzara and myself. I peeked around the partitions of the other cubbyholes, only to find narrow stalls with absolutely no furniture whatsoever.

Zenzie found me there. "What are you doing?"

"Where do they sleep?" I hissed.

She looked taken aback. "I don't know. Why?"

I pointed out the lack of beds. "Do they stand in the stalls, like horses?"

She was horrified, whispering back, "For goodness' sake, don't say that! The Nepheals are twice as highly developed as the Spacelanders! They would take it as an insult!"

"Yes, I won't. But do you think they just stand on all four feet to sleep?"

A large Nepheal head pushed between us. "We sleep on all fours, yes. Why? Don't you?" It was Danaa.

Zenzara shook her head. "We sleep lying down."

Danaa's eyes widened. "Lying down! What do you do if you are attacked? That doesn't sound safe at all."

I realized that the Nepheals' whole culture was about survival. About leading predators away from the main population centers. About being able to run as fast as you could and as quickly as you could. Even now, Danaa's eyes were wide and frightened. Millennia later, the thought of attack could alter her breathing, her calm intelligence.

"But you haven't been attacked for centuries, have you?"

Danaa shivered. It went right through her whole slender body. "We are always ready for an attack. It is in our DNA. We are prey animals. We fear predators. When you are prey you live with fear perpetually."

It seemed strange to me. I would have thought that the fear would have dissipated, after so long. Seems I was wrong. It made me feel sorry for the Nepheals. "So you each take a stall and ... what ... just stand in it?"

She nodded sagely. "Exactly. For us, to be on all four feet is very relaxing. It puts us into what we call the prehistoric state. Originally we only walked on four feet. Developing a bipedal gait is a relatively recent development. We are still quadrupedal at heart. Our racial consciousness is still quadrupedal."

And, suddenly, I realized just what a privilege it was to be able to share something like this with this amazing race. I blushed, causing Zenzie to frown at me.

I held up Scout's lead. "What about Geigas? Where do they sleep?"

There was a giggle as she bent to stroke Scout's head. "He has his own pen, which was brought along especially for him. Along with your hammocks."

"Thank you very much. You have thought of everything."

"Come. There is plenty of food." She bent down to Scout again. "And many, many phyonwe fruits for you, Scout!"

Scout had already scented his dinner. He gave a jerk on his lead that almost pulled the skeletal Nepheal girl off her bipedal feet. She screamed with laughter and allowed him to drag her off.

"Were humans never prey?" asked Zenzie.

I wrinkled my brow, trying to think back along all of human history before we separated into the Flatlanders and the Spacelanders. "I don't think so, no. I mean, there were times when humans killed humans, but I don't think humans had any natural enemies that killed off large numbers of them. It was the other way around, if anything."

"So you were the predators?"

I didn't like that. But maybe it was true. Not something I wanted to think very much about. Not now, at any rate. I was far too hungry for philosophical questions.

"Let's go to dinner."

The next morning we said goodbye to our protectors. They packed up the hammocks and enough food to last us on our journey.

I bent to pick up one of the packs, but Danaa held up one of her long prehensile fingers. "No. I shall carry all of the gear."

"I don't want you to do that. I am stronger than you. I shall carry it." I felt obliged, though the bulkiness of the packs dismayed me.

She gave her wheeze of amusement at the thought. "You would double over with the weight!"

I glared. "I would not!"

Zenzie tried to pick one of the packs up and couldn't. "You would!" she said helpfully.

"I cannot let a young girl struggle with all that weight!"

Danaa swung both packs up, one over each shoulder. I was amazed she could. With such gangly limbs, Nepheals look quite fragile. "See?" she said. "I hardly notice them. We are prone to breaking limbs because our bones can fracture easily transversally. We are quite strong when weight is distributed vertically on our bones."

She settled the packs carefully across her shoulder blades, pointing out to me how the stress vectors would actually pass vertically down her long thin leg and back bones. I saw that she was right, although I still thought that the weight would turn out to be too much for her.

It didn't seem to slow her down at first. I was hard put to keep up with her, even though she was going at half her usual speed. Only Scout seemed eager to overtake her. He pulled relentlessly against his lead, to the extent that I began to be worried whether he was going to throttle himself.

Danaa saw the problem. Her large eyes softened to see his struggle to outpace his own collar. "He will hurt himself," she said.

"He might. I don't think all this pulling is very good for him. Geigas don't take well to being restrained."

She glanced around her at the mountain. "There is nobody near us here. Would he run off?"

I shook my head. "No. He is bonded to me. He might run around a bit, but he would never run away completely." He has never been on his paradise planet before, either, a small voice told me. I ignored it.

"Let's let him loose. We will tether him again before we reach the retreat. He should be able to enjoy freedom as well, should he not?"

I wasn't about to argue with that. I bent and removed the collar. Scout gave a shake of his head as if he couldn't believe his luck, located the nearest phyonwe tree, and vanished towards it. Little grunting sounds came back to us on the light breeze.

"Don't worry," I said, in what I hoped was a nonchalant tone. "He can't reach the fruit. He will just snaffle up the windfalls. Then he will find us. We can go on."

Zenzara was regarding me with doubt. So was Danaa.

I smiled to reassure them. I hoped he would come back. I wouldn't be very popular if I let a grown and hungry Geiga loose on Nephealis. I gestured up the mountain. "Ladies?"

We continued to climb. It was getting harder and harder. The landscape was now quite hostile. The track wove between huge grey rocks that jutted out of the rusty brown dirt under our feet. Not only did we have to clamber up and over and around these, but the path was also littered with shards of loose rock. This made it very difficult to traverse the mountain.

The only vertical interruptions to the lower scrub and small bushes were these boulders and the sparse phyonwe trees. These trees, so much higher up than the ones we had passed the day before, grew shorter, with slimmer trunks and weather-beaten bark. Some of them lurched disturbingly towards the sheltered side of the mountain, having desperately tried to turn their backs on the winds that tore down from the summit. Few of them had fruit.

Even only half way up the mountain, the wind was much stronger. It tore the words out of your mouth and blew them away, making it tiring to talk. The half gravity now felt like full gravity. Whether the altitude was affecting my body, or whether it was because we were battling into high wind, I couldn't tell.

Danaa looked as if the smallest extra gust would set her in flight. She was doubled over as she strode up the steep incline. I wondered where the stress vectors were pointing now. After watching her for several minutes, I tugged at her tunic.

She stopped. "What?"

"Take off those packs. It is my turn now."

A ripple of disquiet spoiled her smooth face. "I can manage."

"No, you can't. I will be taking them from now on." She hesitated. I pressed on. "It is only fair."

Zenzie could also see how tired she was. "Just for a little way, Danaa. To give you time to catch your breath."

I had known I could rely on the Tyzaran girl to offer someone else's services.

"Put them down. You need to rest."

In the end, Danaa agreed. I shouldered both of the packs. Standing up was a bit of a problem, but I managed it in the end. After that, the journey became one long blur of pain and discomfort. It was like ten simultaneous workouts in the *Nivala* gym. Agony.

Not that I intended to let the girls see just how difficult I was finding it. For some silly reason it seemed important to soldier on. I concentrated on trying not to gasp with pain, stared down at the track and placed one shaky foot in front of the other.

Scout scuttled back to me after some time. I wished he were a pack mule. They used to have them on Ancient Earth. Large creatures with long furry ears. They have been extinct for centuries. I remember writing an essay about them when I was around ten.

The Geiga settled to the forefront of our little group and bounded up the mountain with springy steps. I envied him.

Danaa and Zenzara stepped after him. Danaa had recovered. She was walking upright now and seemed to have recovered her energy. Zenzie was oohing and aahing about the views.

This went on for a few hours. Then I noticed that the ground began to change. There was less and less dirt beneath my feet and more and more rock. Finally we were marching only on rock. Scout's hooves slipped and slithered as he tried to keep his balance.

In the end, Zenzie had to put him back on the lead. His enthusiasm for the terrain had vanished. His ears were flat against his scalp and his little tail was pressed in between his legs. She wound the leash around her hand. At least she could help him if he slipped. Though I wasn't sure Scout didn't weigh more than she did. I didn't think she would be able to save him if he actually fell.

Danaa called a halt as the daylight began to fade. She pointed to a rocky crag. Rockier than the rest of the rocks. "That outcrop overhangs the ground. It will give us some protection from the winds and the weather. We can spend the night there."

I staggered up to the overhang. My legs felt as if they were made of wet washing. I grabbed hold of a large ledge and let the packages fall. For a moment I felt as though my whole body was levitating upwards. I blinked, wondering if I was hallucinating.

Zenzie passed me some water. I sank down and drank. The black spots in front of my eyes began to vanish. I was able to breathe more steadily.

Danaa gave me a sympathetic grimace. "The altitude makes any physical effort twice as hard up here."

Tell me about it! I thought I would probably never walk again.

Zenzie was unpacking the hammocks. I waved a hand at her. "Go ahead. Let's see if you can do it on your own."

She may have realized that I couldn't have got up if I had wanted to, for she treated me to a sardonic twitch of one eyebrow. Thankfully, she decided against complaining. I closed my eyes. I ached all over, but the pain along my back was the worst.

"How far do we have to go tomorrow?"

Danaa thought. "A little less than today, I believe."

I nodded, wondering how I would manage it. I don't think I could have walked another ten feet at that moment.

"Tomorrow I will take the weight again," she told me.

I shook my head. "You can't. You are risking a fracture."

Zenzara gave both of us an irritated glower. "Tomorrow we repack the weight and distribute it between all three of us," she snapped. "Honestly, you two are treating this like a competition. Nobody has to kill themselves. There are more intelligent solutions, you know? Divide the weight up, position it better. And we can probably leave a few things here, under this cliff."

She finished lashing one of the hammocks across a space between rocks. "Here, Mallivan. Drink some of the soup Danaa has heated up and get into bed. I think you will fall over if you don't."

I let the warmish soup trickle down into my stomach. Once it was gone I shifted over to the hammock, before remembering something. "Scout?"

"Don't worry about him. We will feed him and make sure he is comfortable."

I was just about able to nod. I crashed backwards into the hammock. That, for me, was the end of the day. I must have fallen asleep immediately, because I remember nothing else until the following morning.

The day was clear and bright, even at the early hour we woke up. As the sun just began to rise over the distant peaks its tenuous rays glistened off the scraps of mica embedded in the rock surrounding us. When I poked my head out from under the rocks I found myself gasping at the sight in front of me.

It was quite magnificent. The rocks lay in pleats along the mountainside, like icing that had been allowed to accumulate into folds and creases on some enormous cake. They flowed down the mountain leaving smooth skirts interspersed with sharp drops where the weight had provoked fracture lines that ran right around the mountain.

In the distance, I could see more and more mountains, all very similar to the one we were on. Even at this height, there were still some phyonwe trees, sticking out starkly into the chill morning air. Apart from the hardy trees, the vegetation had all but disappeared. Looking down, I could just make out the line of green where the shrubs began to survive the harsh winds and cold weather.

It was cold. The wind felt like a battering ram against my skin. I took a deep breath and almost coughed as the icy air raced into my lungs. I ducked hastily back under the overhang.

Danaa was already awake. She shifted her front legs slightly and then yawned. I caught sight of small but solid teeth banked up in her mouth. There were no sharp incisors. They were ideal for grinding up the fruit and tree bark which were the staples of this vegetarian race's diet. Useless for attacking an enemy.

She nodded to me. "How did you sleep?"

"Like the dead. The air up here is very thin."

"It is. I like it." She reached up her long neck to sniff delicately. "It reminds me of my birth year."

"Yes. You all spend the first year in the mountains. Why is that? I would have thought you would be safer down in the valleys, where there is more food and shelter."

I saw Zenzie waking up out of the corner of my eye. She blinked, then lay still. She wanted to hear this story.

"Long ago, when the vulture birds attacked our people, the delicacy they sought the most were the young ones. The babies, the children."

She gazed at me with sad eyes. "They would come in their flocks at the time of birth. They would kill every Nepheal they could find, just to feast on the youngest flesh."

She stopped and took a deep breath. "So it was necessary to protect the entire population by separating the young. That meant putting them somewhere where the birds would find it difficult to go. The birds didn't like the cold. They came from a hotter planet. Their wings iced up in the mountains, and the high winds made it difficult for them to fly."

I could understand that. I found it hard to *walk* in these winds.

"Eventually, it became standard for the females of our species to make the journey up here to the highest mountains, and for them to remain here until their young had developed sufficiently to be able to run as fast as their mothers. That is usually one of our standard years."

"Yes," I said, "but that was all over thousands of years ago, wasn't it?"

She sighed. "Our race has a long collective memory. We value our history very much. We keep up the tradition, because we know that the birds are still out there. One day … any day … they could come back."

"You think the birds are the Vaers?"

"We know they are."

"But the Vaers can no longer fly. Their wings are vestigial only."

She gave a sound somewhere between a bleat and a cough. "So they tell us. We have learnt to distrust the Vaers. All of the vulture birds are liars and cheats. They live only to tear their beaks into flesh – literally or metaphorically."

I couldn't disagree. The Vaers had certainly ripped my life apart when they appropriated *Faraday*. They had known exactly where to attack, what benefit they could reap. She wasn't wrong. They were certainly still predators. "I see. So you were brought up here as well? On this cold mountain?"

She nodded. "We all are. Coming back here for me is like returning to the womb of my mother. It brings back happy memories of my childhood."

"How do you keep warm?"

She laughed. "You will see. Come, let's eat some breakfast and be on our way."

After breakfast Zenzara took charge of all the supplies. First she separated what she considered to be surplus stocks, stashing them deep into a ledge near the ceiling of the overhanging rock. Then she halved the water we were carrying, leaving the rest carefully wedged in front of the food.

Once she had done that, she made three piles. She took the smaller one for herself, leaving one of the hammocks together with half the remaining supplies for both Danaa and me.

I swung my pack onto my shoulders. That was much better. I breathed a sigh of relief. I thought I might even be able to get through the day like that.

Judging from Danaa's happy expression, she was feeling the same. I checked Zenzara out. "Are you sure you can carry all that?"

She grinned. "I have given myself the smallest pack. This will not be a problem for me. Now, can we all stop trying to be martyrs? This is fine for all of us. We should have done it yesterday."

Danaa and I exchanged glances. Neither of us would admit it, but I guess we were both pleased that Zenzie had decided to take charge.

I put Scout back on the leash, in case he slipped on the smooth rocks, and then tentatively put my head out from under the rock overhang once more. I stifled a shudder. Hopefully it would get warmer as the sun came higher up in the sky. If not, walking would keep our body temperature up. I hoped.

As we made our way out from our makeshift shelter, I felt the full force of the wind. It rammed into me, pushing my head backwards and making my eyes tear up. And it was icy. This was not going to be fun.

A whimper from my feet made me look down. Scout didn't look happy. He is more a warm-weather sort of animal. He was lifting each foot off the ground in turn, complaining silently about the temperature of the rocky surface. His bristles were sticking straight out, which made him dangerous but might keep the wind off his hide. He was puffed up to almost twice his normal size. I envied him. My own skin felt very vulnerable to the elements, even wrapped up as it was. The wind chill simply bit through the clothes.

As we climbed, the sun rose higher in the sky and the chill relented, just a smidgeon. It was wonderful.

After an hour, life began to be worth living again. I shook my head. I couldn't think how these spindly aliens could possibly survive for a whole year up here, particularly the newly born.

I could understand why the Avian predators might find it hard to fly, though. I should think their wings would freeze open. That's if they ever managed to unfurl them against the gales that battered these mountains.

I was still musing on considerations like this when Danaa gave a startled cry. She shouted something, but it was carried away by the wind.

She pointed out to one side, to the right of our track.

I peered myopically out into the bluster.

There were two sleds beating over the mountain. They seemed to be heading vaguely in our direction.

Danaa signaled us to cluster near her. "Those are not Nepheals!" she told us.

"How can you be sure?"

"No Nepheal would desecrate the mountains by bringing machinery onto them. It is unthinkable."

"Maybe there is an emergency? Maybe they are coming to look for us?"

She shook her head. "No. That is simply not how we Nepheals work.

You don't understand. The Retreat and the *Phaala* are sacred rites. They may not be interrupted by any technology whatsoever. They have to be kept carbon clean. They have to leave the planet undamaged." She looked again at the two distant sledges. "Those are hover sledges. They adulterate the air we breathe. They are not even allowed on this *planet*, let alone the Mountains."

I squinted more at them. "You mean that they are not Nepheal?"

She scowled. "That is exactly what I said."

I grabbed at Zenzie's arm. She glared at me and pulled it back.

"We have to hide!" I stared around desperately, but could see only jagged boulders with no overhang. "Quick! They may be searching for us?"

Danaa shivered. "You think they are Vaers?"

I felt grim. "I do."

She closed her long eyelashes for a brief moment and then collected herself. "We must protect the Chyzar. That is who they will be looking for."

"Undoubtedly. But I don't understand. I can't believe they would violate Nephealis in this way. There is something going on here that we don't know about."

Danaa was looking around wildly. "The nearest cover is about a quarter of a mile away, up there towards the summit." She pointed. "There is a set of caves."

"Then we need to get there as fast as we can."

She nodded. "Let's go!"

I threw myself up the path, the two girls hot on my heels. I just hoped they were not tracking us in some manner. It would be hard to see us, tucked in as we were amongst the jagged rocks, until they were almost on top of us.

It was soon really hard to drag the frigid air down into our lungs. It actually hurt to breathe. Not only that, but the altitude meant that it was getting harder and harder to suck air in. My leg muscles were protesting and it was progressively harder to keep going. Add to that a pounding behind your eyes and a definite feeling of nausea, and you have a pretty decent picture.

It sounds easy. Only a quarter of a mile. It wasn't. It felt eternal. It felt impossible. Still, I knew that I couldn't let Zenzara and Danaa down. I had to keep calm and as logical as possible, if these were, indeed, Vaers. They would be looking for us and our only hope would be to avoid detection. We were in no state to fight them, and we had no weapons. Well, Zenzie still had her nivala and thoria and her ZR handheld gun. She never went anywhere without them, and because she was the Chyzar nobody had objected. I had been told fairly curtly to leave any weapons on board the ship. In any case, against armed and armored Vaers even Zenzie's three weapons would be of limited use. We might as well spit at them. No, our only chance was to avoid detection, and that meant reaching the caves.

But we didn't. We were still around eighty meters away from the larger cliff when Danaa signed us to get down.

"They are closing in. We need to get behind a rock. They will see us if we move now."

We shuffled quickly around a nearby rock, so as to put it between us and them. It jutted up from the ground, but only a little more than my own height. The leeward side was smooth and vertical. We could crouch behind it, but we would be spotted if they came anywhere near us.

Scout gave his ping of keening and set, his head an arrow towards the incoming sledge, his tail stiffly out behind him.

I pulled gently at one ear. "Thank you, boy. A little superfluous this time though, and a little late."

He lowered his ears and sank heavily to the ground. He had done his duty; what we did with the information he passed on was not his concern.

Now we could hear the sledges. They covered the mountain really quickly, though they can't have been a comfortable ride. They were being buffeted by the winds to such an extent that the edges of the sleds wobbled in a precarious way, threatening to rip against one of the sharp rocks.

We ducked down, trying to make ourselves as small as we could. They must be able to see us now, surely!

But they didn't. They passed around fifty meters down mountain to our position and, by some fluke, they did not see us.

We waited with our hearts thumping in our chests, listening as the hum of the sleds gradually faded a little.

At last, Danaa thought it safe to raise her head. "Right. They are way off to the left now. I think we can get to the caves."

I nodded. "We can try."

I knew that we wouldn't be truly safe anywhere on this mountain. However, a cave sounded one step better than being out here in the open. I wanted to make things difficult for them.

We resumed our run for shelter. I say run, but that is not the right word to describe our clumsy way of moving. We were doubled over, stumbling across the loose rocks that dotted the landscape, struggling to get enough oxygen into our painful lungs. We shambled along, lurching from boulder to boulder. The only member of the group that appeared unaffected was Scout. He had regained his usual insouciance and was trotting along with equanimity. I took this as a good sign.

The caves, when we finally reached them, were dark and gloomy. They still looked fine to me. We ducked inside and took our packs off. I moved towards the back to explore. We had chosen the deepest of the three, and it went back for around ten meters. Not enough, but it would have to do.

I checked for a back door to the place. There was none. We would be trapped if they found us here.

I went back to rejoin the girls and tell them of my exploration. "I will take the packs and Scout right to the back of the cave," I said. "Zenzie, I think you should go with him."

She gave a bit of a sad grin as she shook her head. "You know I can't do that, Mallivan."

I did. The Savior Protocols wouldn't let her save herself at my expense. I shrugged. "Then we put Scout and Danaa back there."

The Nepheal girl's neck went taut. "I shall stay with you," she told us in no uncertain tone. "I do not hide at the back of caves."

I spread my hands. "Very well. We stand together and fall together. Then see if you can put a few of these loose rocks together to form a makeshift barrier if they do get in."

I took Scout right to the back of the cave and boxed him in behind the packs, tying him firmly to one of the rocks. He snuffled at the ground in a rather disgruntled manner, but then allowed me to pack the supplies around him. I gave him a quick pat. "Be good. Don't make any noise!"

He wouldn't, apart from the first high-pitched ping of alarm. Geigas can be very aggressive towards other Geigas, but they are more sanguine when attacked by larger predators. Flight is not in the Geiga dictionary. They fight or they try to live to fight another day by standing very, very still. Vaers are pretty effective predators. I did not think he would be tempted to fight.

When I got back to the penumbra about ten meters into the cave, the girls had already managed to cobble together enough rocks to provide cover for all three of us. It was not much, but it was all we had.

Danaa went cautiously to the cave mouth and, taking care not to show herself in the daylight, looked around.

She ran back to us. "I can't see anything yet," she whispered. "Maybe we will be lucky!"

I was about to answer when I heard an unmistakable ping from the depths of the cave. "We aren't," I whispered back. "Get down!"

Danaa's gentle eyes widened in fear. As we ducked out of sight, we too began to hear the hum of the two sleds close in on our position. No, no luck today, it seemed.

I sighed, and took the ZR pistol Zenzara passed over to me. Beside me, the Tyzaran girl had unraveled her thoria from around her neck and was now twisting it over and over in her fingers. I watched as she fingered the nivala too, checking it was still in its position. I knew from experience that she could and would kill with it. Her crest was now rigidly out from her scalp. The heavy wrinkles that characterized her face were very worried.

I gave her a smile. "Sorry!"

"What for?"

"I knew that something was going to go very wrong. I felt it, just as soon as Bull Cunningham stepped on the ship. I should have been able to foresee this."

"Can we win?"

"I don't think we can, no."

She pursed her lips. "Then I shall try to bargain for your safety," she said.

She saw my indignant look and stopped me with a hand in the air. "Think about it. If they want me, then they want me uninjured. I could get hurt in crossfire if we battle with them."

"So?"

"So I would rather you were alive and looking for me, than dead and unable to."

She had a point. I found that option more attractive too. "Go on."

"Will you come to find me, Mallivan?" Her voice sounded very small, very tentative.

My heart melted. "You know I will."

"Promise?"

"Cross my heart and hope to die."

She frowned. That was a new expression for her. Danaa leant into the conversation. "I promise, too."

"I don't think Denaraz would simply leave you behind either. Nor would the others."

She gave the ghost of a smile. "Then I am not too scared. I will wait for you all to come and rescue me."

I felt utterly despondent. "We don't know what they will do to you." She looked so very young and so very vulnerable.

"I am valuable to them. We know that. They will not kill me." Her mouth wobbled slightly. She made such a brave little figure standing there, trembling but determined.

The trouble about logic is that you don't always like to hear it. I was ready for a fight. I *wanted* a fight. I wanted to keep Zenzara safe, out of the hands of the Vaer. But she was right. There were three of us and around twenty of them. We might manage to pick off three, four even five of them. That would still leave plenty to finish us off if that was their intention.

I felt bile rising in my stomach at the thought of Zenzie being taken away by the Vaers. I couldn't even answer her.

She must have realized how I was feeling, because she gently touched my arm before turning away. I felt her take the ZR pistol back out of my hands, at the same time as she pressed something into my palm.

I looked down. It was her nivala. "No! Zenzie! Don't—"

Too late. She had stood up and was facing the group of Vaers at the door. She was holding her pistol to her forehead.

I think I gasped. So did Danaa, who had been staring down at her own palm, at the curled thoria which Zenzara had slipped her.

"Do not come any further into this cave!" Zenzara's voice was young, but firm. "I am willing to make a deal with you, but only if you stay back. Who is your negotiator?"

There was a generalized cackle from the Vaers. I looked at their insignia. The Vaers who attacked *Nivala* had been Sellica faction. These also had a black stripe tattooed over the top part of their beaks, making them Sellica faction too. I wondered what significance that had. It was less than reassuring. The Propter faction on Vaer Nova had a better press than the Sellicas, who were secretly called 'the exterminators' by even their own people.

Eventually a large Vaer with a rather prominent beak stepped one pace in front of the rest of the group. "I am."

"You have come to take me away with you?"

"Yes."

"I will come to an agreement with you."

"I am listening."

"I will not surrender this gun. However, I will come with you provided you take no action against the two people who are with me. If you ... or any of your party ... attack my friends I shall shoot myself."

The gun was still pointing unwaveringly at her right temple. I tried to will my heart to beat again, but it seemed to have stuttered to a stop.

The leading Vaer considered. I hoped that his instructions had been to deliver her unhurt. I wasn't at all sure she was bluffing. Her face was set and I could see her determination by the set of her chin and her crest.

After some moments, he lowered his own gun and signaled to his men to do the same. Zenzara nodded and took a couple of steps toward him. Then she stopped. She extended her free hand towards them and spread her fingers, encouraging them to move backwards with her.

"Either we all go, or nobody goes," she told them, her eyes never leaving their leader. "I do not trust you. I will not surrender my gun until we are all on the sleds and have abandoned this mountain. Is that acceptable, Mister ...?"

There was a pause while the lead Vaer thought about it. My heart started to beat again, though it was anything but regular. I was still terrified for her. My fingers turned the nivala over and over in my hands, as if doing so would somehow keep her safe.

Danaa gave a small moan.

Then the Vaer nodded. He gave one deliberate step back, inviting Zenzie to continue on her own way out of the cave. "My name is Yseebi. Captain Yseebi. I agree to your terms. You will, however, hand over your weapon once we reach our shuttle."

She inclined her head.

He gave hand signals to the rest of the group to fall back behind him. They were reluctant, but grudgingly obeyed him.

He then took slow and careful steps backward out of the cave, drawing Zenzara after him as though they were connected by an invisible string.

She allowed this to happen, obediently following him as he stepped deliberately towards his sledge.

Danaa was shaking with utter terror, and I could understand why. For the first time in her young life, she had been brought face to face with Avians. Yet she was still on her feet. I reached out sideways and touched her shoulder, hoping the touch would help her to steady herself. She gave an involuntary flinch. Then she tried to give me a smile. I tried to return it. Neither of us could put much sincerity into it, but it did help to know that we were not alone. I hope it helped her, in any case.

Zenzie was already beyond the cave entrance. She was bathed in sunlight. From the darkness of our position, it gave her an aura of gold.

Yseebi took things slowly. Even so, the time flashed past my eyes. I was thinking of ways to stop this and discarding them as soon as they popped into my brain. None of them would get any of us out of this alive. Zenzara's reading of the situation was true. Her solution – however wrong it felt now – was the only one available to us if we were to keep all of us alive and unharmed – at least for the time being. But I hated feeling so impotent. My head was telling me that this was the only way to save us all, my feet twitched with the desire to attack these invaders and pummel them into the icy ground.

They retreated. We edged towards the mouth of the cave, unable to look away.

The sleds were hovering above the ground in a small clearing between rocks some fifty yards below the caves. We watched as, pace by pace, they made their way backwards to the sled. Zenzara clambered onto it, waving the Vaer back when they attempted to surge closer.

The sled lifted. She stood, statue like, as it raised around ten feet in the air and turned back the way they had originally come from. As it sped away in the wake of the other sledge she made no move to turn around. Her head was unmovable, her eyes presumably still fixed on Yseebi's face.

The two sleds picked up speed. Within seconds, they had accelerated up and out of our field of vision.

We were left alone on the mountain.

6

We were only half a day away from the Retreat. Danaa convinced me that we had to continue upwards rather than retrace our steps to go back to Nephealis City. She seemed to think that we would get action quicker in that way.

So we stumbled into the retreat some four hours later, scratched and tired. Neither of us had been able to talk on the journey. I for one, felt so inadequate that there was very little to say. I just wanted to get back to *Nivala* and get started on finding Zenzara. We had to get her back. And we had to do it before they hurt her. I had no idea what the Sellica faction intended to do with the Chyzar, but I did know that I was going to stop them.

A tall, patrician Nepheal woman strode up to us, her face crinkling with worry. "Where is the Chyzar?"

Danaa broke down. She collapsed on her lanky legs into a heap on the nearest rock. "The Vaer took her."

There was a ripple of horror around us.

The woman stared. "The Vaer? They who speak with beaks? Here? On Nephealis?"

Danaa nodded.

The woman turned to me. "I am Agraala, Danaa's aunt. You, I think, must be Captain Mallivan?"

I shook hands with the woman, who towered over me of course. "I am. I am sorry, but we need to get back to my ship as soon as possible. I have to get after the Chyzar. I don't seem able to use my ansible implant?"

She gave a solemn nod. "No. Ansible communication is blocked all over the surface of Nephealis. I am very sorry. Naturally, we will make sure you get back immediately. However, you will pause long enough to take some refreshment, I think?"

Scout was pulling against his leash. He wanted to get to this woman, for some reason.

She reached down and scratched him behind his ear. He promptly rolled over and exposed his tummy for similar treatment.

She obliged. "I was looking forward to meeting a real Geiga. Unfortunately, it seems I shall not be able to spend very much time with him. Can you tell us what happened?"

We were brought a hot drink and some Nepheal equivalent of sandwiches. I realized that I was hungry.

As we ate many other members of the retreat gathered around. Word of what had happened had spread like wildfire around this small community. There were many young Nepheals, even more loose-limbed and wobbly than their elders. Agraala also came up with another woman, rather older, who was introduced to me as Ouraali, the leader of the Retreat.

Their faces were long and fearful as they listened to our story. The possibility of genocide was still a very real one to them. They had to be wondering if this was the forerunner to a full-blown attack on their people.

Danaa only sipped at her drink. She kept her eyes downcast and took little part in the story-telling. Only when I had finished did she raise shocked eyes to the leader of the Retreat.

"I failed. I was granted the honor of protecting the Chyzar, and I have failed."

Ouraali's long face examined her niece for a few moment. Then she sighed. "Yes. You did. Although, from what I have heard, I do not think that you can be blamed."

"But I cannot stay here. I cannot stay on Nephealis. I must go to find the Chyzar. It is the only way forward for me."

There was hesitation. Then Agraala spoke, her voice soft. "If you feel you must go then no-one will stop you."

Danaa's voice almost choked. "I must."

Ouraali nodded. "Very well. Then we wish you luck in your quest. Agraala and I will accompany you both as far as Nephealis City."

"No!" Danaa scrambled to her feet. "No, you can't leave the retreat!"

"This news supersedes the importance of total retreat. The Board of Elders must be informed immediately of all that has taken place here. And the Spacelander would hold us back. I will carry him on my back, along the emergency pathways. I will proceed on all fours. Danaa, you and Agraala will follow as quickly as you can. I do not expect you to keep up with me. Danaa, you are tired; your speed will be affected."

There was a collective gasp. I gathered that such a step was unprecedented. I stared at Ouraali. "I cannot ask you to do that for me!"

"Nevertheless, I shall do it." She managed to crack a weak smile. "I assure you, you will find it to be most uncomfortable."

I felt humbled. How could I take her up on her offer? It would demean her, bring her down to the level of a beast of burden. One the other hand, how could I not? I had to get to Nephealis City and time was of the essence.

There was no choice. I bowed my thanks.

She raised her head proudly. "I hope my dignity will allow me to bend to exigent circumstances. However, if you are to stay on my back during the trip, we must make up some sort of harness for you to hold on to. That will take a little time. Danaa – you will rest after you have eaten."

"I … I am not hungry, Ouraali."

"Nevertheless, you shall eat. Your presence is required in the city. You will control your shame. You will eat."

"Yes, Ouraali." Danaa's head dropped even lower.

"This is not your fault," I told her.

"No. But it is my responsibility."

"Then come with me. I need all the help I can get. But don't blame yourself. That is only going to fill you with negative feelings. If you are to come with me I shall need you to be positive."

Agraala seemed to approve of my words. "Take notice, child. He is right. You wish to be of use. Then you must control your body, your impulses."

Now Danaa looked up at us. She seemed to have found a small degree of encouragement. "I will. I understand." For a brief moment, she looked almost as Zenzie had as she faced the Vaers.

Ouraali was staring down at Scout. "I am sorry. You cannot take him with you. Not only is he extra weight, but I do not think he would take kindly to a journey on my back, no?"

No. He wouldn't. I wished I didn't have to leave him, though. Ouraali saw my face. She scanned the surrounding faces, and beckoned to two young Nepheals. They came forward eagerly.

"This is Elyaan," she told me, indicating one of the boys, "and this is Daagess."

They both bobbed their long necks at me.

She pointed to Scout. "You are to take care of this Geiga, understood?"

They bobbed again. "Yes Ouraali," they chorused.

She turned back to me. "Please use the time to inform them of its diet and needs."

I felt like saluting myself. She had that air about her. I managed not to. "Of course." I passed the leash over to Daagess, who took it with an air of reverence. "Is this a real Geiga?" he asked.

I nodded. He and Elyaan dropped to their knees. Their eyes were like plates. "And we get to look after him?"

When I nodded again they exchanged looks of amazement at their luck. "We will take good care of him."

I was sure that they would. They were tickling his stomach and already Scout was looking smug. I thought he would probably never even notice my disappearance. After all, I would be leaving him in the middle of phyonwe country. He would hardly starve to death. In fact he would probably find it hard to believe his good fortune.

We got started about an hour later. The Nepheal women had managed to strap some sort of harness around Ouraali's neck. It reached back to a sort of girth that went around her waist, so that it could not slip. They had fashioned a looped handle out of cloth which had been twisted around and around until it was almost solid.

It felt sacrilege to be about to leap on her back. But she dropped onto all fours with little ceremony and dipped her shoulder to enable me to climb up.

To my chagrin, she was still too high from the ground. I made a couple of feeble attempts and then she grew impatient, grabbing hold of one of my ankles and tossing me upwards with no more ado. I landed and managed to grasp the looped ring over her shoulder blades.

They had also fastened a thick pad over her shoulders. I was immediately glad of it. Her backbone jutted up through her skin. Even with the pad, I could feel it. This was not going to be a pleasant ride. This was going to be another form of torture. I closed my eyes and hoped I would not moan. Ten hours of this might just cripple me for life, I thought. But it had to be done.

She paused only long enough to give a brief nod to the rest of the Retreat, and then she gave a huge leap that almost unseated me and we began our breakneck race down the mountain. My heart leapt into my throat, where it stayed for the whole journey. I have never been so terrified of anything in my whole life.

Out of the corner of my eye, I saw Danaa and her aunt set off behind us. And I caught the small figure of Scout receding even further into the distance as we sped away. Then the only sound was the wind howling against us, and Ouraali's steady breathing as she found her rhythm.

And what a rhythm it was! No wonder they had managed to avoid complete extinction, even when threatened by predators that could fly. She hurtled over the terrain, her prehensile fingers anchoring us to a rock while her powerful back legs gained enough traction to propel us in giant leaps and bounds down the mountainside.

Within minutes my fingers were white and numb with the strain of holding on. All I could do was attempt to keep my eyes open and hang on for dear life. Keeping my eyes open was not an easy task. She was moving so fast that the effect of the wind and the cold was amplified. I ended up peering down the mountain through thin slits that barely permitted me to anticipate each new and spine-shattering jerk and lurch.

Just as I thought I was going to fall off in an ignominious heap, she stopped.

I gave a cross between a squeak and a moan. It was the only thing that would come out.

She turned her long neck and regarded me. "You feel like a sack of phyonwe fruit! Can't you try to go with the movement? You are all over the place. You are making it very hard to keep my balance."

I gave another squeak and a nod.

She stared at my white face and then huffed. "You are very delicate," she said in a complaining sort of way. "Oh well, I suppose we still have to get down."

We were on our way again with another terrible leap, one that unseated me totally. I only stayed on because my hands were numbly frozen around the ring. I slammed back down onto the pad with such force that I thought I must have broken something vital. I moaned.

Luckily, the first part of the journey had been the worst. The rockiness of the terrain decreased with the slope of the mountain, which meant that the lurching was less too. Her gait became smoother. While she still took huge leaps from one spot to another, it was easier to anticipate these, and they became far more predictable. They still made my teeth jar in my head, however, and I was now so stiff that I wondered if I would ever walk again.

We careened down what were now foothills. Her speed, if anything, increased.

As we neared the city we began to pass occasional wanderers. They all stared in dismay at the sight of one of their own pass them at full gallop on all fours, with someone on their back. They leapt out of the way at once, but their cries of dismay followed us. This was such an unusual event that some of them even dropped to all fours themselves and began to race after us. By the time we reached the city center we had attracted perhaps fifty or so followers.

Ouraali looked neither to the right nor to the left. She hurtled through the streets causing even more dismay. The city was busy.

I realized that our destination was a tall building with a transparent dome covering it. It was huge – easily visible from anywhere in the city. Clearly, it was the home of the Board of Elders.

There were many armed Nepheal around the dome. I had seen no arms when we landed at the Spaceport.

We were flagged down, but when the guards saw who it was, and who she was carrying, Ouraali was waved through. The eyes of those who saw us shadowed with fear. I realized just how extraordinary this mad dash would appear to them.

The escort we had picked up along the road was stopped, however. They straightened up to their full height and began to ask urgent questions of each other. As I was carried towards the main doors I looked back to see many shaking their heads.

Ouraali stopped at the huge transparent doors. These were twice as high as the tallest Nepheal, so they were imposing. She turned her long face to me. "You can get down now."

I nodded, dragging one reluctant foot in front of me and swinging it over her withers to join the other. Then I let myself slide down her flank.

My feet touched the floor. Then my knees, then my face. I found myself unable to stand. I lay there, winded, feeling mortified and wondering whether I would ever be able to get up.

I heard a sigh. As I turned to her, I saw Ouraali rolling her expressive eyes. Then she gave a disbelieving shake of her head, plucked me off the floor with her teeth and flung me up again on her back.

"Why didn't you say you were hurt?"

"I didn't know."

"Do you need a doctor?" Her voice was tense. She didn't want to waste time.

"I will be all right. It may take a little time, though."

She nodded and padded through the vast hall. "I am taking you directly to the Elder General. He is the head of our Board of Elders."

"Will he see you without an appointment?"

She huffed. "He will."

She must be an even more important person than I thought. "Thank you."

"There is no need to thank me. It was necessary to act quickly, which dictated the means. It was my duty to inform the Board of Elders as soon as I could, and you are a necessary part of my report."

"I still thank you."

She showed me her teeth, in what I took to be a grin. It was a little disconcerting. "I believe you may have experienced some discomfort."

No kidding! "A little." *I ache all over and may never walk again.*

"I regret any suffering." She looked at me, more closely this time. "Are you aware that you have blood on your face?"

Of course I was. I had bitten my tongue so many times that at one point I had been worried it might fall off. "It doesn't matter."

She raised an eyebrow. "You should know."

We were waved through various Nepheal guards, each group more heavily armed than the last. I put my hand over the nivala that Zenzie had passed me. It helped me to forget my own aches and pains and concentrate on what really mattered. Finding her again.

The Elder General was the most enormous Nepheal and also the most skeletal I had ever seen. His hind legs shook as he balanced himself on them. His elbows and joints were so angular that they protruded through his skin. He didn't look as though he had much more time in the world of the living.

However, he was surprisingly gentle. He lifted me down from Ouraali and deposited me with great care on a chair that was much smaller than all the others. At his nod, a Nepheal lady approached and laid a small tray with refreshments at my side. He then escorted Ouraali over to a larger chair and made sure she had access to food and drink as well.

Then he sat down. "You have come a long way, and you have come as fast as you could. I fear grave news?"

Ouraali told him what had happened. His face lost all of its green color, turning a pale grey. "Vaers attacked?"

When I explained he drew himself up. "They have feathers: this should have been expected. Our history tells us what they are like."

He gave a small bow to Ouraali. "You did well to bring this to me so quickly. It will give our people time to prepare for war."

I twitched. "War?"

"Naturally. They have invaded our territory. Our people are now at war."

I held up one hand, ashamed to see that it still shook. "They were just one faction – the Sellicas. I believe they came solely to take the Chyzar. Although ..." I frowned, "... I can't quite see why."

The Elder General suddenly looked even more uncomfortable. I stared at him.

"I ... I may have more information for you on that."

"Something else has happened?"

"It ... It has, I am afraid. Yesterday morning both the scientist and the Terran who accompanied him disappeared. Along with one of our most lauded theses." He gave Ouraali a very meaningful stare. "Number 6758."

Bull Cunningham! Of course he would be at the bottom of all this. Why had I ever agreed to let him set foot on my ship? I knew at the time that no good would come of it.

"A thesis?" I still couldn't quite see the connection.

"Yes. A thesis that explores in detail a nonlocal macroscope to examine the far reaches of the universe. It was groundbreaking."

I must have looked blank. Ouraali was looking distinctly grey around the mouth. "The nonlocal macroscope," she repeated dumbly.

He nodded. "I think you know what that means."

She nodded. "I was one of the peer reviewers. It means that they now might have a way to entrap the Chakrans. To extract their cells from the Nexus and funnel them into quantum constraints." Her eyes glazed over. "But how would that benefit them?"

I was a long way behind. "Macroscope?" I asked.

She blew out air. "To enable us to get information about parts of space at the borders of, or outside, the observable universe," she told me.

That didn't help. My face must have showed it.

She sighed again. "Look. If one cell of a Chakran is here on this planet, let's call it the 'head'. Another is in the Coma Supercluster, let's call it the 'foot'. Then the head sends the foot some information – instantaneously, because it is uses quantum nonlocality which happens in that moment."

"Yes?" I hate this sort of thing. It reminds me of physics lessons at school.

"Then information is sent back. In response, if you like. Instantaneously."

"Yes?" I couldn't see what she was getting at.

"But the Coma Supercluster is 300 *million* light years away." She smiled at me in an encouraging sort of way. "Which means ...?"

I frowned. I was getting a headache. "That we see it as it was 300 million years in the past? The only information we have about it is from 300 million years ago?"

I had pleased her. She smiled encouragingly. I felt even more as if I were at school. "Yes! Exactly! And if you are the foot of the Chakran, then your head is ...?"

"... Seen as it was 300 million years in the past, as well."

"It is a bit like the thunder and lightning that exist on nearly all planets. We see the lightning before we hear the thunder. Not because they happened at different times, but because one takes longer to get to us. They are both information about the same event, but the thunder is older information by the time it gets to us."

I thought about it. "Yes. Nonlocality tells about what the foot is like now, whereas light can only tell us what it was like a long time ago!"

"Exactly." Then she moved her giant head from side to side. "Well, not exactly, because that was just a simple analogy, but it will serve."

I tried not to show my relief. "So this thesis was about that?"

"It was. Basically quantum nonlocality can offer us a window into the present. It can help us see what is happening now in galaxies that we only see in the past. Even what may be happening in galaxies that are so far away and traveling so fast that light from them will *never* reach us. Events outside our visible universe."

"But that sounds like a very good thing indeed."

The Elder General and Ouraali looked at each other. The female Nepheal pressed her lips together. "It is. Of course it is. Nepheals only work for the development of positive technology. And the author of this thesis thought so too. She went on to examine just how to build such a nonlocal macroscope. In order to focus quantum events into a steady stream of data, she found a way to collect such phenomena without altering them or causing them to decohere prematurely. However, at the end of the thesis, the author noted as a negative that her technology could also be used to trap any living quantum cells that engage in nonlocal communication. With some small modifications, her ideas could even be used to constrain such cells inside a tiny space and control them."

"And the Chakrans are living quantum cells and so could be imprisoned using these techniques?"

"Yes. The Chakrans are unique. They are so sparsely distributed that they must also see the whole universe as it is now. That is what makes them so fragile. It is a miracle that they have survived so long, over such enormous distances. It is why we must protect them to the very best of our abilities."

My eyebrows were nearly meeting in the middle. I could feel them. "But why would anybody want to harm the Chakrans?"

"Because of what happened on the *Chibuzo*." The voice was new. It belonged to Xynia, who was standing some distance away, flanked on either side by a Nepheal guard. I hadn't noticed her before.

We all turned to her.

"When the Chakrans altered the molecules of the guns on *Chibuzo*," she said, "expanding them, it showed that they had to be a source of negative energy."

The Elder General and Ouraali again looked at each other.

I narrowed my eyes. "And negative energy is important if you want to ...?"

"Build a traversable wormhole."

There was a deathly silence.

"Excuse me," I said, "did you just say traversable wormhole?"

She nodded. "I believe that may be their intention, yes."

"And you just happened to figure that out now, or has the Supreme Council known about this for a long time?"

She looked down. "I ... I ... just discovered it."

Nobody believed her. The two guards flanking her moved even closer at a gesture from the Elder General. I saw the whites of her eyes flash as she registered that fact.

"Won't that destroy the Chakrans in the Nexus?"

Xynia treated me a withering look. "They might not care."

"It would be genocide!" Now I knew why Zenzara had told us that the Chakrans hadn't wanted to demonstrate their ability to expand the molecules of something solid. It made them, despite being immense beings, incredibly vulnerable. It was all making sense.

This was terrible news. Terrible news indeed. Cunningham had the Nepheal technology to extract Zenzie's Chakran strands from their Nexus. And he had been working on wormhole technology.

The Tyzaran Supreme Council *had* to have known about that new development. They *must* have, if Xynia knew enough about it to tell us now. That would put the Tyzarans squarely on the wrong side of the equation. Was that why they had been so keen to offer the scientist an alternative to jail?

"How did they get off Nephealis?" I asked. "Cunningham and Chandrayanan, I mean?"

The Elder General dipped his head regretfully. "The only ship that has been in our system and unaccounted for is a Vaer cruiser. It avoided the Gyre, took up geo-stationary orbit for several hours, and then left our planet when challenged. We think they had time to deploy sledges and pick up the two Terrans."

"And Zenzara, too, I presume." I gave Xynia a look of distrust. "So the two Terrans have sold out to the Vaers? To build wormholes together? Perhaps to develop more RAMP missiles, too? I thought Chandrayanan said he wouldn't do that."

Xynia replied in a very cold voice, "No. He knows the danger now. He would never allow more RAMP missiles to be built. It would be suicidal. His pretensions go further than that. Whoever operates stable wormholes will control the future of the Shells logistically. It would offer military supremacy and billions of credits a month in revenue."

She moved uncomfortably. "However, it would certainly appear that Cunningham and Chandrayanan are working with the Sellica Vaers. We had not predicted that."

I was losing my patience. "I want to know why you were working with them. What were you going to do to Zenzara? To your own Chyzar?" My own voice was chillier now that I wasn't sure of the Supreme Council any more. I found it hard to believe that the leaders of Tyzar would risk Zenzie's life to try to harness the Chakrans, but I certainly wouldn't put it past them. They had, after all, been obsessed with their Chyzars and their Chakrans for millennia. A lot of bad things can be done in the name of science and knowledge.

She went pale.

"Spokesdesignate?" The voice was Denaraz's. He was standing to the back of the room. He must have followed Xynia down to the surface of Nephealis. I motioned to him to come forward. Seeing that, the Elder General nodded for his accompanying guards to step backwards. "Please answer. What were my people planning to do with Chy Zenzara?" I had never heard him talk in that tone to anyone. It was clipped with fury.

"I … I am not privy to that information. I am on the side of our planet." She glared at him and practically spat out the next words. "And so should you be!"

His mouth dropped open. "She is our Chyzar. *The Chyzar!* How could you contemplate hurting either her or the Chakrans?"

"I do not believe that the Supreme Council would do anything to harm the Chyzar."

He huffed. "Says the person who exchanged our ZEPH technology for the RAMP missile specifications?"

She reddened. "I can say no more. I have told you of their intentions. You should thank me for that."

"Now you have been left stranded here with us, you had no choice but to tell us if you wanted them stopped." I couldn't keep quiet any longer. "You had to have known about this. From the beginning."

She looked directly at me. "I had no idea that the thesis even existed. But Chandrayanan obviously did. He asked me to contact the Nepheals and suggest a lecture on the RAMP missile crisis. I acceded. How was I supposed to know that the true aim was for Cunningham to break into the Nepheal Thesis Library while the scientist was lecturing, to steal the one thesis that would unlock the Chakran network for them?"

"But you knew about the other research. The Supreme approved that."

"I am not at liberty to answer you on that question."

"Then you will have to get back to Tyzar some other way. I will not take you on my ship."

Her eyes widened. "I must search for the Chyzar."

"You can do as you wish, but not from my ship. I will not take someone who may be working against the interests of the Interstellar Alliance. You will have to take that up with the other signatories on Ulon Prime. It's above my pay grade."

Her crest stiffened and she looked daggers at me, but I had no intention of giving in. She had put Zenzie in danger. She could not be trusted. I had already made the mistake of allowing Bull Cunningham on board *Nivala*. I wasn't planning on making the same mistake twice. I figured I had to start learning not to make the same mistake twice.

Both Ouraali and the Elder General had been following this conversation with great interest. They exchanged a glance and then the Elder General nodded to a waiting Nepheal. "Please escort the Spokesdesignate to a transit area." He bowed to Xynia. "As you know, we do not usually travel far from our own system. However, we shall arrange for you to be taken to either Ulon Prime or Raksora. I'm sure you will be able to organize transport on to Tyzar from either of those two places?"

For a moment it seemed as though she might spit at all of us. She was having a problem keeping her usual equanimity. Interesting. Finally she dropped her eyes. "That is more than kind, Elder General."

She was ushered out. Ouraali turned to me. "Better?"

I nodded. "I just want to find Zenzara. Who knows what they could be doing to her? What does this thesis of yours say?"

"I am afraid there was only one copy. That has been stolen, as you know."

I gaped at her. "You mean we don't even know what he has stolen?"

The tiniest flash of irritation spread over her face as she shot a slightly accusing look at her leader. "Apparently it was not possible to facsimile all our library of theses. Even though they represent the greater part of our achievements."

The Elder General frowned. "I hardly think this is the time to be bemoaning decisions that were taken long ago," he said in a cooler voice. "Although, naturally, that decision will have to be re-evaluated in the light of recent events."

"It certainly will."

There was a long pause. Then she looked at me again. "Although we do not have a copy of that thesis, the person responsible for writing it is available."

"You said it was a female Nepheal? Where is she? Can I talk to her?"

"You already have."

I spun around to identify the speaker. Danaa and her aunt had finally arrived. They were standing at the entrance to the reception room.

I didn't understand. I squinted past them, still trying to see who had spoken. "Who said that?"

Danaa began to giggle. She lifted her hand and pointed rather sardonically at her aunt.

I may not be the brightest firework in the box, but illumination finally came. "Agraala? You are the author of that work?"

Both she and Danaa looked tired. Danaa, particularly, appeared to be swaying from side to side.

Agraala nodded. "For my sins."

"Can you remember what it said?"

She bristled. "Of course I can. I spent a year writing and thinking about it."

"Then you can tell me?"

She bent her long neck. "I will do one better. I will go with you."

The Elder General gave another of his dark frowns. "That is not convenient, Agraala. If there is no copy of the work, you will be required to re-edit it. I cannot allow you to leave the city until that is done. We must think of the future of the Nepheals, as well as the fate of the Chyzar."

Agraala treated the old Nepheal to a look of disdain. "The fate of the Chyzar is of immense importance, and I will not allow my work to be used to torture another living being. What sort of a Nepheal would I be if I did?"

His expression tightened. "I believe I am still head of the Nepheal people?"

Ouraali glared at him. "Well, you won't be for much longer if you make arbitrary decisions like that one. We will vote you out."

He matched her dark expression. "Is that a threat?"

Agraala shook her head, breaking the deadlock. "It is of no importance what you or the Board of Elders decide. I shall accompany Captain Mallivan. I will not allow my work to be used to enslave the Chakrans or damage the Chyzar. It was a journey into pure knowledge; it was never meant to be used for harm. And, if the Vaers can use it to hurt other living beings, I have no intention of ever rewriting it. Those who read it earlier may remember parts of it, but I will never allow the whole thesis to be stolen or taken again. If I recover it with Captain Mallivan I shall destroy it." She was shaking by the time she finished this revolutionary speech. I felt like clapping.

"The Board of Elders will require its return."

"That does not mean I shall obey."

"If you refuse to comply with the Board of Elders, you will be banned from the city."

Agraala was about to reply, but Ouraali stepped in. "I think that would be unfortunate," she told him.

"Why?"

"Because, if Agraala is banned from the city for refusing to re-edit her work, other female Nepheals may well decide to leave with her. There is plenty of room for all female Nepheals to live permanently in the mountain retreats."

His mouth opened and closed a couple of times, making him look very much like a fish. In the end it closed with a snap. "I will discuss this in session with the Board of Elders."

Ouraali nodded. "That is, I believe, a good idea. I shall be eager to know their opinion on this thorny subject."

His neck muscles were rigid. "You will be informed in due course."

As he walked out with stately steps, Danaa turned to her aunt. "Really? You are going to come with us?"

"Us?" I repeated, raising one eyebrow.

"Of course I shall come. I already told you!"

"I shall come with you," confirmed her aunt. "I cannot believe that somebody has allowed my work to be read by a Vaer! It is the ultimate humiliation."

"Err ... there is just one problem," I told her, looking her up and down. "You ... err ... you are a tall lady. I do not believe that there is sufficient headroom in my ship for you."

Her whiskers twitched. "When I said accompany you, Captain Mallivan," she said sternly, "I meant in my own ship. I have no intention of being crushed inside your tiny vessel. No offense."

I was offended. *Nivala* was a wonderful ship. Though I suppose she mightn't seem that way to these tall Nepheal women.

"You have a ship?" These women were full of surprises. Or I hadn't understood the dynamics of Nephealis society, perhaps.

"That thesis won the Dialectis Prize two years running. As a Dialectic winner, you are automatically granted some honors. They will let me take a ship." She was matter-of-fact about it; there was no boasting in her voice.

"Thank you. If you are joining us, I am sure we will be able to get

Zenzara back."

She smiled. "And my thesis. We have to get that back too. I will not leave that information out there to be utilized by the Vaers." She thought for a moment. "Would you help me to destroy it?"

She was asking if I would commit to helping her in spite of the Elder General's instruction. I bowed. "I would."

Danaa was jumping up and down with excitement. "When can we leave? When?"

Ouraali gnashed her back teeth together, considering the necessary arrangements. "I should go too," she said finally.

"No!" Agraala was adamant. "We need you here. Otherwise the Board of Elders will probably approve some inconvenient law or other to stop us. You are one of the only females they will listen to. You are the most influential woman on Nephealis. You know you are."

Ouraali looked down her long nose at me. I don't know what she was thinking, but I got the distinct impression that what she saw did not impress her overly. She might have been remembering my lack of agility on the long run down the mountain. I couldn't blame her. It was a painful memory for me, as well.

"I will do my best to ensure no harm comes to either of them," I told her.

She gave a skeptical raise of her eyebrows. We both knew that I was unable to offer any guarantees. "You will do your best," she acknowledged in a grudging voice. "Although I am doubtful that will be enough."

Agraala had not finished. "You have to stay here, Ouraali. The population will be outraged by what has happened. They will want to declare war on the Vaers. That has to wait. Full-blown war will only get in the way of our aims."

"Very well." Now that she had made up her mind, Ouraali regained the determined set to her large jaw. "I will hold them back. But do not take long. The Board can be delayed in their decision. It cannot be stopped."

I breathed out in relief. Now I just wanted to get myself back to *Nivala*, brief the others on what had happened and set a course for wherever the Vaers had taken Zenzie, if we could figure out where that was.

7

We finally set sail two days behind the Vaers. I initially laid in a course for Vaer Nova, which had seemed the logical place for them to take Zenzie.

Luckily, we managed to pick up their faint trail, thanks to Mel's expertise with the forward scanner and the Vaers' complete disdain for curtailing their emissions. Because of our remit, *Nivala* had been fitted with state-of-the-art environmental detectors. These were managing to detect traces of radian toxicity even after a few days. The Vaer ship must be off-the-scale for that to happen. It didn't surprise me, but I hadn't been the one who thought of checking for illegal emissions. The honors went to Mel. She was the one who had suggested tracking for contaminants. Thanks to her quick thinking, we now knew for sure where they were going. Their present course would take them straight for Ebyssia, a system lying between Ulon Prime and the Vaer homeworld. It was too far away to be sure, but it looked as if one of the small moons around a gas giant would be their final destination.

I was chafing at the bit to move faster, but we needed the Nepheals in the ship behind us. Nepheal ships were fast, just not as fast as *Nivala*.

It was frustrating, but there was nothing we could do about it. It gave me plenty of time to bite my fingernails and snap at other members of the crew, particularly Denaraz.

Izan and I had been circling each other warily since my return to the ship. He had been there when I banned Spokesdesignate Xynia, had applauded it, even. However, it had given him a bit of a problem. Was he to be loyal to *Nivala* and our new mission, or was he still in part a puppet of the Supreme Council on Tyzar, his home planet?

It was something I needed to know. And soon. But neither of us had wanted to push the subject too soon, so we had been tiptoeing around each other. I was hoping he would come down on the side of the *Nivala*, but I knew it would be hard for him. If he did that, his status as Adjunct would definitely be withdrawn by the Supreme Council. He would become, like all the rest of us, an outcast. It would not be an easy decision for him to make.

Though, come to think of it, even *Nivala* might be taken away from us after my actions. She was, after all, a Tyzaran ship.

I sighed. But I didn't regret my actions.

Izan had come onto the bridge without my noticing him. He now walked up. "Can I talk to you?"

"Sure. Let's go get a coffee."

I nodded to Sammy to take over, and we wandered down the corridor. It felt stiff and unnatural, after all we had gone through together. I hoped he would stay with us; he was fast becoming one of the most valuable crew members.

We grabbed a coffee each from the large galley/kitchen and then sat down in the adjoining mess hall. As usual at that time of the day, it was empty.

He sighed. "It has been hard to choose."

"Yes, I imagine it has."

There was a pause. "Losing your whole identity is hard."

"Tell me about it."

He took another sip of his coffee. He pulled a face. "This stuff is disgusting. I don't know how you ever got me addicted to it in the first place. I think you are trying to kill me."

I was mildly interested. "Don't Tyzarans have coffee?"

He was scandalized. "We do not! What good is it? Stimulants increase the heart rate, break down muscle and make it hard to sleep. What sense is there in that?"

I had to agree with him. "Put like that ..."

"Unfortunately, I have become accustomed to it. I would find it very hard to give up now."

I blinked. Had he just said what I thought he had said? "You are staying?"

He spread his hands. "The so-terrible coffee is difficult to leave, I find."

I gave a shout and pummeled his arm. "Terrific!"

He looked pained. "But you must promise me at least one cup a day."

"Will they drum you out of the brownies?"

That caused a crinkled frown. "Excuse me?"

"Will they strip you of your Adjunct status?"

"I expect so. But I find myself rather at odds with the Supreme Council just at the moment. I do not like that they allowed Chandrayanan to continue with his research. It shows them in a greedy, unfortunate light, does it not? Especially when you consider the number of people who had to die during that extremely stupid war. Especially when you think about what they might have been planning to do to the Chyzar."

I was so relieved that I pounded him again, on the back this time.

Denaraz gave me punch in return, knocking me off my chair. I didn't mind. "Then you will come with us?"

"Did you really think I wouldn't? I have failed in my duty. The Chyzar has been captured. Of course I will come with you. I have to look at myself in the mirror of a morning, you know."

"You weren't there. If anything, it was my fault."

"Maybe."

That irked me. "You mean, you think you could have done better?"

He shrugged. "Hard to do worse, Mallivan. You must see that?"

I would have punched him right on his stupid chin if he hadn't been right. He wasn't saying anything I hadn't berated myself for a hundred times. I turned away. It had been hard to look my crew directly in the eyes since it had happened. I felt that, even if they didn't, they *should* blame me. I liked that Denaraz put it out there in the open.

"You are right. I should have been able to save her."

His crests dipped. "I have to believe I would have made a difference, but I must admit that I can't see how. From what you said, Zenzara was determined to save you and Danaa. Once she makes up her mind, I know just how stubborn she can be. Remember Xynia's door?"

I did. "I should have let her do it. Xynia and the Supreme Council were plotting behind our backs, after all. Plotting ways to circumvent her as Chyzar, if their real intention was to directly control the Chakrans."

He nodded. "I have to believe that they were unaware of the intention to use that research. If they were … well, it would be clear that our political class has betrayed us."

"Don't they always?"

He seemed shocked. "No! They are above such things! The Supremes act only on the best interests of the whole population."

"Really?"

He bowed his head. "No. But I thought they did."

That rang a bell. I had always believed that the Space Trust only had Spacelanders' best interests at heart too. Now, I was not so sure.

"Thing is, Izan, we have to believe in the newly formed Interstellar Alliance. We are part of that. We may not be politicians, but we are in a position to change things. In our own small way."

He cheered up. "You are right. Our example may eventually improve some things."

"—And the Chyzar is crucial to the Tyzarans. Zenzie will have a big influence over Tyzar's politics when she is older. *We* may not be able to influence the Supreme Council; I believe *she* could."

"I will try to make sure she lives that long."

"I am just glad you are staying with us." I offered him my hand and we both shook on it. That moment cemented my trust in him; I was glad not to have been mistaken.

He held up one finger. "What are we going to do about the ansible implants?"

I hadn't thought of that. "Can they be used against us?"

He considered. "Yes, I think they probably can. Certainly against you. I saw how hard you are finding it to adapt and I think Xynia did as well."

Great! Just what I needed. "We are going to have to have them taken out. We will leave the Macers to the diplomatic work of interstellar relations."

"We can't adjust them ourselves, even though I said I would rip mine out. We are going to be vulnerable until then."

"Yes, if you think the Supreme Council could be prepared to go that far."

I could see it on his face. He was horribly afraid that they might. The idea that they had secretly been plotting to undermine the Chyzar was such heresy that it had left him convinced that they might do anything.

He sighed again. "I always thought we were the good ones."

"All governments say that."

"Yes. I suppose they do."

"It's our own fault. They only tell us what we want to hear."

I had a thought. "Is there any way to block the signals from reaching us?"

"No, because ansible technology depends on quantum nonlocality."

We both realized at the same time. I was the first to say it. "And we just happen to have the foremost expert on quantum nonlocality in the ship behind us!"

We hurried to the weapon's bridge, which is on the same level as the mess hall, and contacted the *Aenysia* – the Nepheal ship traveling in our wake.

Agraala listened carefully but shook her head. "I can do nothing. Theoretically it is possible to set up an interference network, such as the one we have in place over Nephealis itself, but I have no access here to the materials I would need. In any case, to be effective everywhere it would also have to be an implant, and the possibilities of some neural damage to one or both of you would be quite considerable."

"Is there anything we can do to prevent some sort of overload? Is that even a possibility?"

"It is not my field of expertise, but I would think it could happen." She thought for long minutes, "I think the Chakrans are the only ones who could influence it. Maybe the Chyzar could, if she now has a fully-established Chakran node inside her body."

So we would be vulnerable. It was not good news, but we would simply have to hope that such a thing would either not occur to the Tyzarans or they would not take things to that extent.

We cut the connexion after chatting for a few more minutes, updating the two Nepheal women with the course corrections and our surmisals.

Agraala nodded sagely. "The Ebyssia system is hard to penetrate. That moon is surrounded by a carbon cloud and is dangerous to approach. The Vaers will bank on that. It will not be easy to penetrate such defenses."

"No, though there is something they haven't thought of. Their emissions are so high that it may be possible to track them accurately through the carbon cloud. After all, there must be a relatively safe way through, mustn't there?"

She smiled with pleasure. "You are right. That would be helpful. We are going to need to take them by surprise though. They will have many more effectives than we do."

"We are going to have to make this up as we go along, I'm afraid."

Danaa tried to look fierce. She didn't succeed because she was a skeletally thin mass of arms and legs with a long neck that looked about to snap at any moment. "We can do it!"

I stared through the tight-beam at them. If I had been a praying person I would have prayed at that moment.

We had a meeting of the crew later that day. I think all of our faces were solemn. The two Nepheals were present on the vid-screen.

Mel was pale. It took her much of her energy to overcome her claustronetia; meetings in confined spaces made it worse. She and Sammy sat together, shoulders touching.

Seyal had left her son sleeping in their cabin. She kept looking at the door in a concerned fashion, as if waiting to see him stride in and demand her presence.

Neema and Anzany were also seated together. Denaraz had gravitated to the only other Tyzaran on the ship. Anzany had abandoned her world because of intolerance. She would know what he was going through. She invited him into their conversations and was trying to keep him engaged.

I cleared my throat and they all looked up expectantly.

"If Mel is right, we should be able to trace the Vaer ship through the carbon cloud right up to the moon's surface. From there, everything will be unfamiliar. There is no way we can probe through that cloud of dust. We have no idea what we are going to find on the far side. They could have built a complete city for all we know."

"They will see us as soon as we arrive?"

"I would think so. So we are going to try to find a pocket in the carbon cloud. That dust is so thick they wouldn't see us in that until they were on top of us. I think we can orbit there without being seen. They chose this planet because that cloud concealed them; let's use that against them. I don't think they will be expecting it."

"And then?" Sammy asked.

"Then we will take two shuttles and try to make our way in without being spotted."

"Who is we?"

I knew all of them wanted to go, but that made no sense. "Denaraz and I will take the first shuttle, and Danaa and Agraala the second."

There was a chorus of indignant voices. Even Didjal and Eshaan thrummed angrily.

I held up my hand. "I can't see the benefit of taking more of us into direct danger."

Seyal's calm voice took over from me. "You are wrong," she informed me in her placid kind of way. "You will need me."

I raised one eyebrow.

"Think about it, Mallivan Bell. I am the only one who can speak Vaer. It is my job on this ship. I will be needed … to translate and possibly to interpret. I shall be coming with you."

Didjal stepped forward. "You will need an engineer to go with you. Zenzara might be locked behind a force field. None of you know how to dismantle one. You have no choice but to take me with you."

Eshaan moved to join its partner, standing stoutly beside it. "Where Didjal goes, I go."

Sammy had got to his feet. "Why should you lot have all the fun? Mel and I want to go, too."

"So do we!" Neema and Anzany glared at us all.

I was surprised little Segaton didn't crawl in to demand a place on the rescue team. I wouldn't have put it past him.

"We can't all go. We need to leave at least two people on each ship."

Faces fell. "That means four of us will have to stay," said Mel. She knew that, with her tendency to freeze in combat situations, she was the one I was most likely to leave behind.

There were glances of speculation amongst them.

"Look," I stepped up. "There are only eleven of us. That means, that if four have to stay on ship, seven can go down. Didjal and Seyal are right; their skills may be needed. That makes six of us who must go. I think the rest of you should stay on board. Three on *Nivala*, and two on *Aenysia*."

Neema wasn't convinced. "Surely one of the two Nepheals should stay on their ship?"

Danaa's face on the tight-beam twitched. "I was assigned to the Chyzar. It is my duty to go down. And my aunt MUST go; she is the only one who understands the theory of what they may be trying to do."

Neema objected. It's not as if any of us know how to fly your Nepheal ship."

I nodded at that. "A good point. I think whoever is to stay on *Aenysia* should go over after this meeting. Get a feel for the ship. I suggest Sammy and Mel stay on *Nivala*. We are going to need Mel's expertise with the scanners, in order to find us a bolt-hole in that carbon cloud, and a way through. Neema and Anzany can cross over to *Aenysia*. And Eshaan—"

"—will be coming with you to the moon." Eshaan's black carapace glittered, brooking no dissent.

I blew out air, uncertain what to say. Then I remembered how useful Eshaan had been when we had been retained on the Vaer ship, during the Terran-Avarak war. He had always been an asset to us, even if his role was undefined because he was an artist. "All right, Eshaan. Mel, apart from your other duties, you and Sammy will be responsible for Segaton."

That more or less put an end to the meeting. I asked Agraala to bring the *Aenysia* alongside so that Neema and Anzany could grapple over. We were going to need all our shuttles.

Aenysia was about twice the length of *Nivala*, but four times the height. She loomed over us and I had to stop myself ducking as I stared at her through one of the ports.

Neema gulped at the sight of the taller ship. She and Anzany were only wearing IEVA suits instead of the bulkier full EVA suits. They were not planning on being out in the vacuum of space for more than a few seconds, a minute at the most. IEVA suits could cope with full vacuum for much longer than that. They were generally reliable up to fifteen minutes, though that depended on make and maintenance of course.

Anzany stared up at the bigger ship. Although they had wanted to form part of the rescue group, this was unprecedented too. They were about to be the only non-Nepheals ever to learn about Nepheal ships. She *had* to be excited. I would have been.

Agraala brought the ship to match our velocity vector and shunted towards us until there was barely ten meters between the two airlocks. I saw Danaa step inside the bigger lock on the Nepheal ship. She was holding a long piece of thin rope with a weight on it.

I had to grin. I wonder what the ancient mariners on Earth would say if they saw their plumblines in use in such a technologically advanced society. It seemed incongruous, to say the least. But nobody had come up with a better way to secure a safety line between two ships. It was still done manually or with a line-throwing adapter kit for an M596.

In this case, with the ships so close together, Danaa was clearly going to throw the plumb across manually. She clipped her safety harness on and then curled the rope into loops which would unfold correctly.

Her first shot missed. It hit our hull with a dull clunk, but was just too far back for Neema to be able to grapple with a boat hook. Another anachronistic implement still in use today.

The second time her plum bob sailed cleanly through the open hatch. It was quickly secured and a metal line drawn over behind it. Both girls clipped onto the line and then thrust themselves out of the airlock, passing quickly hand over hand to the other ship. It took bare seconds for them to be reaching out their hands to Danaa to be pulled inside.

At our end, Denaraz, who had gone into the airlock with them, untied the bob and released the line. This was quickly pulled back over to *Aenysia* and both hatches were secured.

The ships pulled away, *Aenysia* dropping back to her position behind *Nivala*. Now it was only a matter of time. We continued to follow the Vaer ship's track of pollution, hoping it was going to lead us to Zenzara. Hoping we would still be in time.

Two days later we approached the carbon cloud around the third planet of the Ebyssia system. The Vaer ship's track led straight to the edge of the cloud and then vanished inside it. We decided to enter the cloud some distance away from that point. We didn't want a Vaer ship to run over us as we felt our way into the cloud. We would find our own route, gingerly easing forward to find trails through the thinner parts of the carbon dust. At the same time we would attempt to map the larger channel the Vaers were using.

Mel was huddled over the plotter. Her job was going to be extremely difficult. She was so concentrated that her tongue was peeking out between her teeth as she peered at the string of numbers on the screen in front of her, looking for less dense routes, for openings in the thick clouds. Sammy was at the helm, interpreting her painstaking work.

We had positioned *Aenysia* at our stern, her bows almost touching our cargo door. Neema was at the helm there, and had been told to follow us exactly, stepping in our footprints as it were. It would be quite a test as to whether she had mastered the other ship.

The cloud was a filthy place to be. I have been in dust clouds before, but this was thick and cloying. I could see deposits building up on the Nepheal ship behind us. Surely the same thing would be happening to our own hull. The tiny molecules of carbon were attracted to our fuselage.

As we slipped inside the cloud we were submerged in a fairylike world where it was impossible to orient yourself. We were cruising through soot.

We edged forwards. Sammy had us creeping along at only around twenty miles an hour. For a ship like *Nivala*, that was hard to maintain.

We had no idea how deep the cloud was, either. We certainly had no wish to break through on the other side and be picked off at the Vaers' leisure!

After a hundred miles we were exhausted. It had taken five solid hours to wend our way along this open channel through the cloud, and there was no sign of any change. No wonder the Vaers had chosen it for a secret base!

Aenysia was still glued to our tail. The girls had done well. Now Anzany had taken over from Neema, and it was my turn to take over from Sammy on *Nivala*.

I slipped into his station and he went over to Mel, giving her a small neck massage to try to dispel the tension building up there.

I pulled the throttle back and stopped the ship. "Take fifteen minutes," I told her. "Eat something, drink something. Then come back."

She was about to protest, but Sammy dragged her out of her chair. "Come on, we don't want you making any mistakes. Just take ten minutes. Get some food inside you!"

She went, reluctantly. We hung in space, Anzany almost scraping our shuttle bay doors, while our navigator walked and moved and ate.

She was back in ten, slipping into her station and screwing up her eyes at the numbers again. "It is getting harder and harder," she admitted to me. "The carbon absorbs the emissions and the further in we are, the fewer openings I find. If this goes on much longer we may have to stop where we are."

"Couldn't we find our own way through it? Recalibrating the emissions sensors?"

She seemed doubtful. "I guess. The thing is, we would have to write a new algorithm to do that, even if it is possible. And ... and I don't think I could do that. Our only choice then would be to take the same route as the Vaers. It winds and bends a bit, but they keep it clearer."

"All right. Don't worry about it. Are we recording the route?"

"Of course we are. We will be able to find our way out of here. I can guarantee that. It's going on that worries me more."

"It won't be much further. Keep going. Another hour!"

In the end it was another three, and Mel's face was almost desperate by the time the nose broke through the cloud.

Instantly I backed us back into the carbon dust, almost causing a collision with the ship behind. I could almost hear Anzany's comment on my driving skills.

"Now take us closer to the Vaer channel and find us a gap big enough for two ships!" I told Mel.

That took another four hours. We had to retrace our steps and follow a winding area of thinner dust. Eventually this did open out to a certain degree, allowing us to park both ships with not too much dust around us.

We stopped all engines and hung in space.

It was time. Those of us who were going to the moon beneath us struggled into IEVA suits. We wanted none of the bulky full EVA suits, although we would need them later. For the time being, they would simply hamper us as we worked. IEVA would give us minimal protection whilst still allowing us to move.

One shuttle slid out of *Nivala's* cargo bay, and one from *Aenysia's*.

I let Denaraz pilot the shuttle. He was fresh. Fresher.

He tiptoed along the gap and back into the mainstream channel, taking his time to check it was clear.

It was just as well he did. A large Vaer ship tore past our position, heading down to the moon. It was so close that it nearly hit us.

Denaraz had slid us immediately into the thick dust to one side of the meager channel.

We poked our nose out with even more care the second time around, then, seeing it was all clear, followed the Vaer ship to the edge of the carbon cloud.

I took a decision. "We will wait for the next ship, and then piggyback our way into the system. If we cling to an incoming ship, our individual signals won't be detected." I hope.

Denaraz pursed his lips. "They might see us."

"They might. If they are looking. Let's hope they aren't. After all, there really isn't much of a view from this moon, is there? I don't think I would be sitting staring out at a big black cloud over my coffee."

"Hmm. You are not a Vaer. They must know we will try to get Zenzara back."

I couldn't deny that. "Have you got a better idea?"

He shook his head. "No."

I shrugged my shoulders. It might not have high odds of success, but it was our only plan. "We'll do it, then."

"I just hope we aren't hanging around for a week or two, waiting for another ship."

Since the air supply on one of these shuttles wouldn't last that long, so did I.

We burrowed into the thick cloud that formed the sides of the tunnel, tucking ourselves just out of sight, our shuttle to the right and *Aenysia's* to the left.

The idea was to get up to speed alongside the incoming ship and then drop out of the cloud on top of them. Their fuselage should hide us from scanners. We would be detectable, of course, but only as the slightest of slight double blips on a screen. It was going to take a very efficient Vaer to notice us.

We only had to wait an hour. A new vessel was announced by the shaking of the clouds, which gusted away from the bows of the shuttle. I whispered over the tight-beam to the other shuttle. "Get ready!"

We cranked up our engines and began to accelerate. It was like stirring molasses. The clouds of carbon dust dragged at the small vessel, trying to keep it anchored in the black grit.

I nodded to Denaraz, who was piloting the shuttle. He grimaced and pushed the little ship even further. "She may fall apart."

"She can't. Keep your foot down, Izan. We need to get up to their speed. They will spot us if we don't."

"I am trying," he informed me from gritted teeth. The entire craft was rattling like a can of pebbles. I almost fell over, only saving myself by clutching hold of Denaraz's shoulder. He winced.

"They are almost on us!"

"There is another ship behind this one!" shouted Eshaan, who was monitoring the sensors. "Coming in directly behind!"

Now that was a stroke of luck. "Which is the biggest?"

"This one!"

I punched the tight-beam link to the other shuttle. "Agraala, you take this ship. We will hop on the next."

"Understood."

"Good luck. See you down there."

She was gone. Almost immediately, the second incoming Vaer ship swept past us in a scurry of the surrounding particles. The vacuum of surrounding space usually insulated a ship from feeling any effect of outside phenomena, but now the molecules of the dark cloud were forced out of the way by the ship and then rained down on our hull with such insistence that we were physically buffeted from one side to the other. I hated to think what was happening to our hull.

Izan was struggling to keep up the acceleration. His knuckles were white.

I noticed that I was still clinging onto his shoulder. I let go and staggered back to my own station.

He gave a sigh of relief. "Matching speed."

"Get on top of her and drop us to within ten feet. Towards the stern, please."

"Would you like me to settle on the hull?" he said sweetly, causing me to shoot him an uncertain look. His subsequent grin dispelled my doubts.

"Just don't ram the thing."

"What little confidence you have in my flying ability, Captain!"

I would have answered, but the ship had suddenly swerved and dropped at the same time, and I had come close to biting through my lip. I cursed and did my best to ignore the throbbing. The rush of warm liquid inside my mouth was an effective gag. Denaraz was lucky; I would have had plenty to say if I could have.

I wasn't the only one. Both Eshaan and Seyal had ended up on the floor with that unexpected twist of the shuttle.

They picked themselves up with annoyance. Didjal chattered at his *faliif.*

The tone was rebuking and amused. Eshaan's black carapace glittered momentarily. Then it nodded in a rueful sort of acceptance.

Seyal seemed fine, though she was rubbing one of her elbows which had caught on a console. "I am unhurt," she said mendaciously. "Nothing to worry about."

It was not a great start. We weren't exactly looking like superheroes. I hoped the Vaer would not simply laugh when we confronted them.

Suddenly the dark cloud was behind us, though it was still pitch black at the centre of the surrounding carbon shell, because none of the star's light could penetrate the dust barrier.

But the moon was illuminated. Even from this altitude, we could make out many spots of light in the midst of a whole large area of darkness.

The ship we were piggy-backing on was headed for the only completely illuminated area. It appeared to be a docking bay, because we could see several ships against the large gantries that were spotted all along the area.

I gave a silent whistle. This enterprise was much, much bigger than I had thought. The Sellica faction must have been expanding this base for many years to have such extensive facilities here. It looked like an invasion base. Which made me wonder what their targets might be. It was a worrying thought.

I bit my lip. Just in case, we needed to get word about this out. Out to the Macers, if possible.

I let my lids close and tried to flip back inside my head, hoping to activate the ansible connection.

The feedback was instant, and very uncomfortable. I clutched at my skull and my legs bent, making me duck down to the hull plating. "Aagghh!"

Oznard's voice clicked on inside my head. "What do you want?"

It took me a moment to concentrate through the riot of white noise that was deafening me. I cringed down even further. "I want to talk to the Macers, not you!"

Her voice in my head became even frostier. "Really? And what do you expect me to do? Patch you through?"

"How can I reach them?"

She sent blackness through the connexion. She was not best pleased. "I could make you want to rip that ansible right out of your scalp, if I wanted to."

"I know you could. Are you going to?"

"Not yet. You would deserve such action, however. You disobeyed orders. You made Spokesdesignate Xynia leave your ship. Our ship."

"And you know perfectly well why, Oznard!"

The crackle of dislike threatened to blast my head apart. I moaned as I clutched it even tighter, hoping to stop the discomfort.

"Why should I help you?"

"You need to decide whose side the Supreme Council is on. The other members of the Alliance will demand it."

She gave a bark of amusement. It was deafening. "We are the founders of the Alliance!"

"Maybe. That doesn't mean you don't have to abide by its rules, now does it?"

The volume of the white noise dipped momentarily. "We obey all existing laws."

It was my turn to laugh. I hoped it sounded as loud in her large head as hers had in mine. "You obey what is convenient, Supreme. Your actions over the scientist were ignoble, to say the least."

"We did nothing legally wrong."

"Your actions may have led to the loss of the Chyzar!"

"That would be most unfortunate."

I sent what I hoped was a mental raspberry. "Please put me through to the Macers. —If they have completed their installation of ansible technology."

"They have." She was abrupt now. I sensed an opening of some sort of pathway inside my brain. "I have unlocked your access. You can get them simply by thinking of Ulon Prime."

"Thank you."

I did as she asked and was almost immediately in a link with a Macer. I could tell it was a Macer by the absolute calmness inside the link. Even the hated white noise seemed to abate.

"This is the Legacy," it told me. "Welcome, Captain Mallivan."

I explained where we were, what had happened and what we were observing.

"That is extremely disturbing," it said. "The Tyzarans have shamed the chain. Ulon Prime is the nearest inhabited system to Ebyssia. Such a build up by the Sellicas may mean that they intend to invade us."

"This is a courtesy call in case our mission is unsuccessful."

"We appreciate it."

I took some minutes to debrief to them about the Tyzaran part in the recent fiasco. They thanked me, and confirmed that they wanted us to continue. "The Chyzar is a most important being. She should not be risked. You are instructed to use all means to recover her."

I wasn't particularly bothered about their instruction at this point. We were already committed. But it was nice to know that there would be no political repercussions. I cut the connexion, to find Denaraz's sharp eyes on me.

"The Macers?" he asked.

I nodded. "Just in case."

He gave a few short nods. "I was thinking of contacting them myself. Do we have their blessing?"

"We do."

He smiled. "It is comforting to know that not all the Alliance is against us."

I couldn't help giving a long sigh. "They won't be any help."

"We can do this. Look at the Terran-Avarak war. We stopped that, didn't we?"

"I guess."

"Enough of this pessimism. Let's get at them!"

Seyal touched my arm. "They don't stand a chance!" she said quietly.

I felt a surge of pride. We might be just the flotsam of the Shells, but we were a team. Denaraz was right; we had already achieved great things. We might not succeed this time, but we would leave our skin behind trying to get Zenzara out. She deserved it.

8

The moon was now looming in the shuttle visor. I had my eyes glued on the ship ahead of us. The small black speck on its back – a flea from this angle – was Agraala and her shuttle. I wanted to see what she would do. We could hardly just fly into the bay and settle on the deck.

I had already made up my mind to copy her actions. We needed to stay together. Anything else would be suicide. I found myself wishing we had spoken about contingencies. I hadn't realized that we wouldn't be able to communicate once we came out of the carbon cloud that encircled this moon. The dust had blocked us before. It wouldn't now. We couldn't risk our tight-beams being detected.

The blood in my mouth had vanished, washed away by saliva, though the lesion still throbbed. It helped focus my concentration.

What would I do if I were in the leading shuttle? I considered.

We had two options. To enter the hold or to peel away to the darkness at either side. I preferred the latter. Perhaps there would be a way to slip in later on, when the docking area had fewer Vaers around.

As I came to that conclusion, so did she. The larger shuttle waited until the Vaer ship was on its final approach, then the parasite gave a swift leap and vanished to the right of the docking bay, disappearing into the dark shadows.

I did the same, except I leapt to the left. I wanted to keep the two shuttles apart for the time being. The smaller each signal, the less the chance of being detected. Two blips on top of one another might amplify the signal.

We clung to the outside of the huge docking area, hovering unseen in the penumbra caused by the lights. The small moon must have once been riddled with reservoirs of methane, for the docks were housed in a natural cavern which resembled a wedge-shaped bite out of its surface. It wasn't going to be easy to get inside. I asked the others for an assessment, but there was no consensus.

There was nothing for it; somebody would have to go outside the shuttles and take a look around. I decided I would go, but when I told the others of this decision I found the two Enif in my path.

"We will go," Eshaan told me, its fingers flashing on the touch pad so that the synthesizer would have enough to work with. "We do not need EVA suits, which means that we will be quicker and much more effective."

That couldn't be denied. I had to nod.

They chittered together and then made their way down to the top deck starboard airlock. They seemed excited at their adventure.

"We need a way into the complex that will not be detected. See what you can do."

Didjal nodded. "We will find the entry point, Mallivan. We know how important this is."

We watched as they let themselves out through the airlock and floated gently into the darkness. They were soon out of our sight. I would have liked to stay in contact with them, but it wasn't practical. We would risk being picked up by the Vaer sensor array.

Time passed slowly in the shuttle as we waited for news. It would take them hours to reconnoiter the hangar. We used the time to make our own analysis of the situation.

The huge bay was permanently kept open. The gap was so large that it would have been nigh on impossible to fabricate doors big enough to close, or a mechanism strong enough.

It was clear that the force field was of industrial quality. It would have to be, with the carbon cloud so close and individual molecules continually bombarding the installations.

There were guards stationed right around the docking area, and they were well-armed. It seemed it would be suicide to take either of the shuttles inside the bay.

Denaraz was peering out of the viewport, stretching upwards to get a reasonable view. "I don't think we can go through the force field without being detected. Did you notice that the whole thing lit up when that ship went through? It is color-coded with a sonorous alarm too."

"I did notice, yes."

Seyal had been examining Vaer records at the communications station. "I have something about the Sellica Vaers, if you are interested?"

"Go ahead."

"The two factions came about when Vaer Prime banished the Nova Vaers from their planet. There was a race to establish dominance on Vaer Nova and declare independence. Originally they colonized the North. It was hard living and when Vaers became criminals, they were packed off to the Southern continent, where living conditions were so extreme that few were expected to live. Against all the odds, some did. They formed their own faction and have been bitterly against the northern continent ever since. The Propters are the Vaers that inhabited the northern hemisphere of Vaer Prime, the Sellicas the southern hemisphere. Both declared Vaer Nova as their own, on the same day. Since then, they have been battling each other for control of the planet."

"Is there any difference in the hemispheres?"

She shook her head. "Not much. There is little mineral wealth on the planet, and both factions would have starved to death if they hadn't looked outside of their star system for sources of income."

"So they became thieves from necessity?"

"They refer to themselves as facilitators."

I gave a snort. "They would."

"They claim to be flexible to market demand and quick to alleviate trade shortages."

"They are pirates!"

She made a face and her finger ran across a few lines of text before she found what she had been looking for. "They deny that. They claim to adhere to a strict code of conduct."

I may have made a rude noise. "Code of conduct, my left elbow!"

"If you remember, Mallivan, they requisitioned your ship with some legal jargon. That, to them, made it all quite acceptable business practice." She looked up at me, an anxious expression on her face. "You *did* sign their papers."

"I signed because they threatened Zenzara!"

"But you signed. For them, that made it all legal and above board."

I could feel heat traveling up my face. Just thinking about *Faraday* and the ship's loss made me uncomfortable. "They are pirates. Full stop."

She closed the file. "Yes, Mallivan."

That made me feel mean. "I'm sorry, Seyal. You lost your shuttle, as well."

"We all lost something during the war."

She had lost her husband, too, and although personally I wasn't sure exactly how much of an asset he had been, she had probably been attached to him.

The Enif were back after three hours. As soon as the airlock activation light popped up, we raced to the starboard hatch to help them back in.

Didjal was first out of the door. It was humming with excitement. "I think we have found a way in!"

Eshaan stepped in behind its *faliif*. "They have a diamond plant!"

We stared. "A diamond plant?"

Didjal took over. "Yes. There is a large semicircular vent some twenty meters above the hold, and another one about twenty meters below it. Air is pumped out of the inferior vent and sucked into the one above it. They have an electrostatic grid in place outside the force field, so that larger carbon particles can be dislodged and dealt with. They must have been having problems with contamination. The loose particles are then carried in the air to the superior vent."

"But you said a diamond plant." Seyal was looking confused.

Eshaan glittered. "Those upper vents are sucking in a continual stream of the purest carbon! All they have to do is compress it down and they have a pretty inexhaustible supply of industrial grade diamonds."

Trust the Vaers. Turning pollution into diamonds.

"Can we get in through the vents, do you think?" I asked the two Enif.

They flashed. "We already did! There is a huge pumping station, and there are failsafe hatches along the walls. They must be used for cleaning access. Those shafts are metal sheeted but they are coated with carbon cake and they must need scraping from time to time. I tell you, these facilities have been here for a long time, because the cake is quite thick!

"The hatches are small, but we opened one and no alarms sounded. They are not rigged to the general security system."

I couldn't help smiling. "They made a mistake. That is our entry and exit point. Let's get kitted out. We will need full EVA, though, until we get inside the installation proper. Come on, let's go knock on the Nepheals' door!"

We took a mag frame with us. Mag frames are thin boards with opposite-pole magnetic coils set into the front and back. You can fiddle with the controls and be repulsed from one metal source and attracted by another, or simply to move across a surface. They are not easy things to control, but when used well can substantially decrease travel time so long as you are not in open space. They require metal or metal ore to function.

Denaraz dragged the mag frame out of the airlock and lay on top of it. They are quite light, but bulky, being made up of aluminum struts shaped like a surfboard with the electromagnetic coils in protected aluminum boxes at either end.

I hooked a line around his boot, and the others latched themselves similarly onto me. One mag frame was not much for such a lot of us, but we needed to go slowly and carefully in any case.

We sailed across the top of the docking bay entry doorway. I realized just how big the thing was. It would easily have taken even a ship the size of the late *Commorancy*, with her twenty-five decks. Whatever happened, I was glad that the Macers were now aware of this illicit base on their doorstep.

We soon briefed Danaa and Agraala to our plan. They clambered into very large EVA suits and clipped onto the tail of our small group. Then Denaraz raised an eyebrow to the Enif.

Didjal pointed upwards and towards the centre point of the docking bay entrance. Denaraz nodded.

It was strangely quiet out in the vacuum, surrounded by the dampening effect of the carbon cloud. No stars. No light except for the artificial ones left on by the Vaers. It felt like floating through purgatory, through dull darkness that enclosed us all and threatened us in some intangible way.

We arrived at the mid-point of the entry hatch. Now I could see the vents all along this area. They were smaller at the sides of the entry bay, larger at the apex, where we were now. There was certainly room for an Avarak or even a fully grown Nepheal in the vents.

Denaraz fiddled again with the switches. We began to sink down towards the vent, our tail of people stretching out behind us. The two Enif brought up the rear, much more comfortable in open space than the rest of us were.

Didjal and Eshaan had already hacked an opening in the protective mesh that acted as a filter to the system. It was peeled back so that it would not be a hazard for us.

We tethered the mag frame to the mesh. It hung there, nudging the mesh as the carbon molecules which were drawn in pressed it against the metal intake.

One after another, we slipped through the mesh and made our way into the duct itself.

My eyes widened as I took in the size of the operation. These ducts were big enough for Agraala to stand comfortably on two feet. And about twice as wide. On both sides, the air flowed into this collecting duct from smaller tubes that curved and flowed with the curved walls of the spaceport set beneath us into this moon.

We were able to walk comfortably along the passageway, which was made of sheets of steel. Our boots found good traction on it.

The carbon cake that had deposited all along the duct was hard and shiny but with a covering of light ash. This puffed up as we disturbed it, making it hard to see. I noticed trails in the deposit, showing where Eshaan and Didjal had been previously.

We waded through the carbon cake with care. It took around an hour for us to reach the hatch that Didjal had spoken about. We clustered around it.

Didjal reached down and twisted the circular locking mechanism. There was a sharp click; the hatch began to open. We could see a chink of light around its edges.

Didjal had already told us that the atmosphere inside the installations appeared to be breathable. We all shrugged ourselves out of the full EVA suits and left them fastened to the outside of the hatch with a long line. They floated away in the direction of the suction pumps, looking much like somebody's washing hung out to dry. We had brought an extra suit along for Zenzara, in the hope that we would be able to find her. That sat right at the end of the line, a much smaller size than all the others.

Now in our IEVA suits, which made it much easier to move around, Denaraz and I motioned the others back. We had been in this sort of situation before, and felt that we should take the lead. Denaraz slid through the hatch, looked around, and then waved me forward.

I dropped down into a large walkway. It was completely deserted. We were in a long corridor that was also lined with metal plating. Gravity at this point in the moon felt around half Earth standard.

The others followed me down, one by one, until we were all standing on the walkway.

Agraala smiled and showed us a hand-held device. "I have been working on this for the last few days."

"What is it?"

"It's an adapted Nepheal environmental sensor array. Miniaturized, of course. I have changed it to detect quantum nonlocality." She showed us the readout. There were two bright spots amongst our small group.

She explained. "It is picking up the ansible nodes that you and Denaraz have been fitted with."

She began to zoom out, picking up more and more of the surrounding space port. Finally we saw another bright spot on the screen.

"There! That will be the Chyzar. Now, all I have to do is ask it to escort us there. Done!" She held the sensor out in front of us and treated us all to a large grin. "This way!"

I was so glad that she had come. I walked up to her and gave her a loose hug. She tried not to flinch. She was getting used to my strange ways.

The navigation device was leading us off to the right. From what I could tell, Zenzara was being held several stories above us and around half a mile inside the complex. This wasn't going to be easy.

It wasn't. Although we were in an area that clearly had very little traffic, every step was potential detection. I think the only thing that saved us at first was the immensity of the installation and the lack of

Vaers populating it. We saw about twenty of them, but those that we did see were working industriously in the distance, going about their business, unconcerned about and uninterested in their surroundings.

Even so, there were several near misses, especially when we found some stairs and made our way up several flights. Once close to the area where Zenzie was being held, moving became more challenging. We stopped in a relatively unused section to regroup.

I was panting. The others had found the stairs little challenge, but it had been an effort for me to scramble up steps that reached above my knees. I bent over to get my breath.

"How are we going to go about this?" I asked them all.

The two Enif looked enigmatic and had no suggestions. Seyal merely became thoughtful. Danaa turned to Agraala, and Agraala's long face grew still as she considered the options.

Only Denaraz had any ideas. He gave a growl and his crests stood up. "We bowl in and kill them all."

We had all armed ourselves before coming out on this mission, but I couldn't help feeling his grand plan had a few flaws.

"We need to get in and out without being seen. If the alarm is sounded, then we stand no chance of getting back to the ships, of getting the Chyzar away.

Anybody else?"

There was silence. Then Danaa spoke, her voice very hesitant. "I wondered ... I thought ..."

"Go on."

She nibbled at her lower lip. "It's just that it seems to me ... that the only person who can do anything silently is the Chyzar herself. We just need to get to her and remove whatever is neutralizing the Chakran link. Surely the Chakrans will protect their Chyzar?"

She had a point. Once the Chakrans were free to act, they might be strong enough to help us. It was only the beginning of a plan, but everything has to have a start. It would have to be good enough.

Others were nodding as well. "Right. That is our initial plan, then.

We find Zenzara. Agraala is the only one of us who can figure out what is controlling the Chakran Nexus. She is the one the rest of us must protect. Agraala, your only job is to smash whatever is keeping the Chakrans contained." I looked around. "Danaa, you get to Zenzara —wherever she is. Your job is to keep her safe."

The young Nepheal woman nodded.

I turned to the two Enif. "Didjal, you sabotage whatever mechanical systems you find. Try to ensure that any pursuit will be delayed. Try to cause as much chaos as you can."

Didjal gave a solemn nod.

"Eshaan, your job is to locate the thesis. It has to be recovered or destroyed totally. Seyal, since you are the one who can read Vaer, you will go with him. We cannot leave that here."

Eshaan assented, but it was an artist. It knew about copies. Its disjointed face was worried. "What if they have reproduced it? Memorized it?"

Agraala's long neck twisted from side to side. "They couldn't have memorized it. Nobody could. The base algorithms are not something you could just remember. I certainly could never remember them and I *wrote* them. This work is not a couple of lines, remember. Most of the algorithms are over a thousand lines of coding. There are hundreds of algorithms."

"Copy it, then? Once they made the computer program?"

She gave a huff. "You don't understand. The thesis is not in paper form. Our theses never are. They are all set on quantum chips. And each quantum chip is protected from copying. The Vaers certainly do not have the technology to circumvent the safeguards in place. It would have self-destructed had they tried."

That made us all stare at her. She shrugged her bony shoulders. "Sorry. I thought you knew that."

"But they could use it?"

"Oh yes. They would need a key to open it, but they would never have stolen it if they hadn't had the key, I imagine. Once open, the

Terran scientist will have been able to hook it up to any late generation quantum computer and start working with it. My thesis is organic. It can be encouraged to grow in certain directions."

She must have realized that we were staring with open mouths. She frowned. "Don't any of you have a background in quantum computing?"

Since even Didjal was still gaping at her, the answer to that was pretty obvious.

I spread my hands apart. "Anyway. What does this thesis of yours look like, then? You are implying it will be hooked up to a machine?"

"Yes. It is a small titanium box, marked with a bar code. It will also carry the official stamp of the Nephealis Library of Advancement, which is a phyonwe tree in silhouette. There will also be the letters NLA stamped onto the box, with the numbers 6752."

Seyal nodded her comprehension. "Right. I don't think there will be two of those on this moon. How can it be destroyed, apart from copying?"

"It is made of a specific TTN alloy." Agraala checked our faces and realized she had to clarify. "Tantalum, tungsten, niobium. One of the hardest alloys we have found. This particular combination can withstand over a thousand degrees Celsius, or can survive open space. It is the most resistant material suitable for encasing quantum chips that has been found, to date."

"So what do we do? Toss it into the nearest star?"

She nodded. "Exactly that, if we want to be absolutely sure it is completely destroyed. But, just to be on the safe side, it should be something above a red dwarf on the Hertzsprung-Russell diagram."

I blinked. "It might survive a red dwarf?" This was taking durability to extremes. I wondered what other materials could survive being thrown into a star. I had never heard of any.

"It might. This alloy is really tough."

"No kidding!" I surveyed the small group. "Anyway, that leaves Denaraz and I to act as back up for all of you. Our only role will be to protect you. It isn't perfect, because it seems to me that you won't all be in one place, which will leave us spread really thin on the ground. We will do our best. All clear?"

There was a chorus of murmurs. None of us sounded particularly enthusiastic.

We moved out again, edging closer and closer to the flashing white dot on Agraala's navigation aid. Agraala and Didjal were now leading, poised to split and head for their individual objectives. Eshaan and Seyal had moved closer, ready to find the quantum chip. Danaa was tucked in behind them, and Denaraz and I brought up the rear.

The walkway now became a passageway. It was harder to anticipate Vaers. Then it became impossible. We were walking past a closed door when it opened and a portly Vaer bustled out.

Denaraz's weapon flashed. The Vaer collapsed with only a faint squawk of surprise. Denaraz and I dragged him back inside the room, after checking it was empty.

But we were getting closer. Our position showed us to be almost on top of the white light. The corridor that we were in ended just in front of us. It widened out into a vast hold. We edged closer to the opening and peered around it.

We all gasped.

I could hardly believe my eyes.

The area in front of us was huge. It definitely wasn't man-made. Or Vaer-made. This had to have formed naturally. It was big enough to hold a fleet of ships. Instead, the whole cavernous area was empty except for a circular structure which was suspended from the ceiling far above with cables as thick as tree trunks.

It was some sort of building, for we could see light through the open doorway and sets of windows running up the rounded walls. The edifice must have been around 30 meters wide and perhaps 100 high. It shone with a coppery light which glittered in the semi-darkness.

The sets of windows indicated that there must have been about twenty stories above our vantage point and perhaps another ten below. Where the thick cables met the tower they were insulated by huge rubber shock-absorbing compensators so as to isolate the cables from the hanging structure.

Leading from our level towards the laboratory was a pontoon of metal. We would have to find a way around the circular outer wall of the huge chamber we had entered to reach it. It had no railings and looked very flimsy. There was a break in the bridge before it reached the dangling building so that the suspended structure was not touching any of the surrounding metal. The edges of the gap were again overlaid with rubber. The gap was around a meter.

I looked more closely at the bridge. In fact, the farthest part of the pontoon was not a bridge at all; it was attached to the structure itself, and would cover the doorway when pulled up. It was in drawbridge form and could be raised and lowered at will, being kept in place by two tight hawsers fitted to stanchions near the end. Although the doorway itself was small for a Vaer building, about two meters high, the drawbridge when retracted would probably cover six floors.

Our gazes took in the scene in front of us. We were all shocked by what we saw.

"That wasn't built in the last few days," whispered Danaa.

"No." I had never heard Agraala so grim. "They have been planning this for a long time. That whole large-scale structure is a quantum-isolated system."

I stared up at the central building. "Are you sure Zenzara is inside that thing?"

Agraala consulted her navigation device. "Yes. She is on the top floor. Up there!" She pointed, and our eyes followed her arm. From the height of the windows, the very highest floor looked to take up perhaps three stories.

"So, how do we get inside?" The bridge across to the building was about the width of a person and made of metal planking. On both sides of the bridge there was a drop down to the floor of the vast chamber of at least a hundred meters. Nobody who fell would survive that. The planks were the only way in, and the gap where the drawbridge met the bridge swung to and fro. That wasn't going to be a nice leap to make.

It amazed me that the Vaers, who are much larger than we are, could even cross something like this. Perhaps, having been a flying species, heights did not bother them. Maybe their vestigial wings were still good enough to ensure stability in such a situation.

I wished I had wings. I am not normally scared of heights – an advantage in space – but that bridge made something inside me shrivel up and want to go to sleep. I shivered inside my IEVA suit.

Denaraz was peering into the lighted gateway to the building. "Are there guards? Will we be seen if we try to cross?"

Eshaan studied the far doorway. The Enif eyesight is much better than most other species. "I can see two guards," it told us. "They are set back, just outside the illuminated entrance."

The Enif exchanged a glance and then a nod. "We will go," said Didjal. "We can cross on the underside of the walkway."

"Are you sure?" It would have been suicidal for a Spacelander.

The Enif examined the underside of the walkway. "Our physiology is very different to yours. It will be difficult for us, but not, I hope, impossible."

Eshaan transmitted something privately to Didjal, who began to shake with amusement.

I felt left out. "What?"

Eshaan looked back and gave the Enif equivalent of a grin. "Nothing," it said. "I was just pointing out that it would have been a lot easier for us if Didjal had been younger."

The joke was that they were both exactly the same age.

I rolled my eyes. Denaraz was a bad influence on us all if even the Enif were catching his irreverent attitude to life. "I blame you, Izan."

He twisted around, hurt. "Me? What have I done?"

"Never mind. Okay, you two. Go make it safe for us all to cross. Good luck!"

The two Enif checked out the path they would have to take. First, they needed to make their way around the circular walls until they reached the start of the bridge out to the structure. Then they had to make it as far as the drawbridge gap. Once across that, they merely would have to sneak up on two large Vaers and knock them unconscious.

"Don't take too long," I told them.

They both gave me a long look, then left.

It took them only around a minute to plaster themselves to the shiny wall of the massive chamber we were in and shimmy along one of the welded joints. These protruded some four centimeters from the wall. There was little chance of them being seen doing that since all of the available light was concentrated on the pontoon bridge and the doorway. Black as their bodies were, Eshaan and Didjal blended perfectly with the shadows around the walls.

They ducked under the bridge and froze as a large group of Vaers emerged from the passageway leading back to the rest of the moon's installation. They paused, their feet not one foot away from the two Enif. We all held our breath.

Then the group began to cross the bridge. They did so with care, one by one. I was surprised to see that they did indeed unfurl their short wings. These could be flapped and were still enough to momentarily raise them from the ground if need be.

With their wings to help them, it was a moment for each Vaer to cross. However, it did show us how the bridge would bounce and jump when weight was put on it. It was extremely scary.

We watched as the two small figures curled themselves under the bridge. The ease with which they could maneuver upside down on such a fragile walkway was quite notable. I had been around them so long that I had forgotten just how different their makeup was from my own.

They have a backbone, so are not insects, but they also appear to have some insectival characteristics. They possess partial shiny and black exoskeletons, and large compound eyes. They possess two full sized legs and two full sized arms, but also possess vestigial arms set above the main ones. The vestigial arms are very useful as they are still functional and possess extremely dexterous working digits, effectively giving them four hands.

The gap edged by the rubber shields proved quite difficult, though. Due to the light gravity on the moon, their bodies flopped downwards when they released their back legs. And a meter was too far for them to reach across.

They solved it by using the fact that there were two of them. One – I couldn't tell at that distance which one – climbed down the other's body so that they were dangling beneath it. The first one began to swing to and fro, gradually building up momentum. When the swinging movement was considerable, the hanging Enif unfolded until it was dangling off its friend's body, its head and arms loosely pointing downwards.

For one horrible moment I thought that it was going to fall. Then it used the momentum it had picked up to propel itself across the gap and grab a handhold on the other side.

Once that was done, it was easier. The one who had crossed released its own legs and began to swing. The one left behind waited until those legs were close to its position, at the height of their trajectory, and launched itself across the gap.

My heart gave a leap at the same time, fibrillating with fear like a machine gun. All this tension was getting to it. Maybe I should get it checked out.

Then they were across. They appeared to hesitate for a few seconds, getting their bearings, and then they disappeared into the shadows just inside the gate.

We didn't have to wait long. Within around a minute, two slim and recognizable shapes reappeared in the opening and waved to us.

The two Nepheals had already navigated the welding line and were poised ready to start the crossing. I saw Agraala advise Danaa and then pat her shoulder, sending her on her way.

The young Nepheal dropped onto all fours and scampered across, making short work of the gap. A quick wave told us she was safely with the Enif.

The bridge was swinging from Danaa's crossing and I wondered how Agraala would do. I didn't see her though, because Denaraz and I were on either side of Seyal, trying to help her across the weld shelf.

In the end we told her to close her eyes. She hesitated and then nodded. I knew how much determination she had. She wouldn't let us down. She had gone through far too much to fail now.

And I was right. She took a few deep breaths, then told us serenely that she was ready. We guided her across with short instructions and held her against the wall with one hand each.

By the time we made it as far as the bridge, Agraala was waving to us from the other side. I looked at Seyal.

"This is not so hard for me," she said with dignity. "I can do this."

I waved her across the pontoon, which was still quivering from Agraala's passage across it.

Seyal smiled. Then she took a deep breath and whisked herself across the whole thing in very few seconds, hardly making it move. She still had the ability to virtually pass undetected.

Denaraz, as expected, made short work of it.

That left me. I wished for a moment it didn't, then took quick low steps across the pontoon.

I hated every second. The thing vibrated at every step and seemed to be threatening to throw me off. I found myself unable to breathe.

There was only one way to take this. Fast. I threw myself at the thing and ran as lightly as I could across it, taking good care not to look down. I didn't stop at the gap, either. It was easier simply to keep running and propel that step just that much further. I landed badly and the whole long catwalk tilted slightly to one side, threatening to decant me over the side.

My arms flailed as I desperately tried to keep my balance. Then my forward impulse helped to right me and I stumbled across, arriving at the gateway in a tumble of limbs.

Denaraz grabbed at my arm and helped me to pull up. "Good," he said. "We made it. What are we going to do about the drawbridge?"

Well, that was a no-brainer. If they had built the thing to be completely isolated from the rest of the installations on the moon, more fool them. That could be used against them, too.

"Pull up the drawbridge!" I told Didjal, feeling a little archaic as I did.

The Enif activated some sort of mechanism and the last stretch of bridge folded up towards us, until the view across the vast bay was cut off. The section slotted neatly into a recess at the sides of the gateway, cutting the module off from any outside intervention.

We turned and exchanged satisfied looks. We had made it this far. Now we just had to find Zenzara.

9

The passageways shone with the same coppery color that I had noticed on the outside of the structure. It gave us all a distorted mirror image of ourselves as we passed by the walls. It was eerie and yet warm at the same time. More than once I found myself starting at nearby movement, only to find that it was one of my own party dimly duplicated on the wall.

We were lucky. There had been no reaction to the raising of the drawbridge. Perhaps the Vaers were so sure that nobody could get close to their secret suspended laboratory that they had become careless. I don't know. We crept along the shiny passage until Didjal, who was leading us, discovered a door that led to a stairwell. The flight of steps led both up and down, but we directed ourselves up.

Denaraz and I had taken the lead now. Denaraz positioned himself one flight above the rest of us. We wanted to make sure we would hear any Vaer that approached.

I was just coming up to the door of the next floor, which was marked with the number 20, when it was flung open from the other side and two heavy Vaers marched through.

I ducked, but since I was standing directly in their path they couldn't help but see me.

One of them gave a low roar. His beak slashed down towards me; a reflex reaction that almost reached my throat even though I was already leaping backward.

There was a flash from above and then another one. The leading Vaer hung for a moment and then tumbled into me, knocking me off my feet and down several steps. I was winded as the inert body slammed on top of me, pinning me down.

The only thing I was able to do was to lie there gasping as the others attempted to drag the Vaer off me. He was quite dead. Denaraz had not been trained to miss. We had already discussed weapon settings, and his logical argument had prevailed. However much we disliked killing, we had to ensure that any Vaer we came across were quietly and efficiently silenced. Vaers are big animals; if you want to keep one down for long you cannot simply stun him.

I still couldn't breathe. In fact the drumming in my ears was telling me pretty clearly that if they didn't manage to pull me free soon, I would join the two corpses on these stairs. That was a convincing reason to help the rest of the group. I twisted and turned as much as I could, attempting to bring pressure to bear on the dead weight that was skewering me to the floor.

Finally, the rounded body was dislodged. I felt as though I were floating upwards. Somebody was mouthing something at me, and was pushing down on my chest. I wondered why, until some dulled part of my brain clicked into action and forced me to take a breath.

The air rattled down my throat and trickled into my lungs, where it was actually painful.

I propped myself up on one elbow and turned to the side, coughing. Seyal leant over me, shushing at me and trying to cover my lips with her hand.

I pushed her away, but her actions did have some response from deep within me. The air was now circulating inside my bloodstream and I was beginning to realize where I was. The need for silence came back to me at the same time. I gave her a nod, then went back to the hard work of sucking in air.

It seemed like only moments later that Denaraz and Didjal were pulling me to my feet. Denaraz's face loomed into mine. He appeared worried. I waved him back. "I ... I ... am all right," I tried to tell him. The words clumped in my larynx and remained unsaid. I heard a sort of croak come out.

He understood, giving me a hard pat on my back. Then he slid up the flight of stairs again. We had to hurry. There were now two Vaer bodies cluttering up the stairs. The next workers out of that door could hardly miss seeing them, and once the alarm was raised, our possibilities were going to be severely curtailed. Or we would be dead.

We had another ten storeys to go. With Didjal beside me to prop me up, I was able to keep pace with the rest of the group as it surged upwards. We were bringing up the rear now. The two Nepheal women were tucked in behind Izan, and then Eshaan and Seyal were just in front of me.

As each storey flickered by, I found my body responding less and less. My head was swimming with fatigue and the oxygen I was managing to get into my lungs simply wasn't doing the trick. I wondered what I had injured. It seemed to me that if I was breathing again, I should feel better. That wasn't happening. I probed the area around my ribs. It was very tender but as far as I could tell, there wasn't any crepitation. Good. That might just make it muscular. I had probably strained some of the muscle encasing the ribs. Not surprising when a dead weight cannons into you.

I waved Didjal away. There was no time for all this now. I needed to get better, and get better now.

I doubled over for a few seconds and tried to will away the pain in my chest and in my back. I was not going to give in to this. I was needed. I could sit down and feel sorry for myself once we had got Zenzie back.

I did manage to scrape up some determination out of the pain, and I followed the others up the stairs. I was pretty sure there was nothing broken. The muscle pain was tough, but not incapacitating. I had to make my body respond.

And, gradually, it did. The air began to dispel the dizziness. The more I made myself calm and took measured gulps of air, the more I could feel it penetrating down into all the bronchioles and filtering into my bloodstream. As that happened, I was able to move more easily. The pain was still there, but pain could be ignored, at least for a short time.

If any more Vaers had chosen to use the stairway while I was desperately trying to recover control of my body, I would have been unable to defend myself. Luckily, they didn't. I reached the door marked 30 soon after the rest of the group and was able to give them what I hoped was a reassuring smile.

From the worried looks on their faces, it didn't work, but it didn't stop them either. They knew what the priorities were.

"Now or never," said Denaraz, his eyes running over each one of us to make sure that we were ready. "You know what to do."

We all nodded. We just didn't know what we were going to find on the other side of the door.

I pulled out my gun. I wasn't going to be much use as a quick responder. My job was going to be backing them up from the rear. I hated the necessity, but I recognized the change in my own circumstances. I was going to have to take a back seat on this one.

Izan grimaced at me. He could see what I was going through and he knew he was going to have to take the lead on this one. His eyes flickered to my gun. He took out his own and made sure it was in working order.

The Enif preferred hand to hand combat. Their carapaces made them almost immune to pulser attack. It simply bounced off them, sometimes with lethal consequences to both the shooter and to bystanders. This time they were the first through the door.

I thrust myself after them.

The cavernous laboratory stretched upwards for three floors. In the middle of the space there was a large egg-like structure. It wasn't constructed of any solid material, however. It was made of what looked like light. Individual radiant threads were intertwined with others until they formed bars of a cage. It gave out a rose-gold glow. The cage sat squarely in the middle of the space, hovering around a foot from the ground.

The space between the bars of light was completely transparent, so it was easy to see Zenzara.

Seeing her hurt my soul.

She was inside the cage of light. Her body was naked and she was hanging in mid air, facing upwards, with her arms and legs dangling down. Folds of wrinkles were also being pulled downwards by gravity. They dangled down, forming a short curtain. I could see nothing physical keeping her where she was.

She was not moving.

I thought she was dead.

Long nanoseconds ticked by as I stared. My mind went a complete blank and the world turned much darker.

Then I noticed a glint off one of her eyes. I saw that it had moved to look at us.

That one eye met mine. There was a spark of hope that was almost immediately blotted out by anguish.

I felt like screaming. The utter despair I had noticed inside that one eye was so strong that it seeped into me and made me shiver.

We might be too late.

I didn't see how the Zenzara I knew could still be there. How even such an indomitable spirit as hers could survive such treatment.

Agraala, beside me, gasped. "They made a skyrmion chamber." She looked horrified. "It was just a theory. I never expected to see it in practice. I mean, it requires quite a lot more than just establishing two counter-circulating electric currents, after all." She sounded drained. "I was hoping it would be too difficult for them to make."

"What is it?"

"It is condensate latticework formed by creating synthetic

electromagnetic knots and then fusing them together."

"It is made of light then?"

"In a way. Light and plasma and condensate."

There was no time for more. The last part of her sentence drifted back at me as she moved past. I vaguely registered her flying towards a control panel that was set onto a plinth to one side of the tank. Seyal and Eshaan were racing towards a large computer which took up an entire wall.

Denaraz and I raised our guns. But these were scientists, not pirates. It was only necessary for us to singe two of them along their portly waistlines before all of the Vaers present raised their wings and surrendered. Much easier than I had anticipated.

The problem was at the control panel. Ramesh Chandrayanan and Bull Cunningham were standing behind it. Bull was pointing a hand-held ultrapulse pistol at Agraala's head. The whites of her eyes were showing.

I walked towards them. "Bull. How nice to see you again."

"Step back, Rye. And tell your people to do the same. I am sure you don't want to see this nice Nepheal lady hurt."

I stopped advancing and lowered my gun.

"Drop it on the floor." I obeyed.

He turned to Denaraz. "You too." Denaraz obeyed.

I turned my head to Chandrayanan. "You have been planning this all along."

His mouth formed a self-satisfied smirk. "Maybe I have."

"Where did you get the wormhole technology you intend to use? Did you steal that too?"

He bristled. "I have no need to steal anything. I am the greatest living scientist."

I gave a snort.

He looked even angrier. "I am! Who developed the RAMP missiles? And I came up with the wormhole protocol myself!"

I raised a skeptical eyebrow. "You brought the Vaers on board out of the goodness of your hearts?"

He hesitated. "They may have been useful, but only as procurers of the necessary materials." He puffed out his chest. "I am the only physicist capable of developing this technology."

"I am sure you are." If I could keep him engaged it was less likely any of us would get shot. "How did you find out about the thesis?"

He opened his mouth, but Bull held up his free hand. "They don't need to know about that, Ramesh."

The scientist disliked being told what to do. The sour expression on his face was enough to tell me that. I wondered if I could use that to our advantage.

"Are you in charge here, Bull?"

There was a quick flash and I felt a scorching sensation in my left arm. I stifled a yelp and the temptation to grab at the wound. I wasn't going to give him that much satisfaction.

He sighed. "Don't think you can split us by playing one off against the other, Rye. It won't work. I will shoot you or one of your friends dead if you do that again."

I raised my hands above my head, spreading my fingers wide. "Very well. You win."

He hadn't though. Izan had been carefully inching his second weapon out from the secret pocket he had in his IEVA suit. Now he shot at Cunningham.

The tiny pistol he kept secreted about his person at all times was not enough to kill. It was hardly bigger than his crests. But it was enough to knock the ultrapulse clean out of the Flatlander's hand.

I lunged and caught it as it fell, swiftly turning it on its owner.

Cunningham's eyes glittered murderously. He stepped forward. "You would never shoot me, Rye. We had too many good drinking sessions together on *Commorancy*."

I shot him. His eyes showed surprise and then pain. He swayed, then sank to the floor, his hands protectively covering the wound in his thigh.

I smiled. "What was that you were saying, Bull? Reminiscing about the good times on good old *Commorancy*? Before you got her and a great number of innocent people blown to bits? Why, yes. Good old times, weren't they?"

The surge of emotion his uncaring words had provoked ate away at me. I contemplated putting another ultrapulse through him, this time around about where his heart would be if he had one.

Denaraz stopped me. He waved Chandrayanan away from the console. Then Cunningham.

"I will take care of these two," he told us. "Agraala. Your turn!"

Agraala and Danaa slipped behind the console. Their fingers hovered over the panel, but it was clear that they were having some difficulty figuring out what was for what.

I grabbed the left wing of the nearest Vaer scientist and dragged it over to the console. It squawked in fear but made no resistance.

"Explain all this to them!" I snapped.

It cringed as I brought the ultrapulse up to its ample midriff. "I will!" The words rushed out of it. "I will! Don't shoot me!"

"Don't tempt me then." I kept the gun pointing at it, after waving the barrel briefly at the remaining Vaer scientists to corral them into the far corner and make them sit against the outer wall. They obeyed with alacrity. They had seen me shoot Cunningham. That had convinced them to be discreet.

Agraala began to whisper to the Vaer, pointing to the cage containing Zenzara and then to the controls. The Vaer hesitated, then replied. Since Agraala was nodding, I had to assume that she was getting the information she needed.

Denaraz signaled to Didjal and then to all the doors, making scything movements with his hands to indicate closing.

Didjal gave an 'on it' signal back. It knew its job. It had already ripped off two covers that were set into the wall and was manipulating circuits and cables inside.

I checked to see that Seyal and Eshaan were unobstructed at the computer, then turned my attention back to the console.

Danaa had waited until her aunt was safely ensconced where she needed to be, but now her face was tense as she gazed towards the cage of light. There was some doubt there. I had given her the job of helping Zenzie, and it was the same mission her people had entrusted her with back on Nephealis. Her expression showed a stony determination not to fail the Chyzar for a second time.

As I watched, I saw her come to a decision. She said something briefly to her aunt, who looked up suddenly, concerned. They both stared into the cage. Agraala directed some punchy questions at the Vaer scientist, who hesitated and then gave a long answer. Agraala's face twisted. She considered. Then her haunches dropped slightly and she nodded to her niece.

The young Nepheal girl drew rather a shaky breath and edged towards the cage made of stopped light.

I could only follow her progress out of the corner of my eye. Cunningham was watching me like a hawk despite his wound. I knew that if I allowed my attention to wander, all our advantage could be lost. So it was with difficulty that I managed to see what she did.

Nepheals are tall when walking upright. Danaa, still young, must have been around two and a half metres. The solid light looked impenetrable. I wondered how she thought she was going to get through. I didn't see how she could do it.

But I was banking without Agraala's ingenuity. She used the console to focus a tight laser beam at one particular point of the cage. The threads of plasma nearest to the laser beam seemed to twist out of the way, resettling themselves around its edges.

I allowed myself one quick look towards Zenzara, in the middle of the tank. The eye was following Danaa's progress.

I felt sick for the Tyzaran girl's suffering. Sick that any person could contemplate subjecting someone to something like this. As I turned back to Cunningham and Chandrayanan, I was again tempted to shoot them both. But that was not my job. We were supposed to be the

Interstellar Enforcement Agency. We had to submit to due process, not act like a band of old-time vigilantes. I sighed.

Cunningham twitched. I shot a hole in the floor two millimeters to the right of his foot. He froze. It made me feel a tiny bit better.

Danaa was close to the bars of the cage, wrapping her fingers to protect them. I just managed to catch an increase in the intensity of the laser, which enlarged the gap. Her hands managed to grip the sides. She felt her way around the gap for a few moments, trying to get a handhold on the smooth material. Then she hauled her thin body up and through the aperture, dropping lightly into the glittering skyrmion cage. Within seconds she had made her way over to where Zenzara was.

The Nepheal girl put her arms around the suspended body, giving her a hug, I think. Trying to convey something of the shock we had all felt on seeing her. Trying to tell her that help had arrived, that she could hope again.

After the quick hug, Danaa attempted to get Zenzara to move. The Tyzaran girl couldn't. She had no movement in any part of her body. I saw Danaa begin to drag Zenzie towards the gap. It seemed the Tyzaran girl's body resisted. Something unseen was pinning it in place. I saw Danaa looking under and around the prone girl, trying to identify the problem.

The doors to the laboratory were now closed. Didjal was signing that they could only be breached by force. That was now being applied. I could hear thumping and the unmistakable sounds of pulsers being directed at them from the other side.

I asked it how long they could be kept out, but it shrugged. It couldn't know what kind of filling had been used inside the doors. I would imagine that all the doors to a facility like this would be safety doors. It seemed foolish to risk all our lives on that conviction, however.

Didjal was now seated at a smaller console which I hadn't noticed before. It was peering at computer code and nodding to itself. All four of its arms were busy, with twenty-four digits tapping out a furious instruction.

Suddenly, it looked up. I followed its gaze, just for a second.

The suspended chamber was equipped with many windows, some of which were set into the roof of the huge laboratory we were now in. Through these windows it was possible to see the rock ceiling of the vast main cavern, far above even those windows. Now that I looked more closely, I could just make out vents set in that ceiling. There were many of them, and they were set regularly into the rock so far above us.

These vents had just opened. Didjal met my gaze and smiled, holding one thumb up. It made a circular movement with its hand to indicate that it was pumping out all breathable air throughout the entire facility on the moon.

I turned back to catch the look of fear that crossed Cunningham's face. Dying of suffocation had not been in his plans for the day. His head went automatically to the emergency storeroom, behind him.

I allowed my Vaer prisoners to shuffle to their feet. They were so nervous that I was afraid one of them would start a stampede. I motioned to a bank of hanging PSAs.

Since Portable Safety Airbags are generally intended for those of Terran ethnicity, I was unsure how many Vaers to fit into one. They looked to be the standard kind, made to take two or three humans, though we had previously stuffed seven into one. I guessed that we could cram one Vaer to each and still leave them with enough air for about half-an-hour.

I motioned for them to activate the red levers on the wall and deploy the PS airbags. These ballooned outwards, causing the Vaer technicians to leap back. I put up three fingers, pointed at three Vaers and then signaled for them to wait by three of the airbags. There was no point using up emergency air when they could still breathe in here. The Vaer scientists nodded. They had understood.

The other group deployed the rest of the PSAs.

I had been planning to take Cunningham and the Terran scientist with me if we ever got out of this facility. But to do that, I would need at least IEVA suits for them. There weren't any inside the laboratory. There weren't even any full EVA suits. I couldn't take them with me. That annoyed me. But Didjal had been right to release the air in the whole moon facility. It was the only way we stood a chance of escaping with our lives. The Vaers would be too busy trying to get to ships to be concerned with any intruders. I would, if it were me. You don't track down a thief when your oxygen supply may only last ten minutes, believe me.

So I nodded to Cunningham eventually. He leapt to deploy the nearest PSA. The space burlap sack blossomed out of the storage locker, almost knocking him off his one good leg. I couldn't help wishing it had.

He and Chandrayanan stood by the PS airbag, their eyes going from me, to Zenzie and Danaa, to the vents far above all of us. The cold outside the moon facility was causing condensation as the air met the three or four Kelvins of the local surrounding space. Clouds of vapor were forming around each vent. Because of them, we could trace the speed of the air evacuation. It was fast. None of us would be able to breathe for long without some sort of artificial oxygen. Except the Enif, naturally. They had a distinct advantage there over the rest of the species.

Danaa had already freed Zenzie from whatever was holding her in place. She was now able to raise Zenzara up and pull her slowly towards the small hole in the solid plasma cage. The girl was completely unresponsive though. Her reflexes were inhibited. I didn't know what they had given her, but it seemed that the only things she could move were her eyes. I wasn't sure how she was breathing. *If* she was breathing. Zenzie must have been terrified to go through this all alone. I could hardly think of anything worse to do to somebody.

An alarm began to flash on the wall. It was an orange light that was some sort of air quality detector. I had the nasty feeling it was going to go red at almost any moment. Time here was running out.

There was a sudden increase in the light surrounding Zenzara and Danaa. The rose-gold glow in the skyrmions deepened into copper and I saw new beams of plasma forming inside the condensate. The plasma was like coils of rope, twisting and intertwining with other coils, building to form a sheet of blinding luminescence around the two girls and their cage. The gap in the cage that Danaa had entered through was quickly being closed by the new beams of plasma that were forming. They could no longer get through it.

A shout made me check the Terran scientist. He was scrambling towards the center of the laboratory, his hand reaching out towards the two girls. The whole cage was vibrating now, and lights were flashing on the console behind it.

"It is happening! I did it!"

I stopped him with a growl. "Get back!"

He obeyed, and I swiveled towards the plasma cage. It was as if it were filling its own walls in. The coils of condensates were seething in and around the existing bars, touching them, causing small pulses of blue energy to splinter off them. Then some of the strands of fire merged with the original plasma, making a partial wall that looked solid and was growing up around Zenzara and Danaa.

The Nepheal girl's eyes were wide and petrified. She reached out to push at this new phenomena, but snatched her hand back as the light seared her flesh.

I saw her look around the laboratory, first at her aunt and then at me. Our eyes met for a moment. I sensed her absolute terror of what was happening. Then she hardened her gaze, and her mouth, and her shoulders. The determination came back into her stance. She turned her attention back to the Chyzar, cuddling Zenzara's prone body to hers, standing protectively over her.

I swallowed, unable to look away. I don't think any of us could. For a moment, my captives were completely forgotten.

The patterns of light swirling around the center of the room were blinding now. More and more of them were blazing through the condensate, ripping apart the very fabric of spacetime itself.

"The condensate has already formed a skyrmion vortex!" shouted Chandrayanan, his eyes almost fanatic in their excitement, all fear dispelled by the sight in front of him. "They are trapped!" I wasn't sure whether he was referring to the Chakran strands or the two girls.

We had come too late; Agraala hadn't been able to halt the process.

I grabbed his slight frame as he launched himself towards the complicated figure in the center of the room. I had to prevent him from going further. I think he would have thrown himself at the sensors that were recording the seething mass of energy in front of us, if he could have.

Bull Cunningham was regarding the whole thing with interest. He was still detached, though. Still sure of himself. This was merely the enactment of his plan. He even raised one eyebrow at the excitement of the scientist.

"It does appear to be working," he said quietly. "The Nexus is dissolving, Rye. Think of what a great advance this will be for the Major Shells. Think of what it will do for space travel! Now we will be able to get that wormhole technology up and running; now nothing will stop us. You should get those girls out of there. I wonder if you will be able to?"

He didn't care about the Chakrans. He didn't care about the lives of the two girls inside that thing. He cared only for power, for supremacy. His calm voice was full of conviction. My adrenalin spiked so high that I almost dropped my gun.

"Agraala?" I had to shout over the noise.

She shook her head. "The process had already initiated; it reached viability point some time ago. I am sorry, Captain. The process will now accelerate. It will completely destroy the Chyzar's Nexus before going on to attack the rest of the Chakrans."

"No!" I stared wildly at her. "That will annihilate the Chakrans."

Agraala ruminated for a few long seconds, closing her eyes, trying to come up with some sort of a solution. Then she opened them again and stared over the room at Danaa. Her nod was one of conviction, though she looked heavy-hearted too. "There is something I can try. I ... I believe I can interrupt the process."

I was swamped by the horrid feeling that the girls would never get out of that cage now, that I would be forever haunted by their death. But I nodded to Agraala to go ahead. We couldn't allow the Chakrans to be farmed in this way. It was beyond unacceptable. We had no idea what it could do to them. I knew that Zenzie would want to pay the price. I hoped Danaa would too. I hated myself for giving that order, though. It was a detestable thing to have to do. I wondered if I would be able to live with it.

The orange flashing light changed to red. I ushered my two captives into their PSA and zipped them inside it. They weren't going anywhere now, and I might still have a chance of taking them with us to face trial. I activated my own IEVA suit and waved the remaining Vaer into their PSAs.

That only took perhaps thirty seconds, yet it was enough to prevent me from stopping Agraala.

I look back on that moment with huge sadness. Because of me, she did what she did. Because of me, she is gone.

I closed the last of the Vaer PSAs and then, of course, turned back to the plasma cage. I was just in time to see Agraala throw herself against the bars of light, now almost woven into a complete wall.

She had directed some sort of coherent beam at one particular point of the cage, and it was having an effect. Where the laser impinged on the solid light, it wavered. Motes of dust shimmered before the area, piece by piece, began to dissolve.

Soon there was a man-sized gap in the solid light. She left the laser on, still targeting the cage. She ran to the shining walls. Her fingers scrabbled frantically at the thick strands of interwoven rays that were already damaged by the laser, tearing at them, teasing away until she managed to unthread some of them and enlarge the gap. The skin on her fingers was curling away from the bones as the energy inside the walls of the cage ate away at her flesh.

I dropped my weapon and ran towards her position, but I was far, far too late. Even as I took the first steps to cover the distance, she had reached inside and plucked Zenzara out of Danaa's arms. She drew the Tyzaran girl swiftly through the hole and threw her across the laboratory.

Before Zenzie had landed, Agraala had jumped inside the cage through the hole. Her hands were black and the burnt stumps of her fingers had closed around Danaa's thin neck. The Nephealis girl had dug her heels in and seemed disposed to argue. Agraala dragged her summarily head first to the hole and then thrust the thin Nepheal girl firmly out with a solid push from behind. Danaa tumbled out in a splay of limbs, nearly hitting the computer array. Then Agraala herself turned back towards us and seemed to be taking a step towards us.

She wasn't able to. The center of the cage exploded just as she was disentangling herself. There was a huge flash of energy that traveled outwards from the golden structure. It reached out towards all of us, and would have consumed the whole laboratory, but something stopped it.

The explosion stalled. The energy pulse halted, just beyond Agraala. I caught the last light of life in her eyes as time stopped and everything froze. I know I was able to count to five.

I couldn't get to her. I was halted in mid air. Don't ask me what caused the effect; it made no sense to me. One moment I was closing in on her position, the next I was pinned in space and time and only able to watch with horror as the walls of stopped light pulsed outwards.

They enveloped almost her whole body, hanging there for what seemed like minutes, but must have been nanoseconds.

Just as suddenly, the scene in front of me unfroze. The bands of light snapped back towards the centre of the structure, hardening as they retracted. Her body was decimated by them. They passed through her flesh like a thousand knives. The life disappeared from her eyes as I watched. It was so quick that she couldn't have felt pain. One moment she was on the edge of the energy pulse, frozen but still complete; the next she was lacerated by the light beams and her body ceased to exist.

The threads of light didn't stop there. They continued to fall in on themselves and the cage of plasma until the entire construct collapsed backwards, dragging the mutilated body of Agraala with them. There was a fierce ripping sound that was so sharp it hurt our ears. I felt a strong wind pulling me towards it. If I had been a little closer I think it would have dragged me with it.

The solid sides of the cage fell backwards towards the centre. The surrounding air gave a long gasp as if pain seemed to exude from the cage, then the whole construction vanished in on itself and disappeared. So did Agraala's body.

I was thrown to the floor by the void caused as the structure collapsed. I flinched as my shoulder was jolted again. But the pain seemed far away. What I had just witnessed dimmed all sensation.

She was gone. I had seen her body scored through and through. She had died saving the two girls. Tears slipped into my eyes as I struggled to my feet.

Danaa was staring at where the cage had been. Her face was agonized.

I made my way over to her. "She wanted to save you." I put my arms around her. There were angry red marks on her neck where Agraala had grabbed her.

She shook me away. "She was a genius. She is the one who should have been saved. I am nothing. I have done nothing. I have written no theses. I am not worthy. No. No! This cannot have happened. She died saving me! No!"

"She died saving the Chyzar," I told her in more severe tones. "As she promised to do. And the Chakrans."

Danaa's face was stricken. "She should have left me. I don't deserve this."

I felt suddenly angry with her. I should have maintained silence, I know, but I couldn't. "Then you will have to deserve it in your future.

You will have to do enough to make her proud of you."

Her patrician nose twitched. "I suppose," she sniffed, "but how will I ever be able to pay her back for my life?"

"You can't. Talk to Zenzie about it. She knows."

Danaa stared at me, at first uncomprehending. Then her brow cleared. "Oh, you mean the savior protocols. Yes, she would understand."

We both turned towards the Chyzar, but Denaraz had beaten us to her. He was bent solicitously over Zenzara and had already formed an initial opinion.

"She will recover," he told us. "Though I think she will be marked by the experience for the rest of her life."

I stared at the gaping hole in the middle of the laboratory. Burn marks extended outwards from the epicenter of the colossal explosion.

"I think we all will."

Seyal and Eshaan joined the rest of us. So did Didjal. We clustered around the two survivors.

Zenzara was still completely unable to move. Her eyes were the only part of her which could express feeling. Big tears had welled up in the outside corners and were getting caught up in the deep wrinkles down her face. The eyes themselves were full of sadness and fear.

I grabbed at the spare IEVA suit we had brought for her and summarily pulled it over her thin frame, manhandling her outer extremities until they obeyed me. I hoped that I wasn't hurting her. She made no sound and her eyes had closed. Only the tears caught up in the wrinkles showed that she was still with us.

Denaraz gave a jerk of his head towards the exit. He was right. We were all running low on air supply and we needed to get out of here while the Vaers were still preoccupied with breathing. Once somebody switched the air supply back on we would be toast.

We ran down the stairs as fast as was possible when carrying a prone person. Zenzie was only a slip of a thing, but she still slowed us down. Denaraz took her legs and I took her shoulders, and we ran clumsily with her sagging body between us. When we tired the two Enif took over. They were much more agile than we were. Having two sets of arms helped. They could hold her steady.

Danaa ran ahead to lower the drawbridge. There were no signs of angry Vaers. Most of them were slumped in the corridors, having fallen wherever they were. The flashing lights did not extend outside the laboratory and the corridors had a meager supply of air; they would have had no warning of problems with their environment.

We dashed across the bridge, ignoring the piled bodies of unconscious Vaers that were piled up around and on it. We had to clamber over one or two that had collapsed right on the bridge, but they were thankfully unresponsive to such indignity.

Making our way along the smooth rounded wall back to the tunnel we had come out of was possible only because of the Enif. Six appendages enabled them to manage Zenzara and still cross. The rest of us inched along the thin ledge as best we could.

As we reached the relative safety of our scarcely used tunnel, there was a humming above us and a slow hydraulic whirr as the vents far above us closed. They had the system back up and running. We needed to leave. Fast. It wouldn't take the Vaers long to get themselves organized and unless we were safely back in our cocoon of the carbon cloud, we would be easy to pick off. At least we would be leaving them with severe logistical problems; I doubted they had a large enough supply of air to repressurize the whole installation.

I will always remember that race against time. We came across one or two isolated groups of Vaer, but they had either collapsed or were woozy and in no condition to act against us. We sped past them. There was no point hindering them any further. Any Vaer with two brains to rub together would realize that we must have come in through the carbon collector. It wasn't going to be a secret for very much longer.

Denaraz and I were about to take over carrying Zenzara, when Danaa, who had been quietly bringing up the rear, pushed us aside. "I will take her from here," she told us, dropping onto all fours. "Seyal can hold her steady on my back. We will be able to move faster."

I frowned. Ouraali had carried me down a mountain, but Danaa was only young. The Nepheal bones were very fragile. "I am not sure you should do that, Danaa. You could break something."

She shuffled impatiently from foot to foot. "I know my own strength more than you do. I can do this!"

She needed to do it, I saw. "Very well. Thank you."

We gave Seyal a leg-up onto her back and then pushed as the Avarak woman hauled the inert body in front of her. Once that had been done, the two Enif raced on ahead to fire up the mag frame and prepare the EVA suits. We would need them, after all. Our oxygen supply was running really low in the limited IEVA helmets.

Danaa galloped away, following in the tracks of the Enif, Seyal clinging grimly to her back. Zenzara's body was jolted up and down with each step. She would have a few more bruises on that poor little torso of hers.

Denaraz and I found ourselves left behind. We exchanged a glance and began to run. He, of course, being that much taller, was faster than me.

I became well aware of the limitations of the human body as I pounded down that corridor after them all. We Spacelanders usually thought of ourselves with pride, but here I was, last in the race and still finding it painful to breathe. It was a humbling experience.

Thankfully, I was not too far behind when they arrived at the airlock into the carbon collector. Eshaan was already on the other side, and they had passed the EVA suits inside so that we could all suit up. The Enif didn't need it, of course. They were showing no signs of distress.

I, on the other hand, was puffing like a fireblower.

Denaraz bent over and put both hands on his abdomen. I felt secretly pleased that he was showing at least some signs of discomfort.

Danaa slowly dropped to the floor, where Seyal could slip Zenzara off her back. The young Nepheal girl was looking grey. Her journey had not come without cost. The marks on her neck where Agraala had snatched her from certain death were still a pulsing, vivid red. I wondered if they would stay with her forever.

We pulled the IEVA helmets off and put the EVAs on top of the suits. At least, Denaraz, Seyal and I did. Danaa simply pulled a larger, clip-on helmet over her large head. With a quick twist of one of her hands, she was being supplied with ample oxygen. Nepheal vacuum suits were clearly more flexible in use than ours. Her face immediately began to lose the grey tinge, and she smiled and held her thumbs up. She had done very well.

We crowded into the airlock and let ourselves out into the carbon collector, which widened as we went. The two Enif ran ahead to ready the mag frame for us.

When we reached the vent, we lay Zenzara on top of the frame. The rest of us formed a long line trailing behind it, each person attached to the person before.

As we emerged to open space, our suits partially lit up with a blue reflection that flashed on and off every second or so. It was leaking out of the large entryway to the docking area, and was visible even out here in space. Our EVA suits absorbed some of it, but the two Enif, with their high reflectivity, turned blue and black alternatively.

There was a touch to my shoulder and I turned with some surprise. Danaa was pointing to where the Nepheal shuttle was and making question signs.

At first I had no idea what she was trying to convey. Then it dawned on me. With Agraala gone, Danaa would be on her own on the Nepheal shuttle, although she had Neema and Anzany to help her on the Nepheal ship. She was injured and probably in shock. She shouldn't have to get the shuttle back to *Aenysia* on her own through the carbon cloud.

I chewed on my lip. It had to be Denaraz or I who went with her. We were the only experienced pilots present. He was just ahead of me in the chain. I pulled at his leg until he dropped back to my level.

He was quick to appreciate the problem. He looked at me and made a 'you-me' signal and then spread his hands. I nodded. The lines on his face creased even more.

But I knew he would have to stay with Zenzara. He was Tyzaran, after all. He was the same race. He would at least have some idea of first aid, of how to help her. I had none. I was the most dispensable one of the two of us, at least at this time and place.

I pointed to myself and then to Danaa.

He gave a solemn nod. He would have come to the same conclusion. Anybody would.

Danaa's eyes brightened when I signed that I would go with her. I smiled back, before realizing that there was something else we could do. I made a rectangle sign to Seyal and then raised my eyebrows. Who had the thesis?

She pulled a small shiny metal box from a voluminous pocket I hadn't noticed and handed it to me.

I held it up so that Denaraz could see it. I indicated myself and Danaa and then throwing it away.

He nodded.

Then I pointed to him, opening the gesture to take in the rest of the crew. I made signs of water in the dark vacuum surrounding us.

He got it straight away. His intelligent eyes sparked and he nodded. He would take Zenzara to Ulon Prime. It was one of the closest systems to where we were now, and the Macers would keep her safe. We could join them there. I slipped the thesis inside one of the EVA pockets.

First we had to get out of here.

Then we had an appointment with a star.

10

Danaa and I were the first to be dropped off at our Nepheal shuttle. I floated in space outside the hull while the young girl opened the hatch to the airlock. I hoped that the Nepheal ships would be similar enough to ours for me to master the controls easily.

The ship was so spacious that my jaw dropped. It was only a shuttle, yet it must have had almost the same volume as *Faraday*, the ship that had been taken away from me by the Vaers. It was shorter in overall length and in the beam, of course, but so much taller that the volume would be maintained.

Inside, the corridors were five metres high. I looked up, amazed. I had known what to expect before coming on board, but the reality was still quite surprising.

In silence, still in shock from the loss of her aunt, Danaa led me towards the bridge. I made no attempt at conversation; she deserved the mental space to begin her mourning process.

The bridge was quite impressive too. The footprint was about the same size as a Tyzaran shuttle, which were bigger than a human-based ship, but the airiness of the high ceiling made it appear more cathedral-like.

I attempted to slide into the pilot's seat. Impossible. It was so high up that I was like a baby trying to reach a high chair. I had to look around for something I could use as a step. Danaa was immersed in her own sorrow; I don't think she even noticed.

The only available thing was a box full of cleaning products, which I found in a cupboard. I tipped out the contents and upended it beside the pilot's station. Using that, I was able to jump onto the actual pilot's chair. The attempt made me wince as the injury in my chest complained at its treatment.

I tried to ignore the pain, concentrating all of my attention on the console in front of me. I felt immediate relief. It was in Nepheale, but the standard colors and pictograms were all used as well, so it was relatively easy to deduce what each of the controls was for.

I began the pre-flight check. Not that we had much time to spare for it, but I did want to give myself a moment or two to familiarize myself with the position of the most important controls. I might need to access them quickly, and if that happened I didn't want to be wasting time trying to find out where they all were.

The shuttle throbbed into life, sounding deeper and more efficient than the shuttle engines I was most used to.

Everything else was just as optimal, so I checked that the mag frame with the others was way out of danger from the engines, then edged the craft from the moon's surface.

She was reactive. Her bows shot round, which made me hustle to correct and led to an overcorrection. She was a thoroughbred, light on the throttle and the helm. I would need more finesse.

But we gradually got to know each other. I sidled into the shadows to the right of the still-open main entryway to the moon facility.

I made up my mind to travel around the facility, rather than head straight back into the cloud. I would rather they chased us to the wrong place rather than the right place. I hoped Denaraz would do the same. We should have spoken about it before we split up. My ability to keep a straight head on me had been compromised. I wasn't pleased with my leadership skills. They would need some honing if I was to make a success of this new Interstellar Enforcement Agency thing. It was a steep learning curve.

Just as I was considering my lack of prevision, I noticed that one of the Vaer ships was preparing to leave the docking bay. I crept closer to the doors again to try to see what was happening.

Inside, flashing lights announced that they were evacuating all the personnel that they could. Tiny figures in EVA suits were organizing long queues of other figures without EVA suits. They were shepherding them onto the ships. I zoomed in on the sights below.

The Vaers in the queue were still standing. Several of them seemed to have labored breathing, and were looking wildly around them in an uncomprehending sort of way, but there were no prone bodies here inside the vast docking bay.

Of course! The space was so large that it would take much longer for the air to rarefy and also much longer to refill again. Those working around the ships had decided to organize themselves into some sort of emergency procedure in the docking area and evacuate anyway. They had time to get most of those present in the vast hold to relative safety on one or other of the autonomous ships.

I zoomed out and checked the ship that seemed to be hauling out of the docking area. It was a large freighter – an ugly thing with pod after pod of cargo containers dragging its speed down. Each pod was an independent module bolted and shackled into a slot along the backbone structure of the long freighter.

I smiled. That would see one of us across the gap to the cloud. I wouldn't risk it with two, not in the present circumstances. They knew we were here … they could detect a ship leeched onto the freighter if they really tried. But if they saw one shuttle running for the cloud … well, they were unlikely to guess that we had actually come in two, weren't they?

It was clear to me that, of the two ships, I had the one that should draw away any pursuit. Zenzara, the Chyzar, was on the other. Together with the other members of our small team. Although I was loath to risk Danaa's integrity, it was really a fairly easy choice.

I cruised over the top of the massive door, until I spotted the other shuttle. They were just entering the airlock. I saw faces turn towards us, the visors on the EVA suits reflecting the flashing blue warning light that seeped out of the docking bay area.

I wiggled the shuttle slightly to get their attention, and then deliberately turned her nose through ninety degrees until she was pointing towards the freighter that was slowly accelerating out of the dock. Then I repeated the gesture.

A lone arm thrown upwards signaled understanding. I wiggled the shuttle from side to side again, and cruised back over the top of the doors to my original position. Now I would wait just long enough for Denaraz to get his shuttle correctly aligned to the freighter. He would have to stick to her like a limpet across the divide if he didn't want to be detected, but I trusted him implicitly. He was a better pilot than I was; if anybody could pull it off, he could.

I managed to string out the waiting for another ten minutes. It was all I could give him, if we were to have half a chance of getting across to the protective cloak of the carbon cloud.

As soon as the freighter was fully outside the docking bay and beginning to haul itself out of the moon's light gravity well, I knew it was time for me to act. I nudged the controls of the Nepheal shuttle to pile on the thrust, and she leapt to comply. It felt as though she were eager to escape. I certainly was. I took a vector which would lead them away from the freighter.

Our luck ran out when we were about half way across the gap between the moon and the surrounding carbon cloud. About fifty Vaer shuttles shot out of the huge docking station and accelerated towards us.

I looked at the distance left to travel to the cloud and the distance between us and the closing shuttles. I grimaced. It was going to be tight. And, even if we did manage to make the carbon cloud, we were going to have to hammer straight into it, without finding less dense areas. That could be extremely dangerous. I sighed.

Danaa came out of her reverie. "Problems?"

"Will this thing stand up to that carbon cloud? At full strength?"

She gave a sort of half shrug and a sort of half grin.

"Yes. I don't know either," I replied. "But I guess we are about to find out. If we get there first, that is. They have just opened fire."

Danaa reached down to the console in front of her and played with something for a few seconds. A bright blue flashing light started to play around the top of the walls. "We have shields," she said.

Good news. I was extremely happy to hear that. "Will they keep the carbon off us too?"

"I ... maybe?"

"Do you want me to fire back now?"

"No, no. Whenever you think it is a good time!"

She opened her wonderful accepting eyes. "Really?"

I gave up. "No. Fire now, please!"

She examined a screen display. "Firing three anti-ship torpedoes and fifty anti-attack rail guns," she told me calmly.

"Well done!"

There was little time for more. The first missiles from the Vaers had arrived while we had been talking. They exploded against the shields. Everything got very loud and very uncomfortable for a long minute as the ship tried to neutralize the momentum and force of the explosion without passing it on to us. It wasn't as successful as it should have been. The Vaers were using heavy ordnance.

Although I had strapped myself in, the straps were made for Nepheals, which meant that they didn't fit me very well. I fell off the chair and had to reposition the box to scrabble back up again. It made me feel very exposed and vulnerable.

Danaa, who had weathered the bumpiness remarkably well, grinned. She had managed to track our own attack's progress. "We got two of their shuttles and damaged quite a few more!" she shouted.

I clutched at the seat of the chair as we were rocked by further detonations against the shields. "Fire again!"

She did. She looked as if she were enjoying this chance to avenge her aunt. I had never seen such a fierce look on a Nepheal's face. It was incongruous in a species that loathed violence of any kind.

When she saw me looking at her, she blushed. "I regret my feelings," she said quietly, hanging her head.

"You don't have to apologize to me, Danaa. I understand. You can be yourself. You can't help the way you feel, and neither can I."

"No. But we should be pliable and forgiving."

"Sure. That's me. Pliable and forgiving."

She burst out laughing, which helped remove some of the tension. I saw her turn back to the screen. She made a face. "Not so good that time. We damaged only one shuttle."

I nodded. The Vaers now knew what force and what timescale they were facing. It would get harder from now on. "Doesn't matter. We are about to enter the carbon cloud."

Just as I spoke, we were hit again. There was a massive crack from the shields behind the shuttle and she yawed to starboard. It was lucky she did, for another heavy torpedo sideswiped us on the port side. We heard a grating noise as it scraped the remaining shield right along the length of the shuttle.

My heart had done a good impression of bursting, but the shields held and the torpedo didn't explode. The lateral impact had not been enough to trigger it.

I breathed again. "We are at the carbon cloud! I am going straight in a full speed, and will pull the nose right up as we swerve over towards *Aenysia's* position. It might be bumpy."

Danaa had deactivated the weapons panel and was now sitting back in her chair. The aggressive expression had vanished again, though her tension was evident in her posture. She nodded casually to me, as if I had suggested a stroll in space.

The last salvo of missiles hit the rear part of our shields just as the bows of the shuttle met the carbon cloud. The whole ship shuddered from the back and then slammed into what felt like a brick wall from the front. I fell off the chair again and had to ignominiously pick myself up.

The shuttle ploughed through the carbon cloud as if it were cutting through solid rock. The shields groaned and began to dent inwards.

But we had disappeared to the ships following us. Both visually and on their instrument panel. The bad news was that they had disappeared to us as well. One of their ships could have been right on top of us and we would never know until it was too late.

I zigzagged a little, in the hope of obfuscating our real destination. I didn't really have time to manage anything particularly sophisticated; those shields were not going to put up with such mistreatment for very long and as soon as they went I would have to crawl through this black soup.

Then I had to slam the ship to starboard. One of the Vaer shuttles had loomed out of the murk directly above us. We were within an ace of driving straight into her. She disappeared back into the gloom as we wheeled away. My heart thudded so loudly that I thought Danaa must have heard. I looked in her direction.

Her eyes were on the screen in front of her. She may not even have noticed.

"Right," I said – in what I hoped was a cheery voice. "Time to set a course for *Aenysia*. We need to get out of here. We have an appointment with a star."

She looked up at that. I patted the pocket with the thesis. "We have to keep our promise to Agraala."

Tears sprang into those large eyes. She nodded. "We do."

I hesitated. "It will be like a last goodbye to her too."

More tears ran down her long face. "It is what she wanted."

"Make sure you pick a good star, then."

She seemed surprised. "I will."

I wondered what star system she would choose. We couldn't spend time hanging around Ebyssia, that was for sure. And there really weren't that many star systems between Ebyssia and Ulon Prime, where we had arranged to meet *Nivala*.

She would find the right place. I hoped that it would help to bring her peace, to allay some of the survivor's guilt she was feeling. This was going to be a very difficult time for her.

I forced my attention back to the controls of the shuttle. Despite the complaints of the shields, I was impressed by the small ship. She was a much stronger shuttle than anything I had been in before. She twisted and turned in answer to my input in what was almost a dance; she was responsive and quick to answer my requests. The Nepheals clearly knew how to make ships, even if they did rarely take them out of their own system.

I spun her over and under to correct the drastic turn I had just been forced to make. It was time to get to *Aenysia*. It was time to get out of this carbon cloud. Though I was feeling much more benevolent towards it now. It felt safe and sheltering.

At that, the shields gave a final groan and evaporated. I pulled the throttle right back. We were down to a crawl. Anything else would literally eat away at the nose of the ship. I gave a sigh. Served me right for feeling reassured. I should know better by now.

We nosed our way through the carbon cloud at walking speed for the next few hours, thankfully without seeing any new menace in the shape of Vaer ships. All we saw was the same stygian gloom inside the cloud. It clung to the ship and pervaded everything.

I had a set of co-ordinates for *Aenysia*. I hoped that she would still be there. If she weren't, it would be impossible to find her in this sensor-dead space.

I had once been on a firefighting course and we had been placed in a total blackout and asked to find our way out. I still remember the rising panic that the darkness had caused inside me. I had stumbled out, thirty minutes later, feeling ashamed of my inability to control my primitive instincts. I had not been the only one. Even spaceship captains such as myself rarely experienced real darkness. In space, stars were always twinkling somewhere on the horizon, if not closer.

I felt the same thing now. It was a hazy fear which settled deep inside my abdomen, threatening to paralyze me. I hated it.

I suddenly became aware of Danaa. She must have got out of her seat, for she was standing behind me, a cup of steaming liquid in her hand. "You need this," she told me gently, her voice reassuring. "You are shivering with cold."

I cupped both hands around the mug and let it warm my fingers. She was right. I was freezing. No wonder all these negative feelings had taken me over. I sipped at the drink and immediately felt a little better. It was sweet and tasted faintly of vanilla.

"I hadn't realized," she said in an apologetic tone. "We usually set a very low temperature in space. I forgot."

"That's all right." I just felt relieved to have an excuse for my fear. As I sipped, I could feel my backbone straightening.

"I have increased the temperature by ten degrees Celsius. I hope that will be enough? Neema and Anzany find it to be acceptable, on *Aenysia*."

"I am sure it will be fine. Thank you."

She touched me lightly on the shoulder and gave me a concerned look. "Are you really all right? I know you have a serious injury."

"I'm fine. I never have liked pitch blackness."

"No. It suffocates, doesn't it?"

Yes! That was exactly the right word. It made me feel short of breath. I realized that my brain had been slowly tricking me into thinking that my air supply was damaged. No wonder the reptilian part of it was entering into panic mode. I should have been aware of what was happening. There are ways to counter such things, but you need to recognize what is happening to you and why for it to work.

I took another sip. The feeling of unease receded further.

By the time I had finished the hot drink, I felt competent to continue.

I just hoped it wouldn't take too long. My whole body was telling me that I needed to rest, now the adrenaline was beginning to drain away.

We came across the mainstream channel after another five hours. The nose of the shuttle abruptly broke free of the cloying particles.

I was so close to sleep that my reaction time was about three times what it should have been. Luckily, that was enough. There were no signs of Vaer vessels in the channel.

I edged the shuttle back slowly into the enveloping cloud. Then we peered warily both up and down the channel. It looked safe to cross, but those Vaer ships rattled along this channel at a fair old speed. If they caught us half-way across there would be little left of the shuttle.

I was about to push the shuttle out into the channel, when I noticed a disturbance in the carbon cloud around the nose of the shuttle. It was shimmering: rather like the reflection in hot weather off tarmac. Something was coming.

I slid back into the anonymity of the carbon cloud just as one, and then another, Vaer cruiser slammed past us. The swirling of the walls of the mainstream channel was so severe by the time the second one swept past that it left parts of the shuttle uncovered. Luckily, the Vaer cruisers were long gone by then.

I pushed the throttle forward. Time to get to the other side. We would be safer there.

We had barely reached safety on the other side when the same strange dancing of the carbon molecules announced other ships coming through the mainstream channel behind us. We had only just made it.

I turned the ship to watch what was happening. This time three of the Vaer ships sped past us. They had taken the decision to evacuate the moon. Or maybe ships were leaving to set up a blockade on the other side of the carbon cloud? We would have to be extremely careful how we exited the cloud, if we ever got that far.

We were moving even more slowly now. *Aenysia* ought to be within a few hundred meters. If she was still in the same place.

I peered into the gloom. Nothing. Just more darkness. At this rate we would hit them before we saw them. I glanced at Danaa. She was sitting on the edge of her chair, grasping the seat with her fingers, staring out of the visor in front. There was no point watching the sensor screen. The sensors were as blind as we were.

Then the clouds parted momentarily and I got a glimpse of metallic grey – a flash of something lighter than the surrounding carbon. Very close. Too close.

I pushed the shuttle into reverse, but we still bumped the ship lightly. There was a new groaning sound as they scraped together. But it was almost a relief to hear.

We slid along the hull until we came to the shuttle bay, dropping down to line up the bows of the shuttle correctly.

I waited. Did we have to knock?

We didn't. The shuttle bay doors finally opened, and we were able to ease our way in through the force field that held back the carbon cloud. I dropped her onto one of the low circular pads that enabled a turnaround without engines and switched off.

"I'm done."

Danaa nodded. "I think we both are." She fussed with some controls until she was able to let down the main door to the shuttle. It hissed as it disengaged. I slid uncomfortably off my chair.

There was a flash of movement from the doorway. "Did you get her? Where is she? Where is Agraala?" Both Neema and Anzany were giving us questioning looks.

I couldn't help sighing. "We got Zenzara. We lost Agraala."

Neema's eyebrows snapped together. "Lost her? What do you mean lost her? How could you do that? Why didn't you go back for her?"

"There was nothing to go back for." My mouth felt heavy, somehow not my own. I swayed on the spot. I just wanted to lie down somewhere.

Anzany's crest went up. She was sensing our physical state. "Not now, Neems," she said. "We need to get them to sick bay and let them rest. Neither of them are going to tell us any more now."

I waved an arm. "Start the journey out," I told her. "But be careful. There is probably a fleet of Vaer ships waiting for us, looking for us."

She nodded. "All right. Where are we heading if I get us out?"

I turned to Danaa. She tried to smile but it congealed on her tired face. "To MS5602," she said, her voice so tired that it was drained of all emotion. "It is a small but bright blue star, on the way to Ulon Prime. It hasn't got a name."

"Oh yes it has!"

They all stared at me.

It seemed obvious to me. "Agraala's star."

Danaa's eyes filled with tears. "She would have liked that."

"I know she would. We couldn't bring her back from that moon. She deserves to have a fitting memorial. And if we are taking the thesis there, then part of her is going too."

"Yes." Danaa murmured the name slowly, enjoying the sound. "Agraala's star." She took in a ragged breath, and I saw some of the tears trickling down her long face. "Set a course to Agraala's star, please."

She stumbled as she got out of her chair. Neema and Anzany rushed forwards to support her. "We've got you, sweetie," said Neema. "You are safe now. We will take care of you." She patted the Nepheal girl on her forearm. "At least you got Zenzara back."

But Danaa was done. Her eyes turned up in her long-boned face and she crashed out of consciousness.

I trailed along behind. The two girls had brought a wheeled stretcher over and womanhandled Danaa onto it. The legs and arms of the young Nepheal flopped over the edges, catching on the decking.

Neema looked back at me. "You all right, Rye?"

I couldn't find the energy to reply. I nodded instead.

"Was Zenzie OK?"

That was hard to answer too. I had no idea if the Chyzar would ever be OK again.

"She is in one piece," I replied slowly. "But ... but mentally ..." I couldn't go on. I just shook my head. Tears had come into my own eyes now. I was simply too tired to think any more. To talk any more. To walk any more.

They ushered me into the sickbay and I undressed quickly before sinking into one of the Zeroth triage tanks there. I was out before it even began to scan me. White clouds seemed to welcome me out of the darkness. I closed my eyes and felt as though sunlight was flickering behind my eyelids. It was warm and comforting. I surrendered to it. It was so good to sleep.

I woke up with a start some five hours later, with a sense of loss predominant in my mind. It took me some moments to identify the sadness. Although I hadn't known Agraala for very long, I had liked her.

I managed to raise myself on one elbow. There was nobody else in the medical bay, and my Zeroth had switched itself off, so I eventually slid out of the tank, slipped on some space fatigues that had been left out for me and made it as far as the doorway.

Physically, I felt much better. I guessed that the machine had given me some nutrients while I was sleeping, because my body – though aching – felt renewed.

The girls were on the bridge. They turned and smiled at me as they sensed my presence.

Neema bustled over. Her eyes were solicitous. "How are you?"

"Fine. Thank you for looking after me." I stared at the darkness visible on the visor. "Where are we?"

Anzany pulled a face. "We are still inside the carbon cloud. I'm afraid that there is so much traffic along the mainstream channel that we have had to feel our way out through the thicker areas beside it. Every so often I nudge us out to check we are on the right heading. We are still around a half an hour from exiting the cloud. I am glad you are awake; we will need your input as to how to get away without being fired upon."

I nodded. "They will have set up a blockade by now. I hope the others got out before this. Have you seen any sign of them?"

She shook her head. "I couldn't see a supernova at a hundred paces in this stuff."

"I think the best course of action is to stay within the cloud but skirt around the edge. They will probably concentrate most of their efforts on the known channels through. By now, they will suspect that we have already got out. I suggest we take time to plot their weakest areas and then slip through one of the gaps."

"We have low visibility shielding on *Aenysia*," Danaa told me in a small voice.

I pivoted round. "You do? How does that work?"

She shrugged. "It is pretty simple. There is an outside shell which pulls light in from around us and channels it around the hull. The effect is that we almost disappear from sight."

"What about sensors?"

She shook her head. "But we can set off a couple of electromagnetic bombs that would disrupt their sensor arrays for quite some time. They would need a full reset. That takes time."

I shook my head. "I don't think that will work. If their sensors go down they will know where we are. They will simply follow us. I don't want to lead them to Ulon Prime." I tried to get my brain to focus. "However, if we can almost disappear from their view, all we need to do is to flea hop one of their ships again. Once our small signal mingles with theirs, we would be effectively invisible."

"How do we lose the host ship later?" Neema, always practical, always thinking ahead.

I crinkled my brow. "Hmm. That's a really good point. Ideas?"

There was silence. Great.

I bit my lip. "We choose a freighter, to be sure that they won't hang around here as part of the blockade. We stick with them until they engage their EM drive. As soon as they do that, we peel back. Our signal should get disguised by the EM wake."

Anzany wrinkled her lip. "It might. I guess. If they are blind and in the middle of their dinner."

"Don't look so enthusiastic! Have you any better ideas?"

"N-n-nooo."

"Well then!" I clapped my hands together. "We'll go with that one. That means positioning ourselves just on top of the mainstream channel and waiting until something big and full of freight comes along. Then we drop down onto it before it exits the carbon cloud. Easy!"

Even I could feel the weight of the girls' uncertainty. But we had to do something. I could see no point just sitting around letting the Vaers establish a more and more unbreakable circle of ships around the moon and its shroud.

I felt cheered. I am always better when implementing a plan, even a bad one. I hate sitting around. Anything seems better than that, to me.

I walked over to Danaa. She was on all fours, unusually, so my face was almost level with hers. "How are you feeling?"

"I am well, thank you." An expression of anxiety crossed her long face, making it look even longer. "I do not know how I will tell my people of this. I must tell them what happened to Agraala."

I gave her a pat on her shoulder, hoping she would interpret it in the sympathetic spirit it was meant. "You won't have to. I am coming back to Nephealis with you. I will tell them."

Her expression lightened. "Will you? Oh, thank you!"

"Of course I will. What, did you think we would simply push you off back to your system all on your own? Of course not! Anyway, I have a

Geiga to pick up, remember?"

The young Nepheal girl looked so relieved that her face was transformed. "That is good news."

"We will check on Zenzie and the others at Ulon Prime and then I will take you back to your people. We would never leave you all on your own to fly this ship."

She nodded in understanding. "I wasn't thinking clearly. I was worried you would forget about me, I suppose."

"We would never do that, Danaa. You are one of us now."

Her eyes opened wide. "Do you mean that?"

My heart gave a small jump. I hadn't, actually. But, now that I thought about it, I would be happy to have Danaa along with us on any mission. "Yes, I do." There were practicalities that made it impossible for her to travel for any length of time on board *Nivala*, however. "Though you couldn't stay permanently on our ship."

She frowned. "No. You are right, of course. Your ship is too low for a Nepheal to live on permanently. Soon I will be as tall as my aunt was."

I gave her another pat. "Never mind, Danaa. You will always be an honorary member of our crew."

She seemed lost in her own thoughts. "Yes. Yes, I see." I got no more out of her. She turned back to the screen she had been monitoring and turned her complete concentration back on that. At least, that is what it looked like.

We had already reached the edge of the carbon cloud. Anzany positioned the *Aenysia* on top of the channel and moved us back several dozen lengths of the ship. We would need a little time to pick up speed when something suitable did come through. And we would have very little time to decide. Only split seconds to make up our minds on the suitability of the host ship.

"Shall I take the helm?" I wondered if Anzany was worried about the responsibility of such a decision.

She seemed surprised. "No, why? My reflexes are slightly better than yours. I am Tyzaran, after all."

I closed my eyes. She was right. As someone of human DNA, my reflexes were amongst the worst in the Major Shells.

But there was somebody even better.

Danaa cleared her throat and then marched up to the pilot's station. "I believe the Nepheals are the species with the fastest reaction times." She gazed around at all of us in her innocent way. "Of all the species presently on board. I believe I should take the helm."

Neema gave a derisive snort.

She was right; Danaa was very young. But this was a Nepheal ship. It was built for Nepheals to manage. And I had just told her that she had a place with us as a crew member.

"Very well. Danaa, you can take the helm."

The Nepheal eyes that met mine were brimming with emotion. "Thank you, Captain."

The other two sets of eyes that met mine were not so happy. One was outraged, the other accusatory. I waved a dismissive hand at both. "Danaa will do a great job. She is right. Nepheals beat Tyzarans who beat Spacelanders. At least, in this."

Neema sniffed. She didn't appear to agree. Anzany simply got up from her station and ushered Danaa quickly into her seat. The Nepheal girl inclined her head to acknowledge the formal transfer of control. Then she settled so much more comfortably than any of us onto the helmsman's seat. Her fingers began to race across the controls. She had claimed not to have any great degree of skill at this, but even I could see that she was much faster than Anzany. Anzany looked rather subdued. She had eyes, too.

We waited for an hour before the first ship passed underneath us. I thought at first that it would be the one, then realized, almost too late, that it was a military cruiser rather than a freighter.

I slowly released the breath I had been holding back.

Danaa was grinning at me. "You are all very slow," she told us. "I saw that it was military at least two full seconds before you did."

That's right, rub it in. But I was glad to see her slowly able to push

Agraala to the back of her mind. It had been the right decision to put the Nepheal girl in charge of this maneuver. She needed the immersion in work to help her get over the shock and sadness of losing her aunt.

Another two ships rumbled underneath us before Danaa was satisfied. At last, some two and a half hours later, a large freighter came through the mainstream channel.

Danaa had spotted our host quickly. She leapt to match its speed as fast as she could and then dropped us neatly out of the carbon cloud and onto our flea-like position in a gap between two enormous silos. I think they held industrial diamonds. That was a *lot* of industrial diamonds. Still, why not? They would be cheap to make. There was an almost infinite amount of pure carbon dust in the cloud. All they had to do was compress it. Their profit margins had to be huge. It probably funded this whole operation.

Danaa had already activated the shield software that curved light around the shields. We felt nothing on board the ship, but certainly there was no change in our host's pattern of movement. It didn't seem as though we had been spotted. I was impressed at the level of technology on board the Nepheal ship. Perhaps I shouldn't have been. The Nepheals were, after all, second to none in the Major Shells with regard to their understanding of astrophysics. Just because they chose not to travel greatly in space did not mean that their ships would be primitive. It was naïve of me not to have realized that.

The freighter trundled on, exiting the carbon cloud at a stately pace. Immediately, it was surrounded by Vaer ships. They flew over and under her, looking for ships that might be playing pilot fish, like we were.

I stopped breathing, I think. Just in case they could hear me. This whole idea suddenly seemed to be the most stupid I had ever come up with.

Danaa edged us even closer to the coupling between the two silos. To me, it felt as though we were now almost wedged into place. I think there was a bare meter or two between the ship and the coupling.

Another reason to hold my breath.

Our host ignored the inspection, assuming that the smaller military ships would soon abandon their interest. It sailed out of the carbon cloud and adjusted its heading towards Chitran, on the western fringe of the Great Shell. At standard EM drive speeds, it would take the vast ship a journey of two months to reach the large system.

The military lost interest in the ship after around fifteen minutes. I'm not saying I didn't suck in air during all of that time, but it felt as though I hadn't. My diaphragm was sore from being clamped in a vice-like immobility.

They left two of their vessels as escorts and then vanished. I clutched at the nearest console and managed to breathe in and out. The first step was finished. Now for the most difficult part.

We had time to prepare. The ship was taking its time about hauling its bulk out of the gravity well. It piled on the thrust with little result in acceleration. These silos must be crammed with diamonds to have such tremendous bulk.

Over the next day and a half it clawed its way to open space, completely unaware that it was carrying a large flea in its outer coat. The flea was very thankful of that. We played as dead as we could.

Anzany had taken over from Danaa shortly after we left the carbon cloud, and now it was my turn. The freighter was gradually turning her belly away from the moon, a sure sign that she was about to engage EM drive.

This was going to be tricky. I had to sheer away from the larger ship just before she went into EM space. If I left it too late we could be dragged along with her, without any preparation. That might evaporate *Aenysia* completely. If I left too early they would detect our signal and could abort the EM drive and their escorts could come find us. I wasn't keen on that option either.

I had our own engines turning over well in advance. Neema was huddled over her console, eyes peeled for the tell-tale signs of a change from standard drive to EM.

"They're going," she muttered suddenly.

My right hand tightened automatically on the throttle. "Can you count me down?"

"No."

Helpful. Never mind, I could hear a change in pitch. It was hard to detect, but noticeable. It was winding up. Suddenly, I knew where they were in the cycle. *Faraday* had done the same thing. The freighter was on the point of departure.

I swung the nose of our ship out from between the silos, slipping free of the large containers. The pitch heightened one more notch on my imaginary scale.

I set in a course directly back along our tracks. They might just assume we were some sort of flotsam; a chunk of dirt or carbon deposit torn off the fuselage by vibrations at the change to EM drive. My fingers hovered over the signal to engage our own engines.

Long seconds ticked past as the freighter cranked up her long distance engines. Then the pitch reached that certain level that surely signaled transition. I closed my eyes, hoping I was not wrong.

I punched in the instruction to engage our engines, and slid the lever all the way up to the red. *Aenysia* shivered and trembled as she attempted to obey such drastic acceleration. Her hull plating groaned as it experienced new stresses it was not meant to withstand.

Neema's hands, balled up by her side, went white. Anzany made no sound, but stared at the visor in front of her. Danaa made one small whimper and then fell silent.

We rocketed away from the freighter. She slid past underneath us, at first slowly, then with increasing speed. Just as we reached the last part of her cargo train, she blinked and went into transition, disappearing totally from our sensors.

I still didn't feel safe. I let *Aenysia* fall back into a more moderate acceleration, but I was still scouring the space behind us. If they had spotted our signal separating from theirs, they could still come back.

But they didn't. We were able to cruise along for a couple of hours unbothered by any Vaer ships. It was a great relief.

Three hours after the freighter had disappeared we engaged our own Nepheal drive and set a course for MS5602, Agraala's Star.

11

The blue star in front of us sparkled in a sea of black space. It had the look of a diamond itself. It formed part of a very young cluster of stars, some not even 15 million years old. Since even a run-of-the-mill star such as Sol is 4.5 billion years old, they were virtually baby stars. Which is why MS5602 only had a catalogue number instead of a name.

I wondered how I could make this star legally Agraala's Star. Who would be the correct people to assign names to stars? In the end, I decided to start on Ulon Prime when we finally made it there. The Macers ought to be able to table the matter before the recently formed Interstellar Council. I guessed that things like this would eventually become commonplace. We were still at the stage where it was all new. These were uncertain times, but I knew that I had to follow up on my promise to Danaa. It was important.

Aenysia dropped into the closest orbit possible to Agraala's star without being fried by radiation. Blue stars are usually between 10 and 150 times the mass of Sol. This one was only around 15 times Sol mass, so it was pretty small for a blue star.

All the same, it was giving out many thousand times as much

radiation as Sol, which made it a pretty dangerous area to visit. Close was not really close. The surface temperature was registering on our sensors as nearly five times that of the sun.

Anzany had packed the thesis cartridge carefully into a missile casing. When she was ready, we gathered in the weapon's bay for the disposal ceremony. Although Agraala's body was not here, I felt that it was the closest the Nepheal woman would come to a true funeral. I had no idea what the Nepheals did on such occasions, but at least I could set a somber and respectful tone.

"Agraala was one of the brightest minds amongst the Nepheals. Her thesis was ground-breaking and should have brought great gladness to her and to her family. It is with sadness that we consign it to the centre of this star for destruction."

I stopped and looked at Danaa, wondering if she would want to speak for her aunt. She gave me the smallest of small shakes of her head.

I sighed, hoping that my words would be enough. "Agraala gave her own life to save others. She gave it knowingly and willingly, and her selfless act shall not be forgotten. Her last wish was for us to destroy her thesis, so as not to bring threat onto the Chakran people. We undertake to do that now, and respectfully thank her for her great sacrifice."

I gave a nod to Danaa, who activated the launch sequence for the missile, which was set for the heart of the star. It would burn up long before then, evaporated into space by the scorching temperatures as it dropped through the different layers that made up this dense blue supergiant.

Young hot stars such as this one generally became supernovas before they reached maturity. This one would probably burn for only another hundred thousand years or so before its own great conflagration. It would burn bright, but would end its years before its time. That seemed appropriate for Agraala. The beautiful star would still outlast all of the Major Shell races, in all probability. All things die, even stars.

Hot tears ran down Danaa's cheeks as she watched the missile launch. Her mouth quivered. She had still not lost her feeling of guilt. Perhaps she never would. "She was the most intelligent person I know," she murmured.

"She wanted to atone."

Danaa's eyes flashed. "What did *she* have to atone for?"

"She was responsible for the thesis that could destroy the Chakrans," I said calmly. "How do you think she felt about that? How would you feel if your research could be used to exterminate an entire people?"

Danaa gasped. "She never intended to cause harm!"

"But others did. It is why she wanted to come. She was ready to sacrifice herself to undo the damage that her mind had caused others. She wanted the Chakrans to be free. She wanted Zenzara to be free. She was horrified at the use that had been found for her thesis."

"Yes, I suppose she was."

"She died knowing that her last act might stop them from doing harm with her work. That must have given her satisfaction."

"I suppose."

"She was loyal and brave and was prepared to give her life for her beliefs. I feel privileged to have known her."

Neema and Anzany bowed their heads and whispered their agreement with that statement.

Danaa stared into my eyes. "She didn't do it for me? She didn't die for me?"

"She died to save the Chakrans. That she could save you too was what made her happy to do it. I saw her face; she did not regret dying."

Danaa began to sob. "How am I going to tell them all? How am I ever going to live up to her memory?"

I put one arm around her long neck, hoping it would be of some comfort to her. "She would tell you to have a good life. She would tell you that there is nothing to live up to. She made some bad mistakes."

"I shall miss her."

"I know." I gave her another squeeze. "Now, we need to get ourselves to Ulon Prime to see how Zenzara is."

Neema, who had been tracking the missile, nodded. "We have lost track of the thesis. It has been vaporized."

We made our way back up to the main bridge. I felt huge relief. Although Bull Cunningham and Chandrayanan had lived to continue the scientist's research, they would never again be able to use Agraala's thesis material to enslave the Chakrans.

I wished we had been able to bring them back to the Macers for a proper trial, but we would not have escaped ourselves if we had done that. That would have to wait for another day. I had the feeling we hadn't seen the last of them.

We arrived at Ulon Prime some five days later. We made no attempt to find out if *Nivala* had also escaped the carbon cloud, not wanting to announce to the Vaers where we were. They didn't, we hoped, know about this ship, so it seemed rather short-sighted to let them know we were in the area. Even Vaers were probably capable of putting two and two together.

So it was a tremendous relief to see *Nivala* elegantly gliding in geostationary orbit around the blue water planet.

We left the ship automated to a similar synchronized orbit, and then took the shuttle across to *Nivala*. I tried to leave one of the girls behind, but they were having none of it. They all insisted on going to see how Zenzie was. I couldn't blame them.

Sammy and Mel greeted us in the shuttle bay.

"How is she?" I demanded. "Has she recovered? Did you get a doctor to see her? Will she be all right?"

A slim Tyzaran ran into the bay and threw herself at me, almost knocking me over. I grinned when I saw who it was, picking her up and giving her a fierce hug. "Zenzie!"

"Mallivan! Mallivan! You left! I could not protect you!"

"I am back now. Are you all right?"

"Of course I am not all right. I shall never be all right again. But I did well, did I not?" She seemed proud of herself. "I only went with them to save you. You and the Nepheals." She registered Danaa. "Hello, Danaa. I am very sorry about Agraala."

Danaa smiled. "Chy Zylarian. I am very pleased to see you running around."

"You saved me back on the Vaer moon. You came to get me."

Danaa, in her turn, looked proud.

"Yes, yes," I interrupted. "But what about your health? What about the Chakrans? How did you get away? What has been going on?"

Sammy treated me to a look of pity. "A lot. The Tyzarans are furious."

I must have frowned because he pursed his lips. "Denaraz is down on Ulon, trying to sort it out. They want the ship back."

Nivala? Could they even do that? My heart sank. "Why?"

"Something to do with its captain having insulted their representative?"

Oh yes. That. I had forgotten all about it. "Ah."

Sammy was shaking his head. "You are unbelievable, Rye. Did you really think that they would let you criticize their government and take no reprisals?"

I shrugged. "Hadn't thought about it at all. There was too much going on."

"Well, they tried getting rid of you, but that didn't go down well with the other member planets, so they were forced to point out that we only have *Nivala* because of their good graces."

I snorted. "Good graces, my hindquarters."

Zenzie bounced around me. "They can't take the ship away, can they?"

"I don't know."

"You need to get down there as fast as you can. Denaraz is struggling on by himself, but he has been trying to hold off any decision until you got here."

I nodded. "I will go down straight away."

Zenzie nodded. "I will get ready, then."

Danaa, who was finding it hard to stand up in the shuttle due to her height, looked happier. "Me too."

I opened my mouth, but was met by two such identical challenging stares that I gave up. Zenzie would go if I went. Danaa would go if Zenzie went. That was just the way things were likely to be from now on. Get used to it, Ryler.

Our little group of four took the shuttle down to Ulon. We settled easily into the shallow water and I opened the shuttle doors. This Nepheal shuttle only had doors front and aft. The aft door was submerged, so it meant that we had to struggle a little to pull ourselves up and out of the bow exit against gravity.

I reached down to give Zenzie a hand. She ignored it, preferring to make her own way up out of the shuttle. I may have rolled my eyes, because she gave me a long diatribe about Spacelanders who always thought they knew best and interfered with all the other species. Danaa giggled.

We found ourselves on a large floating area. I saw that the Macers had spent the intervening time constructing a type of marine settlement. They had roped many of their rafts together to form a patchwork. Within the patchwork were large gaps, where shuttles could be brought down. There were also small channels of water that had been left between the rafts, presumably to avoid them turning over in turbulence.

There was a cross-looking reception committee waiting for us. Denaraz was the only one with a smile on his face. He may have been happy to see us, but I thought it was tinged with relief.

Spokesdesignate Xynia was standing stiffly one pace in front of him. She had several Tyzarans around her, and was wearing a frown. Her crest was vertical and spiky.

Perhaps I should have been more diplomatic. Something else I was going to have to learn.

Danaa examined those in front of us with interest. She noted the raised crests and the disapproving faces. Her eyes slid to me, and her words proved to me that she had inherited at least one of her aunt's characteristics.

"If the Tyzarans do not want you to have their ship, you can have one of ours. The Nepheals will be happy to oblige the Interstellar Alliance. We are most willing to provide the ships for the Interstellar Enforcement Agency."

Xynia twitched. The Macers who had come to greet us by the shuttle looked on curiously. Denaraz hid a grin.

The Tyzarans all looked at each other. I felt for them. They wanted to show their anger at my comments, but they also liked being at the center of the new Interstellar Alliance. They could become sidelined if we began to use only Nepheal ships.

Xynia examined Danaa with a dispassionate look that seemed to find her wanting. "You are young. You cannot speak for your people."

It was Danaa's turn to stand up straight. She did so, towering over even the Tyzarans present. "I may be young but I assure you that I am entitled to speak for all Nepheals. Our laws specifically allow Nepheal Captains to enter into binding agreements."

The spokesdesignate's voice took on a scoffing tone. "You are not a Nepheal Captain!"

I could have told Xynia that was not the right way to go about things, but I quite liked the way things were going, so I didn't.

"Actually," Danaa looked down at the Tyzaran woman with supreme indifference. "I am. I became one when my Aunt was killed on active service." She opened her large eyes wide. "Although I don't quite understand what gives you the right to question such things. They do not appertain to Tyzar, I think?"

There was a muttering amongst the Tyzaran delegates. One of them leaned in and whispered something to Xynia, who glared at him in return. He gave a firm nod, as if to say: *Do as I say.*

She looked away, her whole demeanor indicating reluctance. Finally, her eyes came back to the thin Nepheal body that was facing up to her with such valor. "That will not be necessary," she said slowly. "We will withdraw our opposition."

Everybody except Danaa and Xynia relaxed. Izan blew out air and I could see the tension drain out of him.

Danaa turned to the Macers. "In any case," she said in a firm voice, "we cannot allow the Interstellar Enforcement Agency to be at the mercy of politicians in order to do their jobs. Such an Agency must be independent if it is to be successful. It is not acceptable that sovereign nations own the ships that are used. Such ships must be made over to them legally so as to nullify any accusations of partiality. That seems quite clear to us. All signing members should be asked to provide ships and funds for Interstellar Agency work.

"The Nepheals will also provide a ship for the Interstellar Alliance. We wish to take part in any new bodies that are formed."

Xynia looked sick. The Tyzarans had clearly thought that they would be the leaders of the newly formed Alliance. This was unwelcome. I wondered if they had thought to orchestrate all its aspects when they suggested the Alliance. I wouldn't put it past them.

She cleared her throat. "The Macers do not have ships."

"No, but they provide tactical support and will no doubt provide part of the funding?" Danaa raised one eyebrow at the head Macer, who inclined his head. She went on. "The Avaraks have plenty of ships. They too can form part of this. There should be a permanent presence around Ulon Prime at all times, if it is to be at the center of the Alliance." Then Danaa swiveled to look at me. "The Spacelander Trust will want to participate too."

Now the Macers were looking askance at each other. This was a conclusion that they didn't seem to have reached yet.

No wonder they say that Nepheals are the Shells' best negotiators! They have a way of making other species feel inferior, and of challenging many of the basic precepts other species live by. I was just glad that I was still *Nivala's* captain.

Denaraz seemed amused. "Are you by any chance a *Dialectis* winner?" he asked her.

One of the major entertainments on Nephealis is the *"Dialectis"*. This is an oratory competition of Weekly logical argumentation where major philosophical or scientific themes are debated and discussed. Nepheals are said to be able to understand all sides of an argument. They have all studied logic, ethics, aesthetics and metaphysics. The most successful orators are idolized by the Nepheals, and command huge sums to give an address. Such Nepheals are very convincing, which makes most of the inhabitants of the Shells tend to avoid meeting them.

Danaa gave Denaraz a formal bow. "I was Junior *Dialectis* winner for three years in a row."

The Tyzarans muttered some more amongst themselves. I looked at the young Nepheal girl with new eyes. Nepheals were so different to Spacelanders. I realized I had put her in a box labeled 'young', and had not looked further. She was obviously so very much more than I had seen. I felt ashamed of myself. Age discrimination was forbidden under the basic tenants of the Spacelander Trust. I shouldn't have made assumptions. I hadn't with Zenzara, so why had I with Danaa?

I stared at the raft beneath me. Water lapped gently at the reeds it was made of. It seemed so gentle in comparison to the harsh worlds we had been exposed to recently.

Refreshments arrived at that point, and the conversations became widespread. I saw Zenzie sidle across to Danaa and give her a congratulatory fist bump. The two girls giggled together. They caught me staring at them and they both went red.

I gave them a thumbs-up. I was just relieved that I hadn't had to take on Xynia myself. She intimidated me.

Izan had come over to my side. "That was lucky."

I had to agree. "Danaa will be an asset to the Agency."

He raised an eyebrow. "She is going to join us? Good." He thought about it for some moments. "So that is why she offered the craft. She can hardly live long-term on board *Nivala*."

"No. She bangs her head all the time on the ceiling. The only place she is comfortable in is the gym, because it has double height."

"She is a terrific negotiator, and we certainly were in need of one." He gave me a long look. "Some of us are too prone to speak our minds."

I lifted my hands in assumption of guilt. "*Mea culpa*, Izan. I know. You are right; someone like Danaa will be able to get us out of all sorts of trouble."

"Will the powers that be on Nephealis have any objections?"

I gave a shrug. "Don't ask me. But I am going over there with her now. We have to explain what happened with Agraala."

His face became set. "I was so sorry that she died."

"We all were. She had a wonderful mind. And I liked her. Very much."

"So did I." He sighed again. "Still, she did save Zenzara and Danaa."

"Yes. "

I told him that the thesis cartridge had now been destroyed.

"Then we don't have to worry about Bull Cunningham any longer?"

I pulled my lips in. "I wouldn't say that. It depends on whether we stopped the process in time. They certainly can't succeed without the strands. We found some of their research material. They had been trying a modified Casimir effect, but that didn't provide enough negative energy. I'm hoping we managed to break up the skyrmion vortex before any of the Chakran strands were separated from the Nexus."

"How do they go about making a wormhole, anyway?"

"It's this ER=EPR conjecture, apparently."

"I have not heard of that nomenclature."

"Sorry. ER is the Einstein-Rosen hypothesis. It refers to wormholes. EPR is the Einstein-Rosen-Polansky bridge, which refers to quantum nonlocality."

"Is that the Terran Einstein who was so famous?"

I had to smile. "He was quite an important figure in ancient Earth."

"He must have been. Does he have many stars?"

I stared.

"You said you were renaming MS5602 for Agraala. Didn't anybody do the same for Einstein?"

He had a point. I tried to remember. "Well, we have Einstein Rings. There are many of those."

"Good. He sounds a great man."

"He found the equivalence between matter and energy."

"Then he was a great thinker. In Tyzar, that was the first Chyzar. It is one of the reasons all Chyzars are venerated."

I looked at Zenzie. She was jumping in circles around Danaa, shouting with glee. She definitely didn't look like somebody who was going to be on a par with Einstein.

Seeing where I was looking, Denaraz pulled a face. "None of the Chyzars since then have been of exceptional intellect, but we still hope."

"Zenzie is strong and brave and very quick, but I don't see signs of a great physicist or mathematician."

"She is young. Who knows what she will be? She has already grown closer to the Chakrans than any Chyzar before her. They have spoken through her. They have acted. That is unheard-of. Many believe she will change the universe."

Now she was sticking her tongue out at her Nepheal friend.

"Do they? She *is* unique; I am just not sure it is in that sort of a way."

It was Izan's turn to grin. "You *are* becoming more diplomatic, Mallivan!"

I walked away. That certainly didn't deserve an answer.

A little later I found myself next to the Macer representative. It was the same one who had been in charge of the original negotiations. I spoke to him about renaming MS5602. He took a few moments to garner responses from his link with the rest of the Macers and then blinked his wonderfully expressive eyes.

"That will be acceptable. The Alliance will gradually be forming departments to deal with such things, but we can find no impediment to Agraala's star being included on all new Alliance star charts."

I gave him a small bow, which made my recuperating torso creak. "Thank you."

"Do you believe that the danger of a traversable wormhole being excavated through the Chakran arteries has been avoided?"

I was struck by the way he put it. Considering that the individual Chakran cells were joined to each other by nonlocal bonds, and that these bonds were precisely what Chandrayanan was intending to blow out into wormholes, he was right. It would be as if they were expanding their very veins into highways.

"I think that would be a dangerous assumption. We destroyed the thesis which allowed them to incapacitate the Chakrans, true, but we may have been too late for the Nexus. We have to hope that the Chakrans themselves might be able to counter any further attempts. We saw during the Avarak-Terran war just how much they are capable of when they are threatened."

"It is unacceptable that any member of the Major Shells could consider extermination of a complete species to further their own interests. We are appalled at the reaction of some of our members."

Yes. I was a little taken aback by the attitude of the Tyzarans myself. I could understand Bull Cunningham. His motivation was simple self-interest. But that a whole people, and one that was considered to be of high integrity, should support that sort of thing was quite shocking.

The Macer's eyes had become saddened. "It is a most disappointing start to the union of the species. We must hope that the future will be brighter. However, you are instructed that we consider the safety of the Chakrans of prime importance. To this end, and to avoid any further complications with any of the signatory species, we are going to insist that all craft donated become the property of the Interstellar Enforcement Agency, as was suggested by the visitor from Nephealis. Members must not be allowed to interfere in policy."

That was a relief. "I understand."

"You will report to the Macers, and only to the Macers."

"That seems better."

"A necessary precaution, I am afraid." He gestured to the skies above us. "Ulon Prime will become your home base, and we would ask that there always be a ship armed and prepared to act. We fear that we have drawn much attention to ourselves by agreeing to form the administrative head of the Alliance. And we have not forgotten how close to us the Vaer base was."

"Very well."

"You may recruit further crew members at your discretion. We would like crew to be as diverse as possible so that all member states are represented."

"That may take time."

"We understand and accept that. Nothing becomes perfect without work."

"I would like to take Danaa back to Nephealis. It is important to support her as she tells them what happened to Agraala. We can confirm the gift of the ship *Aenysia* to the Enforcement Agency at the same time."

"While you are there please ensure that there are no copies of the thesis extant."

My jaw must have dropped. "Copies?"

"We have heard disturbing rumors of a new technology that enables copies to be made, under an extremely sophisticated new process. It is said that the Nepheal Board of Elders has made a full back up of the entire thesis library."

"But ... but that would mean that there may still be a copy of Agraala's thesis!"

"It might, yes."

My heart sank. "Surely not?"

"Our information is as yet incomplete. We cannot be sure. However, it is sufficiently solid as to warrant careful investigation. If we have heard whispers of such a thing it is entirely possible that this Terran scientist or the Tyzaran Supreme has too."

"Then I must go immediately."

He nodded. "The Legacy is in agreement with you."

The Legacy is one of the core beliefs of the Macers. They perceive themselves as part of a long chain traveling from their first ancestors to their distant descendents. They are merely placeholders in a lineage. If they dishonor their ancestors that would erase their whole family chain: something inconceivable to a Macer.

"Then we will leave immediately."

He blinked acceptance and then narrowed his eyes. "One more thing, Captain Mallivan ..."

"Yes ...?"

"The Legacy has decided that your subcutaneous Tyzaran ansible implant ought to be removed. I have asked one of our foremost doctors to perform the small operation. I believe that they have been inactive for some time?"

I nodded. "The implant never worked well, in my case. I found transmissions unbearably loud for some reason. After I spoke to you I have been unable to use my implant. Neither Adjunct Denaraz nor I had access through ansible connection for some time. It is possible that they have been temporarily deactivated by the Supreme Council."

"We find it advisable to remove them altogether. Otherwise they could conceivably be used to manipulate you some time in the future. That would not be acceptable. My doctor will remove both implants. We are in the process of substantially adapting the Tyzar technology so as to avoid any future manipulation. By anybody. When that has been done, you will be given that asset. Until then, I am afraid that we must rely only on previous technology for your reports."

"I shall be glad to get rid of the implant. I was a little concerned that the Tyzarans might be able to access my mind without my knowing."

"Our own technology will carry safeguards against unwarranted interference, but we will not develop our own ansibles to be implants, in any case. All technology is subject to incorrect use. We will not allow that. It would shame the chain."

"If the scientist manages to get his hands on another copy of the thesis, then the Chakrans will be back in extreme danger."

"Your job is to stop that."

My mouth went dry. "What about the moon we found? The moon inside the carbon cloud?"

"The Alliance is still in its infancy. We need time. We should not try to impose ourselves on other species. We are here to protect those who are members. The moon is not ours. We do not have jurisdiction over the Vaers, who are not signatories of the pact. We cannot act openly against them, as this would be construed as war."

I could see his point. I had hoped to close down the secret Vaer base that we had found. It seemed that was not going to happen. But, as they said, we could not take on all of the problems of the Major Shells. It would be impossible. We were just going to have to make a difference in other ways.

Denaraz and I were escorted to one of the rafts that were furthest away from the shuttle. It involved jumping across the deliberate gaps of water. That was a stretch for Denaraz, and for me too, but the Macers found it trivial. They used all four of their hind legs to thrust them forwards, clearing the gaps with some ease. I was surprised; I hadn't expected them to be so graceful out of the water that was their natural habitat. One of them told me when I questioned him that Macers can use four of their legs to impart a thrust that can impel them eighty meters above the water. It is a skill they developed many centuries ago when their survival was threatened by a species of insatiable shark-like creatures.

I asked what had happened to the sharks, my eyes sliding warily to the surrounding sea. I could see no threatening fins.

The Macer gave the sort of belly quiver that indicated amusement. "They died out long, long ago," he told me. "We learned to jump too high and too far for them. They became extinct."

That was good news. I had been feeling distinctly unprotected on these exposed rafts.

There was a doctor waiting for us on the far raft.

I looked for screens, and saw none. Terrific.

Zenzara and Danaa, who had of course been following, jumped onto the final raft, making it rock. Danaa's fine legs threatened to slip through the kelp. She teetered slightly and her eyes opened wide in fear. I could see that she was very unhappy with the raft situation. It must seem like a trap to her. Each footstep could slip through into the water below. Her ears drooped and her usual character was not shining through.

Zenzie greeted the doctor. "Are you going to hurt them?"

"It will be a little uncomfortable."

Our new Chyzar got a look of vicarious pleasure on her small face. "Will it? Oh, good. Will he cry?" She edged close enough to see such a thing if it happened.

"No he will not," I told her in a cross tone. "You are a little sadist, aren't you?"

"It's just that you never show any fear. I am hoping that you will now."

"Why the krikk would you want to see my pain?"

"Because you always seem so ... so ... superior."

"Me?" I began to laugh. "I am not at all superior."

"You get things right."

I did? My own impression was that I was merely bluffing my way through all of this. It felt about six sizes too big for me. But, if somebody else thought I was doing well, then that made me happy.

"You are preening," she told me, her voice now much colder.

"I do not preen!"

"You do so! You got a sort of self-satisfied smirk."

Now I remembered why she was such a pain in the neck. "Can't you go somewhere else?"

She hunkered down. "No, because I want to see what you do when he sticks that great big injection in you."

"What great big inj—" I looked over my shoulder. "—Oh!"

"This will cause you some discomfort," the doctor said in a bright tone. Why do doctors always speak in that bright tone? Do they get taught it in the academies?

I resisted the temptation to swat Zenzie away. I wasn't about to show any weakness with the two girls sitting there. I would never live it down. I set my teeth, ready.

The pain was not slight. It was excruciating. I tried not to gasp, but couldn't help it.

Zenzara cooed with interest. "Is it bad, Mallivan? Very bad?"

"You, young lady, are heartless. Leave me alone." I winced as the syringe prodded around inside my brain. I was clamped into a tight metal constraining band, which, on reflection, was probably a good thing.

Zenzie smiled. "Your blood is so red when it is fresh. It looks like nivala varnish."

"Thank you."

"It is a very pretty colour. Not yellowy like mine."

"I am happy you are entertained."

"Well I am, you know," she confided. "I like to see you when you are not in control."

"I am never really in control. Please go away!"

I felt the most horrific tug at something inside my brain and then it, together with what felt like most of my grey matter, was dragged outside of my skull. I gave an involuntary shriek and had to close my eyes.

When I opened them again the two girls had disappeared. I could hear their laughter as they hopped back over the rafts to the shuttle.

I glared in their direction. "I hope you enjoyed that," I said sourly to their backs.

Izan grinned at me. "Never mind, Mallivan. It is my turn now."

I was battling a very nasty headache. It hurt to look at him. "Just pack me into a box and push me into the nearest sun."

The doctor appeared shocked. "We would never do that, Captain!"

The Macers didn't understand sarcasm.

The way I was feeling, it might not have been sarcasm.

Two hours later *Aenysia* was on her way to Nephealis, to inform the board of Elders of Agraala's fate. Nobody was looking forward to that, so the atmosphere on board was subdued.

I had intended to take only Danaa on this trip, but of course Zenzara insisted on going, which meant that Denaraz took it upon himself to join us as well. Eshaan wanted to see Nephealis in person because it intended to paint a picture in Agraala's honor. I had drawn the line at taking Didjal, who I felt would be needed on *Nivala*, so that made five of us. The others remained on *Nivala*, in orbit around Ulon Prime. We agreed a relaxed schedule of routine updates and some down time on planet for them. They needed a break. They weren't the only ones. Nobody was looking forward to facing up to the Board of Elders about losing one of their greatest ever minds.

We tied up at the Nepheal Gyre and took a local ferry down to the planet, getting some strange looks on the way. Eshaan, particularly, was examined with some surprise. I guess the Enif rarely get as far over as Nephealis. The Enif ignored the interest it was causing, its shiny black carapace reflecting back the locals' stares. The Nepheals seemed bemused by this. It is strange to use somebody's body as a mirror, especially when you aren't expecting it.

The ferry was dingy, as all craft that ply to and fro all day, every day, tend to be. The vid screen was portraying one of the famous Dialectis debates, which Danaa immediately became immersed in. I could see why; the contestants were adept at putting their own points of view across. Interestingly, they were required to put their points twice: firstly in Nepheale and then in Universal. I gathered that all Dialectic winners needed to be fluent in Universal. In the Nepheal mind, it would be pointless to have an orator who was unable to influence the rest of the Major Shells. Having watched Danaa in action, I could applaud this sentiment.

She had grown up on this trip. Although her legs were still long and gangly, her face was leaner and tougher. She had been changed by the things she had lived through. I could feel her energy, whereas the other Nepheals on the ferry seemed almost apathetic in contrast. She was different. I wondered whether going back to her previous life would be even possible for her now. Probably not.

After a bumpy landing at the spaceport, Danaa led our thin file of travelers along the streets of Nephealis City. Her steps seemed to get slower the closer we got to the dome. I tried to encourage her, but her face was rigid with apprehension.

I gave Zenzie a look. She began to chatter in her irrelevant sort of way, commenting on the size of the columns, the color of the ceiling, the distrust of the guards. Gradually the tension in Danaa began to dissipate slightly. She still walked stiffly but her shoulders sloped backwards now and her eyes were more relaxed.

The Elder General was not in the huge chamber when we were ushered in. It was the second time that I had seen the great transparent doors to the Hall of Ages, as it was known. The huge portal towered over even Danaa, who looked up at it in awe.

"These doors kept the Avians at bay for two weeks," she whispered to us. "Look at all the marks on them. Those are the marks of their beaks. One after another, each second of each minute of each hour of each day, they threw themselves at the gates. They were shrieking with anger and disappointment all the time, so much so that those cowering inside had to cover their ears."

I looked anew at the doors. I had realized they were impressive. I hadn't realized just how impressive.

Eshaan seemed to be taking a mental picture of them. I knew that they would appear, sooner or later, in one of his pieces of art. He would be taking in every bump and lump on the glass-like structures.

"They are old, then?" I said.

She nodded. "They were made in the Ages of Pitch, the times when we had no technology. The times before the attacks began. There was one member of the Board who was convinced that something bad would happen to Nephealis. He finally rose to power, and he used that power to construct the Hall of Ages. It was meant as a refuge in times of trouble. A sanctuary, I suppose you would call it." She twisted her neck so as to be able to examine the very top of the door nearest to her. "And his work saved the species. Only those inside the Hall of Ages survived the Avians. They got over a thousand in here. They survived, pressed up against each other with almost nothing to eat or drink, for three weeks. Until the Avians gave up."

I got goosebumps on my skin. "What was his name?"

"Icerius. He was made the first Elder General. The Elders are required to protect the Nepheals from present and future dangers."

A grave voice interrupted us. "That is not always easy."

We turned. The enormous but skeletally thin current Elder General was standing behind us.

"It is good to see you safe, Chyzar," he said, slightly inclining his head in Zenzara's direction. He didn't bother to acknowledge the rest of us.

Danaa gave a gasp and her usually greenish face went starkly white. She dropped onto all fours. "Elder General."

He came forward to examine the youngster in front of him. "So? All did not go well?"

Tears flowed out of her eyes and down her cheeks. She was muted by her pain and regret.

I stepped forward. "Ayaala did not survive. She died to save the Chyzar and Danaa. And the Chakrans."

A look of great pain crossed his old face. I noticed that he had more whiskers than other Nepheals I had met. They made his face seem slightly more ill-defined than most of his species. He must indeed be extremely old.

He raised his head. "What about the thesis they were using?"

"It was destroyed." I explained about the renaming of the star. It did not appear to please him at all.

"I see."

He turned and walked slowly back towards his quarters, leaving us all to gape after him.

The head of the guards in the hall came up to me. "The audience is over."

I frowned. "But he has not heard what happened. I should like to explain it all in detail."

"The audience is over."

I couldn't understand. What leader would not want to know the details of the sacrifice of one of his leading subjects? It made no sense.

Danaa struggled upright, looking instantly older. "We have been dismissed," she said in a low voice. "They do not wish to hear more."

"But ... but ... what about Agraala? What about the ship? What about you?"

She shrugged. On a Nepheal this was a huge gesture. Her shoulders could move up and down by around half a meter. "The Elder General does not wish to hear more."

"But he is supposed to be your leader."

"He has lived through much. He liked Agraala."

"Your people need to do something about all this. You cannot simply sit back. You signed the treaty, for krikk's sake!" I could feel my anxiety beginning to escalate.

"I will take you to the Ayaala Retreat. We will speak to Ouraali."

I felt frustrated. "Ouraali is not the leader of the Nepheal people," I told her crossly. "What can she do?"

Danaa closed her eyes in irritation. "You do not understand. The Elder General and the Board of Elders are men. They conserve. They are not proactive. That is for the females. It is the women's right, and theirs only."

"You mean that there is division of tasks here? That decisions are taken only by women?"

"Of course."

I shook my head. "Then why did Ouraali bring me here, to the Elder General? To the dome? Before?"

"We were attacked by Avians. That involves the protection of the species. It involves conservation."

I couldn't dispute that. It did.

The idea of hiking all the way up the mountain sent my heart to my boots. "It will take a long time for us to reach the Ayaala Retreat."

Danaa again shook her head. "We will carry you. Like Ouraali did before."

My heart sank even lower. I wasn't particularly eager to experience that again. "But there are four of us."

She looked at Eshaan. "The Enif will not require us to carry him. I have heard that Enif are very capable over difficult terrain."

Eshaan agreed. "I will be able to keep up."

That left Zenzie, Denaraz and I. Zenzie and Denaraz were looking at each other. "We can keep up too."

"No. I need to get up to the Retreat today. You can't. We will ask three guards to take you as far as they can. Females from the Retreat will come down to meet us at the half-way point. Male Nepheals may not visit the Retreat."

I grinned at Zenzie. "Pleasure in store for you." She had no idea how uncomfortable her trip was going to be.

She gave me a dubious look. "Yes, I am sure."

I knew how much she would hate it. It was the only thing that would keep me going during the ordeal. That and seeing my Geiga again. I hoped he hadn't frozen to death up there on the mountain.

12

The moment he saw me, Scout went crazy. He threw himself at me with such force that he pulled up the tether that somebody had buried deep into the dirt around the rock he was sheltering behind.

He took a leap from about two meters away and landed in my outstretched arms, his little tail churning around and around in wild circlets of joy. He even tried to nibble at my face.

I jerked away from him. Geiga's teeth are sharper than knives. Even a nibble can rip skin open. "Yes, yes. I like you too. Leave me alone, now." I put him firmly back on the ground. He inched behind me and became my shadow, trailing wherever I went. He wasn't planning on being left behind again.

Ouraali was the first to approach. She took one look at Danaa's face and paled.

"My sister is dead?"

Danaa nodded. Ouraali seemed to falter as she walked towards us. She bowed her head and put both hands together over her heart. "She will be missed." She ushered us all into the central hall of the Retreat. "Please come. Please tell me what happened to her. Please come to honor her with me."

As we walked, Ouraali was signaling to other Nepheal women. Quickly, silently, many fell in behind us. Others hurried to prepare food and brought out a large ceramic bowl which they placed under a metallic arch.

The Nepheal woman turned to Zenzara. "I am happy to see you here, in our Retreat. I apologize for our inability to shield you from the Vaer attackers. I hope you will forgive us."

Zenzie stuttered something, overcome by the formality she now merited as the new Chyzar.

Several Nepheal women approached, carrying a large barrel between them. Some of the contents were poured into the ceramic bowl.

I looked at Danaa.

"We are having the *Mortaala*, our ceremony of death," she explained. "We will all drink from the *Mortaa*. It is to wish Agraala a safe journey through the skies to our heaven. It is to keep the Avians away from her soul as it travels through their lands."

That made sense. In old times, the Nepheals must have thought that the skies belonged to the Avians, and the land to them. Two separate worlds.

A very old Nepheal woman hobbled up to the bowl. She added sugar to it and then cut the peel of some phyonwe fruit into it as well. Then she dropped some berries on the top.

She set fire to the whole thing, all the while stirring it with a deep spoon. Soon, in the gloom of the hall, all eyes were riveted on the blue flames which leapt above the bowl as what must have been extremely high grade alcohol began to burn.

The old woman started some sort of sad incantation in Nepheale and began to dip the ladle into the concoction and lift it high above the bowl. Then she allowed the liquid to flow downwards. It did this in a river of flame. When one of the berries ignited, it did so with a flash of pure white light, so strong that it burnt into the cornea, leaving a strong afterline on my retina. It was quite beautiful. I wished I could understand the words. The ladle rose and dipped, rose and dipped, all the while shimmering with the blue and white flame, leaving traces and lines of light on the walls and the people surrounding the *Mortaa*.

I felt privileged to watch it. It was a truly moving way of remembering somebody.

Eshaan reflected the light on his skin. I was sure that this ceremony would translate into a wonderful work of art, too.

I wondered exactly what the berries were that gave those wonderful flashes of light. It was like watching a mini firework display.

Zenzie was beside me, staring at the lights. Her mouth was slightly open and her eyes glittered with the reflections.

Danaa had bowed her head in respect. I checked the other Nepheal women. They were all in positions of deference. I kicked Zenzie.

"What?" she hissed

"Lower your head."

"Lower yours!"

"Seriously. Look at the other women."

Her eyes travelled around the hall. "Bah! They are Nepheals. What is the point of doing this if nobody looks at it?"

"It is a sign of respect."

"Then you do it."

I dipped my head. Some seconds later Zenzie followed my example.

"Why do you always have to spoil everything?" she demanded.

"Shhh! Behave!"

"I wish you hadn't saved me!"

"Yeah. Likewise."

"What do you mean? Do you regret the Savior Protocols? Don't you want me to be here?"

I gave a long sigh. I should have just kept my mouth shut. Denaraz, who was standing beside me, was shaking with amusement. I directed a rebuking look at him. He gave me a shrug back. Thanks.

The flames had gradually died out while this had been going on. The mass of Nepheal women disbanded as they went back to their daily business. Ouraali escorted us into a comfortable round house made of stone, of around a four meter radius. Brightly colored throws were strewn all over the raised wooden floor on the stone-lined ground, and there was a central wooden stove belching out heat in the center of the circular space.

She sat down on a seating area consisting of several thicker cushions. We sank into similar ones around her.

"Tell me what happened."

Zenzie looked at me, so I began to relate the story of the carbon cloud and the moon it hid. It took some time.

When I finally finished, Ouraali smiled around at us, though her eyes looked moist. "This is how my sister would have wanted to die. Do not feel sad for her. From what you say, it was rapid. She could not have had time to suffer?"

I remembered the moment. As always, it made me feel slightly sick. "No. It was very sudden."

"She risked her life knowingly to save the Chyzar, her own niece and a race of quantum beings. She would have thought that a fair trade, I know."

"Yes. I think she probably did."

"She would have been distraught at the idea of her thesis being used to harm the Chakrans. She spoke to me of her need to put everything right."

"Yes. She *did* manage to stop them consuming the Nexus."

I told her about the star, and the destruction of the thesis.

"Thank our ancestors for that. I hope the Chakrans can never be threatened in a similar way again." She turned to Zenzara. "Have they spoken to you, child?"

Zenzie shook her head. "The connections feel strange ... as if ... as if they had been stretched too far and haven't yet snapped back into place. I am aware of the Nexus, but there is no real contact with any of the strands. Everything is muzzy, hazy. They feel ... thinner, diminished in some way."

"I expect they will be able to reform the links you have with them. Take your time. You have been through a most traumatic experience."

Danaa straightened her back. "I have told the Macers that we will provide a shuttle for the Alliance. For the Interstellar Enforcement Agency. It is our duty as signatories. I wish to go with the ship. I gave them *Aenysia.*"

Ouraali blinked. It took her a couple of moments to take in the new information, process it and come to a conclusion.

"Naturally we must not shirk our responsibilities as full members of the Alliance," she said in a quiet tone. "However, I feel it is not up to one person to take the decision of a people."

Danaa hung her head.

"I understand that you have been upset by my sister's death, Danaa, but you should have consulted before doing anything that bound the Nepheal people."

"I know," she whispered. "But I was in *Dialectis.*"

"Were you? Hmm. That does change things. Come, walk with me. You can tell me of the circumstances."

The two of them left the round house. Eshaan took advantage of the silence to begin to sketch on a flat rock in one of the corners. He deftly began to commit what he had seen to images. He was so immersed in it that he didn't even hear us when we spoke to him.

Scout snuggled up to Zenzie, burrowing his way through the cushions in a most insidious fashion. Soon his full weight was distributed evenly between the two of us. Zenzie idly began to pull at his ears, something that sent him straight into the Geiga equivalent of heaven.

Denaraz was thoughtful. "Do you really feel the Chakrans are trying to rebuild the connection?" he asked her.

She was silent for a couple of minutes. "Yes. I do. I can feel them trying to get back, but they are at a huge distance somehow."

"Try to tell us about it. What it really feels like."

She puffed out her cheeks. "It ... it is ... I suppose it is like an ansible connection. A voice inside your head. Except that the Chakrans don't speak like we do. I feel ... shades. Not of colour, but of something like emotion. At the moment, even though the connection is only tenuous, the shade is of great anger. Maybe of sadness, too."

"Does that make you feel angry?"

"No. They are so immense, so very much bigger than me that their anger is like an approaching thunder storm. It makes me feel scared, but I can't empathize with them. They are too far away, too vast and too different for me to equate easily to them. I am only a mote of dust to them."

"So they make you feel small?"

Her eyes opened wide. "Yes! Yes, that is exactly what they make me feel. Which is why it is so strange to be called the Chyzar, to be thought to be important. The other Tyzarans should try it! I am less than insignificant. The Chakrans whose atoms are embedded in my brain stretch across thousands and thousands of galaxies. Of course I am insignificant!"

"Do the Chakrans have a name? Are they even individuals?"

Zenzie's small face contracted. Her wrinkles deepened. "I think so. But they are all connected, too, so that might not be right. I can feel that my Chakrans are linked to many, many others. Some are so very far away that everything is quite different to here. The stars and galaxies and stuff."

"Then you can see far-away galaxies as they are now? Like Agraala's macroscope?"

"I ...," more wrinkles joined together across her forehead, "I ... I suppose I can."

Denaraz swiveled to me. "Do you realize how important that is?"

"I do. If they knew that, she would never be allowed off Tyzar."

He deflated. "That's true."

Zenzie's crest spiked. "I am not going back. I'm not even going back for the two-week period every year. They forfeited that with their support of Cunningham and that Scientist friend of his! Agraala *died* because of them!"

"That was part of the deal with the ship. With the new agreement, you don't have to go back. I don't think they can make you."

She turned on me. "They had better not be able to! The ship is no longer a favor to us. It is ceded to the Alliance. I am not bound by previous agreements at all. That is what Danaa negotiated."

Izan raised an eyebrow at me.

"Put those claws away, Zenzie! We won't let them take you back. They can't enforce an agreement that has been superseded by something else, but we will ask Anzany to look into it anyway. Just to make sure."

Denaraz gave a solemn nod. "There will have to be many new laws. Interstellar ones. New lawyers to write them. New judges to keep them."

"I suppose there will. So there will be some sort of interstellar hub?"

"Of course. We will be based there."

"On Ulon Prime?"

"Near it, at any rate. The Macers are going to be the cornerstones of the Alliance. Though I suspect they will want to keep their planet as uncontaminated as they can."

I thought back to *Commorancy*. It was not long ago in time, but it felt as though relativity had been acting on the memory. It had been a different life, a different place, a different time. It felt so far away.

"We are going to need some of those lawyers. We are going to have to be in the forefront of any changes."

"I think we are. We are going to have to be flexible."

"I like that," said Zenzie. "Especially if it means that I won't have to go to Tyzar each year for them to put me under their microscopes."

We were in agreement. Flexible it was. New times. New rules.

We had been there for almost an hour when Danaa and Ouraali came back. Danaa looked better than she had since her aunt had passed. Her face, though not happy, had cleared. She had been crying, but she now seemed to have lost some of her burden.

"I can come with you!" she said. "They are going to honor the pact I made."

Ouraali gave her niece a tolerant smile. "I have heard all about the conversation. We will indeed honour the commitment made by one of our number in *Dialectis*."

That was good. I was beginning to realize just how much work was going to be needed if the Alliance was to have a chance of success. It was a huge undertaking, and it was perfectly obvious that one small ship was not going to be able to keep the whole of the Major Shells under control. This was just the beginning.

"Then we should start to get back," I began.

I was stopped by a raised hand. "I am sure that you should. However, we are to have a *Phaala* in a few days, down in Nephealis City. We would be honored if you would attend. It only means staying for one more day."

No foreigner had ever been invited to a *Phaala*. This was an honor that could not be turned down. Even Eshaan had lifted its head from its drawing. The Enif looked at me. It didn't have to say anything.

"We would be honored."

"You would, because up to now no foreigners have ever attended one. But we appreciate all that you and your crew have done for us. You brought Danaa back to us, and you liberated the Chyzar."

"We could not bring Agraala back."

She looked pained. "Sometimes the result is not what we would hope. We must strive to accept what is bad, as well as what is good."

I stared into the fire. "Yes."

"If you leave tomorrow morning you can be down at the Hall of Ages in time for the ceremony. We can always carry you, but I suspect you would rather walk down on your own?" Her eyes twinkled. So she *had* known how much I hated that journey!

"I ... I think walking would be good for us all."

Zenzie agreed with alacrity. "Walk, please!"

Denaraz was more restrained. "We would prefer not to impose

again. You have already been more than kind."

Eshaan ignored all of us. It had returned to its sketching.

The walk down was glorious. The weather had decided to be generous with us and I found that going down was painful, but not so painful as going up. I was able to see the wonderful expanse of the mountain ranges. It was quite exceptional.

We were accompanied on the trail by the oldest of the Nepheal women and the young Nepheal who was the basis of this *Phaala*. Jaaven, despite only being a year old, was able to easily outreach us all on the walk down. He skipped ahead, excited at the prospect of his admission into the Nepheal tribe. He was unfazed to be accompanied by outsiders, chatting breezily with Zenzie, especially, all the way down. He continually treated Danaa to adoring glances. She didn't appear to notice.

Zenzara tended to ignore him, too. As a mature eight-year-old, she was way past such young antics. It was quite funny to watch her. She had suddenly become solemn and contained. Her eyes followed the antics of the young Nepheal boy as she trod with restrained step down the mountain path. He was unable to entice her into undignified play. She was clearly anxious to show herself to be completely above such things.

I couldn't bear to see it.

I gave her a push as she passed me.

She turned on me with fierce anger. "You pushed me!"

"Didn't!"

"Did!"

I spread my hands. "So sorry, Your Royal Chyness."

Denaraz choked, which earned him a disdainful glare.

Zenzie pushed me back. Honestly, I hardly noticed.

"That's better," I said.

"What do you mean?"

"I thought you might be sick."

She put her hands on her hips and stared at me. "Sick?"

"Sick. You were walking down the track like an eighty-year-old. Go play with him. You know you want to."

"He is only a year old."

"About your level, then?"

She hissed at me.

"Come on, Zenzie. This isn't you. Come down off that high horse and be yourself. You aren't the Chyzar yet, you know. You'll have plenty of time to be old. It isn't something you want to welcome early."

Her crest twitched. "I suppose not." She thought about it and then gave a jump of sheer joy. "Come on then, Jaaven. Race you to that rock over there!"

The two scampered off, chased closely by Danaa, who had been trying to copy Zenzara's sudden decrepitude. We heard shrieks of laughter as they tagged each other around the rocks, appearing and disappearing from view.

Denaraz slapped me on the back. "You are right. She needs to enjoy being young."

"She is still traumatized by what happened to her. It will take time for her to recover."

He nodded. "I know. But she is a brave little thing. I don't know many girls her age who would have sacrificed themselves for you."

I stared off into the distance. "She takes the Savior Protocols very seriously."

"She does. But you are right. She does still need to enjoy life a little. And there won't be many days like this, on planets like this."

"No." I wondered what was in our joint future. Because our future was joint. We had been effectively soldered together. Where I went, Zenzara went. Perhaps that would change in the future. When she was truly the Chyzar, would it become where she went I went? I pondered the implications. I didn't like them much. I was getting used to being this new person, this captain in the Interstellar Enforcement Agency. I wanted to stay here. It felt like we were making a difference. At least, I hoped so.

We spent the night in the wooden halfway house, the same one we had used before. We had been given hammocks to carry by Ouraali, so we were able to sleep quite comfortably.

"You sleep lying down."

I jerked awake, startled, and found a Nepheal face only centimeters away. "Oh, Jaaven. You ... Have you been there long?"

"I was watching you. What will you do if you are attacked? You will be eaten before you can escape. It seems a very silly way to sleep to me."

"Yes. I guess it does. But where I come from, you are safe when you sleep."

Even though the Avians hadn't attacked for millennia, he didn't understand what that meant.

"Nobody is safe when they sleep. You cannot look around you when you sleep."

"No. But we have beds in rooms that have locks."

"What is a lock?"

I grimaced. My joints were hurting, my eyes were gritty and I felt like going back to that lovely deep sleep and nice dream he had disturbed. "Tell you what," I said wearily.

"What?"

"Would you like to take Scout out for a walk?"

Scout, on hearing his name, struggled to his feet and twirled his little tail around and around. He was game, it told us.

His eyes lit up. "Yes!"

I undid the lead and handed it over to him. "There you are, then. Off you go! Don't hurry back!"

Zenzie slipped out of her hammock. "I will go with him. He might get lost."

Jaaven's hackles rose. "I will not!"

"You are only little!"

He raised himself to his full height, towering over her. "You obviously don't understand the concept of the *Phaala*," he told her loftily. "It is to declare me a man!"

She made a rude noise.

"I am!" he shouted, waking anybody who was still lucky enough to be in the land of nod. "I will be!"

"Bah! You are a baby."

"Take that back!"

"Won't!"

"Take it back!"

They wandered out of the shack and their voices slowly disappeared into the night.

Denaraz sighed and struggled out of his hammock. He slipped into his clothes with resignation.

"You don't have to go, Izan."

He sighed. "I do. I wouldn't sleep anyway, wondering what they were getting up to. And it is ... was ... my job."

"Was. Not is."

He smiled. "I have got into the habit. And she is the Chyzar. My Chyzar. I wouldn't want anything to happen to her."

"Whatever." I stretched then curled back into the canvas material of the hammock. It wasn't the best bed I had ever used, but I fully intended to give it another chance. I closed my eyes.

The next morning things were much less exuberant. Jaaven was now conscious of his impending welcome into adulthood and apprehension shone in his eyes. He was trying to be as bumptious as the day before, but it was falling flat. Every time we passed adult male Nepheals, his body language changed. They intimidated him. He was scared that he would never match up to them.

Zenzie and Danaa walked on either side of him, the Nepheals

adapting themselves to the Tyzaran girl's slower pace.

The adult males who passed all took a long detour so as to avoid meeting us head on. Danaa explained that it was forbidden for a male to speak to any child who had not yet undergone the *Phaala* ceremony. Only women were allowed to speak to children. It had been that way for as long as history could remember.

I asked what the punishment would be if they did.

Her face crinkled. "Why would they? It is not allowed."

I realized that there probably were no punishments. None would be necessary if the social structure were so rigid that nobody ever went against it. I had known that deference and form were important to them. I hadn't realized just how important. I was beginning to see that for a Nepheal to break the rules was so rare that they no longer thought it was possible.

It seemed to me to be a dangerous way of thinking. It would make life very easy for any Nepheal who did want to break the rules. Which made me remember something. Cunningham had to have had help to break into the library. He certainly could not have done it on his own. The Nepheal who had helped him – as far as I knew – had not been apprehended.

I accelerated to fall in with Denaraz. He agreed instantly. "I had already considered that. Surely the Board of Elders will have investigated?"

"I don't think they will have. From what Danaa just said, the possibility of such a thing happening is not really accepted. I think the Elder General will simply have moved on. He probably thinks that it was all Cunningham."

"Then he is making a mistake."

"Yes. I believe he is. The Nepheals still fear the Avians but they do not fear treason from within. They should."

"Will you discuss it with him?"

"I will try, certainly. He didn't strike me as someone very willing to listen."

"Perhaps it is a female thing?"

I squinted along the road in front of us, which wove between the small bushes and the larger phyonwe trees. At the moment the sun was shining. It was a stunning landscape. "I don't believe it is. I think it would fall into conservation and protection. That is for the males."

"Do you think there is danger?"

"I hope not. Perhaps whoever helped Cunningham has gone to ground. Yet ... I don't know ... I have an uneasy feeling about it."

13

The morning of the *Phaala* dawned dull and grey. The good stretch of weather was over. Clouds were gathering up on the mountain tops and were threatening the fresh air over Nephealis City.

I quickly realized that this was not to be a small ceremony. All over the city the streets were filling with Nepheals. They congregated around the Hall of Ages, leaving only a small gap through which the participants could walk. Each person was greeted with cheers and shouts of encouragement. I looked around with amazement. It was so welcoming that they brought out the whole city just for one or two new children. It made me wonder if they had fertility problems on this planet. It was something I knew nothing about. I certainly had not seen many juveniles. Perhaps the Nepheals were facing some sort of population crisis?

As participants we walked in a stately manner through the throng. At least, I walked in a stately manner. Zenzie skipped from side to side being as annoying as possible.

"Can't you look dignified?" I hissed.

"Why should I? I am young. I am entitled to jump. Think what it must be like to be old, like you."

I may have bristled. "Old? Who are you calling old? I am not even thirty yet."

She gave a 'durr' sort of roll of her eyes. "Like I said, old."

I made my hands cease inching towards her neck. "Stop, anyway. This is a very important day for the Nepheals. And you are an important visitor."

She skipped even more. "I am glad you think I am important."

"Stop it, will you!"

Denaraz took my arm and gave me a pitying look. He was right. I was not her father. I wasn't responsible for her. In fact, the boot was on the other foot. I blew out air. I guess it wasn't really my business how she behaved.

"She just got out of captivity," he murmured to me. "She is just glad to be alive. Yesterday you were encouraging her."

I felt mean. Of course she was glad to have survived. She was entitled to be exuberant. Maybe she was right: I was old. That was a sobering thought. When had I lost all my own enjoyment of life? Denaraz had a point. We had all been through a lot. We should all start to live a little. And she was quite cute, bouncing around the place.

In any case, the crowds were loving their happy Chyzar. Word had got around of her rescue and it was clear that they were celebrating that too. They knew that the Vaers had kidnapped her on their planet and it seemed they wanted to make amends to her. Shouts of encouragement followed her progress.

Denaraz and I trailed along in her wake, receiving more cheers as her liberators.

I saw Caerae, the head of the Nephealis Gyre. He grinned as he saw Scout shambling along in my wake. "Will you be able to keep him away from the refreshments?" he asked. "Only, they are quite an important part of the ceremony."

I showed him the leash with its safety chain. "This is one he can't wriggle out of."

"Good. He really would cause havoc in a ceremony like this."

"He can cause havoc anywhere. Geigas are good at stuff like that." I decided to clear up my doubts. "how often do you have *Phaalas?*"

His face fell. "I ... I prefer not to discuss that. It is a private, Nepheal matter."

He didn't have to answer. I could read the reply in his face. And the math wasn't too hard either. The population of the planet was around a hundred thousand, if I remembered rightly. This was the first *Phaala* I had seen in the time I had been in the city. Say they had one a week, which I didn't think they did. And say each ceremony was for five youngsters, which I didn't think they were. I closed my eyes and tried to calculate. Let's see ... around two hundred and fifty per year. On a population of a hundred thousand, that was ... around a quarter of a percent birth rate per year. And I had the feeling that I had been wildly overoptimistic. It could be a fifth or a tenth of that. Even though the race lived for many years, I was pretty sure the death rate would be at least a half a percent.

I mused on this as we walked. That would seem to indicate that the population of Nephealis was aging and in decline. They certainly would need help before long. No wonder they decided to join the Alliance! And no wonder it was a sore subject for them. Even though they were long-lived, it must be sad to see their numbers declining.

As I walked I was able to look around. There were many, many Nepheals in the crowd. I saw only one or two young ones.

No wonder the *Phaala* had become so important to them. At the same time, it told me why foreigners were not normally allowed to attend. Just as I had done, they would have realized that the numbers didn't add up.

I felt sorry for the Nepheals. They were a great people. Kind, unassuming and very intelligent. We needed to help them. That was something that had to go on the bucket list for the Alliance. I made a mental note to let the Macers know about this. Surely we had some way of investigating what the problem might be? Surely somebody in the Major Shells would be able to help them?

A bell began to toll in the distance. It was a melodious high sound that sent sweet vibrations through the air. I found myself relaxing.

Soon we were inside the Hall of Ages. Our group and what seemed like a thousand others. This must have been what it was like when the great doors were locked against the Avian raptors. At least this time they would leave the doors open.

They didn't. Just as I was thinking that thought, the vast transparent doors began to close. I looked around in panic. Despite the ability to see out through the doors and the dome, both made of the same material, it was claustrophobic. I was glad Mel was not with us on this trip. She would have found it unbearable.

Although the crowd was packed in so tightly, it managed to part before the participants in the ceremony. Three young Nepheals stepped forward with a proud gait. Jaaven was one of them. He was flanked on either side by his parents. The male to his left must be Jarisaan, his father. The tall man was dressed in some sort of a robe which looked as if it had been woven from leaves and twigs. It made him look important, but natural.

Mevaala, his mother, was to his right. She was draped in a riotous silky print in bright red. It was embroidered with many-colored animals and trees that walked majestically across the fabric. I couldn't help staring. It was one of the most impressive pieces of clothing I had ever seen.

Zenzie gave a sigh. She was above me. Denaraz had decided that she was in danger of being crushed by the multitude and so had swung her onto his shoulders, where she was perched in a prime spot to see everything that was going on.

"I want one of those," she informed me from her lofty heights. "Or two."

"You are not Nepheal."

"Well spotted, Mallivan! Did you think I hadn't noticed?"

"Don't get snarky with me, Zenzie. I think that is a garment reserved for these ceremonies. I don't suppose they would be happy if a foreigner were to wear one."

Zenzara raised a skeptical eyebrow. "You don't, huh?" She raised her voice so that it would carry across part of the large dome. "Hey, Ouraali?"

The leader of the Ayaala Retreat pivoted to track down her voice.

"Yes, Chy Zenzara?" In this formal situation, titles were being used.

Zenzie corrected herself instantly. "Leader Ouraali, would I be allowed to wear such a garment? Would that be considered respectful?"

Ouraali's eyes widened. She looked towards the Elder General. He inclined his head in the way statesmen do when they want to add gravitas to a decision.

Ouraali made her way over to us. "Normally none but the mothers of Phaala candidates may wear such ceremonial robes," she said. "However, we would be honored if the Chyzar would allow us to confect her official garments. They could be adapted to include images that were important to her. It would be a great privilege for the Nepheal women to put their hands to such a project."

Zenzie clapped her hands together. "Thank you!"

"What are your favorite colors, Chyzar?"

"Red and orange and yellow," replied Zenzie, her eyes sparkling with excitement.

Now it was Ouraali's turn to give the politician's nod. "It shall be done," she told us with a smile.

I frowned. "You shouldn't feel obliged. It is just a caprice!"

That earned me two sets of reproachful eyes.

"Tisn't," snapped Zenzie.

"The Chyzar should have clothes to reflect her importance," said Ouraali.

Denaraz decided the time had come to change the subject. "Look!" He pointed. "I believe the ceremony is about to start."

He was right.

I'm afraid I found the whole thing rather long. The presentation of the theses, although limited to fifteen minutes per parent, still lasted for nearly an hour. All that time we were standing. By the end I could feel my heart racing and I was beginning to sway from side to side.

Danaa had crept up to me through the crowd. She shot me a worried look. "Are you all right, Captain?"

Terrific. Now I was the only one about to pass out. A sure fire way to improve their opinion of me. I was about to faint like an old Terran woman.

Danaa grabbed my hand and began to pull me backwards through the crowd. "Come with me!"

I was so relieved that I did so without thinking. Zenzie, who was still perched on Izan's shoulders, knocked on the top of his skull and bent to whisper something to him. He turned, and with her instructing him as to direction, they began to follow us. I had no idea where Eshaan was. Being the only shiny black insect-like being in the whole place, it should have been easy to spot him, but he seemed to be nowhere in sight.

Danaa dragged me through the crowd, who grumbled as they were forced apart by her sheer determination. "Let us through!" she cried. "Foreign dignitaries!"

Nothing particularly dignified about the sweat that was now pouring off my body. I was feeling worse and worse and was just trying not to throw up.

Finally we reached the edge of the dome. I had thought that there were no exits other than the enormous transparent doors, but I was wrong.

There was a smaller door set flush with the dome wall. It was made of the same special quartz-like compound as the rest of the dome and the main doors.

Danaa opened it and slipped through, leading us along a long corridor and then turning through into an airy room with some cots on it.

"Here," she said, gesturing at one of the cots. "Lie down, Captain."

Feeling embarrassed to be the cause of all this, I obeyed. I wasn't sure my legs would hold me up for much longer, in any case.

"Thank you."

"You are very welcome. I expect you are unaccustomed to tight gatherings such as ours. It can take some getting used to."

I felt that to be an understatement, and said so.

Zenzie was enjoying my discomfort. "You went through that moon, but collapse in a place with a lot of people. That's funny." She proved it by going off in peals of laughter.

I glared at her.

She appeared not to notice. If anything, her amusement grew.

Denaraz was looking around the room. He gently leaned forward so as to put his precious burden down. "Where is this, Danaa?"

"The Infirmary." She looked around and it was her turn to frown. "There should be at least one doctor and one nurse in here. Especially during *Phaala*. You are not the only one to dislike crowds, Captain. Even Nepheals are sometimes overcome by the heat and the multitude. There should be staff on duty."

I signaled to Denaraz. He nodded and began to edge towards the door. At that moment it opened and a cautious Eshaan slipped in.

"I am glad to find you. I thought the slight ripple in the crowd was you. Are you quite well, Captain?"

Izan put it quickly in the picture. Eshaan immediately stiffened and began to edge towards the corridor.

Denaraz turned to me. "You stay here," he told me. "The rest of us will determine what is happening."

"I will stay with Mallivan," Zenzara said firmly.

So I lolled back on my cot, mortified, as the rest of the group sidled out into the corridor. None of them had any weapons. We had not brought them, knowing that we would be searched before being allowed into the dome.

I lay back and tried to recover from the momentary weakness. Zenzie had found some water and a cloth and bathed my face and arms with it. It helped. So did the amount of space around me. I was soon feeling better.

When Danaa slipped back into the infirmary I was already perched on the edge of the cot, feeling much improved.

She looked relieved to see me sitting up. "Can you walk?"

I nodded. "I am feeling better by the minute. Why?"

"We found the medical staff."

We followed her as she retraced her footsteps. The corridor seemed to be circular, following the outside wall of the dome. Every so often, there were chambers leading off from it.

Danaa led us past several of these chambers, until we came to another corridor. This led off to the right, and seemed quite long. We followed its windowless walls for quite some way.

At last it opened out into an anteroom. To the right, I could see several people.

Denaraz and Eshaan were standing with four Nepheals. Two were dressed in the ubiquitous hospital white gowns of medical staff. The other two were guards.

Izan looked up as we came in. "These men were knocked out with some sort of incapacitating gas," he said in a grim tone. "They called for medical staff."

I shut my eyes for a second. And it had all been going so well. "What is through there? I asked, pointing towards the big double doors leading off the anteroom.

"The mainframe," muttered one of the guards. "Nothing important."

Well, now I knew why he was only a guard. Mainframe computers are always important. But that didn't explain why this one had become a target.

"What did the men who entered look like?" I queried.

"One of them was a Terran. He had some sort of a dress ribbon insignia on his jacket. I don't know what it meant."

"Tall, dark, around thirty?"

The guard nodded. "Exactly! Do you know who it is?"

"I do." Izan and I exchanged glances.

Zenzara's hands had gone to her mouth. "Cunningham?"

"I don't know anybody else in this sector likely to be wearing the Omnial insignia."

"But why? Why would he risk coming back here?"

There was only one possible reason. The Elder General had been lying to us all. "There must be a copy of the thesis. Of Agraala's thesis!"

I noticed that the medical staff and guards had suddenly dropped onto all fours in a respectfully subservient position. The old man himself had just entered the anteroom.

He gave a sigh. "No. There was no copy of Agraala's thesis. It is still not possible to copy theses protected by our adaptation of quantum blockchain, and Agraala insisted that hers was. The thieves cannot have been after that."

"Unless they didn't know it wasn't copied."

The Elder General waved to the staff to stand up. He shook his head. "They knew it had our quantum blockchain protocols. The Terran scientist would be aware of what that means."

"Then what could they have been after?"

He hesitated. "There ... there was a second thesis. One of Agraala's younger nieces recently developed a more streamlined version of the data collection protocols."

I went white. "A second version? Are you crazy? Why didn't you tell us? How could they have found out? Do you know what this means?"

The Elder General was not used to being challenged. His ancient face registered his disapproval. "I am not stupid, Captain Mallivan. Of course I know what this means. I did not tell you for the same reason I told nobody else. The more people I tell, the more are in possession of the facts, are they not? As to how they could have found out, I must assume they found a way to consult one of our Dialectis registers. While little more than the title of the work is given, there are links to works which preceded a particular thesis and works which succeeded it."

"We have to stop them. Call out your guard. The whole city must be searched!"

The quavery old man held up a hand. "We can do no such thing. The *Phaala* is sacred. I may not break it. In another hour it will be over and we can release the guard. If I do something now we would risk a stampede. I will not do that. I cannot risk my people."

I stared at him. "An hour? In another hour it will be too late!"

"I will allow your group to go now. I will give you special dispensation to leave the ceremony. More, I cannot do."

Danaa dropped again to all fours. "Thank you."

I clamped my jaw shut. There was no point in my saying any more. He was not about to change his mind and recriminations would serve no purpose now. I had to remember I was merely a guest on his planet.

The Elder General nodded at one of the guards. "Show them the way through to the far exit. The intruders must have taken that route." Then he turned to make his way back to the ceremony. "Good luck!"

Good luck? We were going to need it. I knew Bull. He would not have been hanging around waiting for us to catch up with him. I feared it would be way too late.

The guard led us through doors that required a bioscan and past a large computer room. It smelt of ozone and metal. On the far side, we came to a small armored door, this time made of metal, not the transparent glass-like material.

This opened with an eight–digit code.

The guard nodded and stepped back inside. The rest of us found ourselves outside in the streets of Nepheal City.

"I don't think he would have used the spaceport," I said. "So we need somewhere close to here that could land a shuttle big enough to carry a Vaer hover sled. That seems like the most likely scenario to me."

Danaa leaped into action. "That will have been seen. There are so many people in the city today; they couldn't have got into the dome without being spotted!" She raced off and began to shout at the passers-by. Eventually we saw in earnest conversation with one of them.

She jogged back over. "They went towards Retaara Park," she gasped. "About five minutes ago."

"Retaara Park, then. As fast as you can!"

Eshaan looked at me, waiting for permission to go ahead. Danaa raised one eyebrow at me too.

"Yes. You two can go on first. We will follow. Do what you can to stop them."

Danaa gave a nod and took off towards the East with a terrific leap. Eshaan was not left behind though its gait was much more even and parallel with the ground.

We broke into a run. Izan quickly pulled away from Zenzie and myself. I was still hampered by the weakness I had just experienced. I decided to keep to a steady jog. It was about all I could manage.

This meant that I was the last of the group to arrive at the park. I found the others grouped in a small despondent circle.

"We were too late," Danaa's head was lowered.

Eshaan's antennae vibrated with frustration. "We were only in time to see their vapor trail in the sky. Unfortunately."

I sat down on a nearby rock. "Then we have to get back to the spaceport and up to a ship. Danaa?"

She looked eager. "*Aenysia* can be ready. I will contact the Operations Team from the spaceport. Then they will be able to use our journey time to get her ready."

"See if they can trace the Vaer ship. I think they will avoid Ebyssia. The faction may have other secret bases in the area."

She nodded. "I will."

I thought it unlikely that they would return to the scene of their previous attempts. Even if they had discovered how we had breached the defenses and somehow managed to eliminate that risk, they were sitting ducks inside that carbon cloud now that we knew where they were and how to get through the channel. Although they might use it if there was nowhere else for them to go, I rather thought that Bull might have a back-up plan. He had always seemed to be a good forward planner.

We straggled back to the spaceport, which was still almost empty. Most of the residents of the city were attending the *Phaala*. We managed to get onto the first shuttle going back to the Gyre. It was going to take us at least four hours before we could be our way in *Aenysia*. That was a long head's start. I closed my eyes. It felt to me like a complete replay of the last mad chase we had undertaken.

As I remembered, an icy thought trickled into my mind. Zenzara!

"Stop!"

There was a commotion. I had been last in the line as we were making our way into the ferry up to the Gyre and my shout had caused them all to bottleneck up and bump into each other.

Denaraz steadied both Zenzie and Danaa before turning to me with an inquiring look. "What?"

"They still need Zenzara. How can they repeat their experiment without her? This may be a trap."

Izan's eyes went slightly out of focus as he considered my words. Then his crests both went rigid. "You are right. Unless they kept some sort of way into the Chakran network, she must be a part of their plans."

Zenzie was looking around suspiciously, her own crest vertical. "You mean that they may be here, now?"

I shrugged. "We don't know. We don't know if they managed to preserve something of the Chakran network last time or whether they will still need you."

Zenzie stared. "You are saying that you don't know if we are chasing them or they are chasing us?"

I huffed. "I suppose you could put it that way..."

Her hands were now on her hips. "Well, which way would you put it?"

"I would say that their motivation is unclear."

"Great!" She looked quite disgusted. I think she was hiding the fear that had overtaken her small body. Her crest was more upright than I had ever seen it.

I reached out to touch her. "I am sorry, Zenzie. It seems we are never going to know what is really going on. I feel that we are continually acting blind. We never seem to have all of the facts."

She shrugged her shoulder to dislodge my hand. "Yes, I understood!" She walked over to Danaa, who looked at her with a worried expression.

"So what is our plan of action?" Izan asked.

I thought about it. "We have to go on. The risk that they already have all the ingredients they need to make traversable wormholes through the Chakran nodes is too high."

"And if we are walking into a trap? If they *do* need Zenzara to complete the transformation, we will be facilitating them."

"Only if they can get her. We will have to make sure that they can't"

"How?"

"That is the part I am not sure of yet. Sorry. I will think about it."

Zenzara allowed herself a disbelieving snort. I couldn't really blame her. I wished we had all the facts, but we didn't. I don't see what else she expected me to do. It was one of those lose-lose situations I was probably becoming famous for.

Eshaan was the one who broke the gloomy silence. "We need *Nivala*," it said, its voice unexpectedly expressive for an Enif. "We may need both ships. We certainly need all of our group on this."

Of course. It was quite right. We should double our assets. For sure. I slapped it on its carapace, which was quite painful. To me. "Good thinking! I will get on to them while the rest of you make sure that *Aenysia* is flight-ready."

"We need to tell the Macers, too." Denaraz said.

"Yes. They need to know this. So do the other members of the

Alliance."

"The question is, what side will they all come down on?" It was Danaa's clear voice that put everybody's fears into words.

"They signed the accords. They will be on our side."

My eyes slid to Denaraz. The Tyzarans had already slipped up on that when they took Chandrayanan in after the war. They had known perfectly well what his plans were. All right, they probably didn't know that he was planning to use the Chyzar in the way that he did, but they certainly hadn't been averse to funding his research.

"They will all be on our side. This technology cannot be allowed to develop. By anybody. It would be genocide. The Chakrans would be exterminated. It is unthinkable. It has to be stopped and banned."

Zenzie's voice was small. "I think they have what they need."

We all swiveled around. Her face was grey.

"I have not felt all the Chakrans since the moon. I ... I feel as though some of them are missing. I think they split at least three away from me in that cage of energy. Probably more. I think they may already have as many as they need in that quantum trap of theirs."

"Are you sure?"

She pulled a face. "No, of course I am not sure. The Chakrans could just be resting, or recuperating, or cross with me, or voluntarily somewhere else. There have been other times I have felt this emptiness, but now it is more specific. I was aware of six different strands before, and now I can only feel two. At least, I think it is two."

That clinched it for me. "Right. Our working hypothesis is that they have all they need to open a wormhole, and that this time they could succeed. We will act on that supposition."

Both Denaraz and Danaa opened their mouths to speak, but I held up my hand. "I know. We cannot be sure. Which is why you two will be in charge of protecting her. We need to put her somewhere where Cunningham and his Vaers cannot get a hold of her again."

Danaa's face was determined. "She will stay on the Nepheal Gyre. The Nepheals can protect her there."

"I will not!" Zenzie's small face was horrified. "I am coming with you. I have to get all the strands of the Nexus back. I am the Chyzar!"

She must have caught my rather sardonic look, because she flushed. "So? I can change my mind, can't I? I know I never wanted to be the Chyzar, but now that I am I have a physical need for the Chakran strands now. I ... I feel as though part of me has been torn out."

"You should have said something earlier."

"I didn't know what I was feeling. Why don't *you* try being suspended for days on a plinth of solid light and see how *you* feel, Mallivan Bell?" Her chin jutted out in my direction.

I held up my hands. "Keep calm! I was just saying."

"Well, don't! And don't tell me to keep calm. It makes my claws come out involuntarily."

I checked her hands. Sure enough, the miniature claws that Tyzaran women had were sparkling like tiny sharp tacks at the ends of her fingers. I took a step back. Those things may be small, but they could do a lot of damage. I had seen them in action. On Bull Cunningham.

It was a rare occurrence to see them at all. They were vestigial traces from earlier eras and were hardly used by modern Tyzaran women. In each successive generation they were becoming smaller and smaller. The geneticists thought they would disappear completely within a few hundred years.

"No offence."

She breathed in and out, trying to calm her innate response. Eventually the claws retracted. "That is all right, Mallivan. You are just very stupid sometimes. I do not think you do it deliberately."

I glared. If I had had claws they would probably have come out. I slumped down in the seat on the grubby ferry up to the Gyre and tried to develop some sort of a plan. If Zenzie's suspicions turned out to be right, the Terrans could be close to establishing a traversable network through the whole local cluster. And that was just for starters. It was down to us to stop them. I didn't see how it was possible. We were just a band of ill-assorted misfits.

We only had one thing in our favor.
We were all prepared to die doing it.

14

We met up with *Nivala* some fifty light years to the west of Nephealis, just on the border of the Atlas and Great Shells. There was a redistribution of personnel by shuttle. Neema and Anzany joined Danaa in the *Aenysia*, as they had before. The rest of us went back over to *Nivala*.

As soon as I stepped through the airlock onto *Nivala*, Mel ran into my arms and gave me a huge hug.

"Good to have you back, Rye. I'm glad you didn't leave us behind in orbit around Ulon Prime. We were getting fed up with so much down time."

"There isn't a lot to do on Ulon Prime," said Sammy dryly. "Seen one kelp raft, seen them all." He strode forward and stretched out his hand. "Welcome back, Rye."

I was glad to see them again. I gave them both hugs.

Seyal and her growing son were standing behind them. She was still carrying him in a wrap that wound around her waist and upper body. She looked surprised when I gave her a hug too. She squeaked.

I squeezed Segaton's tiny hand. He was just reaching the babbling stage. He managed a "*ba-a-a-a-va-a-a*" as a welcome. I ruffled his downy hair. He squirmed.

Eshaan and Didjal were clicking away at each other, using the Enif tactile system of communication. Their skins are equipped with cordotonal organs underneath almost the whole surface area of their limbs. Touching is the normal form of conversation for them. They speak by creating complex patterns of vibrations.

I left them to it. I knew that it is considered the height of rudeness to touch one or other of the *faliifs* when they are in a state of communications. Enif who do this are expelled from the homeworld.

It felt wonderful to be back on board my own ship. That thought brought me sharply to a stop. When had *Nivala* become 'my' ship? I shook my head. It didn't matter. But it certainly must be an indication of how easily I had slipped into this new job with the Interstellar Enforcement Agency.

And, I realized, with these people. Two Avaraks, three Tyzarans, four Spacelanders, one Nepheal, two Enif. Quite a group. Yet I felt part of it. I belonged here as I had never belonged on my home shipstation. All of the diverse parts of this strange cocktail fitted together. We were different but cohesive.

"What are you grinning about?" asked Izan.

"Nothing. Just that we are a mixed-up bunch."

"Nobody would dispute that. What amazes me is how we all seem to fit in here."

"You see? We were thinking the same thing. Even a Tyzaran girl who is to be the next Chyzar fits in." That made me think of Zenzara. "Have you come up with a way to protect her? Just in case she is wrong?"

"I don't think that she is, but if any ships come within a light year of us, we will do our best to hide her. We are going to pop her in an EVA suit and let her out of the pool-side airlock. She will make her way back to the weapon's bridge and sit on the torpedo housing."

I stared. "That can't be a long term thing, can it?"

"More than you would think. There is a small outer access locker just beside it and I will store a case of air tanks there. With that she will be good for over 24 hours. That should be enough. They will never trace her body heat around such a highly shielded area."

"Well done!"

"Funnily enough, Danaa came up with the basic idea. She knows that Zenzara is comfortable in EVA situations. The rest was easy. We just had to find a closely shielded, heavy hull area."

"You had better practice a few times just in case. Make sure that Zenzara is familiar with it."

"We already spoke to her. She said she would be fine. But of course we will put in some practice sessions. We need to make sure it would all run smoothly."

"Good. Do that."

Sammy and Mel had been tracing the Vaer ship for the last few days. It had taken a slight detour to the south, probably to confuse anybody attempting to follow, then curved around towards the West. Ebyssia and the carbon moon was more northerly, as was Vaer Nova, so it appeared that I was right. The Vaers had another hideaway somewhere in the Great Shell.

Sammy called me over to the sensor array. Mel was peering at it with a disgusted expression.

"We lost them."

"Lost them? How?"

"They just dropped off the sensors. How should I know?" Mel sounded quite fierce.

"All right! I'm sorry. That came out a little too accusing, Mel. I wasn't suggesting it was your fault."

"Well, don't. It wasn't. I don't make mistakes like that, and neither does Sammy."

"I know. I already apologized."

"Could this be similar to the low visibility shielding on Nepheal ships?"

She shook her head. "No. I thought of that. I have checked all the sensors. Their signal is clearly being blocked. But we don't have a clue how. Do the Vaers have some sort of device on board that completely masks their signs, like an invisibility cloak? Or have they reached their destination and switched off all power? That would do it, too, though I would expect to be able to pick them up when we get closer."

"Have you got the co-ordinates of where they disappeared?"

She nodded.

"Then let's head there first. I doubt the Vaers have cloaking technology that the Tyzarans don't have." I looked at Denaraz. "You don't have it, do you, Izan? The Tyzarans, I mean."

"Not so far as I know."

"If the Vaers had it, logic tells me they would have bartered it to the Tyzarans. I don't see them keeping it for themselves. They are merchants. They would have capitalized on it."

"If you are wrong we will be giving them even more time to get away from us."

I nodded. "Yes, but I hope I am not wrong."

It was easy to say, but I did find that I was second-guessing myself for some hours after. I tried to tell myself that mistakes were inevitable. It didn't bring me much comfort. Even on *Faraday* I had known that my orders could affect lives. Now that pressure was more intense. We really were on a knife-edge.

Seyal's calm voice broke through my thoughts. "Here, I brought you something to eat."

I toyed with the fork. "Thank you." I found I had no appetite at all.

"Eat it," she urged. "You need to keep your strength up. Eat, rest, get to the gym that you like so much. It will calm you down, help to balance you. It is not good to rethink decisions. It is unhelpful."

She was right there. I smiled at her. "You can tell what I think?"

"I'm an Avarak woman. We survive by knowing what males think."

That was something else we had to change. When we had the chance. The short life expectancy of an Avarak female had to change.

"We can fix my world when all this is over," she said. "In any case, the movement is spreading." Earlier in the year, Seyal had distributed copies of the accords that the Avarak men had agreed to. They included equal rights for women. By suppressing the accords, they had thought to suppress the knowledge. That hadn't happened. The news had swept through the female inhabitants of Rhyveka like wildfire, spawning a new movement amongst them. It was in its infancy, but slowly gaining momentum.

"It is not ready yet," Seyal told me. "Such things take time. And our women die very young. Time is something they do not have."

"Yet."

She looked happier. "Yet," she agreed.

I dipped my fork into the food and took a bite. It tasted good. Very good. I wolfed the rest down. Then I took Seyal's advice. There was time to rest and time to work out. Keeping a balance was very important.

We dropped down to a crawl when we came up to the coordinates Mel had spoken of. It turned out to be a fairly empty area of space in the Aschasi area of the Great Shell. Apart from several dark nebulae which were birthing new stars, it holds little of interest. There are no habitable planets in the region, and it merits no more than a cursory mention on star maps.

The coordinates were close to the edge of the dark nebula. The Aschasi nebulae are classified as Bok Globules, being on average only a little above two light years across. They are small dark areas of space that are just dense enough to block out the light from distant stars, but not dense enough to hamper spaceships.

Coming, as we were, from the Ulon vector, the Globules stood out against the Chitran emission nebulae as dark black patches against an orange firmament.

We brought both ships to a halt in space, and Mel took detailed readings of the surroundings. At length, she shook her head.

"I can't find anything here," she lamented. "I rather think they must be long gone."

"I don't know. I have the feeling ..." I stared out at the dark clumps that were highlighted against the bright background of Chitran. The hairs on my arms were standing straight out from my skin. I couldn't quite say why, but I knew that Cunningham was close by. He was hiding in plain sight. So why couldn't we see him?

Try as I might, I could find nothing that denoted life. "Do you think they are inside one of the Bok Globules? Would that be enough to hide them from us?

Mel rolled her eyes. "Of course not. Bok Globules are only dark because their gas clouds are relatively thick compared to the vacuum of space. They are still only around ten to the four molecules per cubic centimetre. Breathable air is around ten to the nineteen molecules per cubic centimeter. That is fifteen factors higher." Her tone told me what she thought of such ignorance.

"Fine. So we would see them if they were in there. So where did they go?"

Mel glared. "I already told you, they must have some sort of invisibility shield. They are long gone. We should head to Vaer Nova. That is where they will go."

Sammy's mouth was open. He hated having to choose sides. He compromised by looking away from us both.

That irritated Mel. "And don't think you can avoid confrontation like that, Sammy! I am just saying what is logical. The only way they could disappear is by engaging some sort of invisibility cloak."

"Hmm." He shifted from his good foot to his bad foot. "I expect you are right."

I had to smile. Sammy is the worst person I know at prevaricating. Judging from the scowl he got from his girlfriend, she wasn't convinced either. She gave a heavy sigh and turned back to her monitor.

I was about to give in, when I remembered Scout. "Just a minute!"

I made my way off the bridge and down to my cabin. Scout was eager to be let loose to roam around the ship. He scuttled out of the door ahead of me and raced down the corridor past the gym, only stopping when he reached the bridge.I watched him closely. He nuzzled Mel and Sammy, then wagged his little tail at Denaraz and Seyal, who were also present.

After that, he snuffled his way around the room, thoroughly checking everything out. Finally he ended up standing beside the captain's station, staring out into the void as I so often did.

I sat down next to him, and watched his reaction.

At first he was quite calm. Then, suddenly, as he peered with his Geiga myopia at the visor, he stiffened. There were some long ten seconds as he sniffed the air and made little excited noises.

Shortly after that, he began to emit the one high-pitched note of warning that Geigas give on detecting danger. The sparse hairs he possessed stuck out of his body at right angles. He turned several times on the spot and then settled in a pointing position, his snout and his tail horizontal to the deck plating.

I noted the direction, feeling much more certain about the action to be taken.

"He's out there. Scout can sense him, too."

"Great," muttered Mel. "Now a Geiga is navigating!"

"Come on, Mel. You know that they can sense danger."

"Sure. Let's just ignore all the science, shall we? Let's take the word of a Geiga."

I decided to ignore her. She wasn't about to give in. "Take us slowly along that vector. I am going to sit outside on the hull. There must be something to see out there. Geigas are never wrong about danger."

There was more rolling of the eyes, but she did as I asked.

I went to the port airlock and began to suit up. Zenzara appeared beside me and did the same thing.

"You don't have to come," I told her. "I am only going out as an extra sensor."

"Then my eyes will help, will they not?"

"I guess."

We both suited up and slipped out of the airlock.

Outside, the spacescape was fantastic. The bright orange and yellows of the emission nebula off towards Aschasi were almost blinding. They filled your eyes and made it hard at first to see the small black smudges that were the Bok Globules.

For a few moments I was so struck that I was unable to speak. Judging by the expression on Zenzie's face, so was she. I could see her face clearly, which is an indicator of the strength of light reaching us from Aschasi.

Once we had become accustomed to the panorama in front of us, we found places on the fuselage to sit and look with more attention to detail. It wasn't going to be easy, particularly since we had no idea what it was that we were looking for.

We went through three bottles of air each before I caught a glimpse of something. I reached out and touched Zenzara's arm, pointing as accurately as I could at the tiny anomaly I had ... at least I thought I had ... spotted.

She spent many moments in a futile attempt to see what I had seen, her lips pressed together and her forehead crinkled. I was beginning to think that I must have imagined it myself, when she went still. My heart gave a leap. I knew in that moment that I had not been wrong.

Her eyes screwed up, as she tried to focus better. She pulled a face. "There ... there is something there ... but I can't make out what it is."

"It *is* there, though?"

"Yes. I can see where the Bok Globule behind it is just slightly lighter. It is almost invisible. Right on the limit of what my sight can detect." She blinked, as the intent to see more made her eyes hurt. "Is it a sphere?"

"I think so. A sphere hanging in space. They have made an artificial bubble in some way. I think they are inside it."

"So, how do we get in?"

"We don't. We will send the Enif. They are so good at EVA operations;

they will find out what that thing out there is."

"Can the Vaers see us, if we can see them?"

"Good point. We are going to have to be careful about that. We will send a couple of jet skis. They are so small that I doubt anything can detect them. Except a Geiga."

"How do Geigas work? I mean, how do they detect danger?"

"Nobody knows. They seem to see it, as you and I would see an obstacle before us. There have been scientific studies, but they generally don't work very well because if the danger is not real, the Geigas will not react. Of course, if the danger is real, the SPG would step in and the experiments would not be allowed."

"The SPG?"

"Society for the Protection of Geigas. It makes sure they are never exploited too far."

"Is that a Spacelander thing?"

"Yes. I am a member. You can't register a Geiga without going through various tests and a pysch eval."

Her eyebrows nearly touched her crest. "You passed a pysch eval??"

I started to laugh and gave her a push that almost unseated her from the fuselage. "Very funny."

"Yes. I thought so."

I began to take exact measurements of the anomaly. There was no easy way to gauge the distance, but I could pinpoint the other coordinates to within a meter. We would have to judge distance some other way. The sphere in front of us was giving off no signals. As far as our instruments were concerned, it was dead space. The vacuum itself. I wondered how it worked.

Once we were back inside, we filled in the others. I decided to keep intership silence for the time being, in case we could be monitored, so

Sammy took the shuttle over to *Aenysia* to brief Danaa and the others. He had instructions to tell them to dock with us. From now on we were going to be moving slowly. We could do that as one single entity.

With both ships stopped in space, it was easy to twist them around until the intership connection tubing could be deployed. Within an hour of Sammy's leaving, Neema was walking through it and onto our bridge.

Danaa was the one who surprised me. She stared at the almost invisible black circle in the sky and then nodded. "It is about two hundred kilometers away."

We all stared at her. "How can you tell?"

She gave us a blank look of incomprehension. "How can you not? Can't you see it?"

"Yes, but we can't tell how far away it is."

"Nepheals always know how far away things are. I thought everybody did."

"How?"

She gave me a how-should-I-know type of look. "We just do."

"Are you sure?"

Her face showed offence. "To within a kilometer, yes."

I nodded to Sammy. He began to slide the combined ship bundle toward the sphere.

"Go very, very slowly," I told him. "And drop us to a standstill about five kilometers short, will you. The Enif can take over from there."

He gave me a nod. I made my way down to the engine room, where Didjal and Eshaan spent most of their time.

They were pleased to have another mission and nodded when I explained.

"You need to know what this sphere is, and what is inside it," summarized Didjal when I finished.

"Yes. Without them detecting you, though. We are taking the ships in to five kilometers with as many of our systems shut down as possible. We will allow for scant life support and very small engine corrections. That should make us nigh invisible at five kilometers. As long as we stick to the dark side. They would spot us if we were to come between them and the Aschasi radiance."

"We will take the space skis, then?"

"Yes, because they should be undetectable. The mag sleds wouldn't work out there. You should be able to get right up to the thing on the skis."

Eshaan was looking cheerful. "Good. I like to do things like this."

"I thought you only painted?"

The Enif and its *faliif* exchanged a glance. "Our perception seems to be shifting. Although I was brought up to feel that my destiny was to paint, I have recently been finding that I can enjoy other things, can feel fulfilled in other ways."

Didjal stared at its feet. "Eshaan's new painting reflects this involvement. I too have found our new roles rewarding. I feel more ... complete."

You have to know something about the Enif to realize that this was almost a declaration of independence. Enif society is extremely rigid. To break the norms like this would lead to severe castigation. Just telling me about it was probably punishable. No longer were they looking uncomfortable.

"Good," I said, causing them both to look back up at me sharply. "I'm glad."

"You are not shocked?" Didjal seemed surprised.

"No. I believe in the individual. And I don't like putting people in boxes."

"Thank you Captain. That is a relief."

"I don't think anybody on this ship will tell you any different."

"Then we must stay on this ship."

Eshaan chittered. "We are not welcome back on Enifa, in any case."

"Their loss, our gain."

"Thank you, Captain. It is very good to know that you consider us useful."

"You two make little noise, but you are always there when we need you. And we wouldn't be here now if it weren't for you."

Their faces shone. "We will not let you down."

"I know that!"

We came to a complete halt some two hours later. I checked in with Danaa again.

"Yes. We are now around five thousand three hundred meters away from the sphere."

Now we were so close it was very obvious. Not because you could see it, but because it blocked out both light and darkness. It was much darker than the radiance of Aschasi, and slightly ... only slightly lighter than the darkness of the Bok Globules. Against open vacuum it would be utterly undetectable.

We watched as the space skis slid out of the shuttle bay. Space skis or space frames as they are also called, are small platforms with arrow-shaped handlebars at the front and three jet pack engines at the back. The platforms or frames themselves are hollow, so as to be able to carry a reasonable amount of fuel. The Enif had taken one each this time, and had assembled quite a display of technology on the first one. Part of the brief was to discover just what this sphere was, and how to get through it. Didjal had piled many instruments onto the two sleds.

They eased away from the combined ships as we watched. We were now floating in space, and had switched off all non-essential systems. So far, it seemed that we had managed to go unnoticed. I hoped that lasted. I had no wish to get into a space battle with the Vaers. They were bound to win.

The two Enif were soon out of sight. It is hard to spot tiny things in open space. Space is really, really big. The only thing that could have betrayed their presence were the flashes of light which might rebound off the mirror-like carapaces. For this reason they had shrouded themselves in a type of sackcloth that was generally used for stores. With that, they were soon completely undetectable against the immense background behind them.

Waiting was hard. We were concerned about the two Enif, which made it difficult to concentrate. I sent most of the crew to rest. We were likely to be extremely busy once the Enif came back with their intelligence. I don't think they slept, though. There was a sensation of excitement in the air. We all knew that we were going inside that sphere. We all knew that Agraala might not be the only one of us to die tying to stop Bull Cunningham and Ramesh Chandrayanan. It was a strange mixture of anticipation and fear.

The two Enif slipped back on board some eight hours later. Their carapaces were dulled, a sure sign that they had overstayed their time in outer space. Both looked exhausted.

We crowded around them as they opened our side of the airlock.

"What is it?"

"What did you find out?"

"Are they there?"

"Whatever is that thing?"

"Are you all right?"

Eshaan merely nodded. It looked too tired to comment. Didjal held up a hand for a few moments as it began to recover a little of his usual colour, then told us what they had seen.

"The sphere is hollow. What you see is a thin, traversable shell. It isn't a force field at all. It can't block solid objects. What it *does* do is trap carbon molecules seeded with diamond glitter in a spherical shell."

"Interesting. What is the purpose of that?"

"The carbon molecules form a dark barrier. It means that light will not penetrate. The diamond glitter, which is really diamond dust in suspension, blocks sensor arrays from penetrating inside. It is very clever. The concept is stunningly simple."

"They took the lessons they learned on the moon and adapted the tech," I said slowly.

"Exactly. The composition of the spherical barrier is exactly the same as the moon. They simply exported some of the dust. They made the diamond dust on the moon and then mixed it with the carbon dust."

"But how do they keep it in the shell?" I asked. "Why doesn't it simply spill off into space?"

Didjal's antennae twitched. "That is the really clever part. They have kicked out two carbon atoms in some of the molecules and replaced them with enzenium, forming an enzenium vacant center. The enzenium has strong binding properties and because of this they have been able to encourage it to form chains. The end product is a tight spherical sheet of carbon molecules only an atom in width."

"Which they use to trap the normal carbon inside?"

Didjal nodded. "Exactly. There are two sheets of retaining chains, with the normal carbon dust and the diamond glitter trapped inside."

"Very clever. Did you take samples?"

"Of course."

"Good. These carbon bubbles sound like something we might want to emulate one day."

"It is a most effective way to make a ship disappear," agreed Didjal. "I thought so myself."

Zenzie was fed up with so much chit-chat about carbon. "What about the Vaers? Are they in there?"

"We think so."

"Think so? Can't you see them?"

"No. We can't. We believe that there are carbon bubbles, as the captain calls them, inside carbon bubbles. The main area within the shell appears to be empty, though there is a strange structure in the centre. We could see no ships."

Denaraz stepped forward. "What did the structure look like?"

"It was a large construction made of what our sensors told us was solid light."

My heart dropped. "That is why the ships are contained in smaller carbon bubbles. They need the laboratory area to be isolated from anything else. This whole sphere is their next laboratory. They are going to construct the wormhole right here, in front of our eyes!"

Didjal met its *faliif's* gaze. Neither of them appeared to be very happy with what they had seen. "I am afraid so, Captain. And, from what we saw, they are very close to succeeding."

"Can we torpedo them?" I turned to face Denaraz.

He considered. "I don't think so. The Diamond glitter in the shell will destabilize the software. We probably could if we were inside the shell."

"Right. Let's break through then," I said grimly. "The time has come to finish this, once and for all. We will take both ships."

Zenzara grabbed at my hand. "You can't! What about the Chakrans?"

"What about them?"

"That would destroy the strands as well. You can't do that! We don't know if they are still linked to the rest of their species. We can't use missiles!"

"What do you expect me to do," I snapped, "—wait until they have a network of wormholes throughout this cluster?"

"Stop!" She dropped her weight to the ground so that she was acting as a physical anchor. "Stop, Mallivan! You are wrong!"

I ground to a halt, cross with her. "We cannot risk them succeeding. Can't you see that?"

"Of course I can. I am not stupid!" she hissed. Her claws came out of her fingers. She was extremely angry. "But listen, will you? Please?"

I gave a sigh. "Go ahead." She certainly deserved a hearing. She had proved that over and over again. I was only the captain. That didn't make me right. And I was angry myself. That didn't help.

"We need to go in there silently. Not with all guns blazing. We need to get the Chakran strands back in the Nexus. If we can."

"But the Nexus is irrelevant. It just enables the Chakrans to communicate with you. Doesn't it?"

"No. I don't think it is that simple. I believe that if the Nexus is destroyed close to the mouth of a wormhole, it will kill all the Chakrans who have strands inside it. And that could put the whole Chakran population at risk. Agraala explained it to me. She said that they must all be interconnected. And that makes them horribly vulnerable and fragile. The whole race could be in danger if the Nexus is eliminated."

My mouth dropped open. "Are you kidding me? You think that, if we blow up the Nexus here, the whole Chakran race will die?"

"It is what Agraala thought, yes."

"She can't have known that for sure!"

"And we can't know that it isn't true!" she said hotly. "She was an expert on nonlocality. I think she knew a little bit more about the Chakrans than you do!"

I stared at the faces around me. Denaraz took one small step towards Zenzie. He was declaring his support for her in a subtle way.

I felt drained. Every time I made a clear decision it turned cloudy. I looked around the group. Didjal was the engineer. And Danaa was the one who had known Agraala best.

"Danaa?"

Her brow was almost as furrowed as Zenzara's. "I didn't talk specifically to my aunt about this, but if she said it could lead to the annihilation of the Chakrans, we need to take her opinion very seriously indeed. She knew more about quantum nonlocality than anybody else on our planet."

I blew out air in frustration. "So we can't just blow this thing up?"

Didjal chattered to Eshaan for a few seconds, in one of their lightning fast exchanges skin on skin. Then it nodded slowly. "Our knowledge would lead us to believe that exploding one of the nodes might destroy all of them. Nobody on our world has studied nonlocality in living beings. We cannot be sure, but I think that they would at best be severely compromised. I would not recommend it."

"Very well." I ground my teeth. "If we can't go in with all guns firing, what can we do?"

"We have to retrieve the strands. Once that is done, we can destroy the rest of the installation."

"Do we know where they are?"

Eshaan nodded. It held up a storage chip. "I have the detailed scan of the whole sphere here."

"Right. Let's get that up on the main screen and see if we can make a plan."

We all made our way back to the bridge and began to study the data the two Enif had brought back.

"There!" Zenzie looked tremendously pleased with herself. "Right there. See?"

We all squinted at the position she had highlighted. "I can see a blob of some sort," I said doubtfully.

"That is where they are keeping the Chakran strands."

"Are you sure?"

She stood up proudly. "I am."

I shrugged. "You are the Chyzar."

Denaraz frowned. "Then we need to get past the structure of solid light and up to that area right at its center."

"How do we do that? Without them picking us off one by one?"

Eshaan looked thoughtful. "Remember, the carbon bubble works both ways. If we can't see in, I doubt very much that they can see out."

"So we simply walk in and steal it? Surely it can't be that easy?"

That made Izan laugh.

I looked at him.

"Just amused by your idea of easy," he said.

"I meant ..."

"... I know what you meant. And, no, I don't think it will be that easy. I imagine they have some defense mechanisms in place. I would if I were them."

"Do we know where their ship is?"

"Yes. Once we figured out that there had to be inner carbon bubbles, we were able to detect their positions. From inside we could scan the outer walling, which left several areas of decreased depth. There are three inner bubbles ... here ... here ... and here." He pointed them out. Once you knew what you were looking for they were not hard to see.

"All right. I suggest that we split our party into four groups, then. We can each go in from a different angle, and hope one can retrieve the missing strands."

There was some shuffling of feet. I looked around.

"Danaa, you, Zenzara and Denaraz are group one. Ignore anything else that is happening and concentrate on releasing the Chakrans. The other groups will try to protect you."

They gave solemn nods.

"Eshaan and I will take your right hand side. Seyal will come with us."

Eshaan and Seyal nodded.

"Sammy, we need you to stay here. Keep the ships together and be ready either for evacuation or for arms deployment."

He looked disappointed. "Right."

I knew how he felt. "I am sorry, but we need somebody with experience here. It may be vital."

"I know. I won't let you down."

"Neema, you and Anzany can take the lead group's left. That leaves Didjal and Mel for the last jet ski. You will cover the rear."

Seyal bustled away quickly. "I will set up Segaton's playpen on the bridge," she said. "That way Sammy will be able to keep an eye on him without leaving his station."

Sammy gave me an accusing look. I grinned back and spread my arms out. I couldn't help it, could I? She could hardly take her baby into action with her.

He gave a sort of huffy sound and shook his head. "Fine. Just fine."

She responded with a grateful smile. "Thank you Sammy."

"Whatever."

*

It took us two further hours to get everything we thought we might need onto four separate jet frames. It was like going back in time. I was kicking myself for not having foreseen this when we were on the moon. This was all because of Bull Cunningham and Ramesh Chandrayanan. I should have shot the pair of them right there and then. Now we were back. Different place, different time, same aim.

We left Sammy looking forlorn. He was unworried about being in charge of armaments and both ships, but seemed alarmed at being in sole control of a baby.

"What do I do if it cries?" he wailed at Seyal's back. "I don't know anything about these things."

Seyal's inexpressive face regarded him for a couple of moments. "He is a baby," she said, as though speaking to an idiot. "A baby! You give him something to eat and pat him on the back. What do you think you have to do?"

He bristled. "Well, how would I know?"

Seyal rolled her eyes. On an Avarak face, that was alarming. Sammy's eyes widened.

"You *do* know how to change a nappy?" she asked.

"Of course! That is … I … err … I suppose so."

"Don't they teach you Spacelanders anything?"

"That is a female … err … sort of thing."

"You sound like an Avarak man!"

"I don't!" The idea clearly horrified Sammy. "I don't!"

"Yes you do," Mel informed him. "Never mind, Sammy. Segaton won't eat you."

Sammy seemed unconvinced, but we left him to his fate anyway. He glared at me as I entered the airlock, last of all. "I bet *you* don't know how to change a nappy either, Rye!" he muttered.

"How hard can it be?" I replied lightly, quickly shutting the airlock door before he made me admit to it in public. I didn't. And I must say, I didn't particularly want to learn. "By the way, I am leaving Scout here. Don't forget to feed him too!"

His face mouthed at me through the soundproof glass. His expression was threatening.

I waved. "Sure! Whatever! Take care!" Not going to happen, Sammy. Not a chance.

I turned with some difficulty and grabbed onto the space ski Eshaan and Seyal had already aimed towards the carbon bubble. There were nods to each side and then we all set off in a group.

It was an eerie experience. Pushing off from a safe ship into outer space is akin to stepping off a high-rise building. It is terrifying. The only one of us who looked even remotely happy was Mel. She was glad to get out of the ship, though I knew that EVA suits were a bane, too.

As we were dragged along by the jet frames the other groups gradually faded into the darkness of the background. Even the radiance of the emission clouds behind the Bok Globules was not enough for me to be able to pick them out easily. They were simply too small. Zenzie's group, the nearest, were visible, but the others were soon just a pinprick against the backdrop of space. There is nothing like EVA operations to make you feel small. Tiny.

Tiny enough to wonder what possible consequences my one, small human life could have on the universe. At that time and that moment it was pure hubris to think I could have any footprint, any impact whatsoever.

Yet here we were, attempting to help an entity that stretched across thousands and thousands of galaxies. One that was capable of expanding my atoms to infinity and killing me with just a single thought, if I got too close.

Why hadn't the Chakrans done just that with Bull Cunningham and his friends? Expanded them out to infinity?

I should use my brain more often! The only reason for the Chakrans not to act is that they couldn't. Which, in its turn meant that Cunningham still held at least part of the Nexus, still had it contained. And it must also mean that having part of the Nexus contained affected all of the rest. Of course Zenzie was right. I should have been able to come to that conclusion on my own. I felt cross at my own slowness. It stood to reason that the Chakrans would have aborted this whole second effort to build a traversable wormhole if they could have. Which meant that they couldn't.

We *had* to release them from their confinement.

The alternative was Vaer dominance, and war. A war that would involve everybody in the Major Shells. A war that could involve worlds that we knew nothing about. Species living billions of light years away. That simply could not be allowed to happen.

I felt a sudden surge of anger against Bull. He felt some sort of strange justification for his actions, but it came from twisted facts and convoluted reasoning. I couldn't follow it. It simply seemed megalomaniac to me. He had to be stopped. And I was one of the ones who had to stop him. I was amazed that, back on *Commorancy*, I had thought him perfectly normal. He had seemed amusing and interesting, if perhaps a little too bent on restoring the former glory of the Terrans. What a fool I had been!

Now his expansionist plans were a threat to all the Major Shells and beyond.

Our group bumped gently against the outer shell of the carbon bubble. I was surprised to feel its resistance to us. It was only a few angstroms thick yet it pressed back on us slightly, almost a reluctance in space. It was there, yet not there.

We exchanged a look then continued on. The barrier didn't require any effort to break. It represented only a moment of hesitation on our journey. Then we were through, and could see what was inside the huge bubble.

Hanging in space, glistening slightly in what was otherwise complete darkness, was the cage of light. It must have been forty meters in diameter. The thick bands of solid light were woven like scaffolding into a hypersphere, which itself was rotating around its central point. This rotation caused the radiance from the light to flicker, until the whole thing resembled a disco ball.

In front of me I could see Zenzie's group making its way determinedly towards the hypersphere. My mouth was dry. Had I sent them to their deaths? Solid light can be just as lethal as a laser. More, in fact. It might decimate them in seconds.

I tore my gaze away from the nucleus. As I stared around me, I could see the outline of the sub-bubbles quite easily. They were just a shade lighter than the surrounding darkness. The largest was around two hundred meters away, tucked to the side of the hypersphere.

Eshaan nodded when I pointed. He and Seyal began to direct the jet frame in the direction of the hypersphere while I tried not to look sideways at Zenzara's group. Nothing I could do now was going to change their future. I just had to concentrate on doing my part of the operation correctly. We were here to protect them and reach the Chakrans if they were unable to. Worrying about the other groups could only damage the outcome. I grabbed a hold of one of the large weapons we had brought with us. I was pretty sure we were going to see some action shortly. Although the bubbles were opaque, it would be naive to assume that the Vaers had not set up some sort of surveillance system.

They had. Only minutes after we had penetrated the carbon bubble the space surrounding the hidden Vaer ships rippled. About ten groups of their space skis appeared, with four skis to each group.

"Uh oh."

Seyal turned an enquiring face to me. I nodded in the direction of the approaching fleet.

"The odds are not good."

She gave one of her slow, sweet smiles and then lifted a determined chin. "*Avarak Karax!*"

It seemed like the only thing to say at such a time. "*Avarak Karax!*" I told her back. We started to prep our weapons. Eshaan, on the other side of the frame, reached for its M596 rifle.

The Vaer fleet of skis was soon traveling at a faster speed than our space frames could manage, but the few minutes of grace we had achieved played in our favor. We were already closing on the spinning hypersphere. Close up, it was quite petrifying. The spars of light swept by like animated guillotines. There were scant seconds between each one.

The space frame in front of us had already reached the hypersphere. It hovered for a moment. My heart missed a few beats before deciding to continue beating. I crossed my fingers as best I could in an EVA suit.

There was a pause as four of the solid light spars raced past the small vessel, then it darted through the vacuum. I saw sparks flying out of the back end of the frame as the following spar of light caught the space ski on the rear strut. The frame itself tumbled over and over, pushed luckily towards the centre of the rotating sphere.

I saw three small shapes clinging on for dear life as their frame flipped in space. Zenzie was stretched out behind it, only being kept in place by Denaraz's firm hand around her wrist. The rest of her was floating loose.

I just managed to see Izan drag her back to the frame before I became too occupied to watch their progress. The skis behind us had begun to fire. They were aiming directly at the lead jet ski, which was extremely dangerous, because their fire was ricocheting off the solid light scaffolding that made up the hypersphere and peppering our positions.

We all ducked as best we could behind the jet frames. They were better than nothing, though not by much.

There were shouts from the Vaers behind us. The leader was berating them for hitting the hypersphere. They were being told to aim directly at out skis. That put Mel and Didjal, behind us, in the most endangered position. Scores of pulser beams drove through the vacuum to converge on their frame, which bucked and twisted in response to Newton's third law.

Didjal grabbed a hold of Mel with one hand and a portable space pack with the other and pushed off from behind the cover of the space frame. They dove as fast as the hand-held space pack could take them for the hypersphere.

I had come to the same conclusion. We would all be better off inside the sphere than outside. We were never going to get to the other bubbles. The safest place now was inside the hypersphere. It was clear that the Vaers didn't want to risk damaging the thing with weapons fire. If they wanted us they would have to come in and get us.

Nor was it any use trying to get back to Mel and Didjal. They were closer to the sphere than they were to us. They would have to take their chances.

Our jet frame was beginning to come under fire, too. Already several pulses had come near to impacting us.

I signaled to Eshaan and Seyal to abandon the ski where it was. We dragged individual jet packs out of the storage bin and detached a pack each from the ski. Then we did the same as Didjal – abandon the frame to its fate and head with all speed for the hypersphere. I hoped that Neema and Anzany, on the far side, were doing the same.

We covered the intervening fifteen or so meters in record time. Then we stopped, poised. The light framework was terrifying as it axed past our position. There was hardly any time to duck through the gap before the next girder whipped past.

I swallowed. We had formed a line of three, abreast, staring at the depths of the hypersphere, trying to calculate the time it would take to get across. Whatever calculation my brain did, it was too long.

But we equally couldn't stay where we were. The pulsers were getting closer and closer as the Vaers converged on our position. They were no longer aiming solely at the space frame, which now hung, destroyed, in space. They were able to target us individually. If not for the fact that they were trying very hard not to hit the sphere, we would have already been hit. Soon they would be close enough to us to have a safe angle for a killing shot.

We couldn't wait.

I nodded to the people on either side of me.

"Each on his own count!" I told them.

They gave me a thumbs up. Their faces showed panic. Eshaan had gone grey and Seyal's face was just a blob behind her helmet.

I blocked out everything except the rotating shafts of light. Then I realized that there was an easier way to do this. If we could hook a grappler on the spar as it rolled past, we would be dragged up to the same speed as the rotating girder. Then it would be an easy task to slide inside the sphere because we would be moving at equal speeds.

I nudged the people to each side.

They both stared at me. They had been about to jump.

I rummaged in my bag and pulled out the standard foldable grappler. Their faces cleared as they understood what I was telling them. They hurried to do the same.

I made sure that my bag was firmly attached to my EVA suit, and then coiled up the rope so that it wouldn't foul when it was deployed. I clipped the other end to my suit.

Then I clipped the parts into place and began to wield the grappler, twirling it with my hands until it began to describe circles over my head, like an old-fashioned lasso. I kept an eye on the struts of light as they knifed past. Then, just as one bar passed my position, I released the grappler.

It spun into the sphere and I lost sight of it as the following strut bore down on me. Then the rope went instantly from loose to tight.

I was jerked forwards with an impulse that almost broke my back. However, with no air resistance I was soon up to the same speed as the cartwheeling struts. In fact, centripetal acceleration dragged me back. I found myself folded over the second strut.

It took me some moments to disentangle the rope and pull myself up and over the rib that had fouled the line. Then I simply hauled my suit and I up hand over hand towards the grapple. I could have left it behind, but I was worried I might need it again.

Once I got to the grapple, I took a moment to look at my surroundings. I probably shouldn't. They gave me vertigo.

I was perched right on the outermost point of one of the long girders. It was scything through space, turning me from up to side, to down, to side, to up again with appalling regularity. My head was spinning and my stomach threatening to vomit up what little food I had had recently, even though my weightlessness had no direction. It was very unnerving.

However, I was now at a standstill compared to the framework surrounding me. From now on, it was simple. I hoped. All I had to do was drag myself down the tapering triangular corridor formed by the diminishing rafters. As they got closer to the centre, they were shorter and shorter so that the space between them became smaller and smaller. Right at the center, I could discern a small dark spot where there was something positioned in the middle. Hopefully, it contained the missing Chakran strands.

Although I looked to see if the others had successfully mounted the spinning framework, I wasn't able to see anyone else at first. I was wasting time looking, so I ducked back inside the sphere and began to inch along the treacherous way to the inner confines of the peculiar framework.

Each step was extremely taxing. I had thought that I would be at rest with the framework and therefore able to use the space jet. That didn't happen. Because of the centripetal force, I was pulled back from the line of spin. My legs trailed out in space behind me. I did wonder if, by letting go completely, this phenomenon would disappear. I didn't dare attempt it. If I were wrong, I would be spattered on the following strut. The risk seemed too large for the gain in time.

So it became a question of painstakingly progressing along the inside crossbars, all the while feeling that my body was being tugged in about a thousand different directions. It was quite the worst physical sensation I had ever had. That includes having a fully-conscious operation when I was six, when a scalpel was used to scrape off bone spars high up in my right nostril.

I was actually sick more than once, which gave me the pleasant task of continuing through a helmet full of floating lethal vomit. You should try it. Luckily spacesuits are designed to quickly take such effluents away from the head, lest you breathe it into your lungs, where it would kill you. It is not a pleasant thing to happen to an astronaut, however. We generally try to avoid it. I wished I had. I felt increasingly more and more miserable.

Things did not improve when I spotted two Vaers behind me. They had managed to get into the same part of the framework where I was, and were doggedly making their way towards me. They were not there to congratulate me. It was going to be a fight to the death.

With half a cup of my own vomit sloshing around in the base of my neck, I really didn't feel likely to perform at my best.

They came at me just the same. They were twice my size. They had ditched their heavy guns, which were no use to them now, and were carrying knives. EVA suits are strong. They are made to resist being punctured. They are not made to resist hard thrusts with an extremely sharp fighting knife. Terrific.

The first one reached me with a grin on his face. I could see his factions quite clearly through the visor on his helmet. He was delighted to be the first to get to me. He thought the kill was his, for sure.

I wasn't sure he was wrong.

He lunged at me, his arm outstretched, the knife glistening against the whirling hypersphere. My senses fixated on the glint along the edge of the thing. It was almost mesmerizing.

I only reacted at the last minute. I placed my feet below me on the large spar and pushed off with all my might. That impulse took me away from the framework and thrust me towards the next girder.

The Vaer pushed off behind me. He was still looking pleased with himself.

I have never been inside a firework, but I came pretty near it then. The hypersphere was a gigantic Catherine wheel, and I was inside the sparks. Light scattered and rebounded everywhere, but the background was pitch black.

I floated out in the centre of the cell structure I found myself in. I discovered that there was no sense of acceleration once I left the struts. I knew the Vaer couldn't touch me while I was in freefall. He had nothing to anchor himself to, which meant that his knife arm would be unable to bring the full power he possessed to bear.

I smiled at him though my spattered visor. I must still have looked a bit green, because his own grin slipped.

His vector was straight; he would hit me unless I took evasive action.

He looked smug. He clearly wasn't much given to thought. He came at me and lifted his knife arm in order to strike. Then he gave a tremendous push with that arm, attempting to give the weapon enough force to puncture my EVA suit.

The knife came straight at me. I twisted slightly to avoid him, careful not to overdo the response. The move was most uncomfortable because it meant that some of the vomit sloshed back towards my nose and mouth. I had to hold my breath to avoid inspiring it.

The blade missed my torso by the narrowest of margins. It spun past, taking him with it. I gave him a small wave of one hand as he passed me. His eyes were now looking confused.

I knew why. His whole body was following the knife. He had gone into a spin.

Space spins are not fun, let me tell you. They may be one degree better than floating around in your own regurgitated food, but they are still pretty uncomfortable. I watched with some interest. It looked to me as if someone had omitted to give him anti-spin training. The outflung arm now led his whole heavy torso and the spin had become a pirouette. He looked quite cute, rather like a hippopotamus attempting ballet positions.

He was on a track to be expelled altogether from the hypersphere. That might be dangerous for him. I probably should feel pity.

I would have liked to follow his progress further, but a shadow that moved at the corner of my eye pulled my attention back to my own position.

The second Vaer had decided to go for the easy way out. He had dragged a small hand-held projectile gun out of his belt and was aiming at my chest. Such ammunition in such a low caliber was unlikely to damage the hypersphere even if he did miss, which at this distance was unlikely. I opened my hands in a sign of capitulation. He ignored me. I wagged one finger at him in warning. Surely everybody knew you shouldn't fire projectile guns when in freefall? He ignored that, too. On his head be it.

He fired.

The bullet buried itself in my chest.

He was flung backwards and began to spin in a clockwise direction around his pulser arm. His mouth dropped open in shock and his legs scrabbled to get traction on the vacuum. I could have told him that wasn't going to work.

Then he crashed backwards into the crossbar of the solid light framework. His back bent in a most unnatural-looking way. His helmet cracked forward and he slumped near the spar, unconscious.

I assessed my situation. I was in the centre of the cell structure, and I had been shot. I could feel blood trickling out of my chest into the EVA suit, although I could still breathe more or less normally, so it couldn't have hit a lung. Could it?

I did feel woozy and rather unclear about what exactly to do next. I checked the original attacker. He had his own problems. He was still spinning and was about to exit the hypersphere altogether. He was no longer a threat.

I looked further afield, but there was no more pursuit. The Vaers must be concentrating their attack on another area.

I disentangled my jet pack and switched it on. All I had to do now is head along this cell towards the center of the hypersphere.

The hypersphere was formed by large concentric circles of solid light, but these were reinforced every so often by transverse struts. So the outside circle was criss-crossed with bars, making curved rectangles in space. As I looked towards the center of the sphere, I saw a long line of these rectangles, each slightly smaller than the other, forming a diminishing corridor towards the core. There was nothing visible at the nucleus. I wondered why. I should have been able to see the canister.

I engaged the jet pack and headed towards the heart of the hypersphere. Look as I might, I couldn't see any other members of the team. I crossed my fingers that they had come up with Vaers unused to EVA, like my two had been. If they had been more experienced, they could easily have dealt with me.

I began to giggle. In my defense, I had a hole in my chest, and the contents of my stomach in my face. I was not at my best. It wasn't exactly funny, but it did tickle my fancy for some reason. I was hardly the superhero, beaming in to save the situation.

I determined to keep going, anyway. Somewhere in there I would find the rest of my team. That was the thing that I grasped. I wasn't sure whether they would save me or whether I would save them. It didn't matter. I was like a small homing pigeon. I had to find them.

The blood seeping out of my wound was warm, but it cooled rapidly. It was coagulating into a jelly-like substance now. Perhaps it would push back on the wound and help to seal it. I hoped so.

The Catherine wheel spun around me. I was sick again, but there was nothing except a small amount of bile left to come up. That was a relief.

The colors of the revolving structure were evolving the deeper I traveled inside it. It was turning around me with rainbow flashes. The colors were so deep and so bright that I had to close my eyes some of the time. They blinded me. Even through the tightly closed lids, I was aware of the strobing pigments. They mixed together to form a flashing aura.

The world narrowed to my own perception, my own breath, my own small slice of spacetime. It became hard to keep going, hard to persevere in whatever it was that I was attempting to do. I was suspended in a cotton-wool world that was a cocoon of protection.

I lost all track of time.

My hands slipped on the jet pack, so it was lucky that I had pressed the automatic button. I felt myself tip backwards, until I was being towed along behind it.

I thought I was hallucinating, but in hindsight the colors must have been real. I was just weak, confused and unable to focus. I must have been drifting in and out of consciousness.

Some time later I felt the tiniest resistance that indicated another carbon bubble. I must have passed through it, for there was movement nearby. I tried to open my eyes, but could only manage to let the tiniest chink of light through them.

Hands manhandled me onto a platform. I managed to get my eyelids to crack open a little more. I giggled to see Zenzara staring at me, her crest rigid.

"I'm f-f-fine," I told her with a sensation of tremendous relief. "I'm home now."

"He is delusional," said a male voice. It sounded cross with me. "He has been wounded."

I was pulled onto something horizontal. My helmet was unscrewed. The person who had done that took a leap backwards.

"Ugh! This thing is full of vomit!" There were retching noises.

"Get the EVA suit off him. I can't see where he is hit."

They dragged my appendages out of the bulky space suit. Zenzie was still retching. She was also muttering to herself, but her crest had softened a little. She was no longer quite so worried.

"What happened to you, Mallivan?" she asked. I think it was a rhetorical question, but I attempted to answer anyway.

"I ... I ... got shot. And I ... I threw up."

"Yes," she said drily. "I noticed. Very ... appetizing." She retched again.

Denaraz snapped at her. "Get a grip, will you. I need help with this wound."

She glared at him. "Don't speak to me like that. I am the Chyzar!"

"At this particular moment, you are useless!"

"How dare you say that!" Her claws came out of their sheaths. "Take it back!"

He ignored her, much to her chagrin. He gave a sigh. "Ahhh! Here! This is where the bullet went in. Good, good, the spacesuit stopped a lot of the momentum and it was diverted by your ribs, missing both heart and lungs. Looks like you were lucky." I didn't feel lucky; there was a wrench of pain somewhere in my chest and I think I must have lost consciousness for a short time. When I swam back into the real world, Izan was already affixing one of the wound-closing automatic bandages over the wound. He pulled the sides of my IEVA suit back together and slapped my shoulder. "You'll do."

I struggled to prop myself up onto one elbow. "Thank you. Go on, I will be all right."

"You will have to be. We still haven't managed to break into the containment canister. Danaa is working on it."

I tried to look around. My whole body felt as though it might snap at any moment. Danaa was hunched over a control panel and gave me an airy smile. I couldn't see anyone else. "The others?"

He shrugged. "Not made it to the center. Yet. We are in another carbon bubble, so we can't see outside the skin. But the Chakran node is here."

I realized I was breathing. "There is air here."

He nodded. "There is. We presume it was to enable Chandrayanan to work here without being impeded by bulky suits."

"Is he here now?" I couldn't keep the anger out of my voice.

"No." Denaraz sounded regretful, too. "There was nobody here when we arrived."

He slipped me a gun. "We have artificial gravity on this platform, too. You can use this, if you have to."

"Fine." I waved them back. "You three get on, then. I have got your backs."

He slapped me again on the arm. "Good man!"

I was left to recuperate, tensely watching the surrounding skin of the carbon bubble. We had reached the core, or at least some of us had. But we still had to save the missing Chakran strands.

15

I whirled round as I became aware of a slight ripple in the fabric of the small carbon cloud we were currently in. I took careful aim with the pulser. It wouldn't do to miss. Not at this distance.

A split second before firing, I realized who this had to be. The glossy black color of the foot was unmistakable. That could only be an Enif. I lowered the gun and rushed to help the arrival, pulling it through the skin. It was Eshaan.

"Are you all right?" It dropped down, suddenly affected by the gravity inside the bubble. I grabbed at its arm, forgetting that this was one of the few taboos that the Enif have. I dropped my own hands. "Sorry!"

Eshaan looked weary. It took in the air around us and the grayish tinge to its carapace began to disappear. "It does not matter, Captain. I thank you for your help." It looked around. "Seyal and the others are not here?"

I shook my head. "Not yet, anyway. Do you have a weapon still?"

It nodded. "I was unable to use the pulser out there."

"Me neither. Were you attacked?"

"I was. Three of the Vaers made it inside the hypersphere with me. However, they were inexperienced fighting in zero g. I was able to evade their rather clumsy attempts to kill me."

I grinned. "Throw them out of the hypersphere, did you?"

"They are no longer inside, certainly."

I was impressed. Eshaan had done better than me, for sure. "Well done!"

It gave a slight shrug. "The Vaer are large creatures, but they lack the organization and precision necessary to be great fighters."

"You almost sound sorry for them?"

"They were ejected from their birth world. I am unsurprised that they have evolved into the creatures that they are today. They have had to fight for each and every advance. The Prime Vaers have a lot to answer for."

"I suppose they have." The Nova Vaers had certainly been left to fend for themselves on a planet with little or no vegetation and fauna. That could not have been easy. Not only that, but the offenders had been segregated on two separate continents. No wonder they had become rival factions for the scant resources on the planet.

But all that had been thousands of years ago. Now, the Nova Vaers were simply pirates. And they weren't renowned for their compassion. They traded in anything they could, and preferred to grab it rather than buy it. They were cruel and vicious. Eshaan knew that, better than many.

It must have realized what I was thinking. "I will never forgive them," it tried to explain. "They took our life's artwork. They are lacking in any appreciation of beauty. They are boorish creatures. But our history determines who we are. It gave me no pleasure to kill three Vaers who were at a disadvantage because of their lack of training. It was not a proud moment for me."

I sympathized. I hadn't had to kill my two attackers, but they had probably died in any case, unable to regain the safety of their ship. He was right. Such victories are slightly hollow.

I started to agree with it, but there was another interruption. Two jet packs edged their way through the skin of the central carbon bubble, and we leapt to help Neema and Anzany as they slumped to the floor of the central plinth inside the bubble.

Neema was fine, if rather disheveled, but Anzany had been shot. Her right arm was hanging uselessly by her side.

I ushered her to the platform, which I now realized was the space frame that Zenzie's group had come in on. Neema hurried over too, and between us we stripped Anzany of her EVA suit. There was a clean in-and-out bullet wound through her upper arm. Her crest was curled up in pain, but she was still trying to smile at all of us.

"Just wrap it up," she said brightly.

Neema frowned. "You are not a take-away."

"This is nothing. Look, Rye has been shot too. Don't make a fuss, Neems."

Neema peered at my midsection. "Are you all right, Mallivan?"

"Yes." I was busy administering first aid. "Have you seen any of the others? Seyal, Mel and Didjal are still missing."

"We spotted Mel and Didjal. They were all right when we last saw them. They were in the channel next to ours. But there were several Vaers after them. We only had one. Unfortunately, he managed to shoot Anzany before I could deal with him."

I didn't have to ask his fate. It was written on Neema's face. She looked positively bloodthirsty. "Didjal will cope with a few Vaers."

"I hope so."

There was another disturbance in the skin of the carbon cloud and Mel pushed through, towing an inert Enif behind her.

As soon as they penetrated into the gravity field, we surged forward to stop the unconscious Didjal from falling the six feet to the platform.

I stared down at it. Its carapace was a whitish-grey and its huge eyes were clouded over completely.

Neema helped Mel down. I noticed that she was shaking, but I couldn't tear my attention away from Didjal. I knelt down beside it. "What happened?"

Her voice was anguished. "It put itself in front of me. It had taken out two of the Vaers, but there were two more, and they decided to come for me. It somehow managed to get its body positioned to shield mine. Both Vaers fired. It was hit twice."

Eshaan came racing over. It took one look at its faliif and crossed its hands. Then it gave me an apologetic look before dropping its long body to the ground and curling up next to Didjal, adjusting its own thin body so that it touched its *faliif's* in as many places as possible.

"No!" I knew immediately what this meant. They were both entering the Enif state of enlightenment. Eshaan thought that Didjal was dying and was preparing itself to die beside it. *Faliifs* always die at the same time. When the cordotonal organs of one fail, its partner will curl up beside its dying partner, touching it so as to permit the sharing of its own cordotonal organs. This permits both Enif to live until such time as the organs of one of them is not sufficient to feed the bodies of both of them. When that happens, the cordotonal organs of the second Enif will fail, and they will both die together.

Enif usually live for only around sixty years, giving them thirty years of youth, and thirty years of productivity. They decline very suddenly, usually passing from health to death in something like 24 hours.

They will commune for those last hours, and only their nearest *Belofiin* may join briefly with them towards the end of enlightenment to record any lasting insights for posterity. The *Belofiin* will then bless them both, and withdraw to wait solemnly for their joint death.

This is a happy event, as it is said that *faliifs* truly join in the moment of their death, becoming one soul forever. Their local group will rejoice and celebrate such a union for two whole days. These days are called the days of plurality. From the day of their death, their names are also joined into one and all accomplishments are considered to belong to that one new, plural individual.

I shook Eshaan's shoulders, which resembled those of a canine of some sort, sharp and sloping. "You can't do this now! We need you! We need you both."

Eshaan's multifaceted eyes were reflecting the hypersphere

colors with glowing iridescence. "My *faliif* is entering the state of enlightenment. I must accompany it on this journey. We must become one."

I shook him again. "Not now, Eshaan! Stop it! You cannot do this now! Think! We have to save the Chakrans. We have to. Please!"

Its eyes dulled with pain. "I cannot leave Didjal to die alone. I cannot."

"Then help me save it. It has lost a lot of ..." I was going to say blood, but the liquid oozing out of the Enif was not really blood. I didn't know what it was. "... strength," I ended up with, rather lamely. "But we can still save it! I know we can."

"The state of enlightenment should not be halted. It is so written."

I sighed with frustration. "Please, Eshaan. I know I am asking a great sacrifice from you, but we really do need both of you. Let me save Didjal. Let me try to postpone its ... err ... your enlightenment."

There was a long silence. Eshaan seemed to be looking at the center of the carbon bubble, where Danaa, Denaraz and Zenzara were still struggling to find a way into the canister that had been placed at the center. It was not proving easy.

An expression of doubt crossed Eshaan's face. "Our people never interfere with enlightenment. It is forbidden. Only a *Belofiin* may interpret whether or not the time is right. Only a *Belofiin* can determine if lives should be artificially prolonged."

I jumped on that. "Then it is possible for enlightenment to be postponed?"

"By a *Belofiin*. Very occasionally. In exceptional circumstances."

I waved an arm at our surroundings. "There is no *Belofiin*. There can be no *Belofiin*."

"No."

"There are exceptional circumstances?"

He looked down at Didjal. "Yes. Possibly."

"And I can help him medically. I can withdraw the bullets. I can help close the wounds. I know that our medical equipment works on Enif."

"Yes."

"It is up to you."

There was a long pause. I listened to my own heart thumping in my IEVA suit as I waited, just hoping that I had said enough. Twice, I almost spoke again, but something stopped me. I shouldn't pressure it anymore. I should honor its dilemma by giving it the space to make the right decision.

Finally Eshaan's fingers whispered a silent message onto Didjal's arm, its fingers flashing as they spoke in the Enif way. Then it got to its feet. "Do what you can to save it."

I inclined my head to the Enif in respect, waited for a second until it had taken some steps back, then beckoned Mel and Neema over. The bullets were deep. Didjal would be needing more than just my help. The two girls grabbed their own emergency medical kits and bent over the prone figure with me.

Out of the corner of my eye I saw Eshaan walk slowly over towards the center of the chamber we were in. Its feet dragged, but were determined. I had caused it great misgiving. They were, after all, the beliefs of a lifetime. I hoped that I had been right to interfere. I felt convinced that we could not lose either of them, but what right had I to prioritize my convictions over theirs? Yet I had to believe in myself. It was the only way to lead. And I *was* supposed to be the leader, right?

We dug the bullets out and Mel irradiated the whole area with the single-use diathermal cauterizer. The seepage dried up immediately and the patient began to appear less stressed. It twitched, but regained a little of its color.

"Try to get some fluids in it," I told the girls, before standing up. "And make sure to give it shots of antibiotic. Those Vaer bullets are probably full of germs."

Mel, who was so relieved that she could hardly speak, gave a dumb nod. Her eyes shone with tears. Neema leaned over to pat her hand in reassurance.

"It will be fine," she said.

The tears spilled over. "I hope so," breathed Mel. "It risked its life to save mine."

"You did well to pull it all the way here, Mel. Don't start blaming yourself. Didjal saved you; you saved Didjal."

She was struck by that. "I suppose I did, in a way."

"You did ... certainly. I think it would consider the debt well paid. Don't you?"

She hesitated. "Maybe."

"No maybes, Mel. Try to accept what has happened. Move on. Remember why we are here. We have to try to save the Chakrans. That matters more than any of us."

"Yes."

"Good. I'll leave you two with it. Get those wounds wrapped up, and see if you can get enough fluids in it for it to come round. Then it can tell us how it feels. I am concerned I have missed something. We don't have much training in exomedicine, after all."

Neema tried to grin at me but it came out more like a grimace. We were all under a lot of strain. "Yes, Rye."

I moved across to the control panel. They had still had no luck with it, but Eshaan was examining the canister closely. I made my way to its side. "Found anything?"

"How is Didjal?"

"It'll do. We got the bullets out and cauterized the wounds. The girls are trying to get enough fluids back in it, but that will take time, and the number of packs are limited."

Eshaan didn't reply, but it did draw my attention to a small mechanism on the lid of the canister. "Look. I think this is some sort of coded lock. See? If I press here and here, then I detect mechanical movement inside. This is Nepheal technology."

"You think it is independent of the console?"

"I believe so. They will have had it in transit, after all, will they not? It could not be connected at such times. I believe that it can be opened manually." It deflated a little. "However, I am unable to determine exactly how."

Zenzara trotted over to us. When we told her of Eshaan's findings, she called Danaa and Denaraz to the canister too.

Denaraz examined the mechanism, but could see no way to open it.

Danaa peered at the canister. Nepheal women do not have very good close sight. Historically, they have spent so much time up in the mountains that excellent long sight developed, to the detriment of their short vision.

She frowned. "I have seen something like this before, I think. But ... wait ... I can't quite ... Ah! I have it! On the Nepheal Gyre, the weapons cabinets are locked by something similar to this. Only ours are much larger." She thought for a moment. "If I remember correctly, you have to press here ... and here ... Yes, like that, see. This part slides back to reveal another mechanical slide. You press here ... and here ... which reveals a keyboard. Then we just need to input the code!" She looked up, pleased with herself.

"What code?"

She gave a very expressive shrug. "I only know what we would use on the Gyre. Who knows if the same code was used, or if the Vaers changed it?"

"The Vaers are thieves. They steal stuff; they don't change it. Unless Cunningham or Chandrayanan have manipulated it, it will probably be the same."

Danaa bit her lip. It made her long face look very lop-sided. "Well, we would use one of the universal constants. Usually something from quantum theory. But I only have three attempts. If the third attempt is not correct, they whole mechanism will autodestruct, locking the canister. And that canister is made of a TTN alloy. There is no way we will be able to get into it. Not without tossing it into a star." She spread her hands. "And that wouldn't exactly be good for the Chakrans inside it."

Denaraz had been examining the keypad. "It seems to have ten digits."

"Yes. We would use the first ten digits of the constant."

"Like Pi?" I asked. "Could that be it?"

She didn't roll her eyes, but she did come close. "No, Captain. We would only use less ... err ... less well-known constants. Planck time, perhaps. Planck length. Planck charge. Or the Electric constant of vacuum permittivity. Or the magnetic flux quantum. Or even the nuclear magneton."

I knew what the Planck ones were. The others were new to me. "Pick three and input them. We have to get at the strands before the hypersphere matures and they are released automatically. It will be too late by then. Pick three."

Danaa's eyes grew large. "Me?" she squeaked.

I looked around at the others. "Do the rest of you have those numbers memorized?"

There was a general shaking of heads. "Then, you, Danaa. Yes."

"But which shall I choose?"

At that moment there was a rumbling in the floor. Suddenly, the whole small bubble we were standing in began to shake. I clutched at the nearest thing that was nailed down – the canister.

We couldn't see out of the bubble, but something bad was happening outside. I quickly clipped a line to my suit, slammed my IEVA helmet over my head and threw myself through the skin of the carbon bubble, shouting to Danaa as I went to input the first three things that occurred to her.

As soon as my head exited the carbon cloud, I was bombarded by tumbling forms of light. I had to screw my eyes up to avoid being blinded by it.

The hypersphere was changing. It was undergoing some sort of transition. Although the center had not yet moved, the outside layers were transforming. They were not repositioning, as far as I could see, but the cells were deforming, stretching, changing.

My line kept me hovering above the smaller cloud as I examined the structure around me. The cell that stretched from me out to the edge of the hypersphere was splitting down the middle. The left hand side was going in one direction, to my left; the right hand was shaping into a funnel shape.

I looked over my head. The same thing was happening above me. I was so close to the shapes that it was hard to see exactly what was going on. Then I realized. The hypersphere was transmuting into what looked like two nautilus shapes, orthogonal to each other.

My jaw dropped. I had heard of sphere eversion, which is when a sphere turns completely inside-out without splitting apart or tearing. But let's face it – you don't actually expect to live through what are essentially constructs of pure mathematics. It was impossible, yet it was happening.

At least, it was almost happening. But it wasn't quite a sphere eversion, because the wider parts of the nautilus shapes had actually separated from the rest of the construct.

The small carbon bubble, although still stable right at the smallest central part of both nautiluses ... or should that be nautili? ... was not really moving. However, it was vibrating continually, with a force that threatened to shake it apart.

I began to pull myself back to the smaller bubble. Whatever we were going to do, it had to be now. And I didn't fancy our chances of ever managing to get out of this mess. The spin of the hypersphere had been conserved, and now there was a distinct wobble. The irregularity of the new shape was disturbing the previously smooth rotation, which had also speeded up. It was good and bad news. Nobody would be able to come in here and attack as. At the same time, there was no way we would be able to float out of the transformed hypersphere. We were trapped.

A flash of light against something close caught my eye. I turned my head quickly. Something was being buffeted through the spars of solid light. It was close to my position.

I stared. Finally the lump resolved into something I could distinguish. I grabbed at my jet pack and switched it on. The lump was Seyal. Or what was left of her. She was not moving, as far as I could see.

She must have been around a hundred feet out from the bubble, and had clearly lost all power. Her large, thin shape was hanging in space, moving only slowly. She was on a trajectory to pass by the small central bubble, so it was very lucky that I had spotted her.

I hoped she was not already dead. It was illogical of me to think we could all survive something like this, but I couldn't help hoping that we had.

My jet pack crossed the distance between us quite quickly. I was aware of the flashes of pure light that criss-crossed the changing environment as the change continued. Even as I travelled to Seyal, I could see the effect. Parts of the spars of solid light nearest to me were elongating. Others were foreshortening. The geometric shapes they described in space were evolving, twisting and reforming into different patterns.

Here, without the bubble's air supply, there was no sound. It made the experience eerie and strange. I knew that the girders were squealing their refusal to comply with this new layout. Yet I was protected from all of that by the padding of the vacuum. I sailed along as if there were no danger. As if space were not being mangled beyond all recognition at that very moment. It was extremely disconcerting.

Seyal's EVA suit was unmoving. One arm was flung out towards the outer shell of the hypersphere and the other was pointing towards the central bubble. I tried to see if she was breathing, through the visor. She didn't seem to be. But her eyes were closed and her mouth open, both of which I chose to take as good signs.

I strapped her EVA onto the jet pack and began to tow her back to the carbon bubble. She didn't have much time.

We didn't have much time. Whatever was happening was happening now. It wasn't going to wait for Seyal and I to get back to relative safety. And it was big.

We were half way across the stretch of empty space when the light began to change.

I put one arm across Seyal's loose limbs and ducked my head down.

It was then that I realized what the two bubbles really were.

There were huge flashes of light from the proximity of the central bubble and these traveled out towards the outer shell of the surrounding bubble. It started with one small bolt of light and quickly escalated to huge forks of lightning.

They flashed past us as we traipsed back towards the smaller bubble.

I had seen this before. A variation of a Van der Graaf generator. One small metal ball and one large one. It provoked electrostatic discharge from one surface to the other. In this case, the smaller ball was actually contained inside the larger one, so the lightning was moving from the outer surface of one to the inner surface of the other.

As I gaped at this phenomena, it changed. It ramped up, so that the lightning bolts became brighter and stronger. They changed into rings of burning light that travelled outwards in pulses through the space between the two surfaces.

It was blinding.

I hardly had time to close my eyes against one pulse when the next began to flow past me.

I aimed the jet pack at the central bubble and put all the force I could on the control. All this was building up into a climax I was pretty certain I didn't want to be a part of.

We raced through the skin of the carbon bubble and collapsed onto the floor. Seyal hit the metal decking and bounced once before remaining still. Mel and Neema raced over.

"Have you broken into that thing yet?" I screeched at Danaa.

"I tried two of them. There is only one chance left," she wailed. "How should I know which they are using?"

I ran across the decking, grabbed her and began to shake her bony shoulders. "Get a grip, Danaa! You are the only one who can get this right. Do it, and do it now!"

Her eyes stared wildly at me. "I don't want this. What if I am wrong?"

"What if you are not? You have to make a decision."

"Help me?"

Now I was back inside the bubble, I could hear sounds again. Even though we were insulated by the skin, it sounded like the end of the universe was here, and was now. Like Armageddon and the Apocalypse rolled into one.

Those pulses of light that were traveling between the two bubbles were getting larger and closer together. Time really was running out.

"All right. What did you use?"

"I input the Planck constant of length and the Electric constant of vacuum permittivity. Neither of them worked." Her eyes were tormented. "One of those should have worked. They are the last two universal constants that were in use on the Nepheal Gyre. I don't remember any others being programmed. They are only changed every five years or so."

I stored that nugget of intelligence in my reluctant brain. You never know when things like that can come in useful.

"So," I said slowly. "The codes were changed, right?"

She nodded. "We can have no idea what they were changed to."

"We know that they were changed for Vaer use. And we know that the Vaers are less sophisticated than the Nepheals. They steal technology; they don't make it. So whoever changed this code will have used something simple. Something any Vaer would be able to remember."

Danaa now looked even more doubtful. "Y-y-y-e-ss."

"So it will be a sequence any old person would be able to memorize?"

"I guess-s-s."

I smiled at her and at the others. "Stand aside! I know what the code is!"

I didn't. This was going to have to be a stab in the pitch black. But Danaa was right. It wasn't her responsibility. It was, in the end, mine.

I bent over the mechanism. Although a technical person must have changed the code, they had changed it for Vaer end users. I thought it would have been Chandrayanan who changed the code. And I had the impression that he didn't think much of his Vaer co-conspirators, especially the non-technical staff. He would have chosen the simplest code he could think of.

Nine numbers. I know what I would have used.

I covered my hands so that the others wouldn't be able to see what code I was using. Then I began to punch my nine numbers in, very carefully. This wasn't the time to make any mistakes.

I got to the sixth number when things began to disintegrate. Literally.

First, the skin of the carbon bubble sublimated. One second it was there, the next it had vanished. Our oxygen supply evaporated. I slammed my helmet on. In one quick glance my mind took a mental photo of what it saw. People all around me were scrambling to vacuum-proof themselves as fast as they could. Mel and Neema were still bent over Seyal and now were dragging her EVA helmet over her head and trying to secure their own at the same time.

I had managed to get the seventh number in when the gravity disappeared. I began to float away from the canister. I only just succeeded in grabbing hold of one of the handles before I was swept out into the glaring background.

The pulses had now fused together to become one long shimmering funnel of light. It seemed alive; vibrations made waves along it. We were now at the epicenter of some sort of energy that was beyond our understanding.

I grabbed at the handles with one hand and tried to get the other hand back to the mechanism on the canister. I still had two numbers to input. I *had* to finish this sequence.

My hand flailed uselessly in space. The whole canister was jumping up and down. The platform was beginning to disintegrate. My friends were being dislodged from the decking and were now hanging in space, their faces taut with fear and awe.

I got the eighth number in.

The canister bucked and was torn away from my grasp. It, too, separated from its housing and drifted away in space.

I was spinning.

No! This couldn't happen. I had to finish the number. I had to. It was the last chance, the last hope that we had of success.

The canister was beginning to spin too.

I was drifting away from it.

I flailed my arms and my legs, but couldn't change my vector enough.

I gave a cry of despair. No! Not when there was only one number left! Please, not when we could be so close.   ·

I felt a sharp pain in my back, and a thud against the EVA suit. I was suddenly propelled towards the canister, appendages still thrashing at the vacuum uselessly.

My mind registered what had happened. What must have happened. Somebody had managed to brace themselves against something solid and had given me a kick.

I was now on a vector that might ... might just intercept the canister.

Out of the corner of my eye I saw a sardonic Denaraz give me a salute. Perhaps he had always wanted to give me a kick in that area of my anatomy. He certainly looked pleased enough with himself. I noticed that he had grabbed hold of a substantial piece of decking that had come free and was hanging on to Zenzara with one hand. They were both staring at me.

I dragged my recalcitrant mind back to the task in hand. Would I be able to intercept the canister? I tried to calculate trajectories. There were only split seconds to try to correct my course.

I was going to miss. Not by much, but I was going to miss. I needed to correct slightly to the right.

I had practiced this type of maneuver in EVA training. I had to perform a somersault over to the right. Not a full somersault, actually. What is, in space, known as a corkscrew lunge.

That was what was needed now. A corkscrew lunge.

I tucked my legs in as far as I could and tensed all my muscles. It had been some time since I had practiced this kind of procedure. I just hoped it would come back to me.

My body rolled to the right.

I breathed a sigh of relief.

Unfortunately, I had rolled too far and too fast, overestimating the movement. The roll deepened and became a spin.

I would hit the canister, but my body would be whirling like a child's top.

The movement was making me sick again.

I simply could not be sick again into my EVA helmet. The safety system was already clogged up. I gulped, trying to avoid heaving anything more up out of my stomach.

Then I slammed into the canister.

My arms were forced open by the blow, and the air was pushed out of my lungs. I hung there for a moment, pinned in one place by the collision. It hurt like the devil. It must have dislodged the dressing Izan had put over my wound.

Then, luckily, one of my outstretched hands drifted close to one of the handles. I just caught a glimpse of it as I spun away.

I clamped my finger down over the handle.

The rest of my body pivoted and was torn by inertia away from my fingers. I thought for several long moments that I wouldn't be able to hold on.

Two fingers were ripped from the handle. I was left with a slipping grasp.

I tightened the remaining knuckles as much as I could.

My body attempted to pull those fingers out from their sockets.

I closed my eyes and locked the remaining bones as tightly as I could.

My smallest finger broke. I was aware of the brittle snap as the bone decided that the stress was simply too much.

But the remaining two managed to hold. My body was forced to a stop. The force gradually diminished.

I began to breathe again. I dragged my torso back towards the canister. It was still spinning, but now I had matched it. My stomach growled, complaining about the vertigo I was imposing on it.

I scrabbled my way across the canister until I managed to reach the locking mechanism. The numbers were still displaying across the lock, with just the one place for the last, ninth, number.

I took a deep breath and punched in my guess at the last number. Then I allowed my body to relax. There was nothing more I, or any of us, could do. I slumped over the metal container, absolutely exhausted, but still able to see the locking mechanism.

The large digital numbers glowed at me, illuminating part of my IEVA suit. I waited. I suppose we all waited.

The numbers, which had inputted in orange, flashed with the same color for a full ten seconds.

Over that time my heart began to slump. I had chosen something far too obvious. It hadn't worked. I had squandered our very last chance at saving the Chakrans from some sort of enforced slavery.

Then the first number began to flash.

I blinked.

The first number turned green. The second flashed.

My heart gave a tremendous leap. I was surprised it didn't tear its way out of my IEVA suit.

The second turned green. The third flashed.

I closed my eyes. I had never prayed, but now I wished that I could.

The third, the fourth, the fifth, the sixth. Now I had stopped breathing all over again. This was playing havoc with my lungs. My vision was blurring, but I could still see the numbers on the display.

I watched with growing numbness as the seventh and eighth numbers switched to green. Only the last one to go. It had to be right. Surely?

It was. I saw it begin to flash and my head bent over the locking mechanism in sheer relief. We had done it. We were about to die, but we had managed to unlock the canister. Thank the Shells for that!

When the final number became green I threw my free hand in the air and made a thumbs-up to the others.

They had drifted apart now, each trying to anchor themselves as best they could to one of the pieces of flotsam from the bubble. Even so, all of them were staring at me. They replied with their own thumbs-up, as best they could.

The light intensified until it became so brilliant that it whitened the whole universe. It felt as though even the vacuum had begun to tremble. We screamed inside our IEVA suits and tried to protect our eyes as well as we could.

What remained of our small bubble flared like the sun. There was a tremendous outburst of energy and the world ceased to exist.

16

I was comfortable, but cold. Very, very cold. And I was having trouble breathing. Cogs and gears in my mind attempted to make some sort of sense of what input it was getting. I was in a dark space. My eyes were detecting an intense but ghostly green color which surrounded me.

I closed them again and squeezed my eyelids once or twice. The green color was still there when I opened them. I managed to focus as best I could. I was hanging in outer space, in the vicinity of what looked like a planetary nebula. It was certainly a disc of particles that had formed a ring around some central occurrence. I tried to remember my studies. I think one of the few really green things in space were doubly ionized oxygen particles in some planetary nebulae.

I felt absurdly pleased with myself. I knew where I was.

Then it struck me. I began to recoup some of my memory. There was a deluge of information which hit me all at the same time.

I might be in a green planetary nebulae around some dying white dwarf star, but what the fitz was I doing here? Where were the others? Where was I?

And why was I finding it hard to breathe?

I twisted slightly in the vacuum, attempting to scope out more of my surroundings.

I was not alone in this place. I could see large sheets of decking that had come along with me for the journey. With relief, I caught sight of Denaraz, still clinging onto one of those pieces, with Zenzara floating along beside him. I couldn't see if they were conscious, unconscious, or dead.

I realized that my hand was still feebly clutching one of the handles of the canister. It was open and the contents had disappeared. I didn't remember ever seeing what those contents had looked like.

Behind us, taking up a huge arc of the night sky, was the funnel part of the nautilus shape. As I watched, it gave one or two flickers of energy and then vanished, disappearing in fits and starts so that it appeared to be disintegrating as I looked on.

My brain gradually began to whir back into its usual functioning mode of normal inefficiency. I remembered everything. The hypersphere had become a wormhole, and we had managed to release the Chakrans. We had been successful but not in time to totally stop the appearance of the wormhole. It seemed that we had somehow been sucked down the funnel of the space anomaly and transported to a new area of the universe.

And I would die. We all would. We were hanging thousands of miles above an exquisite electric green nebula. There were no planets in sight and there was certainly no air to breathe within two days of space travel, if we had been lucky enough to have space travel, which we weren't.

I think I sighed. I know I yawned. My air was slowly becoming contaminated by my own breathing process. I was feeling progressively more drowsy and my perception was beginning to cloud up.

Then a long black arm grabbed me by the shoulder and shook me.

I opened my eyes.

Eshaan was looking at me, a very irritated expression on its shiny black face with its multifaceted eyes. It appeared to be most put out.

I gave it a lazy wave with one of my hands. I couldn't even attempt to speak, and it wouldn't have heard me if I had.

It shuttered its eyes rapidly a few times, which I took to be an attempt to communicate with me, then it gave a sort of shrug of frustration, grabbed one of the stiff folds of my EVA suit with one of its hands and began to tow me over towards Denaraz and Zenzara. I saw, in a surreal and detached sort of way, that it was still using a jet pack. You had to admire the Enif. How could it have come through a wormhole and still managed to retain its jet pack? Hats off, I thought.

"You should make a painting of all this," I told its back as it dragged me along. Unsurprisingly, it didn't hear me.

I felt like a towel flapping in the wind. My legs were dangling loosely as I was being hauled along.

I giggled. Luckily, Eshaan didn't hear that either.

It pulled me up to Zenzara and then placed my arm on hers, so that I would be able to anchor myself. Then it gave me a small nod and sped off again, presumably to search for further survivors.

Zenzie was awake, I saw. Her eyes lit up as they saw that I was still alive. Mine were glad to see her, too.

She pushed her helmet against mine. We ought to be able to communicate like that. "Are you all right, Mallivan?"

Well that was a waste of last words, if you want my opinion. I shook my head at her. I would have rolled my eyes, but they were hurting so I didn't.

"Did you get them back?" I demanded.

"Get what back?" Her own pupils were slightly glazed. I think she was already suffering from hypercapnia – a build-up of carbon dioxide.

I shook her. "The Chakrans!"

"Oh, the Chakrans." She screwed her eyelids shut and seemed to examine her own consciousness. "Nope. I don't think so."

"Try to talk to them!"

She stared blankly at me. "Talk to them? How can I do that?"

I shook her again. "I don't know! But if you don't we will die. They are the only beings that might be able to help us now. Talk to them!"

She stared at me and I saw when the realization of our position clicked into place in her head. She gave a swallow. Then she clamped her eyelids firmly shut and began to frown.

I let go of one of her shoulders, but kept a grasp of the other. I turned to Denaraz.

The Tyzaran was smiling at me. I blinked, but it didn't change anything. He was definitely smiling. "Captain," he said in a pleased voice.

"Izan." I reached out to touch him on his arm. He had done a good job in caring for Zenzara. "Are you all right?"

I know, another waste of words.

He grinned at me and then waved at the green nebula. "Pretty ..." he muttered.

I patted his arm. "Very pretty, Izan." There was no point trying to get anything sensible out of him; he was past that. Perhaps Tyzarans suffered more quickly from poor quality air.

Something tugged at my shoulder. I managed to turn slowly through ninety degrees. Zenzie had been trying to get my attention.

I placed my helmet against hers again.

"They are here!"

"Then tell them to get us out of here. We are all going to die within minutes if we are not transported to a planet with the right air for us to breathe."

"They don't know how to do that, but they are very grateful to us and they are trying."

I felt my heart slowing from the lack of oxygen. "Then tell them to hurry!"

"They know we are struggling."

"Good. Good." I made to move away, but she dragged my helmet back to hers with both hands. "I am sorry, Mallivan. I am sorry I cannot protect you anymore."

I tried to grin. "You did a great job. I ... I relieve you of your obligation."

"You can't do that!"

"So sue me. I won't care. I'll be dead."

"You can still sue people on Tyzar if they are dead. Their relations are held responsible."

"Now, why does that not surprise me?"

She gave me a small push. I opened my arms and let myself float gently away. I might as well enjoy the wonderful panorama. There wasn't going to be time for much more than a quick appreciation of the view.

She lunged after me and dislodged herself from the grip of Denaraz, which had loosened as he began to hallucinate.

The two of us floated, side by side, in outer space in some unknown location.

She looked at peace with herself. She twisted so that she was lying on her back relative to me, and staring out at the stars.

I copied her.

I had never seen such abundant stars. We weren't anywhere within the Major Shells. I had studied star maps of that whole area, and there was nowhere with the concentration of stars that now surrounded us. We had been transported somewhere else. Somewhere a long, long way away from our home.

My breathing was slowing. I had the sensation of no longer needing it. I had a brief moment of panic and then came out the other side into some childlike wonder at the sight in front of me. I slid into acceptance and found it welcoming.

Zenzara's face was illuminated. She, also, seemed to be enjoying the vista in front of us.

Who couldn't? The brilliant electric green of the nebula was offset by a sky that appeared absolutely encrusted with stars of different colors, from sparkling red on one end of the scale to a shimmering blue on the other. It was like being surrounded by some sort of tapestry of precious stones.

I let myself sink into it. My eyes began to close. I hoped that the others had been able to appreciate the beauty of this last resting place.

Then my neck was jarred again and I felt Zenzara as she pulled our helmets together. It must have been with the last of her strength: I don't think I could have even moved by that time.

"They know what to do!" she told me. "They haven't lost the seed of the wormhole. It is still a part of the strands that are dying! They might still be able to make us another!"

They would be too late. I was sure. I didn't think I had another minute to live. I gripped her hand and tried to squeeze it. I wanted her to know I appreciated her efforts, even if they were going to be too late.

"Hold on, Mallivan!"

After that it was chaotic. I was aware of a thunder growing around me. I could no longer see, even though my eyes were wide open. I was blinded by some physiological reaction that no longer seemed relevant.

I did feel the small lifeline tugging on my hand. It must have been Zenzara, but I was only dimly aware that she was still hanging onto me. I was floating feely, almost above my own body, aware of something rising and something falling. It was time to separate in some way, to leave things behind, to let go.

Then the roaring in my ears increased and the heat on my face flared. All along my body there was a sharp spike in temperature, as though I had walked outside on Beznik during a close conjunction of the planet's three suns.

I began to shake all over, but I was somehow aware that it was not my own body that was causing the shake. The space around me was fracturing. It was convulsing with turbulence. The hand in mine was wrenched away.

I felt bereft and lonely, all of a sudden.

The fabric of spacetime was disentangling itself. Despite my temporary blindness, the light grew stronger, until it scorched everything it touched. There was a blazing flash. Everything seemed to sublimate into pure energy.

I was falling, yet it could have been happening to somebody else. There were no physical symptoms of discomfort. It was like flying through time.

Then there was a crack of something that sounded like stone.

17

I felt the presence of somebody close by to me. My EVA helmet was efficiently removed.

"Breathe!" the voice said. "Breathe!"

I gasped in air. It was icy cold and made me choke. I went into a paroxysm of coughing, which had the advantage of forcing more oxygen into my lungs. Almost straight away, I began to feel better.

I lifted my body up on one elbow, and stared around me. At first, my eyes were still detecting only blackness, but gradually that began to change. Small patches of light seeped into the darkness and slowly expanded. They gave way to clouded images that I could not separate into any distinct reflection of what I was looking at. The lens in my eye had become almost opaque.

However, as I persevered, the scene in front of me resolved. I realized where we were.

The Ayaala Retreat, in the mountains of Nephealis.

I gasped.

Zenzara was lying beside me. Denaraz had already recovered. He was running from person to person, trying to help. So was Eshaan.

I struggled to my feet, swaying slightly as I stood up.

I was able to see the others. Neema and Mel were sitting, but they looked to be intact. Didjal, Seyal and Anzany were prone on the ground. Danaa was trying to struggle to all fours. Her legs were shaking and she looked distinctly tottery.

We were safe.

I bent over Zenzara. "You did it! The Chakrans did it!"

Her eyes fluttered. "Interdicted," she muttered. "It is forbidden."

"What?"

She finally managed to prop her eyelids open. "That way of travel," she explained. "They have told me it is forbidden. No-one must ever try to develop it again."

"But they have just used it themselves!"

"Yes. They will retain the capability, I believe. Now they know how it is done they could probably replicate it anywhere. They were able to use the remnants of the first wormhole to open the second. However, doing so killed two of the strands and very nearly killed the rest. Wormholes interfere with their quantum structure, and the rest of the Chakrans almost didn't survive. They were only able to recover because the energy had been largely dissipated through the first explosion."

Zenzie breathed out rather shakily before she continued, "They are telling me that they will never allow their nonlocal networks to be used by other species. Such travel threatens their very existence. They are calling it 'Interdicted Space'. Even their own Chakran strands will not be allowed to use it."

"Then why did they save us?"

"They know we helped them, and they recognize the concept of being indebted. They also wished to continue their link with me. They decided to save me. The strands that have died to transport you were probably beyond repair. They wanted to help. The rest of you were included because it could be done with no further danger to their cell structure, and because they were pleased that we had all risked our own continuity to rescue them."

"Our own continuity, eh? I am certainly a fan of continuity." I was less pleased to be saved as an afterthought, but I wasn't about to complain out loud. I wasn't sure they couldn't hear me.

Her face wrinkled in confusion. "That is what they call life, I think."

"Then long may they 'continue'. Please thank them."

Zenzie sighed. "I can vaguely feel some remaining strands, but they are withdrawn from the Nexus. I don't think I will be able to reach them for a while." She looked sad. "I think they were damaged by what happened."

There was a pounding on the ground, which began to tremble. I looked up. A herd of Nepheal women were galloping towards us, on all fours. They slid to a stop at the edge of the group.

Ouraali stared down at all of us with deep lines of worry etched on her long face. "What happened?"

I tried to stand up, but then thought better of it. I waved a hand at the debris around us. "The Chakrans brought us back."

She seemed bewildered as her eyes took in the crater that had been formed by the wormhole. "They dented my mountain?"

"I guess wormholes are difficult things to control. Did you bring doctors?"

She nodded and waved a hand to the waiting Nepheal women. "Of course."

"Seyal and Didjal are the worst off, I think."

She nodded. "They will be taken care of." Her kind eyes bore into mine. "Did you succeed in stopping the Vaers?"

"I think so. We only just managed to release the Chakrans in time, though. The wormhole had already begun to form. We were sucked through into ... into ..." Where had we been sucked through to? I had no idea. I shrugged. "Who knows?"

She looked even more confused. "Then ... they brought you back? Here? How did they know to bring you back here?"

"You know as much as I do, Ouraali. But thank you for coming."

A couple of Nepheal women knelt down beside me and started to care for the wounds I had. I peered down at my EVA suit, which was now being deftly removed. It was peppered with holes and gashes which had self-sealed to protect my skin.

They rolled the EVA suit down, leaving only enough to preserve my dignity. I was wrapped up in a sheet of metalized thin fabric, which turned out to be surprisingly warm. It made me aware of the trembling that had overtaken my whole body.

I closed my eyes for a moment, relieved to be alive. I hadn't expected to be. If the Chakrans hadn't brought us back from—

—Wait! Sammy! And Segaton!

I threw the sheet aside and this time did manage to struggle to my feet. Sammy was still at the carbon cloud. We had left him alone.

I grabbed Ouraali's leg and shook it. She stopped talking to one of the doctors and gave me her full attention.

"We have to get back. We left Sammy there. And the baby!"

"Back? Back where?"

"To the carbon cloud near Aschasi. Please! I can't abandon him there! He may have been attacked!"

Her long patrician nose dipped as she considered. I saw her eyes take in the panorama around her.

Denaraz and Zenzara were close by, recovering. Neema and Mel were helping to treat Seyal and Didjal. Eshaan was stretched out alongside its *faliif*, its four arms wrapped protectively around it. Anzany was now sitting, though her arm was still hanging uselessly by her body. Danaa had finally managed to keep her footing and had lurched over to my position. She was listening to my conversation with Ouraali.

"I will come with you," she said in a voice that came out surprisingly firm.

"You will not! Look at you!"

"You are no picture postcard yourself, Captain. I need to finish what I started. Nepheal women do not give up on things. Surely you know that by now?"

I thought of Agraala. I certainly did.

"Besides," she said. "My ship is attached to *Nivala*, remember? You will need somebody to pilot *Aenysia*. I will be needed for that."

She looked at me and I looked at her. There was no need to voice what we were both thinking. *Aenysia* might no longer exist.

There was a shuffling behind me. "We will come too!"

Naturally, it was Zenzie and Denaraz. Of course they wouldn't want to convalesce normally. Of course they would expect to come with me.

"Zenzie, you need to rest."

"I am the Chyzar. I need to go. The Chakrans request it!"

I narrowed my eyes at her. I bet they didn't. I couldn't see the Chakrans wanting to get involved in logistics. "I thought you couldn't hear them anymore?"

She stared at me. Her face was defiant, set. "They managed to get that thought through!"

I believe I ground my teeth together, because her eyes suddenly changed to that expression of pure innocence that all lying children assume. It seems to have crossed species and become universal. She knew perfectly well that I wouldn't risk it. Not after the Chakrans had just saved all of us.

My shoulders slumped.

Neema and Mel had now hobbled over. "We want to come too. The doctors have everything in hand."

"How are they doing?"

Mel gave me a reassuring pat on the arm. "They will all make a recovery. Seyal is going to need very special care. They are taking her straight back to a Zeroth chamber. She will be in that for at least two weeks. However, they think she can make a full recovery."

"And Didjal?"

"Didjal was entering the stage of enlightenment. None of us knows exactly how it will be affected. Eshaan says that it has never heard of the stage of enlightenment being reversed. At least, not in generations. It cannot tell the doctors what such a thing will do to them. Didjal is deeply unconscious. It will go into a Zeroth too. But Eshaan says one of the Enif doctors will need to be brought to treat it."

"Might it recover?"

"They think so, though its injuries are deep. The unknown part of the equation is that its cells had initiated breakdown at the molecular level and this was interrupted. My doctors say that they cannot give a definite prognosis yet."

A dark figure close to Didjal disentangled itself and stood up. Eshaan walked over to us. "Are you going back for Sammy? For Segaton?"

I nodded.

"Didjal would wish me to accompany you."

"Are you sure? I know just how important it is for you to stay together."

"I am sure. It is my duty. We interrupted death for this. My *faliif* would want me to see it through."

If anybody had earned the right to do just that, it was the two Enif. I inclined my head. "Then there will be..." I counted, "... seven of us. Ouraali, can you arrange for us to be taken down the mountain? We should move as quickly as we can. We have no idea what has happened back at the carbon cloud."

"I hope Sammy has a lead on Cunningham and the Indian scientist," muttered Zenzie. "Otherwise they will go straight back to the drawing board and try to do this same thing all over again."

I sighed. Surely not? But I knew, in my heart of hearts, that she was right. Bull Cunningham was not about to give up now. He was nothing if not persistent. "We need to get those two into prison."

Denaraz gave a sort of snort. He didn't have to put his sentiments into words.

"We will see if we can get a lead on them. They may have been destroyed by the wormhole."

Danaa shook her head. "I don't think so. We Nepheals have a saying: *Creatures that fly never die.*" She turned to Zenzie. "Will the Chakrans be all right? Did the wormhole damage their structure in any way?"

Zenzara blew out air. "If that wormhole had been kept open for more than a few seconds, it would have spread throughout their entire body and could well have destroyed all the members of their race. Agraala was right; there was a real danger of a ripple effect that would have decimated them. They are very shaky. You know how fragile they are. As it is, the two strands that we released did not survive."

Danaa gave a gasp.

Zenzie went on, "A permanent wormhole would solidify the links between the cells, fossilizing them. They think that would then propagate to the next cell, then the next, like a cancer. They only just wrested control back just in time when the wormhole was created just now, and that was only open for two very short periods of time. Luckily, we opened the canister just in time for them to prevent it stabilizing. They were in very great danger, which is why they say that wormholes must be interdicted and that they must never happen again."

"I guess we can't blame them for that."

Zenzie's shoulders dropped. "They are going to need time to recover. I am not sure if they will want to reform my Nexus."

Danaa touched her lightly on the arm. "Of course they will. Where else can they find somebody who cares about them like we do?"

Zenzie managed a wobbly smile.

Ouraali replied to my previous question. "I will tell Nephealis City to send sleds to pick you up."

There was a huge silence. I looked up. The Nepheal women in the crowd around us had become stationary.

Ouraali let the silence draw out for several long seconds. "The Chakrans opened a *wormhole* to our sacred mountain to save these people. I think we can bend our rules slightly to help bring that rescue to a successful conclusion."

The silence extended for more long moments before one lone Nepheal woman began to clap. The small noise her hands made suddenly became amplified as more and more of those present joined in.

I realized that we had made history. Sleds were to be allowed to come to the Ayaala Retreat.

Several heavy-duty sleds drew to a standstill near our position. It had taken them less than an hour to come from the Nephealis Gyre. They settled into the hover position some twenty feet away.

Those of us left from the initial group made our way as fast as we could across the icy terrain, slipping slightly on the snow.

We must have made a sorry sight for the pilots on the sleds. We were bedraggled and still clutched our metalized sheets around us to protect us from the chill morning air of Ayaala Mountain.

To my surprise, we were followed by twenty of Ouraali's councilors, led by Ouraali herself. My eyebrows went up.

"What? You think you can put dents into our sacred mountain and then exclude us?" she asked. "We have the right to come with you." She grinned. "And I think you have overlooked one small detail."

I raised my eyebrows at her. "What?"

"You will need a ship. You have mislaid yours."

She was right. I wasn't going to argue with her. The Nepheal women had armed themselves and turned from gentle ladies into ferocious amazons. I had seen female Nepheals in action. I was just glad they were on my side.

The sleds were soon boarded. The pilots turned them back towards the Nepheal Gyre.

I found the journey uncomfortable. Although these were extraplanetary sleds, able to traverse the distance between spacestation and planet, they were extremely basic and very uncomfortable. I thought my teeth would be shaken out on more than one occasion.

We docked alongside a very new, very shiny cruiser. Danaa's eyes lit up. "This is the *Anakraal*," she told us. "The very latest model we have.

Equipped with state-of-the-art technology and weaponry. I thought she was still on trials."

We boarded the new ship. As with all Nepheal vessels, it had very high ceilings and felt a little like a cathedral to the rest of us. We followed the escorting crew in silence, slightly awed by the sheer volume of the vessel.

The captain turned to us. His expression was rather lofty.

"So. You are the aliens. I believe I am to take you to co-ordinates close to Aschasi? Please buckle in. Even at our superior speed, this will take some time. I expect you to remain in your allotted quarters and to follow orders at all times."

I turned to Ouraali. "Superior speed?"

She seemed embarrassed. "Yes. This is the prototype of a new ship. It is still undergoing trials. Since time is of the essence, we have decided to use it now."

I grinned. "Faster maybe than the Tyzaran ZEPH drive?"

She grinned back. "Maybe. I really couldn't say."

"Thank you. We appreciate it. I am sure it was hard to persuade the Elder General to allow us to travel on the *Anakraal*."

"It may have taken a little convincing," she acknowledged. "But I pointed out that he owed you an apology."

"You did?"

She nodded. "And to me. I also was unaware of the second thesis on the nonlocal macroscope. The Elder General forgot to inform me." The way she emphasized 'forgot' told me that Ouraali was furious about the lapse.

The Nepheal woman pursed her lips. "Unfortunately it had only been presented in the month preceding your visit, at a *Phaala* I was unable to attend. I would, of course, found out about it in the normal way of things. However, events intervened and nobody thought to mention it to me. I am very sorry."

"Yes. They have that technology now. We must assume that they were able to retrieve the cartridge with the second thesis installed in it."

"It certainly would have survived the energy release around the opening of the wormhole."

I sighed. Nothing ever seemed to reach a true conclusion. We still had to apprehend the two Terrans and recover the second thesis.

We spent the short voyage in the Zeroth chambers on the large ship. Luckily, the sick bay was as modern as the new engines. We were all triaged and in treatment within an hour. Those of us with the worst injuries were slipped into upgraded Zeroths. It was bliss to just lie back in the gel and let my eyes close. I thought I could feel the injury healing itself as I slept. It was wonderful.

I carefully avoided checking how much time passed. I didn't want to snoop into the details of the new Nepheal engine. It didn't seem like very much, so I think that the new power source outperformed the ZEPH drive and then some. But I kept my mouth shut. They would share the new technology if they wanted to. I was just grateful that they were allowing us to benefit from it.

We were only told of our arrival in time to get ourselves out of the chambers and into protective gear. The Nepheals had provided new EVA suits for all of us. I was very glad not to have to put on my old suit again. I had the feeling it would be smelling pretty rancid by now.

I slapped the Captain on his back in a comradely manner. "Great trip. Obliged to you."

The captain's mouth opened and closed like a fish out of water. He looked horrified at my familiarity.

I smiled up at him. "Please wait here until you hear from us."

He tried to speak several times, then simply nodded.

I met Ouraali's gaze. She was looking most entertained. I got the impression she approved of the way the captain had been taken down a peg or two.

"Let's go," she said quickly. "We can take vacuum-ready sleds. They have all types on board this ship."

As we exited the ship, we found ourselves back in the space that had contained the carbon cloud. Now it was completely different. Shards of metal were still being ejected from the cloud. As we emerged from *Anakraal*, one narrowly missed us. We all ducked. Luckily, it only grazed the edge of one of the sleds, spinning it in space until the pilot managed to get it back under control.

I looked around, hoping to see *Nivala* and *Aenysia*.

I didn't.

There was no sign of life, or of any ships in the near surroundings.

My heart sank. I had left Sammy on his own, with two ships to look after. What could he have done – what would he have done – when the world around him erupted in a wormhole?

They hadn't been transported with us; I was sure of that. So they had been left behind. I turned to Zenzie.

"You said no ships were dragged through the wormhole. Are the Chakrans sure about that?"

"Yes. I asked them that. No ships came through with us. They think the energy would have been too localized to affect the outlying ships."

"Then the remaining carbon bubbles are still here. I think that the Vaers are still here. And I think they have Sammy. He would have been a sitting duck. I can't see the Vaers letting two nice new shiny ships escape their clutches, can you?"

"No. They would definitely want to get a hold of them."

"And they would have no idea where we had gone. There hasn't been time for them to disappear, not without leaving traces of their departure. They must still be here!"

"Then why haven't they attacked us?"

"Because they are trying to hide. They already have two of our ships! They must know that this Nepheal ship will outclass them on weaponry. They plan to sit quietly where they are and hope we go away."

"So, what is the plan?"

"There were two interior bubbles, right?"

Denaraz, who had been listening, nodded.

"They will have hauled one ship into each bubble. And they will not be able to see us. This ship is equipped with the latest version of the low visibility shielding and their scanners won't work through the carbon clouds, remember." I smiled. "They don't know where we are!"

Neema and Mel exchanged a look. It was a little bloodthirsty. Especially Mel's. She had clearly grown extremely fond of Sammy. I was glad I wasn't a Vaer.

"Let's get into those spheres," she growled.

"Yes. One sled to each, I think?"

"Neema and I will take the biggest," she told me. "And don't try to stop me."

It wasn't the time to point out that I was the one who took the decisions. I bowed my head. "Right. Zenzie, Danaa and I will take the smaller one. You, Neema, Eshaan and Denaraz take the larger." The least I could do was give her our two strongest fighters to take along.

She gave me a suspicious look. "Why those two?"

"Because you are taking the biggest bubble. Why? Did you want me to go with you?"

She reddened. "No. Of course not! It ... it doesn't matter."

"Fine."

"Fine."

We separated. The remaining two bubbles had merged so successfully into the background that it was extremely hard to see where they now were. We had the Nepheal new technology, however, and I saw just how far ahead of the rest of the Major Shells they were. They picked up the outline after several passes and a superposition of various frequencies. Even so, it took the scans some time to detect their presence. I decided I wanted one of the machines that made those bubbles. They could come in extremely useful.

Once we had nailed the position, we separated.

The smaller of the two bubbles was furthest away from the original central plinth. We cruised up to it, and then paused. Danaa slipped through the carbon shell as carefully as she could and disappeared for a few seconds.

When she came back she was smiling. "They have *Aenysia* in there! She seems to be intact!"

As we followed her instructions to the nearest entry point to the Nepheal ship, I gathered Danaa and Zenzie with the six Nepheal women fighters who had come with us on our sled. "We cannot hope to board the Vaer cruiser. I think we simply try to break *Aenysia* out of their control. What do you think?"

They nodded. It wasn't practical to board the Vaer ship. We could perhaps try to fire on them once we had wrested control of the Nepheal ship back from them.

"How many Vaers do you think will be on board?"

"If it were me I would have sent a dozen or so over. Any more than that and they would be leaving themselves short-staffed on the Vaer ship. Maybe not so many. From six to twelve, say."

The Nepheal women nodded. "One each!" said the one who was in charge. Ouraali had opted to go with the other group.

Danaa bared her teeth. "Nobody steals my ship!" she grated. "Nobody!"

I opened my mouth to tell them to go, but I was too late. They had already gone.

"Leave one for me!" I said plaintively. I doubted they would. They were pretty determined.

Zenzie was laughing. "You need a command course, Mallivan Bell," she told me.

"The Nepheals are collaborators," I pointed out stiffly. "They do not come strictly under my orders."

"Just as well."

I couldn't really be angry with her. She was right. I did need a command course.

I shrugged and gestured to her to lead the way. She fake-saluted me and then pushed through the carbon skin.

We came through directly over the shuttle bay doors. These were standing wide open, so getting inside the ship was easy. Zenzara and I drove into the large bay. The Nepheals had used jet packs. We brought up the rear with the sled itself.

There was already one Vaer slumped on the decking. The Nepheal women had slipped out into the ship. Any hopes I might have had of taking part in the action disappeared. Nepheal women are very efficient.

Even though alarms were now sounding all over the ship, the Vaers stood no chance. These women knew the lay-out of the ship perfectly, knew where to access the controls, how to trap the Vaers in holds and passageways. Within half an hour all of the Vaers had been dealt with. Most were dead. Some were wounded and had been rounded up and sequestered in the medical bay, with two of the Nepheal women to guard them.

There was no sign of Sammy on the bridge. We searched the ship. Neither Sammy nor Segaton were aboard.

Danaa slid into her seat and began to punch the screen. A thrumming sound told us that the ship was ready to go.

Aenysia turned her bows to the Vaer ship that lay beside her. Danaa punched some more times at the screen.

"You can't fire at them from this distance!" I shouted. "They are too close!"

"But if I move out of the bubble, the attack will be deflected!"

"Grapple them!"

"What?"

"Grab a hold of them. We can drag them out of the carbon cloud!"

Her face lifted. "Oh. I see. Yes, that could work. But I don't need to get a hold of them. I'll just give them a bit of a nudge." Her hands moved deftly across the controls, and then the whole ship lurched. I fell over. "See? Like that!"

I clutched at the console and pulled myself up as another shudder ran through the ship. "Are they out of the cloud?"

Her mouth turned down. "No. They have turned to face us. They are pushing back."

They say there is always a first time for everything. I had never heard of a pushing contest between spaceships.

"Whoever is inside the cloud has the advantage. We have to win this shoving competition."

She nodded, and did something to the controls of the ship. The sound of the engines changed and so did the vibrations, which increased. We were all staring out of the visor at the Vaer ship now. Our bows were buckling against theirs. We could see small Vaer figures running around on their bridge.

I cleared my throat. "I hope they don't decide to—"

It was as far as I got. A flash from the ship in front of us coincided with an explosion that knocked me flat on my back again. I gave a groan.

There was a tearing sound of dying metal against metal.

My heart stopped.

Then *Aenysia* swerved slowly away from the Vaer ship. We were still in one piece.

They weren't. The force of the blast had taken the whole nose of the Vaer cruiser off. The only figures we could see now were floating in space. None of them would ever walk again. Their captain must have had the brains of a Zenubi worm. What a fool. He had blown up his own ship in his haste to get rid of us.

Danaa edged *Aenysia* back a little. She looked at me. "What do you want to do?"

"We have to go inside their ship. Just in case Sammy is being held there with Segaton. And I would like the device that makes these clouds. Apart from that, there might be survivors. We should at least offer them the option of prison. We shouldn't just leave them all to die here."

She nodded. "Can you and Zenzie stay here to watch this ship?"

That was the moment I learned that delegation of responsibility can be really tough. I wanted to go myself, find the machine myself, talk to the Vaers myself. But I was going to have to learn to sit back and let others act. Now was as good a time as any. The Nepheal fighters had already proved just how efficient they could be, and I was still in recovery from a bullet in my chest.

"All right. We will check *Aenysia* for damage and try to start repairs." She touched my arm lightly. "Thank you."

Then they were gone. Zenzie and I began to check the bows of the Nepheal ship. These people made their spaceships to withstand practically anything, I realized. The bows were scratched and dented, but there was no major structural damage. I was amazed. A ship had just blown up right in front of her. Things were made to last over on Nephealis. Good to know.

When they came back their faces were even longer than usual. Danaa shook her head. "There was nobody left alive. They didn't seem to have enough time to suit up. Vaers must need longer than we do. The ones that weren't killed instantly died from the loss of atmosphere." She dragged in a large square metal box. "But we did find the carbon cloud device! The bubble collapsed when we dismantled it."

"Thanks." I hadn't realized, but she was right. The first cloud was gone. "All right. Let's go find the others."

We nosed our way towards the larger interior carbon cloud.

Danaa brought us close to it.

We were still drawing to a standstill when there was a shimmer right in front of us. A Vaer cruiser appeared out of nothing. She hung for a few seconds, and then the large carbon cloud shimmered momentarily before collapsing. The cruiser's engines flared and she leapt into space. She was piling on the thrust and would probably be out of range within a few minutes.

I looked back in front of us. Nivala was hanging in space, now clearly visible. They had opened her port airlock to the vacuum. If Sammy and Segaton were still on board and alive, they wouldn't be for very long.

"What do you want me to do?" Danaa looked at me.

I closed my eyes. I really ... really ... wanted to go after them. This ship was probably faster than any Vaer ship. But I wasn't going to let Sammy and Segaton die."We check our people, then we go after them," I said.

So Danaa stayed with her ship and I took Zenzie and three of the Nepheal fighters over.

We edged up close to the open hatch.

I looked Nivala over anxiously, but, apart from a few dimples in her fuselage, the ship seemed to be in good shape.

We saw Ouraali struggling to get the open airlock shut. I had been going to send somebody over by cable, but she seemed to have it under control. We turned for the stern of the ship and glided into the shuttle bay to land the sled.

We were met by Ouraali, who had clearly managed to shut the airlock. Her face was worried. "We have found your shipmate," she told us, "but he is unconscious. The baby is missing."

Zenzie's crest went rigid. "Have you checked the crawl spaces?"

The Nepheal leader shook her head. "We are too big to fit. Neema was about to go, because Mel won't leave Samuel."

That sounded bad. I needed to get to wherever he was. I nodded to Zenzie to give her permission to search the crawl spaces. That is where Sammy would have stashed the baby if he thought they were in danger.

I followed Ouraali to the bridge. Sammy was lying beside the captain's chair. Mel was bent over him, crying.

I moved closer.

Poor Sammy had been cut with a knife. His cheeks were in shreds and his chest looked as though some sadist had been playing noughts and crosses with a blade. The whole area around him was slick with his blood.

I swallowed. Bull Cunningham would have been there. Would have watched this. He used to play cards with Sammy and me on *Commorancy*. I swallowed again. Had he enjoyed watching this? Had he even held one of the knives?

Mel's face was empty. She was simply staring down at his ruined face, tears streaming out of her eyes and dropping onto his chest.

I turned away.

Neema was standing close by. "Captain?"

"Is the ship pilotable?"

"We don't think any damage was done to the ship. But, Captain, we can't find Segaton. I was going to go through the crawl tubes, but there is nobody else who can pilot the ship here. Except, now, you."

"Take over here. Segaton is either on this ship or he has been taken by the Vaers. I will follow them with Danaa in *Aenysia*. We will rendezvous back at the Nepheal Gyre. Get Sammy under medical care there as soon as you can."

"Yes, Captain." For once, there was no backchat from a member of my crew. Neema's eyes were sad and very, very serious.

I left all but one of the Nepheal women with Neema. Ouraali accompanied me back to the Nepheal ship.

Danaa's eyebrows lifted in a question as we appeared. Ouraali explained.

I strapped myself into the navigator's station. "Get after that Vaer ship."

"Yes, Captain." Her voice echoed mine. Cold, professional. I wasn't feeling like that inside. Inside, I was feeling vicious.

Aenysia swept after the Vaer ship, which had headed at full speed towards Vaer Nova. We were soon at our maximum cruising speed. Suddenly *Aenysia* began to shudder. Things went very quiet as Danaa and then Ouraali bent over the visors. The ship was rattling like an old tin can.

I knew as soon as they straightened up that we had no chance.

"I'm sorry, Mallivan," Ouraali said slowly. "We are not going to catch up with them. This ship is badly damaged. We are only able to get her up to half her normal speed. She will need a full refit. We can do nothing."

"Understood." We could hardly limp into Vaer Nova with one crippled ship. They had won. Cunningham had got away again.

I fought down the wave of frustration and anger that had rushed through me. "We will find them again. It is over, for now."

We made our way back. I opened a tight-beam to *Nivala*. "What about Segaton?"

Neema's voice was calmer. "Zenzie found him. Sammy had wrapped him up in blankets and put him under the pool, like we did when the Avaraks boarded. He was tired and cross and very hungry, but no lasting harm has come to him. Scout was safely tethered to a pipe close by."

Thank the Shells for that, at least. I wondered how Sammy had felt as the Vaers attacked. He must have prioritized the safety of the child before his own. It must have cut into the time he had to defend himself and the two ships. He had even saved Scout.

As if she could sense my thoughts, Neema answered them. "He got off two shots, but there were many of them. He was boarded before he could do more."

"He did well."

"Yes. He saved Segaton. I hate to think what the Vaer would have done to the baby. Sammy knew that. He was brave."

"He was. He is."

I could hear from her voice that she was crying. "He didn't deserve that, Mallivan."

"Nobody deserves that. Nobody. But we will stop them. We will have to take a little time at the Nephealis Gyre to get everyone up to scratch again. Then we will find them."

She sniffed. "Promise?"

"I do."

"Good. Do you think it was the Vaers who hurt him? Or ... or ..."

"Cunningham? I think it was the Vaers. I hope it was the Vaers. He will tell us when he wakes up."

"Yes, I suppose he will. He is going to wake up, isn't he?"

"Sure. Sammy won't let a few scars get in his way. He'll be back on his feet before you know it."

Her voice was tight. "I hope so."

"Catch up with us, then you can lead the way, Neems. It is going to take us a while to get back. Is Sammy in a Zeroth chamber?"

"Of course. He is stable, but still unconscious."

"They will patch him up on Nephealis. And we all need a break."

Ouraali walked up to me. She smiled down and her eyes were caring. "You need to rest too, Captain."

"Yes. We all do."

"Your mission has been very successful, I believe?"

"Too many good people got hurt."

She looked down. "A life is a very fragile thing. It breaks too easily. We learned that many centuries ago. It is why we strive to reach a higher level of understanding."

I thought of Agraala, who would never think again. Of Didjal and

Eshaan, who had sacrificed their beliefs. Of Sammy and Seyal, badly hurt during this mission. Of Anzany. Even of my own chest, which still hurt. None of us had escaped unscathed.

It was a day later when Zenzara and I found ourselves alone on the bridge. It was late at night according to ship time. Most of the others were sleeping.

I was peering out at the surrounding space. The Pallis Ring, where the big battle between the Omnistate and the Averaks had taken place, was just visible off the starboard bow.

"Do you remember?" her voice was small.

"The battle? Of course."

"They got away again."

I didn't have to ask who she meant. They were on my mind too. "Yes. They did."

"What will they do now, do you think?"

"Cunningham and Chandrayanan? Retreat to Vaer Nova and cause more trouble."

She bit her lip. "I am never going to be safe. Not as long as I have the Chakran Nexus inside me."

I looked at the eight-year-old Tyzaran standing in front of me. She looked vulnerable and frightened. Her crest was drooping and the wrinkles on her face were hanging down, quite unlike the fierce little creature I had grown to like so much. I wanted to hug her. Damn Bull Cunningham for taking her unique brightness and breaking it.

Our mission might have been a resounding success, but we still had work to do. And I had never felt more strongly about the need for justice.

I swallowed. "We will stop them."

"Do you think we can?" Her voice was so small it almost evaporated into the air.

I nodded. "I will make it my personal goal. I promise."

We both stared out into the night as the Pallis Ring slipped past. Too many people had died because of those two Terrans. Too many people had been hurt. As the minutes ticked by I noticed her shoulders begin to relax. Finally her chin tilted slightly upwards as some of her usual resolve crept back into her exceptional mind. She stared stiffly straight ahead, but her voice had gained determination. "I will help you."

Those four small words made tears well up in my eyes. I looked away. "Shouldn't you be looking after Segaton?" I demanded, my voice a little gruff.

"He is asleep."

"And Sammy?"

Her crest twitched with annoyance. "Sammy is doing well. They are all doing well. Ouraali has just been talking to her people back on Nephealis. Even Didjal is expected to make a full recovery. So is Sammy. Though both of them will have scars."

"You will have scars too. Of a different sort."

She took offence at that. "Don't talk down to me as if I were eight!"

"You *are* eight!"

"I am not! I turned nine last week."

"Oh. Right. That makes a huge difference, of course."

She preened. "It does, doesn't it?" She skipped a little around the console. "Never mind, Mallivan. One day I will even be as old as you are. Though I can't imagine what that feels like, of course!"

"No. Decrepit, I suppose."

She beamed up at me. "Exactly!"

I shook my head. The thought of a thirty-year-old Zenzara terrified me. She would probably twist the whole universe around her little finger.

She thought about it. "Of course, when I am thirty you will be over fifty. I don't suppose you will still be alive. If you are, you will probably be bed-ridden. An invalid. Never mind, Mallivan Bell. I will come and keep you company."

"Don't bother, Florence Nightingale."

That reference went right over her head. "Really? Hmm. You could be right. You might be a vegetable by then. You probably won't notice I'm even there."

At the expression on my face she danced away. "Not that there is anything wrong with being a vegetable, of course!"

"Why don't you go away and bother somebody else?" I grumbled.

"See? You are getting grumpy already. I believe that is a sure sign of old age!"

I ordered her off the bridge. I had forgotten how irritating she could be.

Aenysia cruised on through the void, eventually giving me a sense of peace. It is the sort of peace you can only get on the bridge of a starship during the night watch. It is a sensation of being wrapped by infinity. Staring at the lights of millions of dead star systems makes you value just how exceptional life really is.

Unfortunately, not everyone sees it that way.

That's why the Major Shells need something like the Interstellar Enforcement Agency.

That's why they need people like us.

We don't always get it right, but at least we try.

Next in Series:
Exceptional Point